Jayne Ann Krentz is one of today's top contemporary romance writers, with an astounding twelve million copies of her books in print. Her novels regularly appear on the *New York Times*, Waldenbooks and B. Dalton bestseller lists. First published in 1979, Jayne quickly established herself as a prolific and innovative writer. She has delved into psychic elements, intrigue, fantasy, historicals and even futuristic romances. Jayne lives in Seattle with her husband, Frank, an engineer.

Rita Clay Estrada is the author of more than thirty romance novels and has served as cowriter and coeditor on two books about writing for Writers' Digest Books. An air force brat who has lived all over the United States and Germany, she eventually settled in Texas to raise a family. Aside from being the daughter of Rita Gallagher, a well-known novel structure teacher and writer, Rita is the creator, cofounder and first president of Romance Writers of America. The industry's annual award statue for best published books is called the RITA® Award in her honor.

Vicki Lewis Thompson may be single-handedly contributing to global warming, since there are more than fifteen million copies of her books in print worldwide! Her distinctive blend of sizzle and humor has earned her awards with *Romantic Times* and *Affaire de Coeur* magazines. She's also a seven-time finalist for the Romance Writers of America coveted RITA® Award. Living in Arizona with her husband and a very spoiled tuxedo cat, she spends much of her time in the pool and is waiting for someone to invent a waterproof laptop.

JAYNE ANN KRENTZ

VICKI LEWIS THOMPSON
RITA CLAY ESTRADA

Bedazzled

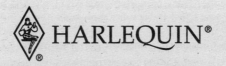

HARLEQUIN®

TORONTO • NEW YORK • LONDON
AMSTERDAM • PARIS • SYDNEY • HAMBURG
STOCKHOLM • ATHENS • TOKYO • MILAN • MADRID
PRAGUE • WARSAW • BUDAPEST • AUCKLAND

ISBN 0-373-83535-3

BEDAZZLED

Copyright © 2002 by Harlequin Books S.A.

The publisher acknowledges the copyright holders of the individual titles as follows:

JOY
Copyright © 1988 by Jayne Ann Krentz

IMPULSE
Copyright © 1988 by Vicki Lewis Thompson

TRUST
Copyright © 1988 by Rita Clay Estrada

Visit us at www.eHarlequin.com

Printed in U.S.A.

CONTENTS

JOY

Jayne Ann Krentz

CHAPTER ONE

ANGUS CEDRIC RYERSON, known as A. C. Ryerson to his business associates, Ryerson to his friends and as A.C. to no one who wished to remain on speaking terms with the man, studied the narrow, twisting road ahead. He swore softly and with great depth of feeling. What there was of the pavement was just barely visible through the pouring rain that was hitting the windshield with an unrelenting rhythm.

Ryerson decided that there was only one major drawback to being stood up by Deborah Middlebrook: he was not getting the chance to indulge the enormous sense of relief he was feeling.

At this moment he should have been sitting in front of a comforting fire, taking further comfort from a glass of good Scotch. He ought to have been allowed to listen to the storm while savoring Mozart and twelve-year-old liquor. It seemed only fair that he be free to wallow happily in his abject misery. Given the circumstances, it was a reasonable expectation. A man who got stood up on the eve of a weekend with a desirable woman deserved a little consideration while he mourned his loss.

Ryerson slowed the silver Mercedes for another hairpin turn and then swore again as he had to decrease his speed even more to negotiate a deep puddle in a dip in the road. Instead of enjoying a fire, a glass of Scotch and Mozart he was driving through one of the worst storms that had struck the Pacific Northwest all year. It was early May. Spring was supposed to be bursting into bloom.

As if the lousy weather weren't sufficient punishment, he was laboring to find a vague address in a rural location on an island where no one spent much money on street signs. At the rate he was going, he would be lucky to find his way back to the ferry terminal before the last boat left for Seattle.

He had only himself to blame for his present situation. Discovery of Debby's note had left him awash in relief. He should have quit while he was ahead and retired at once to his Scotch and Mozart.

Unfortunately Debby's parents had learned that their daughter had fled. They had panicked, afraid their youngest might do something reckless while in the throes of despair from a disintegrating love affair.

Ryerson had made one or two attempts to assure the Middlebrooks that Debby was in full command of herself, but they had not been convinced. He had then attempted to explain as delicately as possible that the love affair they thought was going up in flames had in reality never generated more than a little mild smoke. The Middlebrooks had ignored that bit of reassurance, too.

He'd definitely been a bit too delicate in his explanations. But it was difficult to tell a pleasant, rather old-fashioned couple such as the Middlebrooks that you weren't sleeping with their youngest daughter. To bring the subject up at all suggested one had seriously considered sleeping with their dear darling and that led to additional difficult explanations.

In the end Ryerson had taken pity on John and Leona Middlebrook. He had been feeling so relieved to be free of Debby that he had rashly volunteered to find her and make certain she was safe.

It had been a mistake. John and Leona had immediately taken him up on his offer, gratitude reflected on their worried faces. Too late, Ryerson had realized there had been something besides parental gratitude in their eyes. He was sure he'd also seen a heavy dose of hopeful expectation. He wished now that he'd kept his mouth shut. It was no secret the Middlebrooks had been hoping that the romance between Debby and Ryerson would evolve into something more substantial.

Something as substantial as marriage, to be exact.

Ryerson couldn't blame them. He'd had a few fleeting thoughts in that direction himself in the beginning. Marriage to Debby had seemed eminently logical at one point. Luckily he had come to his senses.

As he fought the storm, Ryerson reminded himself that sooner or later a man paid for his good luck. He was paying the price tonight.

The consensus, after the obvious places had been checked, was that Debby had probably gone to stay at her sister's island home. A phone call had produced no answer, and the Middlebrookses' assumption was that, owing to her emotional distress, Debby wasn't answering the phone. The sister, Ryerson was told, was out of town.

The only solution that would reassure everyone was for Ryerson to take the ferry from downtown Seattle to the island, locate Debby and demonstrate to all concerned that she was in good condition and not indulging in a fit of hysterics or crying inconsolably.

For their sakes Ryerson hoped the Middlebrooks were not harboring too many false expectations about a grand reconciliation. Having escaped Debby once by the skin of his teeth, Ryerson had no intention of getting tangled up again with her. She was a very charming, very attractive young woman, but another week or two of her company would have driven him over the edge.

The road curved again and a small, slanted signpost flashed briefly in the glare of the headlights. Ryerson remembered the directions John Middlebrook had written down for him and turned the wheel of the Mercedes to the right. The road narrowed again, a mere path between towering pines.

Ryerson wondered once more about the mysterious sister whose cottage he was trying to find tonight. Whoever she was, she had the same taste in real estate that he had. His own weekend retreat was farther north but the surroundings were similar. His place was considerably more remote, however. It was on a tiny dot of an island in the San Juans and could only be reached by boat. At least Virginia Elizabeth Middlebrook had ferry service to her island.

Virginia Elizabeth. The name made him think of royalty. There was an old-fashioned dignity about it that appealed to him. Other than the fact that she was a few years older than Debby, which made her about thirty-three, Ryerson knew almost nothing about this sister. Somehow they had always managed to miss meeting. Lately he knew Virginia Elizabeth had been out of town a lot. Something to do with her job as an information retrieval manager.

Ryerson was reminding himself that he wasn't going to meet her tonight, either, because she was still out of town, when the cottage came into view. He could see little of it in the headlights, but from what he could tell, it was a comfortable-looking older home nestled in the trees near the water's edge. Lights glowed warmly in the windows.

Ryerson would have been happier to see the cheerfully lit windows if he hadn't known it meant he'd finally tracked Debby to her lair. He parked the Mercedes in the drive and switched off the ignition. Then he sat for a moment, measuring the distance he would have to cross in the rain before he reached the shelter of the porch.

There was no help for it. He was going to get wet no matter how fast he sprinted to the steps. The umbrella was in the trunk, naturally. By the time he got it out, he would be soaked. Might as well head straight for the cottage.

Ryerson was the kind of man who did not put off the inevitable. Thinking wistfully of Scotch, a warm fire, Mozart and the esoteric joys of celibacy, he opened the car door and loped toward the porch.

He didn't stand a chance against the driving rain. His expensive tweed jacket was soaked by the time he reached shelter and his heavy wing-tip shoes were water stained.

Irritated and resigned to his fate, Ryerson leaned heavily on the doorbell. The sooner this little confrontation was over, the better. All he wanted to do was go home. Alone.

VIRGINIA ELIZABETH MIDDLEBROOK had just stepped out of the shower when the doorbell rang. She paused in the act of wrapping her wet hair in a towel and listened intently. The bell rang again. She frowned. She was certainly not expecting anyone tonight. No one knew she had returned a day early.

It might be a neighbor who needed something and had seen that the lights were on in her cottage, she told herself. Perhaps the Burtons down the road had lost their power because of the storm and needed candles.

Still, a woman living alone could not be too careful. Virginia tightened the sash of her comfortable old terry-cloth robe, tucked in the towel to form a turban for her damp hair and went down the hall to the living room. Her fluffy pink mules flopped comfortably against the aging hardwood floor.

The doorbell chimed once more. There was a distinctly impatient sound to it this time, she decided.

"Who is it?" she asked firmly, and simultaneously put her eye to the tiny glass peephole set in the door. She could see nothing except a broad male shoulder. The shoulder appeared to be covered in wet tweed.

"It's Ryerson. Who the hell do you think it is?" a man's voice growled back from the other side of the door. "Open up, Debby. Your parents are worried sick, and I'm cold and wet. Let's get this scene over so I can go home and languish in peace."

Virginia blinked and stepped back from the door. Ryerson. The name was very familiar because a man named Ryerson had recently bought her father's business. She thought there were initials connected to the name, although she couldn't recall them.

This must be the same Ryerson her sister had mentioned once or twice on the phone, the man Debby had been dating recently. He did not sound happy. Nor did he sound like a doting lover. What in the world had Debby done this time, Virginia wondered.

Tentatively she unlocked the door and opened it. She eyed the large, damp male on her doorstep with considerable misgiving. She had to look up some distance to meet his eyes, an unusual experience for her. Virginia Elizabeth was five feet nine inches in her stocking feet. A quick first estimate put her sister's current boyfriend somewhere in the vicinity of six two—a very solid six two. That same assessing glance told her that *boyfriend* was definitely a misnomer. This man was pushing forty if he was a day, and he looked as if he'd gotten there the hard way.

The missing initials popped into her head. A.C.

It was obvious that A. C. Ryerson was not thrilled to find himself standing where he was at that hour of the night. The harsh glow of the yellow porch light revealed an aggressive, severe jawline and high cheekbones. His eyes glinted at her as they swept her from the top of her toweled head to the toes of her worn, fluffy slippers.

"You're not Debby."

"No, I'm not," she retorted, uncomfortably aware of her freshly scrubbed condition. Freshly scrubbed looked great at eighteen, but at thirty-three it wasn't quite so cute. "I'm Virginia Elizabeth. You're A. C. Ryerson?"

"The last time I checked my driver's license. Is Debby here?"

"No."

"Good." He appeared unduly pleased by the information.

Virginia was taken aback. "I just got home a couple of hours ago. She's definitely not here, and there's no sign that she has been. Why? What's wrong?"

"Nothing as far as I'm concerned, but your folks are frantic. Mind if I come in, or shall I explain everything while I get shrink-wrapped by my jacket?"

Virginia smiled ruefully. "Sorry. Come on in. As you can see, I just got out of the shower. I was about to have a nightcap and go to bed. I've been stuck in airplanes and airports since six o'clock this morning."

"I know the feeling," Ryerson said as he came through the door. "It takes a while to unwind. I would be forever grateful if you would allow me to join you. I've got some unwinding of my own to do."

Virginia's eyes widened in genuine shock. "Join me?"

"In the nightcap. Not bed," he said gently.

Heat rushed into her cheeks. It was an odd sensation. She hadn't blushed in ages. "Oh, yes, of course. Sorry about that. I'm a little groggy. Please sit down," she waved him hastily toward the sofa. "I'll get you something. What do you drink?"

"I've been fantasizing about a glass of Scotch for the past two hours." Ryerson wandered toward the fireplace and examined the supply of kindling. "There was a fire in my fantasy, too. Any objections if I build one? I'm soaked."

Virginia stared at him in astonishment. "Go ahead. Your fantasy life sounds quite tame."

"I assure you it is. I'm a simple man with simple fantasies."

Virginia blushed again under the speculative expression in his silver-gray eyes. "Here, I'll take your jacket."

He shrugged out of it willingly enough, revealing a conservative white shirt and a sedately striped tie. Not at all the sort of clothes she would have expected one of Debby's dates to wear. Virginia put the equally conservative-looking jacket over the back of a chair. "I'll, uh, see if I have any Scotch." She retreated to the kitchen.

Something very strange was going on here, Virginia decided as she located an old, dusty bottle of Scotch and poured a hefty shot into a large glass. She eyed the level of liquid in the glass and added another splash. A. C. Ryerson was a large man.

She was surprised by his massiveness. It gave him an air of granite-hard solidity that was unusual in Debby's male acquaintances who generally tended toward the slender, more devil-may-care sorts. Ryerson was also older than most of Debby's boyfriends. Debby, a vivacious twenty-four, tended to stick to men who were closer to her own age. They were easier to manage, Debby had once explained.

There were a few other things that surprised Virginia about A. C. Ryerson. He appeared to be a good deal more grim and hard than Virginia would have guessed. Definitely not Debby's typical yuppie type. Debby liked her men trendy and adventurous. She preferred the kind of man who liked to dance to hard rock until two in the morning and spend the next day partying on a boat in the middle of Lake Washington.

Virginia had a strong hunch A. C. Ryerson was not the type to routinely rock around the clock.

She poured herself a glass of wine and went back into the living room with both drinks. It was time for a few explanations.

Ryerson was on one knee in front of the fireplace. He had a small blaze going and was feeding it carefully. She saw that he had loosened his tie. He glanced up as Virginia came forward with the Scotch. Reaching for it with obvious gratitude he took one long swallow.

"Thank you," he said heavily. "I needed that."

"You're welcome."

Virginia sat down on the couch and put her wine on the

table in front of her. She watched Ryerson as he carefully placed one more log on the fire and then got to his feet. *A very big man,* she thought again. But it was all lean, muscled strength. There was no softness about his hard frame. *Comfortably, reassuringly large.* Immediately she wondered what had put the words into her brain. Other than her father, she seldom thought of men as being either comfortable or reassuring.

Ryerson started toward the couch and then halted as he caught sight of the compact-disc player on a table. He paused beside the collection of discs long enough to select some Mozart and drop it into the player. When the crystal strains of a piano concerto floated liltingly into the room, Ryerson nodded in satisfaction and sat down at the opposite end of the sofa. His weight put a considerable dent in the cushions.

"To narrow escapes," he said, stretching his legs out in front of him. He toasted the fire with his Scotch.

"Who or what, precisely, have you just escaped from, Mr. Ryerson?" Virginia asked a little tartly.

"A weekend of unmitigated debauchery." He looked at her through lazily narrowed eyes. "Call me Ryerson, by the way. All my friends do. Nobody except my mother calls me by my first or second names."

"Which are?"

"Angus Cedric."

"Hmm. I can see why you don't use them much. They're nice names, though. A little old-fashioned but solid and substantial."

"And dull?" he suggested helpfully.

"No, not at all," she said quickly, startled at the thought. *Dull* was the last word that came to mind when she looked at Ryerson, she realized in mild surprise.

"Thanks," he said dryly. "I'll stick with Ryerson. So you're Virginia Elizabeth?"

"That's right."

"You're not at all like your sister."

"So I've been told since she was in her cradle." Virginia sipped her wine and wondered where all this was leading. "Can I assume that you and my sister have had some sort of lovers' spat?"

"Spat?" Ryerson considered the word for a moment. "No, I wouldn't say that. More like a permanent parting of the ways. Your sister and I had planned to go away together this weekend. We both came to our senses and changed our minds at the last minute. Rest assured, it's a great relief to both of us."

Virginia groaned. "The big romance is over?"

"I'm afraid so."

"Mom and Dad are not going to be pleased."

"They aren't, but I am."

"Yes, I'm getting that feeling." Not at all the stricken, desperate, cast-off lover, she thought. But then, she doubted if this man would play that role for any woman.

"I don't mind telling you, it was a close call, Virginia Elizabeth." Ryerson took another swallow of Scotch and leaned his head back against the sofa. "A very close call. I'm still not quite sure how I let myself get this near to total disaster. Do you know I was even thinking about marriage in the beginning? I've been wondering for weeks how to get out of the mess, but your sister has kindly taken care of the situation herself. Apparently she had the good sense to panic, too. Unfortunately she made a scene out of what should have been a simple matter of saying no, thank you."

"My sister usually does things with a flourish."

"So I've learned. This time she left a note. I think I've got it here somewhere." Ryerson leaned over to pluck a damp piece of paper from his jacket pocket. "Here, read it for yourself."

Virginia quickly scanned the short note.

Ryerson, please forgive me, but I can't go through with it. It's all been a terrible mistake. I must have some time alone to think. I have come to the conclusion that it's all over between us. I'm sorry.

It was signed, "Debby."

"I fail to see the problem here," Virginia remarked. "Debby apparently declined your invitation to spend the weekend with her and you're happy she did. What's the difficulty?"

"Your parents are worried about her whereabouts and her state of mind." Ryerson spoke with acute disgust. "They seem to think she might be sinking into depression and despair."

"Debby? Not likely."

"I agree." Ryerson's dark brows rose slightly. "I think there's a bit more to it than that. Your parents were very happy when she started dating me. They are not at all pleased that the ship of love has foundered."

"Ah. Now that makes more sense. They encouraged you to go after her in the hopes that there might be a grand reconciliation, I'll bet."

"I think so."

"And is there a chance of that happening?" Virginia asked calmly.

"Not a chance in hell. The whole thing was a big mistake. She was right about that."

"I see. I'll bet you don't make many, do you?"

"Mistakes? No," he said blandly, "I don't."

She believed him. Virginia looked at the lean, solid length of him and then her eyes moved to his face. It was an interesting face, she decided. Not particularly good-looking, but definitely interesting. It was an overwhelmingly masculine face—all blunt, roughly carved planes and angles.

Ryerson's hair was still gleaming from the rain. The firelight revealed a hint of red in the thick brown depths. He caught her examining him and smiled faintly. His lazy, hooded gaze revealed a cool, faintly predatory intelligence.

Virginia could see curls of crisp hair where Ryerson's expensive white shirt was open at the collar. She stirred slightly, tucking her slippered feet under her old robe. She was aware of a faint restlessness in herself that was distinctly unusual. She knew the feeling was generated by Ryerson's presence, but she did not understand it. Once more her gaze slipped to the opening of his shirt.

"Wondering what your sister saw in me?" Ryerson asked mildly.

Virginia felt herself flushing again and wished she could have disguised her reaction. "Of course not."

He shrugged comfortably. "I do."

"I'll admit you're not quite her usual type," Virginia allowed cautiously.

"Thank God. Too bad it took us both so long to figure it out. All I can say in my own defense is that it seemed like a good idea at the time."

"I know my parents probably encouraged both of you to think it was a good idea," Virginia said with a smile. "Dad had visions of keeping the business in the family after he sold it. He and Mom thought it would be just ducky if you married Debby."

"Uh-huh."

"Mom and Dad sent you here looking for Debby?"

"When they couldn't locate her at her own apartment they assumed she must have come here. I, being innately gallant and noble, not to mention euphoric over my narrow escape, agreed to make certain she was okay. However, having come this far, I feel I've discharged my duty in the matter. I refuse to feel any further obligation."

"What about your male ego?" Virginia asked before stopping to think. "Isn't that involved?"

His mouth twisted derisively. "My ego will survive just fine, thank you. It's been through worse."

Virginia believed him when he said his ego would survive. There was something about this man that made her think his self-confidence ran deep and was grounded in bedrock. It would take more than a fleeing girlfriend to shake it.

"So now that you've fulfilled your obligation, you're going to turn around and drive back to Seattle?" Virginia asked curiously.

Ryerson cradled his glass in his big hands and stared into the fire. "Right. Just as soon as I've dried out. I appreciate your hospitality, Virginia Elizabeth. I also appreciate the fact that you're not having hysterics or screaming at me for what I've done to your sister."

"Have you done anything to my sister?"

Ryerson caught the underlying question in the words and gave his hostess an assessing sidelong glance. "No," he said bluntly. "This was supposed to be the big weekend. The fact that we hadn't made it into bed before this should have been an early tip-off, I suppose."

She looked at him in confusion. "I don't understand."

He grimaced. "Let's just say that after a month of nothing more than a few uninteresting good-night kisses, one has to assume there was little chance of a grand passion developing at any time in the near future."

"Oh. I didn't mean that. It's certainly none of my business!"

"Forget it." Ryerson grinned briefly at her obvious embarrassment. "I only mention the subject because I want to assure you that your sister and I are not all that involved, in spite of the big plans for this weekend. My fault, I admit."

"Your fault?" she echoed weakly. She stared at him in startled amazement.

Ryerson's grin came and went again. Virginia Elizabeth was good for his ego, he decided. The way she was looking at him implied she could not imagine him having any problems in the bedroom. His ego might not need continuous stroking to survive, but it was fully capable of luxuriating in this kind of attention when it got it.

"I never got up the energy to take her to bed," he said frankly. "Every time we got home from a date, either my ears were still ringing from an excess of loud rock music or I was exhausted from trying to keep up with her on the dance floor. I'm nearly forty years old, not twenty-five. I no longer attempt to party until two in the morning and then try to impress a woman in bed."

"But you were going away together this weekend?"

"I think the idea was a last-ditch effort on both our parts to inject a little vitality into a less-than-immortal love affair. I realized it wasn't worth the effort and was getting ready to tell her so when her famous note arrived."

"Not exactly a thrilling romance."

Ryerson looked at her. "A mistake all the way around. But it's over now. I can relax." He took another swallow of the good Scotch and let the soothing music sink into his bones as the warmth from the fire enveloped him. This was exactly what he needed, what he had been wanting all evening.

Virginia Elizabeth fitted her name, Ryerson decided as he savored the smoky Scotch. Tall, dignified, and wonderfully mature. She was taking his unexpected arrival and the news of her sister's disappearance with great calm. A woman of good sense and intelligence, he thought. Not at all like that flighty, scatterbrained sister of hers. A man could talk to Virginia Elizabeth, really talk to her.

She looked very cozy and comfortable sitting there at the other end of the sofa. Virginia Elizabeth was a fine-looking woman in many respects, he decided.

Ryerson found himself cataloging her assets. Good eyes, for a start. Beautiful eyes, in fact. They were hazel and at first glance seemed to suggest a quiet, womanly confidence. But there was a disturbing wariness, too, he noted.

The lines of her feminine jaw and straight, assertive nose were well defined. Her skin was pleasantly flushed from the fire.

He couldn't tell for certain what lay beneath the ancient terry-cloth robe, but he had an impression of full breasts and well-rounded hips. The woman had some shape to her, Ryerson thought with satisfaction. Not at all like her fashionably skinny sister. Virginia Elizabeth was built to keep a man warm in bed.

The stray sensual thought triggered a dull ache in his lower body that took Ryerson by surprise. He shifted slightly on the sofa, thinking it had been a very long time since he'd had to worry about spontaneous combustion.

"Well, I'm glad we're not going to be dealing with heartbreak and shattering disillusionment here," Virginia was saying briskly. "Could be a bit awkward, what with you just having bought out Dad's business and all."

"I think that might have been part of the problem as far as your sister was concerned," Ryerson said thoughtfully. "She seemed to like the idea of continuing financial security, but she did not care for the notion of being married to a man who was heavily into diesel generators and power systems."

Virginia laughed. "You've got to admit that a career in diesel generators and power systems lacks a certain sophisticated cachet. What made you decide to buy my father's business, anyway?"

"Middlebrook Power Systems is a solid, old-line firm that can be turned into a real money cow with the right management."

"And you're going to milk it?"

"All it needs is some capital poured into it for retooling and modernizing, and the sky's the limit. I've been involved with motors and power systems of one kind or another most of my life. I was the kind of kid who made a career out of shop classes in high school. Always had an after-school job at the local gas station. Then I spent a couple of years in the army, working on tanks and trucks until I finally wised up and went to college. There's more money in managing and consulting on power systems than there is in fixing them. As it happens, I found out I enjoyed the business end of things almost as much as the tinkering end. I know a good investment when I see it. When John Middlebrook put his firm on the block, I grabbed it.''

''And my sister grabbed you,'' Virginia finished shrewdly.

Ryerson groaned. ''You could put it that way. But I'm not sure how much of it was Debby's idea. Your parents were pushing her hard.''

''I know. I can understand their motivations, but what about yours?''

Ryerson gazed into the fire. ''I discovered I wasn't opposed to the idea. The fact is I wouldn't mind getting married again. Under the right circumstances marriage is a pleasant, comfortable institution.''

''But, as someone once said, who wants to live in an institution?'' Virginia remarked dryly. ''To be fair, you may be right. From a man's point of view marriage probably does look pleasant and comfortable. But it looks different to a woman.''

Ryerson glanced at her narrowly. ''You surprise me. I thought most women wanted to get married, especially women over a, uh, certain age—'' He broke off abruptly and grimaced.

''Especially women over thirty?'' Virginia finished for him. ''I'll let you in on a little secret. We're not all desperate.'' She shivered unconsciously. ''I tried marriage once, and it was a disaster. I learn from my mistakes.''

The depth of emotion in her voice caught Ryerson's full attention. ''I was married once myself, and it didn't work out, but I'm willing to give it another try. I think marriage has definite possibilities if two people go into it with their eyes open, a set of reasonable expectations and a willingness to make a commitment.''

"You believe that strongly in the power of love?" she asked in a soft voice.

"No," he said flatly. "I don't believe in love at all. Love is an artificial emotion. It's a twentieth-century fiction created for the fuzzy-brained romantics of this world, and I'm definitely not one of them. I do believe in marriage, however."

"Why?"

It struck Ryerson that this was a rather unusual conversation to be having with Debby's sister. But he found himself intrigued by it. "As I said, I think marriage has a lot to offer. The first time around for me I'll admit was a matter of raging hormones and youthful optimism. We were both too young, and neither of us had any reasonable expectations about marriage. She got restless and started wondering what she'd missed by marrying so young. I couldn't blame her. Things just fell apart. But next time for me will be different."

"Different?"

He nodded. "The next time around, I'll see to it that things are based on more solid, realistic foundations. I know what I want. I've reached the age when I value a comfortable, dependable home life. I guess I'm basically a home-and-hearth type. When I bought your dad's company and moved to Seattle from Portland, I felt as if I'd finally found what I wanted to do with the rest of my life. I felt as if I'd found the place where I wanted to live. I would like a nice, quiet, reliable, monogamous relationship to go along with all that. I'd like to marry someone I could count on. Someone to act as hostess when I entertain business associates. Someone who would share a drink with me in the evening while we talked about our day. I don't know what made me think even for a moment that it would be like that with Debby. I must have gone crazy."

"Either that or your hormones decided to get involved in the decision again," Virginia said with a smile.

"My hormones do nothing these days without my permission." Ryerson took another swallow of his Scotch and wondered about the truth of that statement. He could still feel the tautness in his groin. He wondered if she realized that the top of the terry-cloth robe was gaping slightly, just enough to give him a tantalizing glimpse of soft, rounded flesh.

"So you're willing to marry for comfort and convenience?"

"You sound disapproving."

She appeared to give that some thought. "Well, at least you're honest about it. In some ways I understand and agree with what you're saying. I wouldn't mind having a nice, reliable, stable friendship with a man. I get along very well by myself, but there are times when it would be fun to share things with someone. But I would never marry to get those things."

"You'd rather have an affair?" he asked with grave interest.

"I said it would be nice to have a comfortable friendship with a man. I don't know about an affair. I've never had one," she explained calmly. "I'm not sure I want one. But if I did have one, I would want it to be based on friendship, not hormones."

Ryerson was startled. He tried not to betray the reaction. "When were you divorced?" he asked.

"I wasn't. My husband died a few years ago."

Ryerson cleared his throat. "A few years ago?"

"I was married at twenty-five, and he died when I was twenty-seven. A car accident."

"And you've never… I mean in all this time you haven't gotten involved with, uh…" He let the sentence trail off, aware he was embarrassing her. But the truth was, it was difficult to imagine this woman having lived alone for so long.

"I've never found the kind of friendship that could be turned into a steady, dependable relationship," she answered quietly, "let alone someone I could fall in love with."

"You do believe in love, then?" he asked a little more sharply than he'd intended.

"Oh, yes. I believe in love, although I don't expect to ever find myself involved in a grand passion. I'm not the type. That's for people like my sister." Her mouth curved wryly. "I don't expect to fall in love. I much prefer the idea of a close friendship."

"And you would not want to marry this hypothetical friend?"

"Never in a million years."

Ryerson felt an irrational urge to argue the point. Then he relaxed and chuckled. "I believe in marriage but not love, and you believe in love but not marriage. Both of us agree about the importance of friendship, however. That's reassuring. It's also amusing when you think about it." His humor faded. "Your sister is still at the age when she expects fireworks and drama and a continuous good time."

"True."

"The fact is," Ryerson said as he sipped his drink, "I wasn't the kind of man who could have provided her with those things even when I was twenty-five. Maybe it has something to do with having made a career out of diesel motors and power systems. The field lacks a certain flashiness, and so do I. Do you realize there has been little change in the basic diesel power system in the past fifty years? The fundamental concept is steady, dependable and enduring."

Virginia grinned. "A tried-and-true product."

"Rather like marriage. It works beautifully as long as no one indulges in unrealistic expectations or makes too many demands. Was that your problem the first time around, Virginia Elizabeth? Did you go into marriage blinded by rose-colored glasses? Lord knows I did.''

She stiffened, and anger flashed briefly in her hazel eyes. ''I do not discuss my marriage with anyone outside my family.''

Ryerson backed off immediately. He knew when he'd hit a brick wall. The easiest way to deal with brick walls was to go around them. He let the conversation lapse into silence.

''Now what?'' Virginia asked after a few minutes of uneasy quiet. She was obviously anxious to change the subject.

Ryerson leaned back in his corner of the sofa and loosened another button on his shirt. He probably should be leaving, but somehow he didn't feel like making the effort. The Scotch was soothing, the music was delightful and the fire was comfortable. And if his hostess shifted her position just slightly, the gap in the front of her robe would widen another couple of inches. A man could not reasonably ask for much more out of an evening.

''I ought to be thanking you for your hospitality and seeing myself out the door,'' Ryerson observed aloud. But he didn't move.

Virginia glanced at the mantel clock. She hesitated for a few seconds and then said, ''You've got an hour and a half until the last ferry sails.''

''Plenty of time,'' he mused. ''Now that I know my way it will only take fifteen minutes to get to the dock.''

''Perhaps if you wait another forty-five minutes or so, the worst of this storm will pass. It's a nasty night for driving.''

''Yes,'' Ryerson said. ''It is. There was a regular lake forming across the road a mile or so from your turnoff.''

''I know that section. It floods regularly. It can take hours to drain.''

They both looked at the clock and another few moments of quiet, thoughtful silence prevailed.

''Why haven't I met you before, Virginia Elizabeth?''

Ryerson eventually asked. "Your family mentioned you but said you were out of town a lot lately. I think they planned to introduce us at a dinner party next week. Do you do a lot of traveling?"

Virginia smiled and shook her head. "No, not under normal circumstances. I manage the computerized information-retrieval system for Carrington Miles and Associates. Do you know the company?"

He nodded. "Big conglomerate headquartered in Seattle. They've got business operations all over the Northwest."

"That's right. They're trying to standardize the information-retrieval systems at all their branches, and I've been assigned to oversee the standardization process. Hence the traveling. The job I just finished should be the last for quite a while, though. I think everything's under control."

Ryerson thought about that. "One of the things I want to modernize at Middlebrook Power Systems is the documentation control process. Maybe I should hire you as a consultant."

Virginia shook her head and chuckled. "The firm is hopelessly out of date in that area. Dad never saw the need to update his retrieval system."

She then surprised Ryerson by launching into an intelligent monologue on the wonders of modern computer-aided information systems. He found himself learning more than he really wanted to know on the subject, but somehow it was very easy to listen.

He interrupted finally to get himself some more Scotch. When he returned to the sofa he started talking about the plans he had for the future of Middlebrook Power Systems. Virginia was gratifyingly interested. Unfortunately she had adjusted the front of her robe while he was pouring his drink.

The fire blazed cheerfully, and the storm continued unabated. It wasn't until Ryerson had finished a lengthy, detailed description of his plans to open overseas markets for

Middlebrook that Virginia again glanced at the mantel clock. Her eyes widened.

"You'll never make the last ferry," she said anxiously.

Ryerson followed her gaze. "Damn." But he made no move to grab his jacket and rush toward the door. "Maybe it's just as well, considering how much of your Scotch I've gone through."

Virginia frowned slightly. "There are a couple of bed-and-breakfast places on the island. You might try one."

"Good idea."

They both continued to sit and gaze into the fire as if seeking answers there. Virginia finally spoke up cautiously.

"There's no reason you can't stay here, as long as you don't mind spending the rest of the night on my sofa," she said. "It's a little small for you, but..."

"That's very kind of you, Virginia Elizabeth."

"Nonsense. After all, you're a good friend of the family, even if you and Debby have recently broken off the romance of the year."

He returned her smile. "I like to think so."

Forty minutes later, Ryerson found himself stretched out on the sofa with a fresh-smelling sheet, a wool blanket and a fluffy pillow. It was a tight fit, but he felt remarkably comfortable. The remains of the fire glowed on the hearth.

He listened to Virginia Elizabeth puttering around in the bedroom and then heard her turn out the light and climb into bed. He indulged himself in some pleasant fantasizing, picturing her in prim white underwear. She was the type to wear prim white underwear. Then he imagined her removing the underwear. When the mental pictures got too intense and the heavy, tight feeling in his lower body grew too uncomfortable, he told himself to go to sleep.

But the images didn't disappear completely, and Ryerson still had one in his head when he finally drifted into a deep slumber. It was the picture of a regally tall woman with full, ripe breasts and nicely rounded thighs reaching up to welcome him into her arms.

Ryerson's last conscious thought was that he had been dating the wrong sister for the past month.

CHAPTER TWO

VIRGINIA AWOKE the next morning with the feeling that something rigid and unyielding in her life had been pushed permanently askew. It was a disconcerting sensation. She opened her eyes, gazed at the ceiling and wondered how having one very large male spend the night on her sofa could have any long-term effect on her quiet, well-ordered existence.

The answer was that she was imagining things. The event could not have any such effect. She had simply provided a bed to a business associate of her father's who also happened to be a friend of the family. End of adventure.

Irritated with herself, she threw back the covers, tugged on her robe and padded out of the bedroom and down the hall to the bathroom. It wasn't until she reached it that she realized it was already occupied. The shower was running full force. The experience of having to share her bathroom with a man was a novel one, to say the least. She went on toward the living room.

The pillow, blanket and sheet she had given Ryerson the previous evening had already been neatly folded and stored in the hall cupboard. Only a pair of very large wingtips neatly aligned on the floor and a white shirt hanging over the back of a chair gave evidence of a man's presence.

The shower went off and Virginia stilled, listening intently. She pictured Ryerson drying himself with one of her oversize white bath towels. When she found herself trying to decide if the pattern of his chest hair formed an arrow

below his waist, she knew it was time to go start the coffee.
Her imagination was definitely in high gear this morning.
Very unusual for her.

A few minutes later, the bathroom door opened. Virginia
concentrated on taking two cups out of the cupboard. She
didn't hear Ryerson coming down the hall, which surprised
her, given his size. But she sensed his presence in the doorway behind her.

"Good morning," he said quietly. His voice was deep
and dark with a faint trace of morning huskiness that struck
her as remarkably sexy.

Clutching the cups, Virginia turned around. "Good morning."

She hadn't been quite certain how he would appear to her
this morning. But he turned out to be just as interesting in
the early light as he had been last night in front of a fire.
The fact that he was half-nude undoubtedly contributed to
the overall fascination she acknowledged privately. It had
been years since she'd had a half-nude man in her kitchen.
The last one had been her husband, and she had no warm
memories of either him or his nudity.

But Ryerson was something else again. His red-brown
hair was gleaming from the shower, and his eyes appeared
very silvery in the sunlight. He was wearing only his slacks,
and Virginia realized that the hair on his chest followed
exactly the pattern she had envisaged. It formed a thick pelt
that shaped itself into an arrow before it plunged below his
belt.

"I borrowed your razor. Hope you don't mind." Ryerson
ran his hand over his jaw, checking for stubble. "I'm a little
shaggy in the morning."

"Of course I don't mind," Virginia said quickly. "Here,
help yourself to coffee while I use the bathroom."

"Thanks." His attention was not on the coffee, however.
He was studying her hair.

"Is something wrong?"

"No." He smiled. "I was just realizing that last night you were wearing a towel wrapped around your head. I never saw your hair."

Virginia put one hand to the chaos of her sleep-tousled, shoulder-length brown hair. "It's a mess. I'd better go do something about it." Hastily she put the cups down on the counter and tried to slip past Ryerson.

But Ryerson made no move to get out of the way. Instead he touched her shoulder as she came to a halt in front of him. The weight of his hand was sensual. Virginia found herself very much aware of it. She stilled uneasily.

Ryerson looked down at her intently, and his fingers moved from her shoulder into the thick tangle of her seal-brown hair. Virginia stared up at him, distantly aware of her own throbbing pulse.

"Thank you for last night, Ginny," Ryerson said softly. "I can't remember the last time I spent such a pleasant evening. The Scotch, the fire, the music and you were just what I needed."

She smiled tremulously and wondered when she had gone from being Virginia Elizabeth to Ginny. It surprised her that the familiar, affectionate form of her name sounded so right coming from him. Something astonishingly intimate had happened out there in front of the fire last night. "It was nothing, really. I'm sorry you had such a long drive on a bad night."

"I'm not." There was a long moment of taut silence between them, and then Ryerson bent his head and found her mouth with his own.

Virginia held her breath, not certain what to expect. She knew she was not a very sensual creature. Her husband had made that clear early in their marriage. But Ryerson was not a flaming romantic, either. He had assured her of that. He probably didn't expect too much from her. And it was after all, just a simple, casual kiss.

The thoughts tumbled chaotically through her head as

Ryerson's mouth touched hers and then Virginia relaxed with a small sigh. It seemed the most natural thing in the world to be kissed by this man.

His mouth was hard, warm and subtly demanding. Virginia responded to the kiss instinctively. Nothing had ever felt this right. A. C. Ryerson tasted wonderful, and Virginia realized she had been hungry for a very long time. All her life, in fact.

Her fingertips found his bare shoulder, and she unconsciously flexed her hands, enjoying the feel of strong, smooth muscles under warm skin.

Ryerson groaned softly and raised his head so that his mouth was only an inch from hers. "I think I should tell you something. I've come to the conclusion that I was chasing the wrong sister last night."

Virginia pulled slightly away from him and gazed up into his narrowed silver eyes. She was trembling as if she were on the brink of discovery. The world appeared very new and fresh this morning.

"We hardly know each other," she heard herself say breathlessly and then wanted to scream because of the inanity of the remark. A part of her was convinced she already knew Ryerson very well. How could she not? He was so much like her.

"I would like to get to know you better," Ryerson said, his eyes holding hers. "I think you and I have a lot in common. I do believe, Virginia Elizabeth, that you and I could become very good friends." His fingers tangled briefly in her hair. He was bending his head again to brush his mouth against hers when a key scraped in the lock of the front door. A cold draft of air flowed into the room.

"Ginny! Good grief, it's you, Ryerson! What in the world is going on here?"

Virginia jumped at her sister's startled gasp. Her eyes went to the door behind Ryerson.

"Hello, Debby." Virginia was surprised by the calm in her own voice.

"Well, well, well," Deborah Middlebrook said in a voice that held mingled astonishment and chagrin. "I can't believe it." She came through the door, her slender figure dressed in a chic pair of tight-fitting leather slacks and a huge, glittering T-shirt. Her short blond hair was cut in the latest slightly outrageous style. "What have we here? Finding ways to mend a broken heart, Ryerson? I'm crushed." Her eyes danced. "Positively devastated."

Ryerson turned lazily and examined her with a blandly bored gaze. "I hope you've called your parents. They're worried."

"I'll call them this morning." Debby scanned the tableau of her sister in a robe and Ryerson wearing only his slacks. She shook her head in amazement. "If I hadn't seen it with my own eyes, I wouldn't have believed it. You spent the night here, Ryerson? With my sister? No one in the family is going to believe this. To the best of anyone's knowledge, Ginny hasn't spent the night with a man since her husband died. And she doesn't even know you." The mischief abruptly vanished from Debby's eyes, and her bright gaze suddenly narrowed. "Hey, just what is going on here? Ryerson, if you forced yourself on my sister, so help me, I'll call the cops."

Virginia went a bright pink. Ever since her husband had died, all the Middlebrooks had tended to be a little overprotective. "That's enough, Debby."

Debby glared at her. "No, it's not. Not if Ryerson is playing games." She swung on Ryerson with accusing eyes. "If you're using my sister in some weird way to get back at me, A. C. Ryerson, let me tell you right now, you're in big trouble. My family will be furious. Dad will take you to court."

"Oh, for heaven's sake, Debby," Virginia interrupted

swiftly. "Close your mouth long enough to get the facts straight. I don't need you to protect me from Ryerson."

"I'm not so sure about that," Debby shot back. "You may be a few years older than me, but you haven't had any real experience with men, except for what you got out of your marriage, and you sure didn't learn anything useful from that. I'll admit I wouldn't have thought Ryerson was the type to try to seduce you out of revenge, but you never know."

"I assure you," Virginia said with great dignity, "that there is no question of either seduction or revenge involved here. Kindly shut up, Debby."

"Your sister is right," Ryerson said calmly. "Close your mouth, Deb, before you chew off your toes. I give you my word, Ginny and I understand each other perfectly."

"Is that right?" Debby looked skeptical, but faced with two serenely assured faces, she ran out of argument. She glowered at her sister. "When did you give him permission to call you Ginny?"

"I didn't ask permission," Ryerson said before Virginia could reply. "But Ginny doesn't seem to mind, do you, Ginny?" He smiled down at her.

"Uh, no. No, I don't mind at all, *A.C.*"

"Ouch. I guess I had that coming," Ryerson said ruefully.

"Nobody calls him A.C.," Debby said helpfully. She sniffed experimentally. "Is that coffee I smell? I could use a cup."

Virginia's sense of excitement and discovery had evaporated. She wondered if she should be feeling guilty. But one glance at her sister's face told her there was no reason. Debby's wryly amused expression revealed no hint of anguish or despair. Her main reaction, other than amusement, seemed to be concern for her sister's welfare.

Virginia would have been more touched by her sister's attitude if she hadn't long ago told her entire family in no uncertain terms that she did not need or want their protection. She felt quite capable of taking care of herself when it came to men. Of course, she admitted privately, she had not been in any real danger from a man since her husband had died. She had never allowed one to get close enough to hurt her.

"The two of you would probably like to talk," Virginia murmured. "You must have a few details to discuss. Surely the conclusion of an immortal love affair deserves some sort of postmortem. I'll go get dressed." She hurried down the hall to her bedroom.

"I'll show you my broken heart if you'll show me yours, Ryerson," Virginia heard her sister say as Debby sauntered into the kitchen. "But first I need some coffee."

Virginia pulled on the first things she found in her closet—a pair of soft navy wool slacks and a yellow-and-white blouse. Then she brushed her hair into its usual sleek knot at the nape of her neck. When she was finished applying a few light touches of makeup she glanced in the mirror and was relieved to see her normal, serene, decorous, unexciting self staring back at her.

She listened intently for the sound of voices from the kitchen. The conversation between Ryerson and Debby sounded casual and even rather friendly, as far as she could tell. Whatever had ended between her sister and A. C. Ryerson certainly had not warranted the label *grand passion*. Both parties were relieved it was over, just as Ryerson had said.

When she walked back into the kitchen fifteen minutes later, the room was full of the fragrance of scrambled eggs and toast. Ryerson was doing the cooking. He appeared to have made himself at home with her stove and refrigerator. One would think he'd been waking up under her roof for years, Virginia thought. The idea did not bother her nearly as much as it should have. She turned to her sister, who was sitting at the table, sipping coffee. Debby no longer looked worried about Ryerson's presence in the cottage. Her lovely eyes were alight with a familiar mischief.

"Ryerson says he told you about the *big weekend*," Debby said amiably.

"I understand you called off the weekend with your usual flair, Debby. You must have known you'd put Mom and Dad in a tizzy."

"I didn't think they'd see the note," Debby said, wrinkling her pert nose. "It was meant for Ryerson."

"Then you should have made certain it wasn't delivered to my office while your father was there," Ryerson told her bluntly.

"Why did you open it in front of him?" Debby shot back.

"I didn't. My secretary did. She didn't know it was a personal matter. Poor Mrs. Clemens was so astonished that she dropped it. Your father picked it up and handed it to me. But not before he saw your name and glanced at it. He had a right to ask what the hell was going on. I told him."

"Oh, Lord." Debby shook her head. "So that's why you felt obliged to track me down? My parents made a fuss?"

"They were worried about you," Ryerson said.

"Where did you stay last night?" Virginia asked.

"With a friend in Bellevue. But I couldn't stay more than a night with her, and I wanted to be out of touch for a couple of days. I knew Mom and Dad were going to be upset when they found out I was no longer seeing Ryerson. I wanted to give the heat a chance to die down. They've been hoping for wedding bells, you know."

"I know," Virginia said.

"I came here this morning because I thought you would be out of town for a few more days. Hope you don't mind if I hang around a bit."

It was Ryerson who answered. He was dishing up the scrambled eggs. "Virginia might not mind, but I do. You can take off right after breakfast."

Debby glared at him. "Why should I do that?"

"Because I don't want you underfoot while I get to know Ginny," he retorted calmly, carrying the plates over to the table. "It's tough for a man to get over a broken heart when the old girlfriend is making a nuisance of herself. I've got plans and they don't include you."

Virginia's fingers shook slightly as she took her plate. Her gaze leaped to Ryerson's, and she found his silvery eyes smiling at her.

"For pete's sake," Debby complained, "aren't you even going to mourn our lost, dead love for a few days?"

"At my age one doesn't waste time mourning the kind of romance you and I had." Ryerson sat down and poured catsup over his eggs. "As soon as I realized my hearing had not been permanently damaged from heavy-metal music, I was on the road to recovery. Eat your eggs and leave, Deb."

"I've known you for over a month, and I didn't even realize you could cook," Debby grumbled. She dug into her eggs with gusto.

"Which tells us a great deal about our relationship, doesn't it?"

"True. But I think I realized how hopeless our relationship was the night we went to see Sleaze Train and you complained about the music from the minute we left the concert until you dropped me off at my front door."

"Sleaze Train lived up to its name. I've never heard such bad music in my life," Ryerson told her.

"I'm sure you'll enjoy Ginny's taste in music. Strictly retrograde. But don't count on being able to substitute one Middlebrook sister for the other at the altar," Debby advised around a bite of toast. "Ginny made a decision years ago never to marry again. Didn't you, Ginny?"

Virginia raised her brows at her sister. She was not about to let her outrageous sister drag her into this kind of conversation. "I think Ryerson is right, Deb. Why don't you just finish your breakfast and take off?"

Debby widened her eyes in fake shock. "Hey, what is

this? A conspiracy to get rid of me? I've been through a traumatic experience.''

"You're young," Ryerson informed her dryly. "I'm sure you'll bounce back real quick."

"Oh, yeah? What about you?" Debby retorted.

Ryerson looked across the table and met Virginia's eyes. "Me? I'm going to need plenty of sympathy, consolation and understanding."

"Why do I have this feeling I know exactly where you're going to look for all that sympathy, consolation and understanding?" Debby asked rhetorically. "Ginny, you're not going to let him cry on your shoulder, are you?"

Virginia hid her smile by taking a large bite of fluffy scrambled eggs. "A man who can cook can get just about anything he wants from a woman," she murmured before stopping to think. Her teasing words astounded her more than anyone else at the table.

Ryerson grinned in anticipation. "I'll remember that. Have some more scrambled eggs, Ginny."

"Thank you. Would you please pass the catsup?"

"Lord, how romantic," Debby muttered. "The two of you are going to make a terrific couple. You've got so much in common. People who put catsup on their eggs deserve each other."

Debby left reluctantly an hour later. She complained loudly about having to return to her own apartment where she could count on being hounded by her anxious parents, but her eyes were full of speculative interest as she waved farewell to her sister and Ryerson.

Virginia watched her sister guide the little sports car out of the sodden driveway and then she turned to Ryerson. A slow, satisfied smile edged his mouth.

"Two of a kind," he said softly, sounding pleased. "How do you feel about that, Virginia Elizabeth?"

She thought about it, aware of a distant, beckoning promise of happiness. She did not trust the lure, but she could not bring herself to resist it. She took refuge in practicality. "It's a little soon to know, isn't it?"

"No, it's not too soon to know. Not for me. But I'm willing to give you plenty of time." He stroked one blunt finger along the edge of her jaw. "We don't have to rush into anything. We're two adults who can take our time."

She touched his hand, taking pleasure in the strength in it. "Yes," she agreed. "We can take our time." She could get her feet wet very slowly, and she would not have to wade too deep. Ryerson was the kind of man who would let her run back to shore if she chose.

"I told you I'd like to get to know you much better, but in a way I already feel I know you very well." Ryerson's fingertip moved down the column of her throat to the curve of her shoulder. "You said last night that you would be interested in a friendship with a man."

"I would like that," she said quietly and meant it. She could see herself becoming very good friends with A. C. Ryerson. And perhaps, just perhaps, the association might blossom into something more than a friendship. She knew she was not cut out for a Grand Passion, but for the first time since her husband had died she found herself considering the possibility of a warm, comfortable, safe relationship that would prove satisfactory to both parties.

She halted her thoughts as she realized how far ahead they were spinning. There was plenty of time to see where it all led. It was enough for now just to feel that she was on the same wavelength as Ryerson. In fact, it was the most delightful sensation she had ever had with a man. She wanted to treasure it fully and understand and explore it completely.

"We'll take it slow and easy," Ryerson promised again. "No rush. I think you and I will become very close friends, Ginny."

Friends. Virginia smiled very brilliantly. "That sounds wonderful."

"NO RUSH." The reassuring words echoed again and again in Virginia's mind during the next three weeks. She would find herself pausing for a few minutes at her desk to think about them. They would float through her consciousness just before she went to sleep. She would repeat them to herself in the shower.

"No rush." She had found a man who was content to let a relationship build slowly, easily, naturally into a close friendship before he made any demands on her; a man who was willing to give her time. She and Ryerson would become good friends before they decided whether to take the risk of going to bed together. The knowledge was infinitely reassuring to Virginia.

For the first time since her disastrous marriage, Virginia could accept the fact that she might really be able to establish a close relationship with a man. And if she chose the right man, an understanding, undemanding man, she just might be able to perform adequately in bed. Ryerson wouldn't expect fireworks.

Almost four weeks after she had found Ryerson on her doorstep, Virginia met her sister for lunch at a downtown café. Debby showed up with several shopping bags. She was her usual eye-catching self in a sizzling red short skirt and a matching bolero jacket. She examined Virginia's tailored business suit and sleek hair and frowned slightly but said nothing. She was accustomed to her sister's more conservative ways.

"All right, let's have it," Debby demanded as soon as they were seated. "How's the big love affair going? We all know you and Ryerson have been seeing each other constantly for nearly a month. Mom and Dad are afraid to get their hopes up again, but personally I'm feeling very positive about the future. I think you and Ryerson are meant for each other."

"That's very generous of you," Virginia said blandly. She opened her menu and studied the list of pastas. The dish with olives, capers and basil looked especially interesting. Her appetite seemed to have increased a little lately. Usually she just had yogurt or a salad for lunch. "But just to set the record straight, there is no flaming love affair. Ryerson and I are friends."

Debby peered at her over the top of the menu. "Come on, Ginny, don't be coy. This is me, Debby, your nosy sister. What's going on between the two of you?"

"Well, last Saturday Ryerson and I spent a wonderful evening at the ballet," Virginia said sedately. "On Tuesday we had dinner on the waterfront. Excellent Alaskan salmon, by the way. I think we're going to attend a program of chamber music in the university district this weekend. We haven't quite decided on that, though. Also, there's a new exhibit of cacti at the conservatory in Volunteer Park that we've been meaning to tour."

Debby raised her eyes toward the ceiling. "An exhibit of cacti. Heaven help us. That's not what I meant and you know it. I want to know if you're sleeping with the man, darn it!"

It was Virginia's turn to raise her eyebrows. "You always come directly to the point, don't you, Deb?"

"Sure. Most folks think it's part of my charm. Now level with me, sister dear."

Virginia smiled loftily. "Your question does not deserve an answer, but I'll give you one, anyway, mostly because I know it will drive you nuts. I am not sleeping with him. Furthermore, I'm not at all worried about it one way or the other. Ryerson and I have already decided we have all the time in the world. We're not going to rush into anything. We're more concerned with becoming good friends than we are with being lovers."

"Hmm." Debby tapped the white tablecloth with one long, mauve nail. "Ryerson is a nice guy but I've seen the way he looks at you, Ginny. I'll tell you something. He never looked at me that way. He's got more than friendship on his mind. Does he know about your marriage?''

"He knows I was married once, yes. So was he. It was a long time ago for both of us. We don't talk about it.''

"I mean, does he know just how bad things were for you during those three years you were married?'' Debby persisted.

Virginia's smile vanished. "Not even you know just how bad things were, Deb.''

Debby had the grace to blush. "I've seen the way you've avoided any real entanglements since Jack's death. It doesn't take a genius to figure out just how scarred you were. Your family is bound to be very interested in the fact that you've finally started getting serious about someone. We're all hoping for the best, but we're a little nervous, too.''

Virginia sighed. "I know. Everyone's feeling quite protective. It's touching in a way, but totally unnecessary. Ryerson and I understand each other. We're going to take our time.''

"Is that his chief asset as far as you're concerned?'' Debby asked shrewdly. "He's not the type to rush you?''

"It's certainly a relief to find a man who is content to take things slowly,'' Virginia admitted.

Ryerson was so tender, so considerate, so kind and so content to let her set the pace of the relationship, Virginia reflected happily. A woman could count herself very lucky indeed to have a friend such as A. C. Ryerson.

"NO RUSH.''

Ryerson listened to his own words as they echoed mockingly through his head and wondered if he had been temporarily insane when he had given Virginia the glib promise of plenty of time.

He had been dating her for a full month now, and he was starting to climb the walls. It was ridiculous. It didn't help to remember that he'd dated Debby for a full month and barely noticed the lack of sex in the relationship. Things were vastly different this time around: he was definitely noticing the lack with Virginia Elizabeth. He hadn't felt this constantly aroused, constantly frustrated, sensation since high school. The unrelieved desire was becoming downright painful.

Ryerson got up from his desk and stalked to the window to glare down at the panorama of functional, utilitarian buildings and yards spread out around the offices of Middlebrook Power Systems. The southern end of Seattle was given over to manufacturing, shipping and industrial plants of various sizes and kinds. Generally speaking, this part of town was not the home of high-tech research, accounting firms or stock brokerage houses. This was the muscular side of Seattle, and the grime showed.

But there was money to be made here, as Boeing had proved over the years. Middlebrook Power Systems had always been profitable. Ryerson intended to make it even more so. He was content to have the company headquartered here in the heart of hardworking Seattle. The honest surroundings suited the product. Things were on track in his business life, Ryerson reflected.

The problem in his private life, he decided, bracing one hand against the windowsill as he gazed out over the landscape, was that it was Ginny's nature to proceed slowly and cautiously. He could hardly blame her. He was, after all, a lot like her. And truthfully, he had to admit a month was nothing in the overall time frame of a relationship. In three months he might have legitimate grounds to start wondering if things were headed in a sensible direction, but he certainly shouldn't be getting this anxious after only four weeks.

But he wanted her. Badly. The knowledge flared within him, an undeniable, unrelenting fact that he had to deal with on a daily basis.

Some primitive part of him was awake and prowling restlessly, yet Ginny seemed content to let matters drift in the uncertain territory of male-female friendship. Ryerson didn't doubt that she was expecting the same conclusion he was anticipating, but he was definitely doubting his own ability to last until it all came together for them.

She was enjoying the time they spent with each other, Ryerson told himself. He was certain of that. And he was seeing to it that they spent as many evenings as possible together, though ferry schedules were becoming a damned nuisance.

He was also certain of the extent of her response to his kisses. She went into his arms more and more willingly each time he reached for her, and she trembled sweetly when he touched her breasts. He found the response endearing. Her lips parted eagerly when he silently asked for surrender, but he sensed the lack of expertise in her kisses and wondered at it. She seemed warm and willing but strangely unsure of herself.

Inevitably she always found a gentle, firm way of ending things before they progressed to bed. And Ryerson, trapped by his own promise, had been reluctant to press her very hard.

Ryerson's fingers tightened around the wooden sill, and he felt a cold chill. He was never going to last. He had no way of knowing how long Ginny wanted to spend enjoying the preliminaries, but he suspected she would be content to go on like this for quite a while. She didn't seem in the least anxious to move toward bed.

He would be a basket case within another month.

What he needed was a way of breaking the platonic pattern that was forming in their relationship. Things were too serene, too calm, too sedate, too easy for Ginny to manage. Maybe a trip would be the answer. New and romantic surroundings as well as the sense of being outside the normal routine of life might encourage her to view their friendship in a new light.

Ryerson nodded to himself and walked back to the desk to pick up the phone and call a travel agent.

VIRGINIA WAS ENJOYING the view of Elliott Bay from Ryerson's downtown condominium and eating a marvelous grilled salmon that he had cooked himself when the plane tickets appeared. She was so startled when Ryerson put them down on the table in front of her that she nearly dropped her fork. Her eyes flew to his.

"Are you going somewhere on business?" she asked.

He looked at her, silver-gray eyes intent. "No. We're going somewhere. For pleasure, not business. I want to take you away for a few days. I think we need some time alone together. You mentioned you had some vacation time. Will you come with me, Ginny?"

She went still, sensing that something was about to change in their relationship and not at all sure she was ready for the change. "Where?"

"A little island in the Caribbean off the coast of Mexico. It's called Toralina. I've got reservations at a first-class resort. It's right on the beach. Brand-new. Features dancing every night under the stars, a casino, gourmet food and endless sand. With any luck the sand and the food will be separate. What do you say? Can you get a few days off?"

Virginia swallowed, a wave of uncertainty washing through her. She wasn't ready for this. Only a week ago she had been bragging to Debby about how she and Ryerson were going to take their time developing a close friendship.

But Virginia knew that if she accepted this offer of a trip to Toralina, she was tacitly accepting a radical change in her relationship with Ryerson. She was no fool. She knew that Ryerson was using the trip as a way of asking for a more physical commitment. If she went with him, he would expect her to share a hotel room. He would expect her to sleep with him.

He had been kind enough to suggest an excuse, if she felt

she needed one, Virginia realized. He had asked her if she could get the time off. All she had to do was say no. She knew he would understand that she was not yet ready.

But when would she be ready, Virginia asked herself silently. How long was she planning to take before she went to bed with Ryerson? A few more weeks? Months? She didn't know the answer to that question.

The plane ticket in front of her was Ryerson's way of asking her that same question. Maybe it was time they both discovered the answer. She considered Ryerson her best friend in the whole world, but if she couldn't give him what he needed in bed it would be better for all concerned if they faced that now rather than later.

"I'd love to go with you to Toralina," Virginia said softly and wondered at her own daring.

CHAPTER THREE

SHE WAS FAR MORE NERVOUS than any normal bride would be on her wedding night. But then, Virginia knew better than most brides how devastating a wedding night could be. She had to remind herself that this was most definitely not a wedding night. It was just the first night with Ryerson.

She would not panic, she promised herself.

Nevertheless, another chilling tremor of uncertainty went through Virginia as she dressed with painstaking care for dinner. Words such as *bride* and *wedding night* had a way of doing that to her. Some people panicked at the thought of spiders or airplanes. She panicked at the thought of marriage.

Deliberately she pushed the feeling aside. The last thing she needed to do was start rehashing the memories of her all-too-real wedding night and the nightmare of a marriage that had followed.

She was perfectly safe, Virginia reminded herself for the thousandth time. After all, she wasn't marrying Ryerson; she was merely attempting to start an affair with him. And Ryerson was nothing like her dead husband. Ryerson was her friend, her companion, a man with whom she had everything in common.

Virginia had been repeating the litany to herself since the evening Ryerson had put the tickets to Toralina down in front of her and asked her to go with him to the island. Amid the flurry of packing and getting ready for the trip, she had done a good job of convincing herself that everything was going to be all right. But tonight a lot of suppressed anxiety was surfacing. The evening was balmy and warm, but Virginia felt little chills down her spine and her palms were alternately hot and cold.

She was not marrying the man. She was only going to attempt to go to bed with him. Ryerson wasn't the sort to expect too much from her.

Or was he?

He was, after all, a disturbingly virile man. She might not be the passion queen of the century, but that didn't mean all her female instincts were blunted. She was perfectly capable of sensing the strong vein of controlled sexuality that ran beneath the surface in Ryerson. It was why she had agreed to this trip. Virginia had known that sooner or later the sexual issue had to be settled between them. Both of them had to learn the truth about this side of their friendship.

She finished zipping up the flower-splashed yellow silk she had bought especially for the trip to Toralina. The full skirts of the gown drifted weightlessly around her ankles. The wide sleeves were caught in deep cuffs that emphasized her elegantly shaped hands. The neckline was discreet, displaying a hint of throat and shoulder but no cleavage. Debby had argued for a dress that did more to showcase her sister's magnificent bosom, but Virginia knew she would never have been comfortable in it. She wasn't the sort to wear low-cut dresses.

She wore her hair down tonight. It fell in a smooth, heavy curve on either side of her face, just brushing her shoulders.

Virginia slipped on her high heels and walked over to the window to examine once again the dreamlike view. Beyond the gardens outside the luxurious suite an endless vista of turquoise water and sky stretched to the horizon. A wide strip of sand marked the beautiful beach below. Hillsides that were lush with tropical vegetation embraced the resort. The elegant hotel was a picturesque cluster of brilliant white walls and red-tiled roofs. The place didn't look at all like

Seattle, Virginia thought in amusement. It was a fantasy setting. And that was a good thing.

It was a perfect place to begin a full-fledged affair, and there was no doubt but that Ryerson had brought her here with that purpose in mind.

What she needed, Virginia decided as she turned away from the window, was a drink. A large one.

She crossed the wicker-furnished bedroom, ignoring the wide bed that dominated it and opened the door into the sitting area. She took a deep breath as Ryerson put down the *Wall Street Journal* he had been reading and got to his feet. For a moment she simply stared at him, distantly aware of a sense of longing.

He looked so good, Virginia thought wistfully. The kind of man who had the calm self-assurance it took to look terrific in the conservative black-and-white evening clothes he was wearing.

"I think that must be the original power suit," Virginia said lightly. "You look fabulous."

Ryerson searched her face for a few seconds, and then he smiled slowly. "You're the one who looks fabulous tonight." He came toward her, his eyes drinking in the sight of her. "Very exotic and a little mysterious."

"I don't feel quite like myself tonight," she admitted.

"Neither do I. I haven't given more than two minutes' thought to diesel engines since we got here." Ryerson's silver eyes gleamed. "Maybe the tropics are good for us, Ginny. Maybe this is just what both of us needed." He slid one large hand under the bell of her hair and cupped her nape. Then he bent his head and kissed the curve of her throat.

Virginia closed her eyes and yielded momentarily to the small shiver of anticipation that went through her. It was going to be all right, she told herself. When she lifted her lashes again, Ryerson was looking down at her with an expression that was both infinitely possessive and infinitely tender. She gathered her courage to ask the question that was seething within her.

"Ryerson," she whispered, "I have to ask you something. Something important."

He nodded patiently. "Anything."

"Will you…that is, if things don't…don't quite work out tonight. I mean, if it's all a big mistake and everything goes wrong will you still want to be my friend?"

"Ginny." He groaned as he dropped a feather-light kiss on her nose. "What's the matter with you, honey? Nothing's going to go wrong. We're friends and we're going to become lovers. What could possibly go wrong?"

"But if it doesn't work out. If we don't become lovers, will we still be friends?" She had to know, she told herself.

Ryerson's eyes met hers in a steady, reassuring glance. "You're really nervous about this, aren't you?"

"A little." And that was the understatement of the century.

"Honey, we've been friends since that first night. Nothing's going to change that. What's going to happen between us in bed will only deepen our friendship. Now what do you say we take these two people who happen to be good friends out for an evening in paradise?" His large hand closed around hers, his eyes asking for much more than a dinner date.

Virginia retreated from the issue that was worrying her so much and took refuge in humor. "You're not even talking like a man who's very big in diesel motors."

He trailed a finger across her bare shoulder. "We're even. You're not dressed like a lady who's made a career in information storage and retrieval."

Virginia grimaced. "Don't remind me. Do you think the dress is a bit much?"

"I think the dress is perfect."

They stepped outside into the warm, fragrant evening and walked along a secluded, flower-lined path. The main build-

ing of the resort was located some distance away, hidden
by the thick greenery that provided privacy for the individual suites. The hotel gardens were virtually a tropical forest—heavy, lush and wild. As they walked, Virginia occasionally caught sight of other guests who were also making
their way toward the resort's core.

"I thought we'd have drinks on the terrace and then go
in to dinner. The casino opens at nine," Ryerson said.

Virginia slanted him a curious glance. "Do you gamble?"

"Rarely. I play poker once in a while but that's about it.
This trip is the biggest gamble I've taken in years. How
about you?"

She went pink at the obvious meaning in his words.
"Same here," she admitted dryly.

Ryerson grinned and tugged her a little closer to his side.
"Think of me as a sure thing."

If only she could guarantee him the same in return, Virginia thought fleetingly.

The terrace bar was already crowded by the time they
arrived. They found a small table in a secluded corner, and
Virginia ordered a large margarita instead of her usual white
wine. Ryerson stuck to Scotch.

Some of Virginia's nervousness slipped away as the tequila took hold. Conversation with Ryerson, which had been
a bit stilted prior to the drink, resumed its normal easy flow.
The island felt like another world.

By the time they went into the open-air dining room to
feast on conch chowder, crisp, fried plantains and fish
poached in lime juice, Virginia was feeling a little better.
She was a million miles away from Seattle and her own
past. The bottle of wine Ryerson ordered with the meal
added to the effect.

"I'm feeling lucky tonight," Ryerson announced after
dinner. "Let's try the casino."

He took Virginia's hand in his and led her into the glittering casino where tuxedoed croupiers dealt cards and rows of silver slot machines tinkled merrily.

The room was full of fashionably dressed hotel guests. The atmosphere could not have been more removed from reality. Virginia's feeling of having stepped into a different world intensified. She watched Ryerson play blackjack for a while, and then she tried her hand at the slots. Ten dollars worth of tokens tumbled into her hands the first time she pulled the handle. She added them to Ryerson's blackjack winnings.

"You were right," she told him with a laugh. "This is our lucky night." When a hostess came by with a complimentary glass of champagne, Virginia helped herself. She couldn't bear to have the marvelous sense of unreality begin to fade.

But as she tipped the flute to her lips, Ryerson gently captured her wrist. He looked down at her with a half-amused, half-concerned expression.

"Careful," he advised. "It's easy to lose track when you're enjoying yourself the way you seem to be tonight."

She frowned slightly. "Lose track? Oh, you mean the champagne. Don't worry, Ryerson. I'm feeling great. Never felt better, in fact. I promise not to pass out on you."

"I'm not so sure about that." Deftly he removed the glass from her hand. When she started to protest he laid a finger against her lips. "Trust me. You're not used to this kind of wild living. Don't overdo it or you'll pay for it all day tomorrow, and that would be a shame. We don't have forever here. Only a few days. I don't want us to waste a single one."

He didn't understand, Virginia thought resentfully. She didn't care how bad she felt tomorrow as long as she got through tonight without disgracing herself. "I'm not worried about tomorrow. Why should you be?" she asked.

"Not worried about tomorrow?" Ryerson mocked.

"Come now, that doesn't sound like my Virginia Elizabeth."

"Maybe I don't want to feel like Virginia Elizabeth tonight," she retorted.

"Who do you want to feel like?"

She blinked at the question. "I'd like to be the woman you want me to be tonight."

The laughter faded from his gaze and the silvery eyes. "The woman I want you to be is the woman you are, Ginny. You don't have to become someone else."

"That's what you think," she muttered. Then she brightened, determined not to lose the ground she had already gained. "Let's go watch the poker players for a while."

Ryerson said nothing, but he allowed her to lead him over to a roped-off dais where several men in evening dress sat playing poker. One of the players, a young, redheaded man in his late twenties, seemed more intense than the others. Smoke drifted upward from the cigarette in his fingers. He was winning heavily.

As Virginia and Ryerson watched, the players dropped out one by one until the redheaded man was left with the pot. As he collected his winnings, he glanced up, and Virginia was startled by a pair of feverishly bright blue eyes. The man was obviously high on his victory. As Ryerson started to turn away with Virginia in tow, the stranger spoke.

"Hey, there, you with the lady in yellow. Can I interest you in a game? You look like a man with a sense of adventure."

Ryerson glanced back over his shoulder and shook his head politely. "Not tonight, thanks. Maybe some other time."

"Anytime, but why not tonight? The name's Brigman, by the way. Harry Brigman. I'm riding a streak of luck that just won't quit."

"So am I," Ryerson said with a small smile. He squeezed Virginia's hand. "So am I."

"Well, why don't we get together with a few of these other gentlemen and see what happens?" Brigman said cheerfully.

Virginia felt Ryerson hesitate. She looked up at him. "If you want to play for a while, go ahead. I don't mind."

He considered the matter. "You know, the funny thing is, I do feel lucky tonight."

"Then go ahead and play." Virginia knew she was deliberately buying a little more time for herself, but she ignored the fact. "I'll watch."

Brigman gazed at them speculatively. "Maybe the lady's your good-luck charm, friend."

"Maybe she is," Ryerson agreed casually. He looked down at Virginia, his decision appearing suddenly in his eyes. He brushed her mouth with his own. Then he stepped up onto the dais and took a seat at the card table. He glanced back once to make sure Virginia was nearby.

She rested her elbows on the polished wooden rail that surrounded the playing area and smiled reassuringly. A poker game could last for hours, she reminded herself. Plenty of time for her to work up a little more courage.

She was right about one thing—the poker game went on for some time. As soon as it started, Ryerson, along with every other man at the table, quickly forgot about her. Virginia watched the game for a while, but most of the subtleties were lost on her. She knew next to nothing about poker. After a while she wandered off to get another drink at the bar.

When she returned, there was no sign of any letup in the intensity of play. Ryerson had his jacket off, as did most of the other men at the table, but that was the only concession made to the tension. Virginia did notice that the pile of chips in front of Ryerson seemed to be growing. She took that as a good sign.

She leaned against the railing again, drink in hand, and admired Ryerson's calm, unruffled technique. Nothing seemed to faze him. He could have been doing paperwork in his office for all the emotion he displayed. Brigman, on the other hand, appeared to be getting more and more tense and agitated. It was obvious he was starting to lose, and the experience appeared to be new to him. He did not care for it.

Another hour passed. Virginia wandered away to listen to the band. Two men asked her to dance, but she politely declined. When she returned, she realized the poker game had reached a crisis of some kind. Everyone seemed to have dropped out except for Ryerson and Brigman. There was sweat on Brigman's brow. It trickled down his nose. He wiped it off with an angry, impatient hand before saying something in a low voice.

He spread his cards on the table, and Ryerson did the same. From where she stood, Virginia could not see the hands and wouldn't have been able to decipher them if she had, but she knew a loser's face when she saw it. Harry Brigman had just lost badly. He got to his feet with a jerky movement and murmured something to Ryerson. Then he turned and strode out of the casino. Ryerson rose more slowly, stretching his shoulders. He glanced around and saw Virginia.

"I'll be back in a few minutes," he said quietly.

"Where are you going?"

"Brigman and I are going to talk privately. Stay where you are." Without waiting for her reply, he followed Brigman out of the casino.

Virginia waited impatiently, curious and somewhat alarmed. She wondered what had happened during the game that required a private consultation between Ryerson and Brigman. She was about to follow the two men out of the casino when Ryerson unexpectedly returned. Brigman was not with him.

"What in the world is going on?" Virginia demanded softly as she hurried to meet Ryerson.

Ryerson's eyes were glittering. A tightly leashed excitement radiated from him. "Brigman just covered his losses, that's all."

"But how? Why did you have to leave? What's happening?"

"Hush. I'll tell you all about it. Let's get out of here."

He took her arm and led her out into the balmy night. When they were safely out of sight, he drew her to a halt near a garden light and reached into his jacket pocket. "Take a look at this."

Virginia studied the small jewelry box in his hand. It was old, covered in green velvet. A strange sense of exhilaration gripped her. "What is it?"

Without a word Ryerson opened the box and exposed the contents. Virginia caught her breath. For a second she could not move. Her gaze was riveted on what lay inside the velvet container.

It was a bracelet. An incredible bracelet. Unlike any bracelet Virginia had ever seen. Green flames frozen forever in clear stones shimmered in the soft light. Gold linked the individual emerald fires to small diamonds. The whole piece glowed with a warmth that was surely unnatural for a cold piece of jewelry.

Virginia could not find words as her sense of reality shifted slightly. Tension seized her. For a timeless moment she had the disconcerting feeling that she was looking at an object that was not bound completely to the same dimension in which everything else around her existed. The object in the box seemed to be simultaneously part of the past, the present and the future.

An unfamiliar sense of possessiveness leaped into life within Virginia. *The object in the jewelry box belonged to her and Ryerson.* She knew that with a deep, absolute certainty.

Virginia shook off the unsettling sensations that had taken over her emotions. She finally found her tongue.

"It's a bracelet."

"Emeralds and diamonds linked with gold," Ryerson said. "Or so Brigman claims."

"Do you believe him?"

"I'm not sure. I'm no jeweler."

"It's stunning, Ryerson. Absolutely beautiful. Even if it's a fake, it's the most fascinating piece of jewelry I've ever seen."

"If it's a fake, it's a very good one. Look, here's a formal jeweler's appraisal of the age of the bracelet." Ryerson indicated a folded piece of paper lying under the velvet cushion. "It doesn't indicate the value but it does claim the thing is late seventeenth century."

"Incredible."

Ryerson closed the box, his gaze very brilliant. "I felt the same way when I saw it," he said roughly. "The minute Brigman opened the box and showed it to me, I knew I had to have it. I told him I'd accept it as full payment for what he lost to me tonight."

"Did he lose that heavily?"

"When the game ended, he owed me over ten thousand dollars."

Virginia's mouth fell open. "Ten thousand dollars?" she squeaked. "Ryerson, you gambled for that kind of money?"

"I told you I was feeling lucky." His brief grin was wicked.

"Yes, but *ten thousand dollars*? I can't believe it. What if this bracelet is a fake? Unless those stones are real, it won't be worth anything near ten thousand."

Ryerson dropped the box back into his pocket. "And if the stones are real, it's probably worth a lot more than ten thousand. Brigman didn't have any choice. He didn't have ten grand on him. This was the only thing he could use to cover the debt. One way or another, I have the feeling I've got my money's worth." He smiled at her with satisfaction.

"Come on, Virginia Elizabeth, let's go have a drink. I could use one."

"So could I," she agreed weakly. She felt dizzy and not just from the drinks she'd already had. The idea of a ten-thousand-dollar poker game was enough to make anyone light-headed. "It's so unlike you," she murmured wonderingly.

"What?"

"Playing for those stakes."

Ryerson grinned again, looking arrogantly triumphant. "Lady, the evening is young, and I'm still feeling lucky. This is my night."

She wasn't sure how to take that remark, so she let it slide. Besides, she was beginning to feel some of Ryerson's triumph. She had never seen anything in her life as beautiful as the emerald-and-diamond bracelet.

"Maybe I really am your lucky charm," she murmured daringly.

"I never doubted that for a minute," he assured her.

For the first time, Virginia began to look forward to the end of the evening.

They danced until shortly after one o'clock, and Virginia was amazed by the small but definite sense of anticipation within her. Instead of the anxiety that had been gnawing at her all day, she was now filled with a delicate excitement that was completely unfamiliar.

Maybe everything really would be all right tonight. Maybe her friendship with Ryerson could be extended to include a successful affair with him. She nestled closer to him on the dance floor, and Ryerson's arms tightened around her. She was aware of the hard edge of the bracelet box inside his jacket. And that was not the only hardness she felt when Ryerson held her this close, Virginia realized.

She and Ryerson were in the middle of a slow, sensuous number when the decisive moment arrived. She had been cradled contentedly in his arms, her head on his broad shoulder and her eyes almost closed when he spoke softly in her ear.

"Let's go back to the room, honey. It's way past our bedtime. I think it's time to see just how lucky I'm going to get tonight."

The gentle, unreal feeling of happy anticipation that she had been enjoying wavered slightly. Virginia tried to cling to it as she stirred and lifted her head. With a twinge of anxiety, she realized she was not quite ready. She made a small show of glancing at the watch on her wrist.

"It's just one o'clock. The night is still young by jet-setter standards," she pointed out with a false cheerfulness.

"I'm sure the rest of the jet-setters will excuse us," Ryerson murmured, taking her arm to guide her off the dance floor.

Maybe another drink would help, Virginia thought. "How about a nightcap under the stars?" she suggested brightly.

He looked down at her, silver eyes silently questioning. "All right, if that's what you want."

She nodded quickly. "I'm sure that's the sort of thing real international jet-setters do."

"Far be it from me to spoil the image."

Ryerson took her to the terrace bar and sat her down in a wicker chair. He ordered two brandies and then settled back to sip his.

"It's beautiful, isn't it?" Virginia said, taking a too-large swallow of the brandy. Her throat burned, and she barely stifled a cough.

"The sea is fine. But you're the most beautiful thing on the horizon," Ryerson said quietly.

Virginia's head snapped around, and she found him watching her with eyes that were the same color as the silvery sea. There was no element of teasing or flirtation in his gaze. Ryerson wanted her, and his need was starkly evident in his face. Virginia raised the brandy snifter to her lips.

But Ryerson reached out and stayed her hand. "Does it really take another dose of alcohol to make going to bed with me seem like an interesting thing to do? I'm your friend, Virginia, remember? You can tell me the truth. If you don't want to go to bed with me, just say it."

Instantly Virginia was swamped with despair. None of this was his fault. She struggled for a weakly reassuring smile. "I guess I'm a little nervous."

He answered her smile with a faint curve of his hard mouth. But his eyes were full of understanding. "If it's any consolation, so am I. Under the circumstances, I don't think that's so strange. This is beginning to feel like the first night of a honeymoon, isn't it?"

Virginia stiffened and then forced herself to relax. It was not the first night of a honeymoon, she reminded herself. Ryerson hadn't really meant that. Just a poor choice of words. "You're nervous, too?"

"Yeah."

For some reason she found that vastly comforting. "We have a lot in common, don't we?" she asked wistfully. "Right down to getting nervous about something like this."

"I think we'll both be fine once we get started," Ryerson said gently. His eyes were bottomless pools of silvery moonlight.

Virginia moistened her dry lips. It was going to be easier knowing Ryerson was a little uncertain, too. She tossed down the rest of the brandy with a flourish. The time for action had arrived.

"Well, if you think we'll both do all right once we get started, then by all means let's get started. Let's get the whole thing over and done with and see what happens," she said with brisk determination. She shot to her feet and imperiously held out her hand to Ryerson. "You're right. It's time to go for it. No pain, no gain. Onward and upward. I'm ready if you are."

Ryerson eyed her summoning fingers for a few seconds

and then looked up at her with a strange expression. "This isn't the Charge of the Light Brigade, you know. If you'd rather wait..."

"No, absolutely not. Never put off until tomorrow what should be done tonight," she declared in ringing tones. Her decision was made. It had been made from the moment she had accepted the ticket to Toralina. Her courage was as high as it would ever be. "It's now or never. No more waiting. You invited me on this trip for a specific reason and I came along knowing that reason. I'm sick of being a coward. It's time we both found out the truth once and for all." She grabbed his hand and tugged him to his feet.

"The truth about what?" Ryerson asked as she pulled forcibly on his hand. He allowed himself to be drawn slowly to his feet.

"Never mind," Virginia said as she swept him out the door and down the stone path that led to their suite. "The main thing is to keep the momentum going. Ride the wave. Go with the flow. Mustn't get cold feet now. It's do or die. Now or never."

"I was wrong. This does seem to be turning into the Charge of the Light Brigade, after all," Ryerson observed warily as he obediently let himself be dragged down the path. "I can't help wondering why. Is there something we should talk about first, sweetheart? Are there cannons out there in the valley that I don't know about?"

"This isn't a time for talk; it's a time for action," she told him stoutly.

"If you say so. But, Ginny, there's no need to rush into this. You said yourself it's still early. We've got all night."

She came to a sudden halt and whirled to face him. "This was all your idea. Have you changed your mind?"

Ryerson barely avoided colliding with her. He stared down into her fierce expression. "No, honey, I haven't changed my mind. But I'll admit I don't understand your attitude."

"There's nothing to understand," she told him aggressively. "I'm ready. You're ready. Let's go do it."

"Right," he agreed blandly. "I won't argue with that logic." He took the key out of his pocket and inserted it in the lock. When he stood politely aside, Virginia sailed into the room, pulling him after her.

As soon as she had him over the threshold, she slammed the door and locked it. Then she swung around to confront him. She was trembling with something that might have been excitement or terror. In that moment she honestly did not know which emotion was causing her pulse to race.

With her eyes never leaving Ryerson's intent gaze, she quickly unbuttoned the wide cuffs of the yellow silk gown. Ryerson said nothing. He just watched with an unreadable expression as she reached behind herself and fumbled with the zipper.

She lost a little nerve as the bodice started to crumple to her waist. Hastily she caught the soft fabric in both hands and held it over her full breasts.

"Want some help?" Ryerson asked with grave politeness.

Virginia shook her head quickly. "No. No, I'm fine. Excuse me, please." She rushed into the bedroom and flung the door closed behind her. Frantically she hunted through the closet for the new nightgown she had purchased for the trip. It was in there somewhere. She distinctly remembered unpacking the thing. Clutching the dress to her breasts, she bent over to see if the nightgown had somehow slipped to the floor of the closet. Behind her the door opened.

Virginia gave a small gasp of alarm and stood up so quickly that she hit her head on the closet doorknob.

"Damn!" She groaned and rubbed the injured spot. The silk dress fell to her hips, revealing her prim cotton bra and the waistband of her equally demure white cotton panties. Belatedly Virginia grabbed the bodice of her gown.

"Are you all right?" Ryerson came slowly into the room,

loosening his tie. He had already discarded his jacket. He was carrying the jeweler's box.

"I'm fine," she assured him breathlessly.

"Ginny, are you sure nothing's wrong?" Ryerson slung the tie down over a chair arm.

"Of course there's nothing wrong. What could be wrong? This is a very straightforward situation, isn't it? I mean, you and I here together. We're just good friends who are going to...to go to bed together. A very friendly thing to do. It was bound to happen sometime, wasn't it?"

He came closer, unfastening the buttons of his white shirt. "Yes, it was bound to happen sometime." He looked down into her wide, anxious eyes. "I've been wanting you since the first night I met you."

She swallowed. "You're absolutely sure of that?"

His eyes narrowed thoughtfully as he studied her tense face. "Absolutely certain. But it's no good unless you feel the same way. Do you want me, Ginny?"

"Yes," she gasped. "Yes, I want you." It was true, she realized with an inner start. For the first time she acknowledged to herself that she really did want him. She wasn't doing this just to please him; she actually wanted to go to bed with Ryerson. But wanting him and being able to satisfy him were two entirely different things.

"Then I don't see any problem."

"Lucky you," she murmured under her breath.

"Honey, it's me. Your friend. Remember?" His shirt fell open. Ginny stared at the broad expanse of his chest.

"None of my friends have ever looked like you," she heard herself say in a faint voice. Her eyes followed the trail of dark, curling hair down his flat stomach to where it disappeared beneath his belt. The strong, aggressive outline of his body below the belt was ample proof of her statement. Most definitely none of her friends looked like him. Ryerson was a big man, and he would have big appetites. She had to satisfy him. She just had to. She couldn't bear it if she failed tonight as she had failed with her husband.

"Ginny, honey, I promise you that none of my friends have ever looked like you, either. None of them have ever turned me on the way you do."

"Oh, Ryerson." She gave a small cry and without pausing to think she released the bodice of her dress and flung herself into his arms.

Ryerson chuckled softly, sounding relieved and very pleased. He wrapped her close against him. "It's going to be okay," he said into her hair. "Everything's going to be all right."

Opening the jewelry box behind her back, he removed the bracelet and carefully fastened it on her wrist. He tossed the empty box down on the dresser and studied the glittering stones on her arm.

"It was made for you," Ryerson said softly.

Virginia looked down at the bracelet and knew somehow that he was right. It had been made for her to wear. With Ryerson.

The bracelet felt unexpectedly warm on her wrist. Virginia was surprised. She had thought it would feel cool to the touch. "You want me to wear it? Now? In bed?" she asked uncertainly.

"Does that seem a little too kinky to you?"

"No, no, not at all. A bit exotic, perhaps, but not really kinky. It's just that I've never worn anything like this to bed before."

"We're even. I've never been to bed with a woman who was wearing emeralds and diamonds," Ryerson interrupted gently. "Tonight is going to be very special for both of us." He touched her shoulder lightly, his fingertips a little rough against her soft skin.

Virginia clutched him around the waist. Everything would be all right as long as she kept going forward and didn't lose her nerve, she thought. Ryerson felt good. Warm and heavy and right. Just as the bracelet did on her wrist. Her nerves seemed to be humming with genuine excitement now, not fear. For the first time she allowed herself real hope. She was beginning to think she might be able to get through this, after all.

The important thing was not to lose her nerve.

Under no circumstances must she give herself a chance to lose her nerve. *Forward.*

Driven by a sense of urgency, Virginia reached up to push Ryerson's shirt off his shoulders, and then she quickly fumbled with the zipper of his trousers. She had his pants halfway off when she remembered his shoes. Things were already getting awkward, she thought uneasily as she knelt at his feet and struggled with his shoelaces. Ryerson reached down and tangled his hands in her hair. She sensed the sexual tension in his touch. It sent a ripple of response through her.

Ryerson patiently allowed her to undress him down to his briefs, his expression half-amused and totally aroused as he watched her. When she was finished, she stepped back with a small frown to see if she had overlooked something. Not that anything about Ryerson was easy to overlook. He was very large and very male standing there in front of her, wearing only his briefs. Virginia chewed on her lower lip.

"Hey, it's me," Ryerson said softly. He stepped forward and tilted her face up so that she was forced to meet the desire in his eyes.

"Let me undress you now," he said thickly. He tugged her gently into his arms.

Virginia could feel the unmistakable hardness of his body as he pinned her close. He was hard all over, she thought in vague wonder. His shoulders, his thighs, his smoothly muscled back all seemed strong and tight and hard. She inhaled the earthy scent of him and realized she found it tantalizing. Something unfamiliar vibrated within her.

Then she felt his hands on the silk dress, pushing it carefully down over her hips. It fell to the floor near his trousers and shirt and Virginia was now violently aware of her near nakedness. She searched Ryerson's face anxiously for any sign of disappointment.

"You're beautiful," he said in a voice that was dark and vibrant with his desire. "You're all a man could want." His hands drifted down over her full breasts. He unclasped her plain, functional bra, dropped it on the floor and took the weight of her into his warm palms. His thumbs moved slowly over her nipples. Virginia shivered and closed her eyes for a moment. His hands felt so good on her body.

Before she had completely adjusted to the feel of his touch on her breasts, Ryerson's strong, sensitive hands slid downward to settle on the curve of her hips. He flexed his fingers on her buttocks and groaned. Then, as if unable to help himself, he lowered his head and kissed her deeply.

Reassured that nothing had gone wrong yet, Virginia resumed her rush toward bed. She gave herself no chance to respond to Ryerson's kiss. There was no need to dawdle over that part, she told herself. She already knew he liked kissing her. The worst was still ahead of her, and she wanted to get it over with so that the truth would be out at last.

Pulling free of his arms, Virginia turned and dashed over to the closet. She yanked on the nightgown, which, mercifully, was quickly located on the closet floor. The garment was new, but it looked very much like all the rest of her lingerie. It was made of plain, practical cotton, long sleeved with a prim neckline.

Using the soft material as a screen, she wriggled out of her panties. Then she scooted over to the bed and ripped back the covers. She bounced down onto the mattress, grabbed the sheet to her breasts and pasted on what she hoped was a welcoming smile.

"Maybe you should have had a little more brandy," Ryerson observed ruefully as he walked slowly over to the bed.

"Come to bed, Ryerson. Let's not waste any more time."

"If you're sure this is the way you want it," he muttered, "who am I to complain? I sure as hell am ready. And there will be time enough later to take it slowly. I want you so much, sweet Ginny."

He stripped off his briefs, revealing the hard, thrusting reality of his manhood. Virginia sucked in her breath, and her sense of resolve wavered again. Ryerson was definitely built to scale.

She was no lightweight herself, Virginia thought bravely. Theoretically she and Ryerson should fit very well together.

Before she could give herself any more pep talks, Ryerson was beside her on the bed, putting a hefty dent in the mattress as he reached for her. She was trembling when she went stiffly into his arms, but she was more determined than ever to finish what she had started.

When her arm went around his shoulders, moonlight glanced off the emeralds on her wrist. Virginia saw the gleaming flash and felt oddly reassured. She was doing the right thing, she told herself.

Ryerson loomed over her, all massive shoulders and lean, hard muscle. She felt one of his legs snag hers, and a tiny frisson of panic escaped in spite of her determination to contain it. She squelched it at once.

This was Ryerson, she told herself over and over again. It was going to be all right. Dear heaven, it had to be all right. She wouldn't be able to bear it if he wasn't satisfied with her.

Ryerson ducked his head to kiss her breast, and Virginia held her breath. She thought she liked the feel of his tongue on her nipple, but she couldn't concentrate on the delicious sensation it caused. She was too busy worrying about what came next. When his hand moved down her side to her thigh, she tensed.

"Ginny?"

"Yes, Ryerson?" She clutched at him, her nails digging into his shoulders.

"This is going to work a lot better if you relax."

"I can't relax," she wailed. "I told you, I'm a little nervous. How do you expect me to relax?"

"I might have been right earlier when I said this was like the start of a honeymoon. This is beginning to feel like a wedding night, all right. A Victorian wedding night. What are you planning to do? Lie back and think of England?"

Virginia froze. If he got impatient or lost his temper she wouldn't stand a chance of pulling this off. "There's no need to get angry. I'm doing my best." Her voice was barely audible.

Ryerson made an impatient movement and cupped her face between his hands. His expression revealed concern as well as desire. "You're not making me angry. I'm just trying to figure out what the hell is going on here."

"We're supposed to be making love," she reminded him through gritted teeth. "Why don't you get on with it?"

He stared down at her from suddenly narrowed eyes. "I will," he finally said. "But I think I'll do it my way, not yours."

Virginia wanted to scream. "What's wrong with the woman taking the lead?" she challenged in an unnaturally shrill voice. "I thought men liked to get it over with fast."

He shook his head, smiling faintly. "Believe me, I have no objections to your taking the lead. But first you're going to have to catch up with me."

"What do you mean, catch up with you?" she asked in utter bewilderment. "*Ryerson*, what are you doing?"

"I'm going to give you a small head start."

He caught both her hands in one of his and gently held them together above her head.

"Wait. Ryerson, what's going on?" Her voice was a soft shriek of genuine alarm.

"Sorry, sweetheart, but at the rate you were going, you were about to draw blood."

She closed her eyes in humiliation as she realized just how deeply she had been digging her nails into his shoulders. The poor man must have been suffering terribly. "I'm sorry," she got out.

"Don't be sorry," he said as he carefully parted her legs with his free hand and inserted his knee between her thighs. "There's a time and a place for everything. We'll get to the point where I won't mind having your nails in my back. But first we need to cover a little more territory."

"I don't understand."

"I'm beginning to realize that. Just relax, sweetheart, and pretend you're involved in an information retrieval search on your office computer."

"A search!" A small, despairing laugh was forced out of her.

"That's better," Ryerson said approvingly. Continuing to anchor her wrists above her head, he bent down to kiss her again.

He took his time, inviting her to remember the kisses they had shared in the past. She had enjoyed those kisses, knowing they were safe, knowing he would not demand more of her than she could give.

Virginia gave a tremulous little sigh. She knew and loved Ryerson's kisses. She could enjoy them without fear. Slowly she gave herself up to the familiar caress and parted her lips willingly when his tongue stole into her mouth.

For a long time he made no further demands. It was as if he were perfectly content to go on kissing her all night long. Virginia moaned softly and ceased thinking about the immediate future. Her senses began to swim with pleasurable anticipation. A deep restlessness started to uncoil within her.

"That's it, sweetheart. That's my beautiful, sexy Ginny.

Honey, you don't know what you do to me. You feel so good. I've been wanting to have you like this for weeks."

He kept talking to her in that soft, rough, warm voice. She heard the words of encouragement and reassurance, but what really registered was the tone of them. Ryerson's voice was dark and thick with passion. He told her over and over again how much he wanted her and described in graphic detail exactly what he was going to do to her. To her utter astonishment, Virginia found herself responding to the promise of passion in his words.

It was unlike anything she had ever known. Hesitantly at first, she allowed herself to explore the sensations pouring through her.

At first she simply floated. Ryerson's hands continued to move on her, and something hot and demanding stirred to life within her. Slowly she let herself be tugged deeper into a mysterious whirlpool. She twisted against Ryerson, unconsciously seeking more of him.

"That's it, Ginny. That's the way I want you to feel." His hand slipped down over her stomach to the soft nest below. Virginia started to return to reality with a rush. She knew what came next. She was prepared for it. She tensed again and opened her eyes as she struggled to free her hands.

Ryerson held her still, soothing her carefully. "I'm just going to touch you. It's all I want to do right now."

"It's not all you want," she retorted achingly. "I'm not stupid. And I want what you want, Ryerson. I want you to make love to me. I'm ready now."

He trailed a finger into the warm dampness between her legs. Virginia shuddered in startled reaction. "You're a lot readier than you were a few minutes ago," he agreed in satisfaction. "But you still haven't caught up with me. You wanted to take the lead, remember?"

"Yes, but..."

"Hush, love." He kissed her back into silence. "We really do have all night. I swear to you that all I want to do at the moment is touch you.''

Virginia searched his silver eyes and decided he was telling the truth. There was nothing to worry about yet. He was just going to touch her. She relaxed once more and made no move to resist when Ryerson opened her legs a little wider.

Ryerson began to tease her with his hands, probing gently, coaxing forth a response. Virginia gasped. She had never experienced such erotic sensations. Instinctively she began to move, urging him to explore her more intimately, frustrated when he continued to tease and tantalize.

She tried to free her hands again, not because she wanted to push him away but because she needed to persuade him to carry out the intimate promises he was making.

Ryerson loosed her wrists and groaned appreciatively when she instantly grasped his hand and held it more tightly to her.

"Oh, yes, baby," he muttered. "Show me what you want. Show me exactly how hard and how deep you want it.''

Virginia could no longer contain the unfamiliar sensation that was pouring through her. She arched against Ryerson's hand once more, feeling his fingers go deep inside her. She cried out and clutched Ryerson.

He came to her then, moving quickly on top of her and sheathing himself tightly within her just as the full force of her climax gripped her.

Virginia cried out again as her body sought to adjust to the masculine invasion. But she gloried in the tight, hard feel of him within her and another amazing wave of release went through her. She clung to Ryerson, wrapping her legs around him and whispering his name over and over again as he thrust deeply into her softness.

Then Ryerson went rigid. He shouted her name in a strangled gasp as he surged into her one last time. He held on to her as the storm washed through his body, and then they were both tumbling into warm oblivion.

Moonlight drifted through the window, seeking emeralds and diamonds and gold. Flames flickered within crystal-green stones. The bracelet seemed warmer than ever on Virginia's arm.

CHAPTER FOUR

RYERSON AWOKE at the first hint of the Caribbean dawn. He lay quietly for a few minutes, conscious of the warm, soft, womanly weight on the bed beside him and of the spectacular clarity of the pale light outside the window.

He realized he had never felt better in his whole life.

Briefly he entertained the fantasy that he and Ginny were alone on a distant planet, the only two human beings on a fresh, young world waiting to be populated.

Ryerson decided he could really get into the concept of populating planets with cute little Virginia Elizabeths and some little Angus Cedrics. The job would require a lot of effort and dedication on his part, of course. He would probably have to spend most of his time in bed with Ginny, but a man did what he had to do. Populating planets was important work.

Virginia shifted slightly beside him, and the sunlight danced on the bracelet on her wrist. She had forgotten to take it off before going to sleep, he realized. Idly he eased the sheet down to her waist, enjoying the view of wildly tousled hair, full breasts and gently rounded arms. He smiled with possessive satisfaction. Ginny was glorious in her nudity, his very own lush, pagan goddess. The glitter of the bracelet added to the impression. He was getting hard just looking at her.

Ryerson let his mind drift back over the events of the night. Nothing had ever been this right. Last night had been the most deeply satisfying night he had ever spent in his life. But then, he'd never gone to bed with such a good friend before, he reminded himself with a small, triumphant grin.

There had never been anyone like Ginny for him. Soft and generous and passionate, yet filled with a womanly strength that was ideal for his own size and strength. He remembered her initial anxiety and wondered at it again. How could she have doubted herself? Or was it him she had doubted? Some of Ryerson's arrogant satisfaction faded slightly at the thought. He wondered if she had been hesitant about going to bed with him because she was afraid he wouldn't live up to the standards set by her dead husband.

Ryerson forced himself to relax again as he recalled the way Virginia had eventually responded to him. She might have been nervous and skittish at first, but in the end she had given herself completely to him. Ryerson wondered how his fierce and growing possessiveness fitted in with Virginia's definition of friendship.

More memories of the night floated into his head. Hot, sensual memories that triggered hot, sensual reactions in his body. Ryerson recalled the way Virginia's legs had circled his driving hips and the way she had clung to him as her release washed over her. Her eyes had widened first in shock and then closed in ecstasy. Remembering her silent astonishment the first time she had surrendered to the demands of her own body, Ryerson again questioned just what had gone on in her marriage. Maybe her dead husband's standards hadn't been so high, after all. Maybe her dead husband had been a jerk.

Ryerson glanced down at where the sheet covered his lower body and grinned to himself. Too much early-morning fantasizing. It was time for this particular Adam to wake his Eve.

He turned on his side, intending to kiss Ginny into wakefulness, but something stopped him. Ryerson found himself studying her intently, instead. It was the first time he had awakened beside her, and he wanted to savor the moment.

She looked simultaneously innocent and sensual in the morning light. She was lying on her side, her back toward him. Her thick brown hair was fanned out on the pillow, and her long lashes hid her clear hazel eyes. The sheet foamed below her ripe breasts and flowed over the enticingly full curve of her hips. He had been right about one thing, Ryerson reminded himself. Virginia Elizabeth had some sexy, solid shape to her.

And she'd had the damnedest effect on him, he thought ruefully. Never before had he felt compelled to pin any woman down and make love to her until she shivered helplessly in his arms. It was a side of himself that he'd never experienced. He'd never been so desperate to have a woman respond to him before, either.

Virginia stirred again, one long leg shifting under the sheet. Ryerson propped himself on his elbow, ran his fingertips across the stones in the magnificent bracelet and then leaned over and dropped a warm kiss on her bare shoulder.

"Wake up, woman; we have work to do."

Virginia twisted luxuriously, letting herself come slowly to wakefulness. A small smile played around her lips as she realized where she was and who was with her. The morning sun was just beginning to stream through the open window, bringing with it the scent of exotic flowers and a mysterious sea.

Last night the waves had been crashing on the beach, she remembered. Last night, she had been caught in those breakers, swept out on the crest of a gem-green sea and tossed up onto a golden shore. It had been a glorious, exciting, intensely erotic experience. She was involved at last in the kind of affair she had never dreamed existed in reality, at least not for a woman such as herself. She opened one eye and surveyed Ryerson's face.

"Work?" She yawned. "What work? We're on vacation."

"That's what you think. We have a whole planet to populate." He closed a hand over one breast, teasing the nipple with a gentle scraping action of his palm.

Virginia opened both eyes and stared at him. "We *what*?"

"Don't panic. We can handle it. If we get busy."

She blinked. "You're losing me, Ryerson."

"Not a chance. Now that I've finally got hold of you, I have no intention of letting you slip away."

Virginia saw the warmth in his eyes and blushed in spite of herself. "What's all this about populating a planet?"

"Just a harmless morning fantasy. I had to fill the time somehow while I waited for your majesty to awaken. Look out that window. Doesn't it seem as if we're the only people in the world?"

Virginia glanced out at the fresh dawn. "Mmm. I see what you mean." She covered his questing hand with her own, her eyes searching as she gazed up at him. "It does seem as if we've stepped into another world. I don't feel at all like myself this morning. This is going to be a very special week, isn't it, Ryerson?"

His hand slipped out from under hers, tugging the sheet a little farther down over her hips. "Very special." His thumb grazed over a budding nipple, and he watched with satisfaction as the nipple went taut. "What do you mean, you don't feel at all like yourself?"

She hesitated, thinking of the joys of the night that had been hers. "Let's just say I don't feel like an information storage and retrieval manager this morning."

"And I've hardly given a thought to diesel engines or power systems since I woke up. But that doesn't answer my question."

Virginia sensed the direction of his probing and tried to deflect it. She put on what she hoped was a deliberately inviting smile and began to toy with the crisp, curling hair of his chest. Her eyes dropped meaningfully to where the sheet covered his lean hips. "I don't think this is the time for questions. It looks like you've got more urgent problems."

Ryerson grinned wickedly. "You learn fast. What makes you think you can use sex to distract me?"

She widened her eyes in mocking innocence. "I don't know what gave me the idea. It just sort up sprang up out of nowhere. Will it work?"

He gave the matter a moment's close thought. "Maybe. Temporarily. If you really work at it."

She tossed back the sheet and rose on her elbow. "I'm a very hard worker," she promised. Then she pushed experimentally and Ryerson obediently went over onto his back. He lay looking up at her with anticipation, silver eyes full of sensual challenge.

Virginia responded to the look in his eyes out of the newfound self-confidence she had gained during the night. She knew now that Ryerson would react satisfactorily to her touch, and the knowledge filled her with the kind of pleasure and power only a woman can know.

She touched him with daring intimacy, gliding her fingers down his chest to his thighs. There she found him hard and heavy and waiting. She caressed him delicately until Ryerson groaned and started to reach for her. Evading his grasp, she boldly bent her head and tasted him with exquisite care the way he had tasted her during the night.

Ryerson sucked in his breath. "Oh, Ginny, you don't know what you're doing."

"No? What am I doing?"

"Playing with fire." He pulled her down astride him, guiding her legs around his hips. She braced herself on her knees and looked down at him, enjoying the position. He gave her a smile that said he knew exactly how she was feeling. Then he began to stroke her, playing with all the dark, secret places that quickly grew warm and moist at his touch. When she arched her neck and sighed, he deepened the touch.

"Ryerson." She reached down and cupped him gently.

"A little closer, sweetheart." He cradled her hips in his hands and began to ease her onto his manhood. "That's it." He probed her carefully and began to fill her with himself. "That feels so good, so damned good. I think you must have been specially built just for me. Definitely one of a kind."

Virginia delighted in his muffled groan of desire, feeling him sink deeply into her softness. Then she began to move slowly, aware of his fingers continuing to tease her even as she set the pace.

The thrilling release blossomed quickly, swamping both of them for a few timeless moments. Virginia collapsed languidly on Ryerson's chest and sighed in contentment. Nothing in her life had ever been this good or this satisfying. Nothing had ever made her so aware of her fundamental femininity. For the first time she was learning that she could, indeed, please a man and take her own pleasure in return.

In that moment she decided she was content to be friends for life with A. C. Ryerson.

She was given little chance to enjoy the afterglow. Ryerson recovered all too quickly. He slapped her lightly on her bare bottom and eased her down onto the bed. Rising to his feet, he stretched magnificently.

"Let's hit the showers. I'm starving and breakfast is waiting."

Virginia blinked. "Are you always this perky in the mornings?"

He cocked one brow. "Perky? I don't know about perky, but I am definitely hungry in the mornings. Usually it's just for food, but this morning it was for you and food. Now that I've had you..." He let the sentence trail off meaningfully.

"Now that you've had me, you're ready for the food," Virginia concluded ruefully. "Nice to know your priorities in life."

He leaned over her, caging her briefly between his hands. His grin was all-male. "Hey, you were at the top of the list, weren't you? Stop complaining. If you're very sweet, I might let you come into the shower with me."

Virginia batted her lashes at him. "The thrill of a lifetime, I'm sure."

He laughed and scooped her up in his arms. "Judge for yourself," he told her with lofty arrogance as he carried her into the bathroom.

Virginia, who hadn't been carried in a man's arms since she was a small child, was too startled by the position in which she found herself to argue.

A short time later she conceded that showering with Ryerson was definitely a thrill.

But the early-morning sensual romp did not deflect Ryerson's questions. She knew she had only bought a little time. When he led Virginia down onto the beach for a walk after breakfast, she was resigned to the inevitable. She supposed it was only fair that really close friends shared this kind of information about each other. Mentally she prepared herself.

"I'd like to know," Ryerson said deliberately as he clasped her hand in his, "what was going on in your mind last night when you were working so hard to get up enough nerve to go to bed with me."

Virginia winced. "It wasn't like that. Not exactly."

"It was exactly like that."

"I told you, I was a little anxious. It had been a…a long time, and I guess I felt a bit awkward."

"It was more than that, Ginny." He glanced down at her, his eyes thoughtful. "You were scared to death. Once you'd made the big decision, you just wanted to get it over with as quickly as possible. What did you think was going to go wrong?"

She kicked sand with her bare feet and stared out to sea. He had a right to know, she decided. After all, she had behaved in what must have seemed a very peculiar fashion for a woman of her age and experience. "It's a little hard to explain."

"Was it me? Were you afraid I wasn't going to live up to expectations?" he asked roughly.

Ginny was shocked. "It wasn't anything like that!"

"So talk to me, Ginny. I'm a good listener."

She smiled in spite of herself. "Yes, you are. Well, if you must know, I was scared to death of going to bed with you."

"I got that feeling," he said wryly. "But why, Ginny?"

"You think of me as a confident, mature woman, but in that one area of my life, I'm not at all sure of myself. At least, I wasn't until last night." She turned her head and looked up at him, her eyes narrowed against the bright morning sun. "I want you to know how happy you made me last night, Ryerson."

He released her hand and put his arm possessively around her shoulders. "In case you haven't realized it, the feeling was mutual."

She took a deep breath. "I'm glad."

"It has to do with your marriage, doesn't it?" he asked when she didn't volunteer any more information.

"My nervousness?"

"It was much more than nervousness. I was nervous myself. What you were feeling was more on the level of outright panic. It took a hell of a lot of courage for you to go through with it. Why?"

"I guess there's no need to drag this out any further," she said, willing herself to get it all said. "It's obvious you won't be satisfied until you've heard all the gory details. To put it simply, my marriage was a terrible mistake. And I was naive enough to believe it was all my fault."

"What made you think that?"

Her mouth twisted grimly. "I'd better start at the beginning. Jack worked for my father. He was a rising star in management. Everyone approved of him, and when he started courting me, they all approved of the marriage. I was rather dazzled by him, I admit. He was good-looking, charming and charismatic. But on some level I felt I didn't really know him. I ignored that, though, because everyone liked him."

"In other words, you didn't quite trust your own judgment in the matter, so you relied on everyone else's judgment?"

She smiled wryly at his perceptiveness. "Not entirely. I really did think I was in love. I would never have married him otherwise. Jack was a dynamic, fascinating man. But things started going sour on our wedding night. My husband managed to perform his, uh, husbandly duties, but it was obviously not the supreme moment of his life. And it was a crushing disappointment for me. Nothing like knowing you've failed to satisfy your husband to make a woman start married life feeling like a total failure. Jack had a lot of subtle techniques for ensuring I assumed all the responsibility for that failure. He was good at that kind of thing, I eventually discovered. A real con man. Manipulative and clever. He had a real talent for controlling people."

"So you managed to marry a real bastard first time out of the gate." Ryerson's arm tightened comfortingly around her shoulders. "It happens."

"I suppose so. But I never dreamed it would happen to me. Jack made it clear I was not his ideal woman. He let me know I was too big, too, uh, full figured for his taste. He preferred dainty, petite types. I floundered badly for months, trying to figure out what I was doing wrong and wondering why he had married me in the first place. Like a fool, I kept making compromises, giving ground, deferring to him, trying to please and placate him. I had a mental image of what a good wife should be, and I kept trying to live up to that image. But nothing worked. The truth didn't dawn on me for some time, however.''

''What was the truth?''

Virginia shook her head grimly. ''I finally came to my senses and realized that Jack had married me because he hoped Dad would eventually turn over Middlebrook Power Systems to his new son-in-law.''

''Ah, the picture becomes clear. Why didn't you file for divorce and get the hell out of that situation, Ginny?'' Ryerson gave her a small, admonishing shake.

''It took me months to figure out that the only way out was divorce. For some idiotic reason I kept trying to patch up the marriage. I felt I had to try. Everyone kept saying how great Jack was. What a perfect husband for me. What an asset he was to Dad's firm. But in the end, I gave up. I found a lawyer and started divorce proceedings. When I informed Jack I was leaving he was furious. He threatened to ruin my father if I went ahead with the divorce.''

''How the hell did he manage a threat like that?''

''Jack had become very powerful at Middlebrook. On the pretext of taking a load off Dad's shoulders, he had assumed a great deal of control. I knew him well enough by then to believe he might actually be able to hurt the firm. I felt trapped.''

''Did you talk to your father? Tell him what was going on?''

''I was afraid Dad wouldn't believe me. He and everyone else were really mesmerized by Jack. They trusted him completely. Everyone did. I had to agree to stay in the marriage until I could figure a way out. I could not bring myself to share a bedroom with him, but that was just fine with Jack. He had made it clear he was bored with me in bed, anyway. I nearly went crazy trying to find a way out of that terrible situation. I felt absolutely desperate. Talk about stress. I nearly collapsed from it. I had finally decided I had to talk to Dad when I got the news that Jack had died in a car accident. I know it's an awful thing to say, but frankly, I have never been so relieved in my life as I was the night the hospital emergency room phoned to tell me Jack had been brought in DOA. I was suddenly free.''

''You did a two-year sentence in hell, and you've decided never to risk the trap of marriage again.''

Virginia took a deep breath. Ryerson was the first person who had ever really understood what it had been like. ''The irony of the whole thing was that when it was all over, my father confided that he'd begun to have serious doubts about Jack, but he hadn't wanted to say anything to me.''

''Ah, my poor Ginny. No wonder you've never been tempted to remarry. You got nothing out of that relationship except the feeling you were a failure as a woman.''

''I guess that sums it up. A real disaster.''

Ryerson came to a halt and turned to take her face between his large hands. His eyes burned into hers. ''Virginia Elizabeth, how could you ever have doubted yourself that way?''

She clung to his wrists. ''I made up my mind after Jack died that I would never marry. Marriage holds nothing for me. For me it will always symbolize being trapped. But there were times when I longed for a companion and a friend.''

''Never a lover?''

''I was afraid to want a lover,'' she said honestly. ''I was convinced I could never really satisfy a man. When you showed up on my doorstep I knew you could be my friend and companion, but I didn't know what I would do when you tried to become my lover. I also knew that sooner or later that bridge would have to be crossed.''

''But you kept trying to postpone sex?''

''I knew I couldn't keep postponing it indefinitely. You were very tolerant but I knew you were getting restless. When you bought those tickets, I understood what you were asking, and I knew I had to face the inevitable. I tried to tell myself that if I worked very hard at it and if your expectations weren't too terribly high, I just might be able to get through it without turning you off completely.''

Ryerson shook his head in exasperation. ''With an attitude like that, it was no wonder you felt obliged to down a few margaritas, half a bottle of wine and a glass of brandy before you did your duty. What a little idiot you were,'' he added fondly. ''The idea is to enjoy yourself, not twist yourself into a nervous wreck.''

''Enjoying myself was the last thing I was worried about,'' Virginia admitted. ''I wasn't even thinking about that end of things. But I was petrified that you would find me less than satisfactory. I didn't know how I was going to deal with that. I told myself that you were a lot like me, that you were my friend, that you wouldn't expect fireworks. But I was so scared I wouldn't even be able to create a small blaze.''

Ryerson grinned slowly. ''You're wrong. I did expect fireworks. Every time I kissed you, I could feel the fuse being lit. I knew damned well that when the time finally came, we were going to cause an explosion.''

Virginia went pink. ''Well, I'm glad you had so much faith in me, because I certainly didn't.''

He pulled her close, pushing her head tenderly against his shoulder. ''Did you enjoy the fireworks when you finally discovered them, sweetheart?''

She sensed the masculine satisfaction in him and chuckled. Lifting her face, she smiled into his eyes. ''You know perfectly well I did. I suppose you're going to take full credit?''

He laughed deeply. ''I'm willing to let you have some of the credit. You're the sexiest thing I've ever encountered in or out of bed.'' He kissed her thoroughly, and his hold on her tightened. The laughter went out of him, to be replaced by a more intense emotion. ''Ginny, I can't remember the last time I felt anywhere near this sure of things. We're going to be so good together.''

Virginia relaxed into his embrace. The affair was well and truly launched. She had found a man who was right for her at last. Her good friend had become her lover.

The emerald-and-diamond bracelet on her wrist flashed in the sunlight.

THAT AFTERNOON Virginia browsed through the resort boutique and found a new dress that appealed to her. Her sister would have approved instantly. It wasn't at all the sort of dress Virginia would normally have glanced at twice, and she wasn't sure what made her so determined to buy it. It was made of light, gauzy emerald-colored cotton and had a series of flounces around the hemline that were edged in gold ribbon. It had a multicolored sash. But its most interesting feature was the low neckline.

It was far more daringly cut than the yellow silk she had worn the previous evening. In fact, it was more daringly cut than anything she had ever owned. But a sense of adventure was compelling her, and before she gave herself time to consider too carefully, Virginia bought the dress.

When she emerged from the bedroom that evening, Ryerson looked up expectantly. His expression altered almost comically when he saw the new addition to Virginia's wardrobe. His face revealed a variety of expressions ranging from mild shock to a severe frown. Somewhere in between was a flash of what looked like pure lust.

''Like it?'' Virginia twirled around to display the whole effect. ''It's a perfect dancing dress. And the bracelet goes perfectly with it, don't you think?''

''I like what there is of it,'' he retorted dryly as he came forward to take her arm. ''But for pete's sake, don't slouch or drop anything tonight.''

''Why should I worry about that?''

"Because if you have to bend down, the top half of that dress is going to fall off."

Virginia grinned. "It only looks as if it might fall off. It's actually quite well engineered."

Ryerson arched his brows skeptically and drew a finger slowly along the line of her décolletage. When Virginia trembled delightfully in reaction, he smiled knowingly. "It's my business to know good engineering when I see it, honey, and I can tell you right now, this dress is as shaky as a bridge made out of toothpicks. Remember what I said about minding your posture."

"I'll remember," she promised demurely as she straightened her shoulders. She smiled a secret smile as they went out the door.

Ryerson glanced down at her, a cryptic smile of his own edging his mouth. "Fireworks can be a lot of fun, Ginny. But you have to be careful when you play with them."

"Why?"

"Because you might get your fingers singed."

Her eyes were alight with mischief as she slid him a sidelong glance. "I'll be very careful."

"Why do I have trouble believing that?"

The evening air was heavy with the fragrance of flowers. The dying sun left a residual warmth in the stones of the path that wound through the gardens to the main building of the resort. Virginia could feel the heat through the thin soles of her delicate high-heeled sandals. She was about to comment on it when a familiar figure stepped out of a neighboring suite directly into their path. His back was toward them.

"Hello, Brigman," Ryerson said easily.

The redheaded man spun around, looking startled. Then he relaxed and gave them a rather forced smile. His eyes darted to the bracelet on Virginia's wrist and then flicked back to Ryerson. "Evening. Heading for dinner?"

"Thought we'd have a drink first," Ryerson responded.

"Good idea. I'm heading in the same direction. Mind if I join you?"

Ryerson hesitated, and Virginia knew he was trying to think of a good reason to refuse the casual request. Apparently nothing came to mind, because he finally nodded brusquely. "Sure. Why not?"

"Thanks. I see you're enjoying your winnings," he added with another glance at Virginia's wrist. His smooth gambler's voice almost succeeded in concealing the underlying tension that radiated from him. "I'll have to admit that emeralds and diamonds do something for a woman. When are you going to give me a chance to get my bracelet back, Ryerson?"

Virginia instinctively moved the bracelet out of sight behind a fold of her dress as Ryerson said something bland and noncommittal. Virginia glanced at Brigman. "Do you play poker regularly?"

Brigman shrugged modestly. "It's how I make my living."

Virginia was startled. "You make your living at cards?"

He smiled thinly. "What can I say? I'm good at it, and I manage to earn enough to be able to afford to live in hotels like this one." He waved a hand to indicate the elegant resort. "It's a good life. Never gets boring, I'll say that for it. The one thing I can't take is being bored. There are a lot of places like Toralina with easygoing gambling laws. Around here they don't mind if a few of the guests get into a private game and set their own stakes. I'll be honest with you, I don't generally lose." He glanced at Ryerson. "You surprised me last night. I would never have pegged you for a pro."

"I'm not. I surprised myself," Ryerson said coolly. "I told you, I felt lucky."

Brigman's eyes narrowed speculatively. He did not appear convinced. "Well, my offer is open. If you feel like trying your luck again, let me know. I expect to earn enough tonight at the table to stake myself to another game with you. I'd like to get that bracelet back.''

''Thanks for the offer,'' Ryerson said. ''I'll think about it.''

''You do that. I don't mind telling you that bracelet was pretty special to me. Old family heirloom, you know. Came down to me from my grandmother. It's been my good-luck charm for years.''

''I see.'' Ryerson's tone was still noncommittal.

Virginia was relieved when Brigman took himself off to a far corner of the bar. She touched the bracelet to reassure herself it was safe. ''I don't like him,'' she said as Ryerson found a private table. ''He's too slick. Reminds me of Jack, in a way. You're not really going to let him talk you into another game, are you? Not with the bracelet at stake?''

''Relax. I've lost all interest in poker. Last night was the first time I've really felt like playing in years, but the urge is gone now. I have no intention of gambling away that bracelet. It belongs to you and me. I think I'm beginning to see it as a symbol of some sort.''

''A symbol of what?''

Ryerson looked at her across the table, his gaze serious. ''I'm not sure. Maybe a symbol of what we found together in bed last night. Emeralds and diamonds and gold go nicely with passion, don't you think?''

Virginia's eyes were glowing with happiness as she leaned forward to touch his hand. ''I think they go beautifully together.''

Instead of answering her glowing look with one of his own, Ryerson frowned abruptly. ''Sit up straight, Ginny. You're going to fall out of that dress.''

''I had no idea you had such a prudish side to your nature,'' she remarked as she straightened obediently.

''Any woman who buys the kind of prim, plain white cotton underwear you collect has no grounds for calling anyone else prudish,'' he retorted.

Virginia blinked uncertainly, wondering if he really had found her underwear terribly unexciting, and then she saw the teasing glint in his eyes. She relaxed. "Well, you'll be happy to know I've learned my lesson. Take a good look down the front of this dress, Ryerson. I'm definitely not wearing my Sears bra tonight."

"So I see." He eyed the roundness that was exposed by the daring neckline. "I take back what I said about prudishness. What are you wearing under that dress?"

"Nothing at all," she returned blithely. "I told you the dress was beautifully engineered." She propped her elbows on the table, folded her hands and leaned her chin on them. The net result was to enhance the cleavage. "I feel different tonight, Ryerson. What about you?"

He made a production out of having to force his gaze back to her face. When he saw that her eyes were serious, he bit back the outrageous remark he had been about to make and said instead, "I know what you mean. I feel different, too."

"Maybe it's part of the transformation."

"What transformation?"

She shrugged. "The sense we both have of being in a different world down here. I think we're both feeling more adventurous or something."

"Or something," he agreed dryly. "Be careful when you move your shoulders like that."

"Wouldn't it be strange if this were the real us?" Virginia went on whimsically. "Maybe we were born to be a pair of exotic adventurers, cruising from island to island."

Ryerson's mouth curved faintly in amusement. "And how were we born to support ourselves while we cruise exotically?"

Virginia thought about that. "I don't know. You seem very good at poker. Apparently there's a living to be made from that sort of work. Brigman's surviving by playing cards here in the islands."

Ryerson laughed. "Don't get your hopes up. I'm a fair poker player, but that's about it. I was feeling lucky last night, and I took a chance. Normally I would never have risked a game with a professional like Brigman. I'm still not sure what made me do it. But last night I was on a roll. I got lucky in more ways than one last night." He paused to leer cheerfully. "I'll tell you one thing, we wouldn't get very far on my poker-playing talent if we had to rely on it for a living. I'll stick to diesel engines."

Virginia's eyes flirted outrageously with him. "I have great faith in your talents, Ryerson. I'm sure you could make a living playing cards if you really tried."

"Oh, yeah? What happens the first time I lose?"

"I'll think of a suitable consolation prize," she promised softly as she hunched her shoulders slightly and leaned forward again.

"I'm going to have two very suitable consolation prizes in my hands in another minute if you don't sit up straight."

Virginia's smile became even more brilliant.

Ryerson groaned and ordered his Scotch in a low growl that made the cocktail waitress jump.

He was under a spell, Ryerson decided later that evening. It was the only explanation. He'd had some experience with sex and some experience with friendship, but he'd never had any experience with the kind of magic he was sharing with Virginia. He felt as if he were getting tangled up in a glistening, shimmering web.

The magic was changing him in some indefinable ways, he discovered. It was releasing some very old instincts, for one thing. He couldn't remember the last time he had felt so territorial, for example. The precarious cut of Virginia's dress was never far from his mind. He found himself glaring at other males frequently.

It was totally out of character for him to tell a woman what to wear and what not to wear, but by midnight he had decided he was not going to allow Virginia out in public again in her new dress. Not that the thing didn't look fantastic on her. But she was too tall and too magnificently proportioned to go unnoticed when she was attired the way she was this evening. It seemed to Ryerson that every man on the dance floor had sneaked a peak at the woman in his arms.

One man in particular was edging closer. Ryerson noticed him first when he was sitting at the bar. He was nearly as tall as Ryerson, which made him just the right size for Virginia. That fact alone was enough to irritate Ryerson. But there were some additional, equally annoying facts.

The stranger had the kind of looks Ryerson knew women usually admired. The guy was built along lean, slender lines with light brown hair, a mustache and a pair of dark eyes. He appeared to be a couple of years younger than Ryerson, and he was dressed in white slacks and a blue blazer. It was the kind of outfit that belonged on board a large, gleaming yacht. Ryerson's newly aroused territorial instincts sent up several warning signals when the man turned again to gaze at Virginia.

"Ouch! You're squashing me," Virginia complained as Ryerson gathered her closer.

"I'm trying to cover the gap in that dress."

She looked up at him with bewitching eyes. "You love this dress. Admit it."

Ryerson summoned his most intimidating stare. Strong men had been known to break and bleed when Ryerson used that particular stare. "That dress is going in the trash tonight."

"Hah! That's what you think," Virginia said with relish.

"We'll see," Ryerson muttered, aware that he was not doing a very effective job of intimidation. It was tough to intimidate a goddess.

The music came to a halt, and Ryerson eased Virginia through the crowd to their table. He was about to continue the lecture on the dress when the man in the blue blazer approached them.

"Mind if I borrow the lady for the next dance?" Mustache asked with easy confidence. The question was officially addressed to Ryerson, but the stranger was looking at Virginia, who smiled back with sparkling innocence.

"Yes, I mind," Ryerson said roughly and added the first explanation that popped into his head. "The lady and I are on our honeymoon. I'm not in the mood to share."

The man's brows rose mockingly, and he made a point of glancing at Virginia's ringless hand. "Sorry about the intrusion. My name is Ferris. Dan Ferris. I didn't notice a ring so I assumed—"

"You assumed wrong," Ryerson cut in.

"Don't mind Ryerson, Mr. Ferris," Virginia said kindly. "He's in a bad mood because he doesn't like my dress."

The stranger nodded gallantly. A lot of white teeth gleamed beneath the mustache. "Personally I think the dress is very charming."

"Thank you."

"If you'll excuse us," Ryerson said bluntly, "we'd like to be alone."

"Sure. I understand. Well, congratulations on the marriage," Ferris said regretfully. "I guess that leaves me out of the picture."

"Oh, there is no marriage," Virginia said so sweetly that Ryerson was tempted to strangle her.

Ferris looked confused. "I thought there was something said about a honeymoon."

Ryerson caught one of Virginia's hands and crushed it warningly just as she opened her mouth to reply. He gave Ferris a baleful glance. "We're taking a few liberties with tradition. Whoever said a honeymoon had to come after the marriage? Good night, Ferris."

Ferris held up his hands, palms out in mocking surrender.

"I get the point. I'm gone." He looked at Virginia again. "It really is a nice dress, though."

"I'm glad somebody likes it," Virginia said irrepressibly as Ferris disappeared in the crowd.

"Ninety-nine percent of the men in this room would be glad to tell you how much they like it if they got a chance." Ryerson got to his feet and pulled Virginia up out of her chair. Clamping a hand around her wrist, he started toward the door. "Come on, let's get out of here."

"Where are we going?"

"For a walk on the beach."

"At midnight?"

"I feel the need for some exercise," Ryerson told her grimly. "I would prefer to get it by making Ferris eat his own mustache, but I'll settle for a walk."

"Very civilized of you."

They walked in silence through the moonlight until they reached the endless stretch of white sand that ringed the island. Without a word they stopped and took off their shoes.

"Are you really angry about this dress?" Virginia asked finally.

Ryerson tightened his hand around hers. "Does it bother you that I'm acting like an overprotective, jealous male?" he countered. "Maybe I didn't handle that scene with Ferris properly. It's not my fault. I'm not used to feeling so possessive."

Virginia flashed him a molten glance. "I wore the dress to seduce you, you know. Maybe I overdid things. I'm not accustomed to dressing up to deliberately seduce men."

Ryerson felt the aggressive tension drain out of him as he stopped and gathered Virginia close. "So maybe we're both having to deal with some new emotions and reactions these days."

"Why did you tell Dan Ferris we were on a honeymoon?"

"I don't know," Ryerson admitted, aware of the lingering harshness in his voice. He could not really explain that stupid slip of the tongue. "I wanted to get rid of him as quickly as possible, and that was the first excuse that came to mind."

"Oh." She went still against him.

Ryerson tangled his hands in her hair. "The thought scares you, doesn't it?"

"Honeymoons and weddings and marriages are generally scary thoughts for me." She lifted her face and smiled tremulously up at him. "But I am very much enjoying having an affair."

"So am I," he muttered. He kissed her, tasting the moonlight he saw on her lips.

Her hands stole around his neck, and Ryerson felt her fingertips in his hair. Deliberately he crushed her closer so that he could feel her luscious, firm breasts against his chest. His hands slid down to the curve of her buttocks, and his mouth strayed to her throat. She felt so good. He was already hot and ready for her. He wanted her now.

Ryerson lifted his mouth from Virginia's and glanced down the length of the beach to where the lights of the resort gleamed in the distance. There was no one in sight.

"Ryerson? What are you doing?" Virginia gasped as she felt his fingers on the zipper of her dress.

"It's a great night for a swim."

She laughed up at him in astonishment. "We can't possibly. Not like this. We should go back to the hotel and get our suits."

"We're alone on this planet, remember?"

She sighed in pleasure and put her arms around his neck again as the gauzy dress fell to her bare feet. Moonlight gleamed on her breasts. "How could I forget?"

Ryerson shed his own clothing with casual disregard for sand and wrinkles. When he was naked, he picked up his quasi bride and carried her into the warm, silvered sea.

He didn't care how nervous the idea of marriage made Virginia. He did feel as though he were on a honeymoon, and he intended to enjoy it.

CHAPTER FIVE

THE WATER WAS LIQUID SILK. The only other thing Virginia had ever experienced that was as deliciously seductive was Ryerson's lovemaking. Swimming nude in the sea had the same effect on her senses. She shed old inhibitions as easily as she had shed her clothing.

She swam and frolicked around Ryerson, playing sea goddess in the silver moonlight. She had never felt so wild and free. It was as if she were another species of female altogether. And Ryerson was made for her, a helpless male on whom she could test her wiles.

Slipping and sliding through the waves, she circled her victim, taunting him with soft laughter and teasing touches. Ryerson responded with a primitive passion that thrilled her to the core of her being.

He reacted to the sweet torment with a deceptive clumsiness, tempting her closer until she recklessly came within reach. When at last she finally grew too bold and too careless, he seized her.

"Got you, sea lady. Now what are you going to do?" He held her by her waist, lifting her up out of the water so that she had to grip his shoulders to maintain her balance. His eyes gleamed with his victory.

Virginia smiled down at him with mischievous sensuality. "That's a good question," she murmured. "What would you like me to do?" Deliberately she drew slow circles on his damp shoulders. "You've won the battle. I'm yours to command." The water heaved gently around them, foaming lightly when it broke against her thighs. Her smile was very ancient and very pagan, and it disclosed everything she was feeling.

Ryerson saw the smile and sucked in his breath. The pale gleam of tropical moonlight revealed the stark desire on his face. "Mine to command?"

"Yours," she agreed softly. Virginia touched the side of his face. "What would you like me to do, sea lord? I want only to please you."

"I've never had a sea nymph at my disposal," Ryerson mused. "I'll have to experiment a little to find out what works best."

"By all means, feel free to experiment." Virginia felt her own excitement skyrocketing. "If I might make a few suggestions?"

"Anything," he breathed, his voice thickening rapidly. "Try anything you want. I'll let you know what's working."

"How about this?" She drew her fingertips down to his flat nipples and found them already puckered. When she gently scored him with her nails, Ryerson shuddered.

"That definitely works," Ryerson assured her. He lowered her slightly in the water until she was standing on the sandy bottom.

Virginia's smile became more mysterious as she experimented further. She trailed her fingertips through the hair on his chest and then slowly reached around his waist until she could sink her fingers into his hard, muscled buttocks. Deliberately she brushed against him, teasing Ryerson with her taut nipples.

"How about this?"

"I appreciate the suggestions," Ryerson said in a husky voice. "But I think I'm getting some ideas of my own."

"Tell me," she whispered. "I'll do anything you want."

He looked down at her with a searching gaze. "You mean that, don't you?"

"I mean every word. I want to please you tonight, Ryerson. I surrender completely to you, sea lord. I want only to make you happy."

"Touch me," he said hoarsely. "That will make me very happy."

"Where? Here?"

"Lower." He grinned with devilish challenge and told her graphically exactly what portion of his anatomy he wanted her to caress.

If his thought was to tease her or embarrass her, he had another think coming, Virginia decided bravely. Boldly she took him in her hands, playing with him under the surface of the foaming sea. Ryerson's wicked grin quickly disappeared.

"Ah, that's it. That's exactly where I want to feel your hands. You have such beautiful hands, sweetheart. I think I could really get into this conquering-hero bit." He drew in his breath as she squeezed gently. "*Yes*, honey. A little tighter. Perfect. Harder now. Faster."

Virginia gave him exactly what he wanted, delighting in her newly discovered power to do so. She kissed his salt-sprayed chest as she coaxed his body into a hard, heavy state of sexual expectation.

Ryerson tangled his fingers in her hair and slitted his eyes against the rush of excitement that was gripping his body. He pushed his hips against her, seeking more of her hand.

His powerful reaction fed her sense of feminine daring. Ryerson responded to her. Totally. It was a wonderful high for her. Virginia took a deep breath and sank gently beneath the waves.

She felt Ryerson's fingers tighten violently in her floating hair as she guided him into her mouth. His whole body was taut now. She knew he was about to explode.

"*Ginny*." Abruptly he yanked her above the surface. His silver eyes were glittering. "You're a sea witch, all right.

You've put me under a spell, and now you're going to put me out of my misery.''

"Misery?" She laughed softly. "Is that what you call it? And here I was just trying to please.''

He grinned with rough sensuality. "I'm not sure who's the conqueror and who's the sex slave around here right at the moment. But I do know one thing.''

"What's that?''

"You're going to finish what you started.''

"Of course, my lord. I wouldn't think of leaving you in this condition.''

He cradled her face and kissed her heavily. "Wrap your legs around me," he ordered thickly.

Bemused, but willing, Virginia did as instructed. The water buoyed her and Ryerson's hands under her buttocks steadied her. She felt him slide two fingers into her, and then he hesitated no longer. She gasped as he entered her completely. Then she clung to him, burying her face against his throat. The sea surged around them, establishing the rhythm for them. It was a timeless cadence, one their bodies adjusted to automatically.

When the inevitable release tore through them, Virginia cried out. She was distantly aware of Ryerson's harsh, guttural shout echoing hers, and then there were only the sea and silence.

"I think," Ryerson finally said, "that we had better move toward shore.''

"Why? I'm perfectly happy where I am." Without opening her eyes, Virginia nestled closer.

"There's a small but growing problem with staying where you are," he retorted with a chuckle as he carefully disengaged her.

"Really?" She was mildly interested. "A growing problem, did you say?" She tightened her legs around his thighs.

"Not that kind of problem," Ryerson explained wryly.

"Another kind. The tide's coming in. In case you hadn't noticed, the water is getting deeper by the minute."

Virginia's eyes flicked open as she slid to her feet. The foaming water hit her now around the shoulders instead of the waist. "Good heavens! We could have come to a rather embarrassing end out here. Just think what people would have said at the funeral."

"It would have been a new twist on the old 'lost at sea' verdict. Come on; let's get moving, woman." Ryerson tugged her out of the surf.

The incoming tide was already lapping at their crumpled clothing. Virginia laughed as she struggled into her wet dress. "If you think this dress was a bit daring when it was dry, just wait until you see the effect now that it's soaking wet."

Ryerson scowled at the clinging material that revealed far more than it had earlier. Even in the shadows, he could see the clear outline of her nipples. When she turned around, he could easily make out the dark cleavage of her lush bottom. "I'm sure as hell not taking you back to the room via the main lobby. We'll go through the gardens." He fastened his pants and reached for his shirt.

Hand in hand they ran back along the beach, slipping into the hotel's gardens like two illicit lovers returning from a clandestine meeting.

"I think we were born for this kind of thing," Virginia said enthusiastically as Ryerson eased her soundlessly through a mass of huge ferns. "Look how good we are at sneaking around through the underbrush."

"I'm glad you're getting off on it," Ryerson said with mild irritation. "Personally I'm not into creeping around. If you hadn't worn that ridiculous excuse for a dress tonight, we wouldn't be in this position.... Shush—" He broke off suddenly.

"What in the world?" Virginia almost stumbled into him. He caught her, steadying her silently.

"We're not the only ones sneaking around through the bushes tonight. There're a couple of people up ahead." Ryerson's voice was a low whisper, containing none of the disgruntled humor it had held a few seconds earlier. "I think they're coming this way. Let's give them a chance to move on before we head for our room."

Obediently Virginia went still beside him, aware of the wet gauzy cotton turning cold against her skin. The clumps of ferns and flowering bushes hid them from the view of the two men who were striding briskly through the foliage. More people creeping around in the gardens. She wondered what their excuse was for not sticking to the stone paths.

Virginia caught only a brief glimpse of two masculine heads bent in intense conversation, but she recognized the voices immediately. Harry Brigman and Dan Ferris. Ferris's voice cut through the balmy night.

"Dammit, Brigman, we've fooled around here long enough. You've had your fun. I'm getting nervous. We've done all right. It's time to get the hell off this island."

"There's no rush. I've told you that a hundred times. We have to cool our heels somewhere. It might as well be here on Toralina. Besides, this place is ripe for the picking. Lots of rich tourists just begging for a friendly game of poker."

"There are other islands with casinos. Hell, you don't even need a casino. You can set up a game anywhere, as long as you're discreet."

"I like it here," Brigman said stubbornly. "I've been on a winning streak since I arrived."

"You didn't win the other night when you played Ryerson. Exactly how much did you lose, Brigman?"

"Not enough to concern you," Brigman retorted sullenly. "It was just a temporary setback. The man got lucky. It happens occasionally. But he's not a real pro. I'll talk him into another game and get my money back before he leaves. Now, if you'll excuse me, I've got some people waiting for me in the casino. It's about time you got on with your end of things, isn't it?''

Whatever Ferris said in response was muffled as both men moved off through the bushes.

''Okay,'' Ryerson said softly after a few seconds. ''There's the path up ahead. Let's go. But keep it quiet.''

''This is so exciting,'' Virginia said happily. ''I wonder if we—oh, no!'' She yelped helplessly and tried to keep her balance as the wet skirts of her dress snagged on a jagged palm frond. ''Darn it, my new dress! It's ruined.''

Ryerson muttered a resigned oath and turned to untangle the torn dress. As he swung around to assist, he glanced automatically toward where the two men had disappeared. ''Damn. So much for sneaking around in the gardens.''

''Why? What's wrong?'' Virginia followed his gaze and caught a glimpse of Dan Ferris, who must have stepped out onto the path a few seconds ahead of them. Ferris paused for an instant and glanced back over his shoulder when he overheard her startled cry. He looked directly at her. ''Oh, dear. Well, can't be helped. And no real harm done. It's not as if I'm naked.'' She smiled and waved cheerfully at Ferris, who nodded brusquely and disappeared around a bend in the path. Brigman had already vanished.

''No, it's not as if you're naked.'' Ryerson freed the snagged material. ''But it's the next best thing. Good thing Ferris was a long way down that path or he'd have gotten an eyeful. The way that wet material is clinging to you, a man can see just about everything.''

Virginia arched her brows as she realized where Ryerson's own eyes were focused. ''Only a man with exceptionally good night vision could see *everything*.''

''I must have exceptionally good night vision.''

''Either that or an overactive imagination. You know, I didn't realize those two even knew each other,'' Virginia remarked as Ryerson urged her out of the bushes.

''Neither did I.'' Ryerson sounded thoughtful. ''I wonder

why they were running around out here in the gardens?"
Then his voice changed. "Come on, let's get into a hot
shower. You're getting cold."

"How did you know?"

Ryerson chuckled and deliberately traced a blunt fingertip
over the rigid outline of one of her nipples. "My terrific
night vision."

RYERSON SUCCESSFULLY IGNORED Brigman's offer of a card
game right up until the last night of the vacation. He was
not even vaguely tempted, as he had been the first time
around. Having won the bracelet, Ryerson was more than
content. Brigman was right. He was no cardplayer. He'd just
gotten very lucky one night. Now his luck lay in other directions.

On the last night of their stay, Virginia had a few qualms.
She touched the bracelet protectively as they moved out
onto the dance floor. Then she glanced toward where Brigman was playing cards in the casino.

"Do you think the bracelet really is a family heirloom?"
she asked Ryerson.

"It may be somebody's family heirloom, but I'd bet Middlebrook Power Systems that it doesn't belong in Brigman's
family."

Ryerson spoke with such conviction that Virginia relaxed.
"You're sure?"

"Why would he be traipsing around the Caribbean with
a valuable heirloom? The man's a professional card shark,
Ginny. He won that bracelet from someone else. And now
it's ours. Fortunes of war."

She breathed a sigh of relief and glanced at the beautiful
stones. "And now it's ours," she repeated.

Ryerson followed her gaze and smiled possessively.
"Think of it as a souvenir of the start of our affair."

Virginia gazed down at the gems shimmering on her
wrist. When she lifted her eyes again, her smile had become

a little less certain. "I wonder if things will be the same when we go home tomorrow."

The possessive pleasure that had been in Ryerson's eyes as he looked at the bracelet faded away slightly. "What the hell do you mean by that?"

She shifted uneasily in his arms. "I don't know. Somehow everything seems so different here on Toralina. You said yourself it's as if we're two different people in a different world. I guess I'm wondering whether it will last after we return to Seattle."

Ryerson wrapped his hands around her nape and used his thumbs to lift her face so that she had to meet his eyes. His silvery gaze was intent and full of a fierce energy. "We're the same two people we were before we left Seattle. The only thing that changed for us here on Toralina is that we started sleeping together. I'll tell you right now that's not going to change back when we reach Seattle."

RYERSON AWOKE an hour before dawn. It wasn't the faint glow in the sky that brought him out of a sensual dream of making love to Virginia. It was the soft sound of footsteps on the tile in the outer room. Someone had broken into the suite. Utter quiet followed the small noises.

Ryerson sat up slowly and silently. But Virginia must have sensed his movement because she stirred and started to open her eyes. He covered her lips with his palm. Her lashes lifted in alarm.

There was just enough light in the room for him to shake his head in silent warning. She didn't move, just stared at him intently. He knew she had gotten the message.

The faint sound came again from the other room. This time Virginia heard it, too. She stiffened but said nothing as he took his hand away from her mouth.

Indicating with his hand that she was to remain unmoving, Ryerson eased slowly off the bed and got to his feet. Naked, he padded toward where the door to the other room stood slightly ajar. When he glanced through the crack, he caught the flickering beam of a tiny, narrow flashlight. A figure moved briefly into view. Ryerson saw nothing in the man's free hand. As far as he could tell, whoever the prowler was, he was unarmed.

Ryerson slid one arm out to the side and touched the dresser. His hand closed around the handle of Virginia's travel-size blow dryer. It wasn't much, but it was all that was available. The sturdy plastic nozzle should be capable of inflicting some damage. He started to ease open the door and simultaneously heard a drawer close in the outer room.

Ryerson hadn't seen a gun, but as he leaped through the door he belatedly wondered what the hell he was going to do if the prowler pulled a knife. Something about launching a defensive assault without even a pair of undershorts on had a disturbing effect on a man's concentration.

The thought of whoever was in the other room getting past him to attack Virginia, however, was a powerful motivator.

The figure at the writing desk spun around with a hoarse, hissing sound of dismay as Ryerson came through the door. The prowler was wearing a stocking mask. He threw up his hands in an instinctive attempt to ward off his attacker and then he plunged for the door.

Ryerson was only a split second behind him, but that instant was enough to enable the prowler to clear the door and race out into the dark safety of the gardens.

Ryerson was halfway through the door when a movement in the bedroom doorway brought him to a brief, slamming halt. Virginia stood there, her eyes huge and anxious. He saw she was clutching a high-heeled shoe in one hand as a weapon. She was as nude as he was except for the faint glitter of the bracelet on her wrist. She had insisted on wearing the thing to bed, as usual.

"Call the front desk," Ryerson ordered tersely. "Have them get the cops." He didn't wait for a response.

A few minutes later, Ryerson had occasion to reconsider the wisdom of dashing out into the gardens without a stitch on. He lost his quarry almost at once. The man disappeared quickly in the thick foliage that enveloped the hotel. But the commotion caught the attention of a young man in a white hotel uniform who was obviously just returning from a late-night room service delivery.

"Mind loaning me a napkin?" Ryerson asked grimly as the young man stared in openmouthed amazement.

"Of course, sir." The young man recovered his aplomb immediately. He had obviously been in the resort business long enough to know that one could expect almost anything from the guests. He deftly plucked a large pink napkin from the tray and offered it to Ryerson with a proper flourish.

"Thank you. Suite 316. Have the front desk put a couple of bucks extra on my bill for your tip." Ryerson turned and strode back toward the room with the napkin held discreetly in front of him and the blow dryer cocked at a rakish angle. The important thing, he reminded himself, was to appear casual and nonchalant.

THE TORALINA POLICE were sincerely regretful of the incident but were unable to do much about it. These things happened occasionally, they explained with great sadness, and just lately they'd been troubled with a rash of hotel prowlers. It was probably an out-of-work island fisherman or farm laborer who had had a little too much rum or tequila before getting up the nerve to go through the hotel rooms where the rich people from the States stayed. The police would certainly keep an eye out, but since there was little or no description there really wasn't much to go on, et cetera, et cetera.

"Something tells me the case was closed the minute we boarded the plane," Ryerson said through his teeth as he fastened his seat belt a few hours later.

"Stop worrying about it," Virginia soothed. "Nothing

was taken, thanks to you.'' She gave him an ingenuous smile. ''My hero. If I live to be a hundred, I'll never forget the sight of you racing off naked after the bad guy and returning with a pink napkin.''

But Ryerson was not in the mood for jokes yet. He stared out the window, watching the lush island landscape fall away as the jet lifted off the runway. ''I wonder what he was after.''

''Wallets, jewelry or anything else a hotel guest might have stashed in his room,'' Virginia said. ''Let's be honest, Ryerson. The people who live on this island live in a different world from those of us who vacation here. There's a lot of poverty in the Caribbean.''

''Jewelry,'' Ryerson repeated softly. ''I wonder if whoever it was knew about the bracelet.''

''How could he? We didn't open the box in front of anyone. The only one who knew you'd won the bracelet from Brigman was Brigman himself.''

''That's right,'' Ryerson said meaningfully.

''You don't think Brigman tried to get his bracelet back last night, do you?''

''It's a possibility. He wasn't pleased about losing it to me in that card game, and he turned downright sullen when I kept refusing his offer of a rematch.''

''It was Brigman who insisted on that first game of cards, and he didn't have to bet the bracelet. You won it from him fair and square, and it's ours now,'' Virginia declared, feeling very possessive. She clutched her purse more tightly. She had the emerald bracelet safely tucked into an inside pocket of her bag.

Ryerson glanced at her, and then his mouth curved enigmatically as he reached out and took Virginia's hand. ''You're right,'' he agreed quietly. ''It's ours now.''

''You're sure we won't have trouble bringing it in through customs?''

''No. I checked. Anything over a hundred years old gets

into the States duty free. And the jeweler's appraisal report we found in the box verifies that the bracelet is too old to concern customs.''

''It's really ours,'' Virginia said again. ''I can hardly believe it.'' But the truth was, it was even harder to believe in what she had found with Ryerson. That was the real treasure she was bringing back from Toralina.

CHAPTER SIX

NOT UNTIL she was back into the routine of her daily life did Virginia allow herself to admit just how nervous she had been about returning home. She had felt like a different person on Toralina, and a part of her had wondered uneasily if she would revert to the woman she had been before the trip once she was back in her normal surroundings.

But as she dressed for a dinner date with Ryerson a week after the trip back to Seattle, Virginia looked at herself in the mirror and smiled with secret delight. She had changed, and the change appeared to be permanent, even if it wasn't clearly definable. It was there in her eyes, and she knew Ryerson could see it, just as she could. The change was visible in other ways, too.

The dress she was wearing tonight was not as daring as the infamous one Ryerson had disapproved of on Toralina, but it was decidedly more adventuresome in style than the sort Virginia had been accustomed to buying before she went to the Caribbean. It was true the bra and panties underneath were still made of functional, plain white cotton, but things were changing.

The woman who looked back at her from the mirror was far more confident now in her sexuality. She was bolder, more free spirited. The woman who had swum naked in the sea off Toralina Island was quite capable of contemplating sitting nude in a hot tub with A. C. Ryerson, for example.

Unfortunately neither she nor Ryerson had a hot tub.

But that was a mere detail, Virginia thought as she started

to fasten the bracelet in place on her wrist. The point was, she could actually consider the idea.

The light flashed on a small mark inside the clasp of the bracelet. Virginia paused and gazed at it closely. It was a tiny crest, she realized. Someday it might be interesting to see if a jeweler could identify it.

An hour later when she was seated across from Ryerson at a cozy restaurant in the old section of Seattle known as Pioneer Square, she decided to bring up the subject that had been on her mind earlier.

"Have you ever thought about putting in a hot tub?" she asked breezily, chewing on a bread stick that had just been brought to the table.

Ryerson glanced up from buttering his own bread stick. There was a flicker of surprise and then a suspicious glitter in his eyes. "A hot tub? Now that you mention it, no. I've never considered the idea. Until now, that is." He paused thoughtfully, his gaze drifting to the bracelet on her wrist. "It could be done. There's a spot that would be perfect for it at my island place. I want to take you out there soon, by the way. What made you start thinking of hot tubs?"

Virginia shrugged innocently. "I was just remembering that night we went swimming in the sea and that thought just sort of naturally turned to hot tubs."

"A logical chain of thought," Ryerson said approvingly. He chomped down on the bread stick, his strong white teeth snapping it neatly. "You know, I can see us sitting in that hot tub right now."

Virginia smiled demurely. "Really? What does the image do for you?"

"Makes me hot as hell. You really want to finish dinner, or can we go straight back to my condo now?"

Virginia nearly choked on her laughter. "Ryerson, we haven't even started dinner and I'm hungry."

He sighed with mocking regret. "Okay, okay, I guess I can wait. I wonder how long it takes to install a hot tub. I could handle the pump motor installation myself. All I would need is the tub. If I called someone in the morning and could get it delivered to the island quickly enough..."

"Forget about trying to install a hot tub this weekend," Virginia said on a laugh. "We have to go to the Andersons' party on Sunday, remember? You specifically asked me to go with you to introduce you to people." The Andersons were old business friends of the Middlebrook family, and one of the reasons they were giving the party this weekend, Virginia suspected, was to welcome the new owner of Middlebrook Power Systems.

"You're right. Business before pleasure. I'll worry about the hot tub later. I've got other things on my mind tonight, anyway." The sexy humor faded from his gaze to be replaced by something much more serious. "You are planning to stay the night with me, aren't you?"

"I brought some things in an overnight bag," she admitted softly.

Ryerson relaxed. "I hoped that gym bag you had in the car wasn't really full of old sweats and dirty sneakers. Ginny, I think it's time we talked about moving in together."

Wine splashed precariously in the glass Virginia had just picked up. She tensed. "Move in together? You and me?"

"I wasn't talking about getting a cat," he muttered. "Of course I meant you and me. Think about it, Ginny. It's the next logical step in our relationship. This business of commuting on the ferry is going to get old really quickly. It's already made things damned difficult this week. Next week probably won't be any better. I've got some late meetings and an early-morning appointment with a potential client."

Virginia felt her insides twist. Her first shattering thought was that Ryerson was getting bored with her almost as quickly as her husband had. The confidence she had gained on Toralina began to dissipate. Virginia made a grab to hang on to it. She fought to keep calm and not jump to conclusions. This was Ryerson, not Jack.

"You're getting impatient with the commuting problem already?" she asked unsteadily. "But we've hardly even begun our relationship. I mean, we've just been back from Toralina for a few days. I thought we were getting along well together. I thought you were happy. I thought things were going nicely. I didn't realize you were getting bored."

"Sweet hell, lady, you're not listening to me." Ryerson's eyes narrowed abruptly as he realized what she was thinking. All the joy had evaporated from her face. She was watching him now with a deep wariness that tore him apart. It also angered him. "I'm asking you to move in with me. I'm not suggesting we call a halt to our affair. Just the opposite. What's the matter with you? Can't you understand plain English?"

She put her hands in her lap. Ryerson couldn't see what she was doing, but he was willing to bet she was crushing her napkin into a crumpled ball. Her face was strained.

"You said the commute to my place was going to get old. I assumed that meant you were already getting bored with the idea," Virginia said stiffly.

"And from that you deduced that I was getting bored with you." Ryerson shook his head in disgust. "Your logic is screwy, but I'm willing to overlook that for the moment. The topic I'm trying to cover here is very simple and straightforward. Ginny, I'm asking you to consider moving in with me. I am not getting bored with the commute. I am finding it a pain in the ass. There's a difference."

"What's the difference?"

Ryerson wondered if there was any law against a man shaking some sense into his woman in a public restaurant. He assumed there was. "The difference is this: when I am bored with a situation, I get out of that situation as fast as possible. When I am finding something to be a pain in the rear, I look for a way to fix the problem. The way to fix this particular problem is for us to live together.''

Virginia was eyeing him cautiously now. "You want us to try living together?''

"Congratulations. You are now beginning to grasp the concept,'' he retorted as the salad arrived. He watched her chew on her thoughts as the waiter arranged the plates.

"Living together would be a lot like marriage,'' she said finally, making no move to pick up her fork as the waiter left.

Ryerson recognized the direction of her thoughts. He had moved too quickly. If she knew just how quickly he wanted to move, she would be literally terrified. He looked for a way to reassure her.

"Virginia,'' he stated in his best lecturing tone, the one he used to sell doubtful clients on the merits of diesel engines, "living together is not like marriage. Not a bit. Granted, there are a few of the advantages of marriages, but...''

"And all the disadvantages,'' she concluded quickly.

He scowled at her. "Not necessarily.''

"Have you tried it with anyone else?'' she demanded.

"Well, no, but it's easy to see how it could work very well for two people like us.''

"I don't see how it would be any different than marriage,'' she insisted.

Ryerson was beginning to lose his patience, which was rare for him. "You're being willfully stubborn about this. I can see you're anxious. Trust me. Living together is fundamentally different from being married to each other.''

"I don't see how.'' She waved a hand in a small, desperate little movement and leaned forward intently. "Think about it. Living together would involve everything from sharing expenses to relatives. It would mean figuring out who would do the laundry this week and who would clean the bathroom. It would mean breakfast every morning together. It would mean sharing *closet* space, for heaven's sake. Do you realize what you're talking about here? I'd take over half of your dresser drawers. I'd leave dirty coffee cups in your sink. I'd fill up your bathroom with my shampoo and cosmetics and deodorant. Living together would not be like sharing a hotel room on Toralina. It would be much more complicated.''

Ryerson almost laughed aloud at the frantic look on her face. The only thing that stopped him was the knowledge that she was so serious. ''The idea really traumatizes you, doesn't it?''

She sat back in her chair, her eyes watchful. ''I find it very unsettling. It goes against everything we've decided we want out of this relationship.''

''It might go against everything you think you want out of this relationship, but it doesn't bother me in the least. I don't have your bias against marriage, remember?''

''That's right. You think it would be a very comfortable arrangement with the right person, don't you?'' she shot back. ''And you probably feel the same way about living together. You think it would be comfortable. But that's probably not the way it would be. All the problems would be exposed. All the little things that can be overlooked while we're having an affair would become major nuisances if we lived together. Some of those little things might prove to be more important than you realize. You might not be able to tolerate them.''

He was getting nowhere fast. Ryerson backed off temporarily. ''Ginny, all I'm doing is asking you to think about it. I guarantee it would not be the same as getting married. There would be no formal commitment, for one thing. You would not be trapped in any way. We'll go into it slowly. I'll let you get your feet wet gradually, if you like.''

''How?'' she asked suspiciously.

''You don't have to move in all at once,'' he said persuasively. ''We'll take it in stages. Try spending some portion of the next few weeks here in town with me and we'll see how it goes."

"But everything's working so well the way it is," she wailed. "We're happy this way."

"You think living together will really spoil what we have?" A quiet anger began to simmer inside him. He had been so certain he could overcome her fears.

"I don't know," she whispered.

He realized she was genuinely frightened of the whole notion. Far more so than he had imagined she would be. Hell, he hadn't even broached marriage yet. Until now he had assumed her resistance to the idea of marriage was a minor thing that would be easily handled with a little trust, passion and time.

His long-range plan had been to introduce her to the notion of marriage slowly through a living-together arrangement that would allay her old fears. He had assumed the passion between them would give him all the leverage he needed. Time would do the rest. Now he wasn't so sure. The woman was just plain scared.

"Your husband did a real number on you," Ryerson said, aware of the impotent fury inside him. "If he weren't already dead and gone, I'd be tempted to look him up and give him a hand with his departure."

Virginia looked taken aback by his vehemence. "Ryerson, I thought you understood how I felt about marriage."

Ryerson lost his temper. "For the last time," he said forcefully, "I am not talking about marriage. *I am talking about living together.*" A sudden silence in the atmosphere around them made him realize that his words had been clearly overheard by neighboring diners. Several surreptitious glances were cast in his direction, some amused, some curious and some distinctly disapproving. "We will finish this conversation later when we're alone," Ryerson ground out between his teeth.

Virginia hesitated, looking as if she wanted to say more,

but she must have seen the grim determination in his eyes because she wisely held her peace.

The meal was finished in near silence. Ryerson alternately cursed himself for having ruined the evening and then reminded himself that he had to start somewhere. He had known when he came back from Toralina that he would never be content unless he had Virginia living under his roof. That wasn't the end of it, either. The raw truth was that he would not be content until he had her committed to marriage.

The emerald bracelet glittered in the lamplight as she lifted her wineglass. Ryerson glanced at the old piece of jewelry. It looked good on her, he thought. It called attention to her graceful hands and delicate wrists.

Dammit, he had to pin Virginia down. He had to find a way to talk her into his home as well as into his bed. She should realize by now that he was different from her dead husband. She was going to have to learn to trust him.

The green flames flared in the depths of the gems, beckoning and promising and enticing. He stared at the bracelet.

"Is something wrong?" Virginia asked uneasily, seeing the direction of his gaze.

Ryerson shook his head, frowning as he realized how intently he had been studying the bracelet. "No, nothing's wrong. Are you ready to leave?"

She nodded. "I'm ready."

"Then let's get out of here." He pulled out his wallet and located a charge card. "It's time we went home." He used the word *home* deliberately, testing her to see if she would bristle in reaction.

But Virginia said nothing. She finished her wine in silence while Ryerson scrawled his name on the charge slip.

VIRGINIA TRIED HARD to forget what had been said in the restaurant. On the way back to Ryerson's condominium, she made a concerted effort to introduce bright, cheerful, non-threatening topics of conversation.

Ryerson ignored her part of the time and gave her monosyllabic responses when he did deign to participate in the conversation. He maintained a dark, brooding silence as they drove through the old brick structures that dominated Pioneer Square. It was Friday night, and the area was filling with the crowd who had come to this part of town to enjoy the small theaters, restaurants and the numerous taverns with their popular jazz and rock bands.

Ryerson held his peace as he drove north on First Avenue toward his high-rise condominium building. He still didn't say a word as he parked the Mercedes in the garage and escorted Virginia into the elevator.

When they reached his floor, he shoved the key into the lock, opened the door and stood aside to allow Virginia into the darkened apartment. She went in quickly, sneaking an uneasy glance at his hard face.

"Ryerson," she said softly as he closed and locked the door behind him, "I think we had better talk. We need to settle this."

He eyed her as he shrugged out of his jacket. "We've done enough talking for now. It's obvious we're not communicating in some areas. Might as well stick to the one area in which we do communicate." He loosened his tie.

Virginia took a step back, unsure of the expression in his eyes. She could usually read this man like a book. It was one of the things she liked about the relationship. She felt she understood Ryerson. But tonight she was not so certain.

"I disagree," she said with a calm she was far from feeling. He had the tie undone and was unbuttoning his shirt. "This business of living together is clearly going to be an issue. I hadn't realized you were even thinking in those terms. It changes everything. We must talk it out."

He came toward her deliberately, not bothering to turn on any lights. His shirt was hanging open. In the shadowy room the roughly hewn features of his face were cast into forbidding lines. His eyes were trapped pools of moonlight. He reached for her, his hands closing over her shoulders. Without a word he pulled her to him and captured her mouth. The kiss was heavy, thorough and deep.

All thought of protest and rational discussion faded from Virginia's mind. "Maybe you're right," she whispered dazedly against his lips when he finally raised his head. "Maybe this is the best way for us to communicate."

His body was hard and taut against hers. She felt his fingers tighten on her soft shoulders. "Don't get the idea that you can distract me with sex every time we're on the verge of arguing about our future," he warned harshly.

She shook her head quickly. "I didn't mean that. Besides, it was you who cut off the conversation a minute ago."

"True. I just thought I ought to warn you that we will be returning to it, sooner or later."

"But not right now?" she asked hopefully.

"Right now," he told her, "I've developed other priorities." He picked her up in his arms and carried her down the hall to his bedroom.

HOURS LATER Virginia awoke in the darkness, aware of a burning thirst and a bad headache. Her first thought was that she must have had too much to drink at dinner. She lay quietly for a moment, trying to figure out why the room did not look familiar.

Her stomach was churning. She frowned, remembering that she had had only two glasses of wine earlier. Whatever was causing the headache and the nausea couldn't be related to overindulgence.

She turned her head restlessly on the pillow, annoyed because the normal outline of her bedroom would not come into focus. Maybe she was dreaming.

She was so warm. It was far too hot in here tonight.

Virginia shoved aside the sheet and blanket. She had to open a window.

It wasn't until she tried to sit up that she finally began to realize something was really wrong. She was dizzy. When she got to her feet she almost collapsed. She felt the carpet on the floor and knew it wasn't the rug in her own bedroom. Then she saw the heavy, dark shape on the bed.

She was in Ryerson's bedroom.

Relieved that she had finally figured out what was wrong with the room, Virginia took a grip on her whirling senses and aimed for the window. She wondered how Ryerson could sleep in such heat.

Her stomach threatened to betray her halfway to the window. Virginia wavered for a moment and then changed course for the bathroom. First things first. She was going to be violently sick.

Sick. She was ill. The room was not too hot; she was feverish. Horror shafted through her. She couldn't be sick. Not here. Jack had hated it when she was sick. Virginia staggered to the bathroom and closed the door behind her. She barely made it to the commode.

A few minutes later, the spasms were over. Shaking, Virginia clung to the sink, rinsing out her mouth while she tried to gather her senses and think.

She had to get out of Ryerson's apartment. She must not let him see her like this. If Ryerson saw her like this he would be disgusted and impatient with her, just as Jack had been.

This was one of the many reasons she could not take the risk of living with him, Virginia reminded herself as she forced herself to move to the bathroom door. A stupid thing like her getting sick would spoil everything.

She looked around frantically, knowing she had to get out of the condominium. She had to get back to the safety and comfort of her own home where she could be ill without the added burden of worrying about Ryerson's reaction to that illness.

The pain in her head was excruciating, but at least her stomach seemed temporarily under control. If only she didn't feel so hot and dizzy. It took every ounce of will-power Virginia possessed to stagger back into the bedroom and find her clothing. Ryerson did not move on the bed. The man was sleeping like a bear in winter.

Out in the living room, she concentrated hard on dressing. It was no easy task. Her fingers were shaking, and she kept having to steady herself to keep from losing her balance. It seemed to take forever to get the zipper of her dress pulled up.

When she was finished, Virginia stood panting for a moment, trying to catch her breath. Then she glanced around thinking vaguely that she should leave some sort of note. Ryerson would awake in the morning and wonder where she had gone.

With the aid of the pale light filtering in through the windows, she managed to locate a pad of paper and a pen near the telephone. She turned on the lamp and stared at the paper, trying to compose her thoughts. She could not think of anything to write for a long moment. After concentrating fiercely she finally put down, "Dear Ryerson. Had to go home. I'll call."

It wasn't much of a note, but it was all she could manage. Virginia switched off the lamp and started toward the door. When she stepped into the hallway she collided with a large, warm, immovable object. The object was naked and quite obviously male.

"Going somewhere?" Ryerson asked far too blandly.

Virginia nearly lost her balance. She clutched his arm to steady herself. He made no move to assist her. She released him at once and leaned against the wall.

"Have to go home," she whispered.

"You were going to leave without bothering to wake me? Very considerate."

She could hear the anger in him but she was too weak to react to it. "Left a note."

"I'm touched."

"Ryerson, please. I have to go home." She closed her eyes as she propped herself against the wall.

"Why do you have to go home at three in the morning?" Ryerson asked roughly. "Because you're panicked at the thought of spending even one night under my roof? You didn't feel obliged to go rushing off in the middle of the night while we were on Toralina. Or was that different because you were enjoying the free vacation I was providing?"

"Please." She tried to ease past him but he did not budge. "I have to go home."

"How do you plan to get there? The ferry stopped running an hour ago. There won't be another cne until morning. How were you going to get to the docks, anyway? Steal my car?"

She hadn't thought clearly enough to figure out how to get to the ferry docks, Virginia realized. "I'll call a cab."

"Not much point, is there? I just told you, there's no ferry until six-thirty."

The words finally penetrated her brain. No car and no ferry. She was trapped. Virginia licked her dry lips, trying to think. "I'll call my sister."

"No, you damned well will not call your sister." Ryerson's fury was barely leashed now. "If you think you can spend the night in my bed and then sneak out before dawn, I've got news for you. I'm not going to let you get away with it. You owe me a lot more than that. What is it with you, Ginny? You want to be able to have your cake and eat it, too, don't you? Now that you've discovered the pleasures of sex, you want more, but you don't want to pay the price in terms of commitment."

"You don't understand." Dear Lord, she was going to collapse if he didn't get out of the way.

"That's what you think," Ryerson said bitterly. "I'm finally beginning to understand what's going on. You're too damned selfish or too scared or some combination of both to make a commitment of any kind to me, but you like what you find in my arms, don't you?"

"Ryerson, please, I must go."

He ignored that. "You like sex with me well enough to accept a trip to Toralina or a dinner at an expensive restaurant from me, but you won't accept any real bonds. You know what that makes you, Ginny?"

"Stop it," she breathed, a tiny flame of anger giving her a small shot of energy. "Stop calling me names. Just get out of my way. I'm leaving."

"The hell you are. You're going to stay right here in my home and in my bed until you learn you have to give as well as take if you want an affair with me."

Ryerson moved, reaching out to catch hold of Virginia's arm. She struggled briefly and the effort cost her what was left of her energy. The darkness whirled around her.

"Ginny!" Ryerson caught and held her as she collapsed. "You're burning up. What's wrong?"

"Tried to get out of here. I tried. You wouldn't let me go." Virginia turned her head fretfully. "I'm hot. Need a drink of water."

"A drink of water isn't going to put out the fire that's burning in you, honey. We need a little more help than that." He eased her down into a chair. "Wait right here while I get some clothes on."

"Why?" The chair was uncomfortable.

"Because I'm going to take you to an emergency room and the hospital staff would probably prefer I didn't walk in naked with you in my arms."

Hospital. "I don't want to go to the hospital. I'm all right."

"Sure you are. And I'm the lead dancer for the Pacific Northwest Ballet." Ryerson spoke from the bedroom where he was pulling on a pair of jeans and a shirt.

Virginia sat huddled in the chair, too feverish to even cry. Everything was going wrong. "All right," she whispered in defeat, "I'll call a cab to take me to the hospital."

"A cab will take too long at this hour." Ryerson strode back out into the hall, checking for his keys and wallet. "Can you walk or do you want me to carry you down to the garage?"

"I'll walk." She got unsteadily to her feet. There was no point arguing further. He was determined. Virginia surrendered to the inevitable. This might be the beginning of the end of the affair, but she could no longer fight it. "Oh, Ryerson, I feel so awful."

He steadied her with his arm about her shoulders as he half walked, half carried her to the elevator. "Stop worrying, honey. You're going to be fine. I'll get you to the emergency room and they'll give you something to break the fever. Then I'll bring you home and put you to bed."

"Home? You mean you'll take me back to my place?" she asked. Maybe there was hope, after all.

"I said home. I meant here. My home. You're not in any condition to be left on your own."

"But, Ryerson..."

"Hush, Ginny. I'm taking over now."

CHAPTER SEVEN

"FOOD POISONING." If Virginia hadn't been so drowsy, she knew she would have been even more indignant. Two hours after leaving for the emergency room, she was back in Ryerson's bed with the probable verdict. "I can't believe it. It was such a good restaurant!"

"They weren't absolutely certain it was food poisoning," Ryerson reminded her. "It might be the flu. You heard the doctor—it's hard to diagnose gastrointestinal disorders. They just treat the symptoms and let nature take its course."

"It's food poisoning," Virginia said firmly. "I'm starting to feel better already. If it was the flu, I'd feel worse. I'll tell you one thing: I'll never go back to that restaurant again."

"It might have been caused by whatever you had for lunch. One of the nurses said it can take several hours for the symptoms to show up." Ryerson moved efficiently around the room, plumping pillows and adjusting the blinds. "It can happen in the best of restaurants. If it is food poisoning."

"I'm voting for food poisoning."

Ryerson grinned. "You're not the only one who's voting for food poisoning. If it's the flu, I'll probably be joining you in bed soon, and as much as I'd enjoy the excuse I'd prefer not to be feeling nauseated when I'm making love to you."

She looked up at him, still a little uneasy about the situation. There was no doubt but that Ryerson had been wonderful. He had been calm and caring, and he had handled everything in the emergency room. He did not seem the least put off by having to play nurse.

"I'm sorry to be such a nuisance," she murmured, hugging the sheet to her chin. She was still suffering from occasional chills.

Ryerson gave her an exasperated look. "For the last time, stop worrying about it and stop apologizing for it. If you say one n.ore word about being a nuisance, I'm liable to lose my temper. I'm going to make some tea. I'll be back in a few minutes."

Virginia nodded, still not trusting herself to speak. She closed her eyes and dozed until she sensed his presence beside the bed. "Thank you," she said, sitting up against the pillows to accept the teacup.

"You're welcome." Ryerson sat down on the bed, a mug in his big fist. "Are you feeling well enough to talk?"

"What do you want to talk about?"

"I think you know the answer to that. Now that the crisis is past, I'd like to know why you felt obliged to try to sneak out of here when you woke up so sick you could hardly stand."

Virginia focused on the dawn-lit sky outside the window. "I didn't know how my being ill would affect you," she finally admitted. "My husband couldn't stand sickness in others. He could be very cruel about it. Once when I had a bad cold, he told me I looked ten years older. He insisted I stay with my sister until I was well."

"So you just naturally figured I'd react the same way— is that it?"

Virginia flinched at the cool disgust in his tone. "A part of me didn't want to take any chances," she said honestly. "I didn't want you to see me like this. I didn't want to ruin things between us."

"You mean you didn't trust me to be able to tolerate your being sick. What kind of a man do you think I am, Ginny?

We're involved with each other. In my book, that means we take care of each other.''

She sighed. ''An affair isn't marriage. An affair is based mostly on fantasy. Things seemed to be working for us on that level. I thought it best if reality didn't intrude.''

''Tell me something, if I had been the one who had gotten sick tonight, would you have tried to ship me home before I became too big a problem?''

Her eyes flew to his. ''Of course not,'' she said instantly. ''How could you possibly think that?''

''Guess where I got the idea?'' he replied laconically.

''But that's different,'' Virginia tried to explain.

''Is that right? Why? Because you're a woman, and women are just naturally nurturing? Bull. I'm demanding equal rights, you little female chauvinist. This attitude of yours is obviously another legacy left to you by your dead husband. Get rid of it. You're going to have to learn to trust me.''

''But, Ryerson...''

Ryerson said something rude under his breath. ''Ginny, you'd better face some obvious facts. There is no way for two people like us to have an affair and still stay free of all obligations and commitments. It doesn't work that way. We can't live in a total fantasy. Even if it's possible for some people, it's not possible for us. We're not the right types. We're too practical by nature. Things might have seemed unreal for a while down on Toralina, but that feeling won't last long now that we're home. Reality does intrude sooner or later, no matter how hard you try to guard against it. I, for one, have nothing against reality. The truth is, I'm better equipped to handle reality than I am a full-blown fantasy. And I think you are, too.''

She hesitated and then leaned back against the pillow, closing her eyes. She thought of how sick she had been during the night and of how well he had handled everything. It was the way she would have handled things if the situation had been reversed. He was just like her in so many ways. "Yes," she said softly, "I'm beginning to see that."

There was silence for a long moment, and then Ryerson said calmly, "When you're feeling better, we'll talk about the details of moving you in with me."

In her mind Virginia heard the door of a velvet cage swing open invitingly. Maybe it would work, she thought for the first time. Ryerson was different. Maybe, just maybe, she could take the risk of living with Ryerson.

After all, if it didn't work out, they both would still technically be free. Perhaps she had been wrong earlier when she had argued against living together. Maybe living together wouldn't be quite the same thing as being married.

Or would it?

Virginia fell asleep with the question whirling in her mind.

For a long while, Ryerson sat watching Virginia with brooding, thoughtful eyes.

It still shook him to remember how he had felt in the early hours when he had awakened abruptly and realized she was trying to sneak out of the condo. He had been torn between rage and anguish. No doubt about it, Virginia was a living example of the once-bitten-twice-shy syndrome. She was going to drag her pretty heels every inch of the way.

Quietly he collected the tea mugs and started to leave the bedroom. He was halfway to the door when he saw Virginia's purse standing open on the nightstand. Green-and-white fire laced with gold winked at him from inside the leather bag, and Ryerson smiled. The bracelet was never far away these days. It symbolized the fantasy he and Virginia had found on Toralina.

With any luck, it would soon come to stand for the reality they were going to find here in Seattle. *With any luck?* Hell, he'd been getting lucky since the night he'd found himself standing on Virginia's doorstep. He was on a roll. Nothing was going to stop him now.

VIRGINIA AWOKE about noon and knew for certain she was going to live to eat in another restaurant. She breathed deeply a few times and decided her stomach was almost back to normal. Even the headache had disappeared. She wriggled her toes and thought about a shower. The idea was enough to propel her out of bed.

Once on her feet, she found she wasn't quite as steady as she had thought, but other than that, she was in fair shape. She made her way down the hall to the bathroom, peeled off her nightgown and stepped under a hot spray.

The shower door opened a minute later, and Ryerson peered in with great interest. He examined her lush, wet curves, a faint smile in his eyes. "Does this mean you're ready for raw oysters and steak tartare?"

Virginia grinned. "Not quite. But I think I am going to be able to make the Andersons' party tomorrow evening. As far as today goes, though, I'd better stick with soup and crackers."

"You're in luck. That's one of my specialties. I assume all this interest in food means you're not coming down with the flu?"

Virginia shook her head quickly. "Nope. It must have been food poisoning."

"Well, don't look so pleased with yourself. You're not going anywhere," Ryerson warned darkly.

She stared at him. "What's that supposed to mean?"

"It means I'm keeping you here for another night."

He appeared very determined. Virginia had to admit the idea was not nearly as upsetting as it ought to have been. And it was, after all, the weekend.

"Why?" she asked cautiously.

"For observation," he said with a wicked grin. "Close observation."

Virginia was left staring at the shower door as he closed it firmly behind him. It was happening, she thought. Slowly, inevitably, she was becoming entangled in his life, and he was becoming entangled in hers. This was not the fantasy world of Toralina where she had felt like a different person. This was reality, and she had to face the fact that Ryerson was right. There was no way to conduct a safe, fantasy affair with him. The man was far too real to be treated like a dream lover.

She discovered that afternoon that it was very pleasant to be pampered by Ryerson. He went shopping in the Pike Place Market and brought home flowers along with the groceries. He prepared soup and served it with a flourish. He played checkers with her and allowed her to win twice. And that night he did not try to make love to her. Sensing that she was back to normal but still very tired from the ordeal, he simply held her close until she was sound asleep.

The whole experience gave Virginia an insight into just how comforting a passionate friendship could be. The question now, she knew, was whether to risk a live-in relationship. A part of her was still frightened of jeopardizing everything she was finding with Ryerson.

The next day was Sunday, and Virginia discovered that Ryerson's routine was almost identical to her own. They shared a lazy brunch together and then read the paper over a pot of tea while Mozart played softly in the background. It all felt very comfortable and very homey. Virginia began to imagine a string of such weekends extending into the future.

It just might work.

Ryerson sensed the wheels turning in Virginia's stubborn brain and smiled to himself. His luck was holding.

The Andersons' party was a crowded event held at the couple's Mercer Island home. The modern two-story house fronted Lake Washington. A spectacular garden led from the terrace down to the water where a private boat dock jutted out into the lake.

The house had been built for entertaining, and tonight it was filled with people. Virginia knew many of the guests because of her family's longtime presence in the Seattle business community. She introduced them to Ryerson, who, in turn, found himself readily accepted.

He also discovered that his relationship with Virginia was the source of much speculation. He should have anticipated that, he thought ruefully, as well as the veiled questions about Debby. The truth was, he'd been so involved in plotting to get Virginia into his life that he'd literally forgotten about his brief dating relationship with the younger Middlebrook sister. Funny how a little thing like that could slip a man's mind.

"Heard you were seeing one of the Middlebrook sisters," a balding, middle-aged man remarked confidentially to Ryerson as Virginia smiled across the room at someone and moved off through the crowd. "Thought it was the other one, though. The younger one. Must have been mistaken." He frowned, staring after Virginia. "What's the story? Are you two serious about each other or what? Name's Heatherington, by the way. Sam Heatherington. Known Ginny since she was a kid. She always was a nice girl. She'll make some man a good wife one of these days."

Ryerson's fingers tightened around the glass of Scotch he was holding. His eyes flicked to Virginia who looked poised and regal tonight in blue-green silk that was artfully draped around her magnificent figure. She looked sparkling and animated and utterly charming, her beautiful hazel eyes full of life. The perfect wife for a nice, respectable businessman such as himself, he thought with satisfaction. A lady on the surface, a passionate, adventurous lover underneath.

She was wearing the bracelet and Ryerson liked the way it gleamed on her wrist. He was coming to think of that bracelet as a substitute for a ring, he realized. Whenever he looked at it, he was vividly aware of the bond he was forging with Virginia. It annoyed him tonight that others didn't yet understand that bond, and it infuriated him that he had no way of explaining it.

Ryerson realized he was longing to be able to stake out his territory in the traditional ways, but so far he had no official claim on Virginia. Something within him seethed restlessly. He did not like living in this shadowy world between friendship and marriage. He turned to Sam Heatherington.

"I agree with you," he said smoothly, "Ginny is very nice. For the record the two of us have an understanding."

"Oho! Just good friends, eh?" The man winked knowingly. "Don't worry, I get the picture."

"Is that right?" Ryerson eyed him coolly.

"Sure," Heatherington said with a worldly air. "Can't say that I'm surprised. Everyone knows Ginny went through a terrible time with that bastard she married. I'll admit he had everyone fooled for a while, but ultimately it was obvious he was only after Middlebrook Power Systems." He glanced at the attractive older woman who was gliding up to stand beside him. "Isn't that right, dear? Ryerson, this is my wife, Anne. Anne, this is A. C. Ryerson, the man who bought out Middlebrook."

"How nice to meet you, Mr. Ryerson." Anne Heatherington smiled up at him, her eyes betraying her curiosity. "We've been friends of the Middlebrooks for years. My husband is right, you know. The only favor Jack Winthrop ever did Virginia was to kick the bucket. But he did a lot of damage to her before he finally made his exit. I said at the funeral that I doubted Ginny would ever marry again. I'm happy to see I might have been wrong."

Ryerson cleared his throat. This was getting more than a little annoying. But he was in no position, dammit, to claim he was marrying Ginny. Hell, he couldn't even claim she was living with him yet. "I was just telling your husband that Virginia and I are, uh, good friends. We have an understanding.'' Lord, what a weak way of phrasing it. He wanted to shake Ginny for putting him in this position.

Anne raised her eyebrows. "Is that right? An understanding? How do the Middlebrooks feel about their daughter being 'good friends' with the man who bought the family firm?"

"Why don't you ask the Middlebrooks that question?" Ryerson said through his teeth. He'd had enough. He turned around and plunged into the crowd, aware that his temper was on a short leash.

No one else proved quite as blunt as Anne Heatherington and her husband, but the curiosity and the questions were there in the eyes of several people who knew Virginia. As the evening wore on, Ryerson became increasingly frustrated and angry that he couldn't make his claim plain to one and all. Virginia herself seemed unfazed by the subtle curiosity around her, as far as Ryerson could tell, and that irritated him further.

As time passed, the leash on Ryerson's temper got shorter. Shortly after ten o'clock he glanced around the room, locating Virginia easily. She was half a head above most of the women guests, regal as a queen. And just as proud and stubborn as one, Ryerson told himself grimly. He finished his Scotch and started toward her with sudden determination.

Virginia saw him approaching and smiled happily. He looked so good, she thought with warm affection. Tall and strong and utterly virile. *A man a woman could trust to be there when the going got rough,* whispered a voice in her head.

"Hello, Ryerson," she said as he walked up beside her. "Enjoying yourself?"

"Not particularly. I've been too busy fielding questions about our so-called relationship."

"Oh, those questions." She laughed. "I've had a few

myself. Everyone's very curious. First people can't figure out whether it was me or Debby they'd heard you were seeing, and then they want to know how serious we are.''

''I hope you've been telling them we're very serious,'' Ryerson muttered meaningfully. He reached out and took the wineglass from her hand. ''Let's go outside. I want to talk to you.''

''Now?'' She was startled. ''Is something wrong?''

''Nothing that can't be fixed. Let's go.'' He took her hand and led her out of the crowded room onto the terrace. Then he started down into the garden.

The June evening was cool but not chilly. Virginia followed Ryerson willingly. It was a relief to take a short break from the party.

''Look at the city lights across the lake,'' she said chattily as they walked down toward the water's edge. ''Aren't they beautiful tonight? So clear and sparkling. I haven't been in the Andersons' garden for quite some time. I'd forgotten how spectacular it is. Bill Anderson has made it a full-time hobby, you know. He's always putting in little ponds or exotic roses.''

Ryerson ignored her running commentary. ''I want to talk to you about us, Virginia.''

She tensed. *Here it comes,* she thought. Ryerson's patience had finally run out. He was going to pin her down and extract an answer from her. ''Do you think this is the time or the place, Ryerson?'' she asked softly and knew she was instinctively stalling.

''I was planning to wait but I don't think I can,'' he said bluntly. He released her wrist, his fingers gliding over the bracelet. The moonlight was in his eyes as he looked down at her. ''Everyone inside that house wants to know if we're going to get married. I'm not asking you that. I just want an answer to the question I asked you the other night. Will you come and live with me?''

Virginia hesitated an instant and then turned away from

im and walked a few steps down a tiny, pebbled path. There was a pond at the end of the path. She reached out and touched a rose that was gilded with moonlight.

"Are you sure that's what you want, Ryerson?"

"I want you," he told her. "Not on a part-time commuting basis or for occasional weekends. I want you full-time."

Virginia took a deep breath. "I've been thinking about it," she began carefully.

"Hell." Ryerson's disgust was plain. "Going to wimp out on me, Ginny? Do you really think you can maintain a fantasy affair with me indefinitely? Do you think that I'll let you treat me that way?"

She frowned and swung around to face him. "Ryerson, listen to me. I told you I've been thinking seriously about the problem, and I have."

"It's not a problem, dammit, except in your mind!" He took two threatening paces toward her, his features grim in the shadows. "It's the logical next step in our relationship. I've had it with your shilly-shallying, Virginia Elizabeth!"

He was looming over her in the moonlight. Instinctively she backed up a pace and lifted her chin. "Don't shout at me. I'm trying to conduct a reasonable discussion here. After all, this is a major decision for both of us."

"*Reasonable.* You call your arguments *reasonable*? Your arguments against us living together are as dead as your former husband. Bury them all, lady—the arguments and him."

She was alarmed by his intensity. She took another step back out of his reach. "Please, Ryerson, this is a big move for me. I would appreciate it if you would—"

"If I would what? Give you some more time? Forget it. I want an answer and I want it now." He took another pace toward her.

Virginia lost her temper. "What the hell gives you the right to push me like this?"

"I'm not worrying about rights tonight. I'll push as hard as I have to in order to get an answer. Come on, you little coward, tell me you'll come and live with me."

"I am not a little coward!" she yelped just as her high-heeled sandal slipped on a mossy stone at the edge of the pond. "Furthermore, I am not… *Oh, no!*" She lost her balance and grabbed frantically for a nearby branch, which promptly snapped in her hand. A second later she toppled into the pond with a resounding splash.

"Virginia." Ryerson leaped to the edge of the pool and waded in after her, heedless of his shoes and expensive suit. "Dammit to hell, are you okay?"

Virginia spit out a lily pad and glared at him. "No, I am not okay. This water is freezing." She ignored his extended hand and struggled to her feet. Her dress was a sodden mass of clinging silk. "Now look what you've done."

"What *I've* done!" He stood knee-deep in the water and stared at her in outrage. "This isn't my fault. If you hadn't been such a wimp about answering my question, this wouldn't have happened."

"Is that right? Well, let me give you my side of the story," she hissed. "If you hadn't been so pushy and demanding, neither of us would be standing here soaking wet. You didn't even give me a chance to answer your stupid question in a civilized fashion."

"So what is the answer?" he roared.

"The answer is *yes*."

Ryerson stared at her speechlessly for nearly thirty seconds. Eventually he found his voice. "You mean it? No more arguments? You'll live with me?"

"If I don't catch my death of pneumonia first," she retorted tartly.

"Ginny!" He caught her wet body close, his mouth warm and fierce against hers. "Ginny, honey, I swear you won't be sorry. It's going to work—you'll see."

She melted against him, her arms going around his neck. "If you say so, Ryerson."

"I say so." He kissed her again with rough urgency, and then he stepped back and gave her a charming, sexy, rather crooked grin. "Come on, let's go home. We've got the perfect excuse to leave. You're soaking wet." He took off his coat and slung it around her shivering shoulders.

She nodded quickly. "That's a fact. I'm freezing. We can sneak around the corner of the house without anyone seeing us."

"We're not sneaking anywhere," Ryerson declared. "We'll go back through the house and say a proper goodbye to our hosts."

"Ryerson! Are you serious? Look at me; I'm a mess. And you're wet up to your knees. What will people think?"

"That we're a couple of passionate lovers who tried to get in a quickie out in the garden and managed to fall into the pond instead."

Virginia laughed softly. "Don't be silly, Ryerson. No one's going to believe that. Neither one of us is the type."

"That's what you think. We're going to answer once and for all the questions they've been asking this evening. After this, no one's going to wonder whether we're serious about each other. They'll know."

An hour later, Virginia was snuggled once more in Ryerson's bed. He turned out the last of the bedroom lights and crawled in beside her. She eyed him with accusing eyes.

"You let them think the worst, Ryerson. You did it deliberately. I heard how you explained our little dunk in the pond to Mrs. Anderson. You made it sound as if I'd gotten so carried away with passion that I lost my balance, tumbled into the pool and pulled you in after me."

"Isn't that fairly close to the truth?" He smiled contentedly as he reached for her.

"It's not close at all. I wound up in that pond because we were arguing, not because we were making love."

"In a way we were making love," he informed her.

"How's that?"

He leaned over her, trapping one of her legs with his own. He framed her face with his forearms. "You were telling me you would take the risk of living with me. I consider that an act of love."

"An act of love." The phrase hung in the air between them. Virginia tasted it on her tongue and knew Ryerson was hearing his own words echo in the room.

"An act of love." The words had a variety of connotations. One of them was an euphemism for having sex. But there was another meaning, one that implied the emotions were truly involved. Until now, Virginia knew, she and Ryerson had both been very careful not to use the word *love* in any ambiguous sense. Now the four-letter word was smoking in the air between them.

"Don't panic," Ryerson said softly. "We're going to do very well together, you and I."

"Do you think so?" Ryerson didn't believe in love, she reminded herself. He was much too practical, too unromantic and too realistic to buy into such a fuzzy emotion.

"I'll stake money on it. The same way I staked money to win that bracelet."

Virginia smiled tremulously. "It's a little nerve-racking going through so many changes so quickly."

"We'll adjust."

"You're so confident."

He smiled. "Now that I've got you under my roof, I can afford to be confident." He bent his head and kissed her throat, his mouth warm on her skin.

"I can't believe we're the same two people who once calmly discussed a pleasant, undemanding little friendship that would require almost nothing from either of us." Virginia shivered delicately with passion as Ryerson found her breasts with his lips. She laced her fingers into his hair and held him close, lifting herself against his mouth.

"If it's any consolation," Ryerson said as he moved down her breasts to her soft stomach, "I don't think we are the same two people."

"What happened to us?"

"I'm not sure. Has it occurred to you that we're changing in some ways, Ginny? That maybe Toralina wasn't just a fantasy world that we stepped into for a while and then left behind? Maybe we're not quite the same two people we were before we went down there."

She sucked in her breath as his fingers moved persuasively on the inside of her thighs. "Yes," she whispered. "It's occurred to me." Then she giggled in delight. "And judging from the expressions on the faces of the Andersons' guests tonight when we came back in from the garden, I think it's occurred to a few other people, too."

Ryerson laughed softly and began to stroke her tenderly. Deliberately he sought out the warm, damp, hidden places that he had claimed before. Virginia curled into him, twining one leg around his strong thigh. She touched him as intimately as he was touching her, glorying in the near-violent response she called forth.

Ryerson drew out the lovemaking, teasing and tormenting his passionate victim until she cried out for release.

"Soon," he promised over and over. "Soon."

"Now," Virginia pleaded, clutching at him. "I want you so. I need you."

"Tell me exactly what you need."

Virginia clung to his shoulders and wrapped her legs around his waist while she whispered the words in his ear. In a soft, seductive voice she made the plea as graphic as possible, and she knew her throaty descriptions of what she wanted nearly sent Ryerson over the edge. He shuddered in her grasp.

"Oh, Ginny," he muttered hoarsely. "Sweet Ginny. You're going to drive me out of my mind."

"Tell me exactly how you want me to do it."

Ryerson did exactly that.

THE NEXT AFTERNOON after work, they took the ferry to the island where Virginia's cottage was located. Ryerson had it all planned, as usual. He explained everything to Virginia as he parked his Mercedes in the driveway and walked her to the front door of her home.

"We'll pack your clothes and whatever else we can get into your car, and I'll have a mover come in and do the rest. We can send some of your things over to my island place. It could use some furniture. I've always kept it pretty bare." He turned the key in the lock of her door.

"Maybe I shouldn't give up the lease on this place," Virginia said hesitantly. It was still hard to believe in a long-term future.

"You won't be moving back here anytime soon," Ryerson said harshly as he pushed open the door. "So don't worry about the lease. Let it expire."

Virginia started to say something else, but the words died as she stepped through the front door and confronted the shambles that awaited her.

"Oh, my God," she breathed as she surveyed the chaos in her front room. "I've been burglarized."

CHAPTER EIGHT

"How DARED THEY do this to me? How dared they? They had no right to come in here and tear this place up. I'm going to put traps in the front yard. I'll get a huge dog. I'll get a gun. Yes, that's exactly what I'll do. I'll buy a gun. If they ever come back, I'll be ready for them." Virginia stormed back and forth across the living room, picking up magazines, shoving things back into their proper drawers and righting the furniture with furious energy.

"Calm down, Ginny." It wasn't the first time Ryerson had tried to soothe her. He had been saying "Calm down" and "Take it easy" on an average of every two minutes since the police had left. That had been over an hour ago.

"I mean it, Ryerson. I really am going to get a gun."

"You are not going to get a gun, Ms Amazon," he told her. "You're going to come and live with me, instead— remember? You won't have to worry about anyone coming back here, because you won't be living here." He examined a pillow that had been ripped open with a knife. The stuffing was scattered all over the rug. His hand clenched in silent fury, but he kept his voice calm.

Virginia glared at him. "I'm not so sure about moving in with you now. I don't want whoever did this to think he can scare me off."

Ryerson's expression turned stony. He tossed aside the pillow and walked over to close his big hands around Virginia's shoulders. "Ginny, you are not the brave widow lady trying to hold the farm against a bunch of gunslingers sent over from the neighboring ranch. The local kingpin is not after your property. You rent this place, remember? The police said this was an act of vandalism, pure and simple. I know you're angry and you've got a right to be. But you're going to stay rational.''

"Meaning I'm supposed to just pack up and move out of here?'' She glanced around at the mess the invaders had made. A desire for revenge was burning in her. The knowledge that she would probably never get it was enraging.

"Right.'' Ryerson released her and took the stack of magazines from her hands. "We're going to put this place back into some semblance of order, and then we're going to pack your suitcases and get you out of here.''

"I don't know, Ryerson,'' she said fretfully. "Maybe I ought to stay here a night or two. After all, whoever it was might come back.''

"And you want to be here when he does?'' Ryerson asked incredulously. "Don't be a fool, Ginny. You don't have a gun, you don't have a big dog and you don't have any booby traps for the front yard.''

Virginia thought about that. "You could stay here with me.''

"I could, but I'm not going to. Neither of us is going to spend the night here. We've already agreed that you would move in with me, and that's the way it's going to be. Why don't you start packing?''

She turned reluctantly. She was still simmering with outrage, and she knew that was probably having an effect on her thinking processes. Maybe Ryerson was right, but she didn't like admitting it.

"I really am going to get a gun,'' she mumbled as she started down the hall.

"No, you are not going to get a gun.''

"That's what you think.'' Virginia scowled at him over her shoulder. "I'm going to buy a gun, and I'm going to learn how to use it.''

Ryerson sighed. "Virginia, you know the statistics as well as I do. If you did get a gun and if you did have occasion to use it, odds are you'd either get shot yourself or you'd kill some innocent victim and have to live with that fact the rest of your life. What if it was a couple of little kids who did this? What if they had broken in and found the gun in the course of tearing this place up? They could have used it on themselves or one of their playmates. That's a far more likely scenario than you shooting it out with the bad guys."

"It's the principle of the thing!"

"Don't you think I know that? That doesn't change things. You're not getting a gun."

"You can't stop me!"

"I can and I will," he retorted with icy calm.

"What have you got against a woman defending herself?" Virginia demanded furiously.

"Nothing. But you're not going to do it with a gun."

His implacable attitude infuriated her. "That's what you think," she said.

He swung around with such suddenness that Virginia gasped and stepped back.

"Ryerson?" she whispered, not understanding the cold grimness in his eyes.

He walked toward her until he was standing directly in front of her. "No guns," he said distinctly. "Got that? You know nothing about them, and you can't possibly learn enough in a few days to make yourself an expert. Which is what you would need to be to handle an intruder. Hell, even experts screw up. That scenario I just painted for you? The one where an innocent person gets shot? I didn't just borrow that from an antigun ad."

Her eyes widened as she realized how serious he was. "What is it?" Virginia whispered. "What happened?"

"My father was an expert, Ginny. He kept guns in the house and he made sure my brother and I learned how to use them. He said it was safe to have weapons in the house as long as everyone knew how to use them and respected them. Then one night my kid brother, who had been out on a late date, tried to sneak back in without waking anyone. But he didn't quite make it. Dad heard a noise in the hall.''

Virginia closed her eyes, aware of what was coming. ''Oh, Ryerson.''

''Yeah. Dad shot him, thinking he was an intruder. Jeremy lived, but it was a miracle. Dad never did forgive himself. The next day he got rid of every gun he had ever collected.''

''How terrible for your family.''

''It was. No guns, Virginia.''

It was useless arguing with him, Virginia decided. Exasperated, but considerably subdued by the grim tale he had just related, she started back down the hall.

''What I don't understand is why they didn't steal anything,'' she muttered. ''They just trashed the place. And why me? Do you realize this is the second time someone's broken into a place where I've been staying? There was that prowler down on Toralina the night before we left the island and now this. It's not fair.''

''Yeah. I know.''

Something in his too-quiet tone stopped Virginia. There was a long silence as she stood there in the hall, thinking. Intuitively, she knew Ryerson was doing exactly the same thing. Slowly she turned around and stalked back toward the living room. Ryerson was standing where she had left him, the newspapers in his hands.

''You don't really think there could possibly be…?'' Virginia let the sentence trail off.

''Any connection? No. It's too unlikely. Too bizarre. Toralina is a couple of thousand miles away. And that guy down there was no vandal. He was definitely a hotel prowler looking for valuables.'' But Ryerson kept watching her with a thoughtful, hooded gaze.

Virginia licked her lips. ''Whoever did this might have

been looking for valuables, too. He might have done a messier job of it this time because he figured he had the place to himself and he could be more thorough.''

"But nothing was taken," Ryerson pointed out softly.

"True. Maybe he didn't find what he was looking for.''

"Virginia, you're letting your imagination run away with you. There couldn't be any connection between the two crimes. That would imply that someone followed us all the way from Toralina. Highly unlikely. Why choose us to follow home? There were people staying in that resort who were a lot wealthier than we are.''

Virginia sat down slowly on the arm of the sofa. She clasped her hands and put them between her knees. "The bracelet.''

Ryerson betrayed no evidence of surprise, and she knew at once the same thought had been drifting through his mind. He put down the newspapers and sat down in the overstuffed armchair. He stretched out his legs and regarded the toes of his large, sturdy wingtips. "As far as we know, the only one who knows we have the bracelet is Harry Brigman.''

"Maybe he wants it back. Perhaps it really was a family heirloom, one that he had no right to lose in a card game. Maybe it's more valuable than we realize.''

"Or maybe he just doesn't like losing at poker." Ryerson put his elbows on the arms of his chair and rested his chin on laced fingers. His silver eyes fastened on her. "You do realize we're really reaching here, don't you? The odds are the incident on Toralina was exactly what it appeared to be: a hotel prowler. Happens all the time in the best hotels.''

Virginia nodded glumly. "To tell you the truth, I don't really want to think there is a connection. It's too scary.''

"There is one thing we could do that would instantly relieve our minds," Ryerson said after a moment.

Virginia looked up quickly. "What's that?''

"I could contact the Toralina police and find out if the

prowler was ever picked up. If by chance they caught someone and he's been in jail all this time, we could be certain
that whoever broke in here was not the same person.''

Virginia brightened. ''Great idea. Let's do it.''

Ryerson surged up out of the chair. ''Okay. I'll take care
of it tomorrow. In the meantime, let's get this place put back
together. It's getting late and we've got a ferry to catch.''

''Ryerson, if there is some connection between what happened here and what happened on Toralina, I might have to
seriously consider getting a gun,'' Virginia said quietly.

Ryerson lost his patience. He put a firm palm on Virginia's nape and propelled her down the hall to the bedroom.
''For the last time, you are not getting a gun. Guns are
dangerous. Innocent people get killed with guns. Forget the
whole idea. Now pack.''

''Ryerson, if you're serious about living with me on a
full-time basis, I think I ought to warn you that I've been
on my own for a long time. I don't take orders well.''

''If you're serious about living with me on a full-time
basis, you ought to know that I don't respond well to veiled
threats and muttered warnings,'' he told her cheerfully. ''Go
pack.''

VIRGINIA WAS AT HER DESK two days later when her sister
phoned and invited her to lunch.

''Is this a genuine invitation, or are we going to split the
check?'' Virginia asked.

''This is an honest invitation,'' Debby assured her. ''I
thought we'd celebrate your surrender.''

''My *what*?''

Debby laughed on the other end of the line. ''I talked to
Mom last night. She said you had just called to give her
your new address.''

Virginia tapped a pencil on her desk. ''How is everyone
taking the news? Mom sounded a little taken aback on the
phone, but she didn't say too much except, 'Oh, I see.'''

"She's torn between delight that you've finally decided to give another man a chance and shock that you're moving in with the guy instead of marrying him. I told her that, knowing you, this was probably as close as she was going to get to having Ryerson as a son-in-law. She's still disgusted with me for failing to snag him, you know."

"Well, I trust she's not harboring any false hopes in my case. Ryerson and I are not getting married."

"That's what they all say in the beginning," Debby warned darkly. "Now, how about lunch?"

"I'll accept if you'll guarantee there will be no toasts to my so-called surrender."

"All right, but you're spoiling my fun."

Virginia hung up the phone with an uneasy feeling. But then, the word *marriage* always made her uneasy. She and Ryerson were living together, not getting married. Nothing had been said about marriage. This was an arrangement of two equals who happened to have a lot in common, including a mutual passion. She was not trapped and neither was Ryerson.

The uneasiness faded, and Virginia went back to work on the report in front of her.

Two hours later, she sat down across from Debby in a chic Pike Place Market restaurant that was crowded with business people and office workers. It was a warm, sunny day, and the jagged Olympic range was silhouetted against a brilliantly blue sky.

"Just imagine what a glitz-book writer could do with a situation like this," Debby said cheerfully. "Here we are, two sisters who have shared the same man. There should be great tension and high drama here. This has all the makings of a best-seller."

Virginia smiled, but she looked carefully into her sister's beautiful eyes. "Is there any cause for real tension and drama, Debby?"

"Nope. I'm glad I'm out of it, and I'm glad you're in. I

think you and Ryerson make a perfect couple. By the way, in case you're wondering, we haven't exactly *shared* Ryerson.''

Virginia buried her nose in the large menu. ''I know,'' she mumbled.

''Oh, yeah?'' Debby chuckled. ''Ryerson made that clear right from the start, I'll bet.''

''As a matter of fact, he did.''

''He would. He's very blunt about things, isn't he? Well, it's the truth. To be honest, I found him a dead bore in that department, and I have to assume the feeling was mutual. Oh, he was attractive enough at first. He was different from the other men I've been dating. Bigger and stronger and tougher, somehow. Not just in size but in some other ways I can't explain. But I also found him intimidating on occasion. And when he wasn't being intimidating, he was a bit dull, I'm afraid. He always seems so solid and substantial. An immovable object, if you know what I mean. At least, I never found a way to move him. I never saw him get excited about anything. When I realized he wasn't even getting excited about the prospect of going away for a weekend, I knew we had a problem. Maybe there was just too much of a difference in our ages.''

''Debby, I'm not sure we're required to discuss this in great detail. It's enough for me to know you're not pining for him.''

''Ah, come on, Ginny,'' Debby retorted with great relish. ''We're sisters. I love dissecting men. Great fun.''

''Let's pick another man to dissect. Who are you seeing these days?''

''Tom Canter,'' Debby responded promptly. ''He's a stockbroker. Made two hundred and fifty grand last year in commissions. He's hot. He also happens to love Sleaze Train.''

Virginia glanced up from the menu. ''Sleaze Train? Oh,

yes, that hard-rock group that made Ryerson's ears ring for two days.''

Debby grinned. ''The man's taste in music is as boring as your own. What are you going to have for lunch?''

''The linguine with hot peppers and smoked salmon.''

''Sounds good. I think I'll try the Cajun fish. With maybe a small salad.''

Before Virginia could respond, a large shape moved between her and the window and a familiar male voice asked easily, ''Mind if I join you?''

''Ryerson!'' Virginia laughed up at him, aware of a frisson of pleasure at having run into him unexpectedly. He leaned down and gave her a proprietary kiss. ''Sit down. You don't mind—do you, Debby?''

''Of course not. We've already finished talking about you, Ryerson. We're on another man now. Have a seat. What are you doing downtown? I see you've been shopping. Get anything exciting?'' She noticed a paper sack he carried in one hand. The sack was emblazoned with the logo of a major downtown department store.

Ryerson shoved his purchase under his chair. ''Nothing important. Just a small item I've been wanting to pick up.'' He reached for a menu. ''I figured as long as I was downtown, I'd take Ginny to lunch.'' He glanced up. ''But when I called your office, your secretary told me you were here having lunch with your sister.''

''We're just about to order,'' Virginia said happily. ''I'm glad you found us. You're in luck. Debby is picking up the tab.''

Debby gave a dramatic gasp of dismay. ''Hey, wait a second. I volunteered to take one other person to lunch, not two.''

''Think of all the money I wasted on those Sleaze Train tickets,'' Ryerson pointed out, unperturbed. ''You owe me.''

''This, I will have you know, is a lunch designed to cel-

ebrate Ginny's new living arrangement,'' Debby told him
loftily.

Ryerson grinned complacently. "Well, I'll have to admit
I've already celebrated that a few times privately with
Ginny. Okay, okay—I'll pay for my own lunch."

Virginia broke in before the conversation turned embarrassing. "If you two will kindly stop squabbling, we can
put in our order and get back to work before quitting time."
But inside she knew for certain she could relax. Whatever
her sister might once have felt for Ryerson, it was over.
Debby was treating him the way she would treat an older
brother, and Ryerson was responding in kind.

They were finishing the meal when Ryerson spotted a
business acquaintance across the room. "Have the waiter
pour me another cup of coffee, will you, Ginny? I'm going
to go say hello to Rawlins. My secretary tells me he's been
trying to get hold of me all day."

The package under the chair crackled as he got to his
feet. Virginia glanced at it with interest. Ryerson had made
no mention of having to go shopping this morning when he
had left the condo. She was the one who worked in the heart
of the city. It would have been easy for her to pick up any
small item he needed. She wondered why he hadn't asked
her to do just that.

"So," Debby said as Ryerson moved out of earshot, "tell
me the truth. Any chance the two of you might eventually
get married?"

Virginia's pleasure at the unexpected luncheon faded.
"That particular subject is not open for discussion, Deb.
You know that."

"You're willing to live with the guy, but you won't marry
him?"

"It's not an issue. Ryerson and I understand each other.
Let's leave it at that."

"If you say so, but how does Ryerson feel about it? I
don't think he sees himself as a trendy, fun-loving bachelor,

which is just as well since he'd be a failure in that role. He's the type who wants to wallow in all the comforts of domestic bliss.''

"I've told you, Ryerson understands. He's quite content the way things are, and so am I. Let's talk about something else, Deb.''

"Dang. Older sisters never let younger sisters have any fun. If you ask me— Oops! Look out!''

Debby's exclamation came as the waiter who was bringing the coffee dodged to avoid a collision with a waitress carrying a tray of sizzling fish. The glass coffeepot in his hand tilted precariously and hot coffee slopped over the side.

"The package!'' Virginia yelped as the coffee splashed down over the chair and threatened to splatter on Ryerson's purchase.

"I've got it,'' Debby announced. She leaned down quickly and scooped up the paper sack.

Unfortunately she grabbed the sack from the wrong end. The bag fell open as she yanked it out from under the chair.

A wickedly sexy, Ferrari-red teddy fluttered gracefully to the floor.

Virginia stared in shock at the silky scrap of lingerie. She wasn't the only one staring. Both the waiter and Debby were gazing at it, too. Debby's eyes flew to her sister's startled face, and she burst into giggles.

"Never in a million years would I have pegged A. C. Ryerson as the kind of man who would buy a sexy little teddy for his ladylove. Oh, Lord, Ginny, this is priceless. Utterly priceless.''

The waiter wiped the chair and backed off with a hurried apology as Virginia leaned down to scoop up the red teddy. She was very much afraid her face was the same shade as the undergarment. But she was struggling to contain her own laughter, too.

Without any warning, Ryerson's large hand closed around

the teddy a second before Virginia could reach it. The red silk appeared delicate and extremely fragile in his strong fingers. The sight made Virginia remember how tenderly Ryerson used his strength in bed and she blushed an even more vivid shade of crimson. Her eyes met his, and he smiled at her with sexy amusement.

Then Ryerson straightened and calmly thrust the lingerie back into the bag. Checking to make certain the coffee had been wiped off his chair, he sat down with the same aplomb he would have demonstrated at an annual meeting of Middlebrooks' board of directors.

"When the two of you have finished giggling, we can drink our coffee and leave." He glanced at the thin steel watch on his wrist. "It's getting late."

Virginia felt a wave of sisterly gratitude when Debby proved able, for once in her life, to keep her mouth shut. No one said another word about the red teddy until Ryerson kissed Virginia goodbye outside the entrance to her office building.

"I bought it for you to wear for me tonight. It's our anniversary, you know," he murmured in her ear.

"What anniversary?"

"It was a week and a half ago tonight that you and I seduced each other on Toralina."

"Oh." Virginia snatched the paper sack from his hand. "That anniversary. Since I get home before you, I'd better take it with me."

"Going to wear it to fix the margaritas?"

She smiled brilliantly. "Margaritas would be a nice touch, wouldn't they? Very appropriate." She nodded briskly and turned around to stride through the glass doors.

Ryerson watched her go, aware of the fact that he was aroused just thinking about seeing Ginny in the red scrap of lace and silk. She was going to look as sexy as hell. The bracelet would add a nice touch, too. He felt like the luckiest man on the face of the earth.

Whistling softly, he walked toward the Mercedes.

HE WAS NOT WHISTLING that evening when he strode into
the condo after work. Ryerson was in a deadly serious
mood, and when he realized that Virginia was not yet home,
the concern he had been feeling transformed almost instantly into outright alarm.

"Ginny?" He called her name as he went hurriedly
through the condo. She was always home ahead of him. Her
office building was not that far away. She could walk the
five blocks in ten minutes. He grabbed the phone and dialed
her office. There was no answer.

Ryerson slammed down the receiver and paced to the
windows. He stood staring out over Elliott Bay and told
himself to calm down. She could have stopped at the state
liquor store to get the ingredients for the margaritas, or she
might have remembered an errand she hadn't recalled earlier
when she'd said she'd be home before him.

He'd give her fifteen more minutes.

And then what, he wondered. He could hardly start calling the cops because Ginny was twenty minutes late getting
home from work.

He switched on the answering machine to see if she had
left a message. There was none. Ryerson glanced at his
watch and picked up the phone again to call Debby. He
punched out the number with short, vicious stabs. No answer.

Her parents' house.

He was dialing the Middlebrookses' number when he
heard the key in the lock. Ryerson dropped the phone into
its cradle and lunged for the door.

"Where the hell have you been?" he said through his
teeth as Virginia swept into the hall with a load of packages.
One of the sacks she was carrying was the one containing
the red teddy.

She looked up, startled. "I just stopped off to pick up

some dry cleaning. You're home a little early. What's wrong, Ryerson?''

"You're nearly half an hour late. You should have been here by the time I got home."

"I would have been, but at the last minute I remembered the cleaning. Ryerson, I don't see why you're so upset. There's plenty of time to change into the teddy and get the margaritas going."

"Forget the damned teddy," he grated. "From now on you let me know when you're going to be late. I want to know where you are every minute, is that clear? Leave a message on the answering machine or leave word at the office. Better yet, I want a daily schedule from you and you're to stick to it. No deviations."

"A schedule!" Virginia bristled. She set down her packages and turned to face him. "I think we'd better get something clear around here, Ryerson. I told you I am not accustomed to taking orders. I am also not in the habit of having to account for my every waking minute. If this is your idea of how a live-in arrangement is supposed to work then you're laboring under a severe misapprehension. Who do you think you are to fly into a rage like this just because I'm a few minutes late getting home from work?"

He raked a hand through his hair and made a grab for his patience. He was hitting her like a ton of bricks and he knew it. But she did not yet know what he knew. "All right, calm down."

"I'm not the one who needs to calm down. You are. If I had known you were going to behave like this whenever I'm a little late, I would never have agreed to move in with you. We aren't married, Ryerson. Remember? And even if we were, I wouldn't tolerate this kind of treatment. I put up with enough garbage from my husband to last a lifetime. I will never allow another man to jump on me with both feet."

She was getting hysterical, he thought and it was his own

damned fault. He *had* jumped all over her. He held up a hand. "Take it easy. Let me explain."

"I will not take it easy. I'm angry. You have absolutely no business yelling at me like this. I won't let you get away with it. I won't let you do this to me. *You have no right.*"

"I have all the right in the world," he retorted. "I've been going out of my mind waiting for you!"

"Because I was a few minutes late?" she asked in furious disbelief.

"No, not because you were a few minutes late!" he roared. "The reason I've been going crazy is that when I got back to my office this afternoon, there was a message from the Toralina police waiting for me. Somebody down there finally got off his rear and returned my call."

That stopped her in full flight. She looked at him, her mouth open. "From Toralina? A message about our prowler?"

"Not exactly," Ryerson said bluntly. "The Toralina cops didn't worry too much about our prowler after we left. They were too busy dealing with a homicide in one of the other suites."

"Somebody was murdered? Right there in the hotel?"

"Somebody we knew, Ginny. Harry Brigman. The guy who lost the bracelet to me in that card game. There is a possibility that the prowler in our room later that night was the murderer."

CHAPTER NINE

"I SHOULDN'T HAVE YELLED AT YOU the minute you walked in the door," Ryerson said quietly.

"Sure, but I'll let it go this time since there seem to have been mitigating circumstances," Virginia told him magnanimously. "Who knows? If the situation had been reversed, I might have done the same thing, given the same sort of provocation."

His mouth curved faintly. "You're very understanding."

"You can carry on with the apology later. Tell me everything you know about this mess," Virginia directed. She leaned her head back in the chair and peered up at him. The poor man really did look as if he'd been through a half hour of hell.

Ryerson began to pace the room in front of the windows, frowning. "I don't know all that much. Just enough to get worried. I gave you the gist of it. Shortly after we left the island, a maid found Brigman's body."

"You said you didn't think the prowler who got into our room was armed. If the man had just killed Brigman, wouldn't he have had a gun or something?"

"Or something. Brigman was killed with a knife. In the dark I could easily have missed seeing a knife."

"Oh." Virginia thought about that, and the thought sent little shivers down her spine. "And there you were running after him wearing nothing but your family jewels."

"Quality jewelry goes anywhere."

She smiled wryly. "Nevertheless, the whole thing is unsettling, isn't it?"

"That's putting it mildly. I don't like the outline. We meet a high-strung gambler who thinks he's riding high with Lady Luck. His luck runs out when he plays with me. He can't cover his gambling debts with cash, so he gives me the bracelet, instead. The next thing we know, he's dead and someone is searching our hotel suite. We leave the island in blissful ignorance, and a week after we get home, someone tears your cottage apart."

"You're wondering now if whoever ripped up my place really was looking for the bracelet?"

"The possibility has crossed my mind," Ryerson admitted. "I talked to the cops who handled your vandalism complaint. They agreed to check with the Toralina police and exchange information, but I'm not holding my breath. International police cooperation is more efficient in the movies than it is in real life. In real life, it involves a lot of paperwork, from what I understand."

"And cops, like most folks, probably hate paperwork."

"Probably. Besides, the general impression I got was that no one really thinks there could be any connection between what happened to your house and the murder on Toralina. Highly unlikely, I was told. The Toralina police said that as far as they could tell, Brigman was a loner who liked to island-hop in the Caribbean. He gambled heavily, but had no close friends or acquaintances."

"Did you tell the cops about the bracelet?" Virginia asked.

Ryerson hesitated. "I told the Toralina police I had won a piece of what appeared to be old jewelry from the murder victim. They didn't see any connection."

"In other words, no one really thinks someone followed us from Toralina just to retrieve the bracelet."

Ryerson shook his head. "You've got to admit, it doesn't sound very likely. How would this mysterious someone have even known we live here in Seattle? The logical assumption, Ginny, is that Brigman was killed by a hotel prowler who was just hunting randomly for valuables, and the vandalism at your place is an unconnected event.''

"Agreed.'' Virginia took a deep breath. "All the same, I'm glad I'm living here with you right now instead of riding the ferry back to my cottage on the island. I don't think I'd enjoy being alone there tonight.''

Ryerson stopped pacing. "I'm glad you're finding some positive aspects to this arrangement,'' he muttered.

Virginia smiled serenely. "Other than your jumping on me a few minutes ago because I came in a little late, it's been a pleasant experience.''

Ryerson shot her a scowling glance. "A pleasant experience. Is that how you think of it? You're living with me, Ginny. That's not the same thing as checking into a motel for a few days, you know.''

Her smile disappeared as she realized he was still annoyed. "I didn't say it was, Ryerson.''

"A pleasant experience.'' He shoved his hands into the back pocket of his slacks and stalked over to the window. "That's a hell of a way to describe it.''

Virginia began to grow uneasy. Ryerson was not in his customary comfortable mood this evening. The man had had a rough day. "I didn't mean to offend you,'' she said quickly. "I just meant that things seem to be working out rather nicely. You know I had a few qualms at first. I wasn't sure I could live successfully with anyone again. I had grown to value my independence and my own space.''

"But now that you've seen how generous I am with my closet space and my bathroom cabinets, you figure everything's going to work out, is that it? Just a couple of friends sharing an apartment and a bed. What do you think we are? Roommates?''

She straightened in the chair. "Ryerson, I understand that

you're a little upset this evening, but there's no need to pick a fight with me.''

"A little upset. The woman tells me she finds living with me a *pleasant* experience and then she wonders why I'm frothing at the mouth.''

Virginia grinned in spite of herself. "Are you frothing at the mouth?''

He swung around. There was no answering humor in his silver eyes. "One of these days, lady, you're going to discover you can't have it both ways. You're either going to commit yourself to this relationship, in which case it won't matter if we're married or living together, or you're going to have to run for your life.''

Her brief amusement vanished. She stared at him, shocked to the core. "What do you mean? Why would I have to run anywhere?''

"You'll have to run to escape me,'' he told her bluntly. "Because I'll be right behind you. Sooner or later I'll catch you, and when I do, you're going to find the courage to make a commitment. This roommate business sucks.''

Virginia paled. "I didn't realize you were so unhappy in this relationship. I thought this was what you wanted.''

"You want the whole truth? I'll give it to you. I'm tolerating our present arrangement because I see it as a stepping stone to marriage. Living with you is a whole heck of a lot better than not living with you. I am not unhappy, Virginia Elizabeth, merely impatient.''

Her hands tightened on the arms of the chair. Carefully she pushed herself to her feet, aware of a dull anger. "I didn't realize you were thinking of marriage. I thought we understood each other. I already tried marriage once to a man who did not love me. It was a disaster. Why should I try it a second time?'' Without waiting for a response she walked down the hall to the bedroom.

"Virginia."

She didn't pause, though she heard him storming down

the hall behind her. Without a word, she slipped off her pumps and reached into the closet for a pair of jeans.

"Don't you dare draw any parallels between me and that fool you married," Ryerson grated from the doorway.

"I'm not drawing any parallels." She sighed as she stripped off her panty hose. "You're totally different, and I know that. But you don't love me."

"Is that right?" he roared sarcastically. "You think I'd go through all this nonsense for the sake of acquiring a roommate?"

Virginia looked up in astonishment. She stood holding the panty hose in one hand and her jeans in the other. "Ryerson, what are you saying?"

"I love you," he bit out, sounding not the least bit like a lover. "Do you hear me, lady?"

"Ryerson." She dropped the panty hose and jeans and ran to him. "I'm so glad. Because I love you, too. More than anything else in the world." She wrapped her arms around his waist and hugged him fiercely.

Ryerson's arms closed tightly around her. "Say that again," he ordered thickly.

"I love you. I've known that for several days now."

"Exactly how long have you known?"

She raised her head and saw the molten silver in his eyes. "Probably from the start, but most certainly since the night I fell into the Andersons' pond," she admitted with a small smile. "What about you? When did you first realize you might be falling in love?"

"The night you got sick all over my bathroom." He grinned down at her. "What a pair of wild, flaming romantics we are, huh?"

"I thought you didn't believe in love."

"I was a fool. I didn't believe in it because I hadn't ever experienced it. Once you've been knocked on your ass by it, though, you recognize it instantly."

"Oh, Ryerson." Virginia leaned into him, parting her lips

for him, giving herself to him without words. She had always believed in the possibility of love. She just hadn't expected to find the courage within herself to take the risk again. Now that she had, she was slowly becoming aware of an amazing sense of freedom.

"What are you smiling about?" Ryerson asked against her lips.

"I was just enjoying the feeling of being free."

Ryerson held her fiercely and groaned. "Ginny, honey, you're not free. I thought you understood at last. There's no real freedom in this relationship of ours. We're both bound by a million strings, large and small, and the longer we're together, the more chains there will be between us. I want you badly, but I don't want you living here under an illusion."

She touched his nape with gentle fingers. "You're the one who doesn't understand, Ryerson. The freedom isn't in the relationship, it's in being able to choose the kind of relationship I want. I never thought I would be sufficiently free of the past to risk falling in love. But I've discovered that I am free to make that kind of choice again. And I have chosen to fall in love. With you."

He kissed her again, hungrily, and eased her down onto the bed. Virginia was aware of his fingers on the fastener of her bra. Ryerson was whispering husky words of love and desire when an image flashed into Virginia's head.

"Ferris," she said starkly.

"What?" Ryerson smoothed the skin of her breast with his rough fingertips. He lifted his head and frowned down at her in puzzlement. It was obvious his mind was elsewhere.

"Dan Ferris," Virginia said slowly. "You said the Toralina cops told you Brigman had no close friends or acquaintances on the island, but he wasn't a total loner. He knew Dan Ferris. Remember the night we snuck back to our room after that swim in the ocean? We had to wait for Ferris and Brigman to get out of the way. They were arguing in the garden.''

Ryerson sat up slowly. ''Something about leaving the island. Ferris was getting restless. He told Brigman it was time to go. But Brigman refused.''

''He and Brigman never gave any indication of knowing each other when they were both in the casino or at the restaurant,'' Virginia recalled. ''And I never saw them sharing a drink. In fact, they acted like strangers every time we saw them together.''

''Except the night we overheard them arguing in the garden,'' Ryerson concluded. ''I wonder why they kept their association secret?''

''We can't be sure that they did. It might be that we just never saw them together except for that one evening.''

Ryerson grew more thoughtful. ''Ferris turned around on the path that night. He saw us.''

''Which means he knows we saw him arguing with Brigman.'' Virginia clutched the front of her bra together and gazed up at Ryerson with troubled eyes. ''You don't suppose he's the one who killed Brigman, do you?''

''They were arguing about leaving the island, not about the bracelet.''

''True, but what if the part we heard was only a small piece of the argument? What if they had discussed something else more incriminating that night on the path? Ferris would have had no way of knowing how much we'd overheard.''

''The one thing he could be sure of is that we were the only ones who could link him, even slightly, with Brigman,'' Ryerson said. He got to his feet.

''Where are you going?''

''I'm going to put in another call to the Toralina police. You might as well start dinner. This will take a while.''

Virginia glanced down at her rumpled clothing. ''I take it the big seduction scene is being postponed?''

Ryerson grinned from the doorway. "To be continued."

But Ryerson had other things on his mind after the phone call finally went through to Toralina.

"I don't like it," he told Virginia twenty minutes later. "They were very polite and agreed to check into Dan Ferris's background, but that was it. Ferris was just another tourist on the island, as far as they're concerned. He's long gone. They seem convinced, however, that the murderer was the hotel prowler and that Brigman probably interrupted him while the guy was going through Brigman's suite. After the murder, the prowler went on to the next likely looking hotel room."

"Which was ours?" Virginia started in on her scallops. "It's possible, isn't it?"

"Anything's possible, but you'd think the average prowler would be a little shaky after committing murder. Hard to picture him calmly going on with business as usual. It would take a real pro to be able to do that. After all, a prowler's specialty is sneaking around hotel rooms, not outright violence."

"But if it's true, it would mean there's no connection between what happened here and what happened down on Toralina. Which, in turn, would mean we're as safe as we ever were."

"I still don't like it." Ryerson pushed aside his plate and contemplated Virginia. "I think we're going to take another couple of days off."

Virginia looked at him. "But why? Where are we going?"

"To my place up in the San Juans. We'll take a long weekend. It will get us out of the city and it will give the Toralina police a couple of days to do some checking. Maybe by the time we get back, they'll have something. Can you get another couple of days off?"

"Yes. I still have some vacation time coming," Virginia said slowly. "You're really worried, aren't you, Ryerson?"

"If Ferris or someone else is after us or the bracelet, we're sitting ducks here in town. There are too many opportunities for him to make a move and get away with it. We'll be safer on the island. As far as anyone looking for us will know, we'll have dropped out of sight. Very few people know where my place is, and even if someone did locate it, the only way to reach it is by boat."

Virginia stirred uncertainly. "All right, I guess it won't hurt to disappear for a few days while the cops are checking things out. But what about the bracelet?"

"We'll wait until the banks open in the morning, and then we'll stick the thing in a safe-deposit box."

That night Ryerson double-checked all the locks before going to bed. When he walked into the bedroom, Virginia was sitting up against the pillows, waiting for him. She watched him undress and slide into bed beside her. Instead of reaching for her, however, he turned on his side and groped under the bed.

"What are you doing?" she asked.

"Just checking my insurance policy."

"You keep it under the bed?"

"Why not?" He settled back on the pillows and smiled at her. "There's a lot of unused storage room under a bed, you know. Now that I'm sharing this place with you, I have to find creative ways to use the available space."

"Ryerson," Virginia began very seriously.

"Maybe we should look for a bigger condo. If we had a two-bedroom place we could use the second room for storage."

"Ryerson," she tried again, leaning over him with a frown, "what have you got under the bed?"

"At the moment just a couple of suitcases and the insurance stuff I told you about. But if we got one of those special storage lockers designed to fit under a bed, we could store all kinds of junk."

Virginia planted her palms on his chest and glared at him ferociously. "You've got a gun under there, don't you?"

He wrapped his fingers around her wrists. "Don't be silly," he told her roughly. "You know how I feel about guns. Come here and tell me again how much you love me." He pulled her down on top of him and silenced her muffled protests with a kiss. No need to tell her he'd bought the damned gun the morning after they'd found her cottage ransacked.

VIRGINIA AND RYERSON were at the bank when it opened the next day. Ryerson's Mercedes was already packed, and they were ready for the trip to the San Juans. He was impatient to be on his way. Virginia had been aware of his restlessness all morning. His mood would not have been very obvious to someone who did not know him well, however. Even when he was at his most volatile, Ryerson still appeared controlled and contained. But Virginia was coming to know him very well. The appearance of self-control concealed an alert readiness that reminded her of a hunting animal that senses prey but has not yet spotted it.

"Sign here, Virginia," Ryerson said briskly. "I want your name on the access form. The bracelet is half yours."

Obediently Virginia picked up the pen. She had her name half scrawled on the signature line when something stopped her. "Ryerson?"

"What, honey?"

"I don't want to put the bracelet in the vault."

He glanced at her in surprise. "Why not? It will be safe there. One less thing for us to worry about."

She shook her head, suddenly sure of herself. "I'd rather keep it with us."

"But, Ginny..."

"Please, Ryerson. Let's keep it with us." She put a hand on his sleeve. "I know it seems logical to store it here, but I just have this feeling we should take it with us."

He looked down into her anxious eyes and hesitated. "Ginny, it will be safe here."

"I know. But I want it with us." She had to convince him, she realized. It was crucial, though she had no idea why she was so sure of that. "Please, Ryerson. Humor me. If we're in danger, it won't matter if we have the bracelet with us. Whoever's after it will assume we have it, anyway."

"Dammit, Ginny, it doesn't make any sense to drag this thing around with us."

"You've got your insurance policy. This is mine." She dropped the bracelet into her purse.

Ryerson groaned in resignation. "The hell with it. If that's the way you want it, I'm not going to argue. We've wasted enough time as it is. Let's get out of here."

He wasn't pleased, Virginia realized as she followed him out to the car. She waited out his mood in silence, letting him concentrate on getting them clear of downtown traffic. When they were finally on Interstate 5, heading north toward the ferry docks that serviced the islands scattered from Seattle to Canada, she broke the taut silence.

"I can't explain it, Ryerson. This morning I agreed with you about putting the bracelet into the vault. But at the last minute I got this overwhelming feeling we should keep it with us."

"Save me from a woman's logic," he muttered.

"Well, I happen to be a woman!"

He shot her an unreadable glance. "I'm not arguing that."

Silence settled down on the Mercedes once more. Virginia decided Ryerson was brooding. Neither one of them said more than a few words until they were on board the ferry that would take them on the first leg of their journey. Then Virginia tried to reopen communication.

"Will this ferry take us to the island where you have your vacation place?"

Ryerson leaned against the rail, watching the islands, large and small, float past the ferry. "No. We'll get off at the next stop. I keep a boat in a marina there. We'll use the boat to get to my place."

"Are you going to spend the whole weekend glaring at me?" Virginia asked.

Ryerson turned his head in surprise. "Is that what I was doing? Glaring at you?"

"When you're not actively brooding about my lack of common sense."

He gazed at her for a long moment. "Do you want to know what I was thinking about, Ginny?"

"If you want to tell me."

"I was thinking that I've been behaving a lot like a husband instead of a lover during the past couple of days."

She flicked him a quick glance. "I see."

"I doubt it. In case you haven't noticed, I sometimes have trouble playing fantasy man. I lost my temper with you yesterday, and I got annoyed with you again this morning. I can't guarantee it won't happen again. I wasn't cut out to be a dream lover."

"You did a good job on Toralina," she couldn't resist pointing out.

"Is that why you think you're in love with me? Because of the way I treated you while we were on Toralina? If so, Ginny, you're setting us both up for a fall."

"I don't think I'm in love with you. I know I'm in love with you. I can handle the real you, Ryerson."

"Even when I come off sounding like an irate husband?"

"The real question is, can you handle me when I sound like a shrewish fishwife?"

Ryerson's smile was his first in hours. He put his hands behind her neck and slowly, inevitably, drew her close. "I can handle you, regardless of what kind of wife you turn out to be."

She looked up at him, trying to determine if he was teasing her. There was no sign of it. She moved in his arms and decided the safest thing to do was to ignore the reference to wife. After all, she had inadvertently brought the word into the discussion.

Two hours later, Ryerson guided his small cruiser into a tiny, secluded cove on the east side of what appeared to be a deserted island. Virginia stood in the stern, watching with interest as he tied the boat up at a private dock. There was a small boathouse attached to the planked dock. Both were designed to float on the tide. Nestled in the trees several yards above the shoreline was a cabin.

"Does anyone else live on the island?" she asked. "It looks uninhabited except for your place."

"There are a couple of other vacation cottages on the opposite side. The owners rarely use them. For all intents and purposes, I've got the whole island to myself." Ryerson began unloading the suitcases and packages they had brought with them. "It's a little primitive, Ginny. I didn't build the place to be a love nest."

"No mirrored ceilings or red velvet wallpaper?"

"Afraid not. Also no phone and no dishwasher. Disappointed?"

"That depends. What about hot water and electricity?"

He gave her an offended look. "Honey, I'm a man who knows power systems, remember? Don't worry. You'll have hot water and electricity. Also a stereo. Just as soon as I get the generator started."

Virginia smiled cheerfully. "In that case, I'm a contented woman."

The small cabin was cold and damp from having been closed for months, but the atmosphere changed after Ryerson spent several minutes out back with the generator that supplied power to the cottage. When he had finished with that, he started a fire in the stone fireplace. By the time he had the blaze going, Virginia had his Scotch poured and dinner on the stove.

"Perfect," she mused as she sat down beside him on the old sofa after the meal had been served. "Brings back fond memories of our first meeting. The only thing missing is the storm and Mozart."

"You're not going to have to wait long for either," Ryerson told her as he fished a compact disc out of its plastic storage container and put it on the player. He glanced out the window. "The rain is starting already."

"Ah, that's a nice touch," Virginia murmured, sipping her wine.

"I special-ordered the storm." Ryerson settled back down beside her as the strains of a violin concerto filled the room. He smiled slowly as he picked up his glass of cognac. "You know something? I had a hell of a hard time getting to sleep that night in your cottage. All I could think about was how nice it would be to wander down the hall and crawl into bed with you. I knew then I was in serious trouble."

"You weren't the only one," she confessed. She leaned her head against his shoulder. "I just wish we were here tonight because we really had decided to take a long weekend, not because we're trying to lie low while the Toralina police come up with some answers."

"I know," Ryerson said quietly, his tone hardening. "This is only a temporary hideout, at best. We sure as hell can't stay here indefinitely. But I don't like the idea of you being vulnerable in the city. It's too hard to keep an eye on you there. Any creep could snatch you off the street."

"The Toralina cops are probably right. There's no real reason to think there's a connection between Brigman's death and the bracelet. I'll bet no one even knew he had the bracelet."

"Ferris could have known. That's what worries me. If he knew about the bracelet, he might also know how Brigman lost it."

There was no real argument on that score. Virginia sighed

and finished her cognac. Then she smiled a secret smile and got to her feet. "Stay where you are, Ryerson."

"Where are you going?"

"I'm going to get ready for bed."

"I'll help you," he volunteered with an expression of lazy lechery in his eyes.

"Not at this stage. Just wait right where you are."

She went down the hall to the bedroom and closed the door behind her. Then she quickly opened her suitcase and drew out the scandalous red teddy she had secretly packed. Eyes alight with sexy mischief, she undressed and slipped into the sensual concoction. When she was finished, she stood in front of the small mirror and tried to determine the effect.

The teddy was nothing but a cobweb of silk and lace. It concealed very little of her ripe figure. Virginia faltered slightly in her resolve. This style in underwear was still new to her. What she needed was something to give her the confidence it would take to sashay out into the living room. She opened her purse and took out the bracelet.

When she had the emeralds clasped around her wrist, Virginia felt much bolder. She took a deep breath, opened the door and strode down the hall.

Ryerson was down on one knee, fiddling with the fire, when she arrived in the doorway behind him. He glanced over his shoulder and his eyes burned brighter than the flames on the hearth when he saw her.

"Come here," he murmured softly as he replaced the iron poker. He didn't move.

Virginia went slowly toward him, excitement and love and a glorious sense of abandon leaping in her veins. "Debby said she thought you were just about the last man on earth who would buy something like this for a woman," she whispered, "but you know something, Ryerson?"

"What?" He reached up and tugged her down onto the

rug beside him. His fingers slid beneath the silk strap of the teddy. He seemed fascinated with it.

"I wasn't surprised at all when this thing fell out of the sack at the restaurant." She laughed up at him with her eyes. "Somehow it seemed exactly like something you might buy on a whim."

He grinned, stretching out beside her. He watched the way the firelight played on her skin. "It's the first time I've ever been struck by that particular whim. Do you have any idea how much nerve it takes to walk up to a lingerie counter and ask for something like this? Greater love hath no man." He slid the straps of the teddy down over her shoulders so that the lace was barely cupping her breasts.

Virginia put her arms around his neck and drew him down to her. "Maybe one of these days I'll find the guts to buy you a pair of those itty-bitty black bikini briefs they make for men."

"Don't bother," he advised. "I've got some limits." He eased the teddy slowly down to her hips, his fingers gliding over her breasts with obvious pleasure. "Tell me again that you love me, Ginny."

So she told him. Again and again, she told him as he stripped the teddy off her completely and opened her to his touch.

He rewarded her with tantalizing, seductive caresses that made the secret parts of her blossom. When he bent his head and kissed the dew from the petals, Virginia clung to him, crying out her release in his arms. He held her as she shivered delicately.

"I love you, Ginny."

She looked up at him as he loomed over her. The truth of that statement was in his eyes as he sheathed himself tightly within her.

CHAPTER TEN

RYERSON SLID OUT OF BED much later that night and turned to look at the sleeping woman on the bed. They had both been exhausted from making love, but he hadn't been able to sleep since he had carried Virginia into the bedroom. That had been over two hours ago. It was after midnight now.

There was a strange restlessness driving him tonight. He had experienced it before around Ginny, and he knew how to ease it temporarily. All he had to do was go back to the bed and make love to her until she awoke and welcomed him into her soft, hot warmth. Sheathed within her with her silken legs wrapped around his thighs, he could ignore everything but the glorious sensation of losing himself in her. The wonder of possessing her and being possessed by her would wipe the restlessness from his mind for a time. He was a simple creature at heart, he decided wryly. Sex with Ginny satisfied him as nothing else ever had.

But it was not enough. Reluctantly he turned away from the bed and went out into the hall, scooping up his jeans as an afterthought. The cabin was cold.

Out in the living room, Ryerson pulled on the jeans. The fire had started to die hours ago, and he had not turned on any auxiliary heat. Outside, the rain was still falling with a soft, steady beat. It wasn't a particularly heavy rain, just a light, continuous drizzle. A typical Northwest rain.

Ryerson didn't bother with a light. He didn't want to wake Ginny. In any event, he knew his way around well enough to get by with the glow from the embers on the hearth. He remembered leaving the cognac bottle on the low table beside the sofa. A little fumbling recovered the glass he had set aside earlier. He poured a shot of cognac and moved to the window that overlooked the cove.

The sky was a slightly different shade in the distance. The rain was going to end soon. A watery moon was already trying to squeeze through the clouds. There was enough of a glow to see the cruiser bobbing in the water down at the dock. Ryerson sipped the cognac and watched the boat, remembering how Ginny had looked earlier that afternoon when she had sat in the stern, her seal-brown hair whipping around her expressive face.

Virginia was the first woman he had brought to the island, the first one he had ever really wanted to bring here. This place had always been his private retreat. Then he pictured Ginny as she had been a couple of hours ago, trembling in his arms. When he brought her sexual release, he felt like a conquering hero, master of all he surveyed and most important, master of Virginia Elizabeth Middlebrook. He gloried in his own manhood when she experienced the full potential of her femininity.

When she brought him release, he knew a satisfaction and peace that went to his soul.

He understood now why the primitive side of a man tended to get possessive when the right woman walked into his life.

Ryerson knew he needed Ginny. He acknowledged in that moment that he would do anything to keep her. He stood at the window and looked out at the cove and admitted the truth to himself. He needed her and wanted her as he had never needed or wanted anyone before in his life. He had to find a way to tie her more securely to him. He did not trust the bonds of a live-in relationship. He was damned if he would be roommates with the woman he loved.

The words hovered in his mind like a hawk. Words of

great power; words he had always avoided. Words he had never really understood until he had met Ginny.

He had reveled in hearing her confess her love for him today, but it was still not enough. He was a greedy man. He loved her too much to want her as his roommate. He wanted her as his wife. He wanted her bound to him with all the chains modern civilization could provide.

Which put him squarely between a rock and a hard place.

If he truly loved Ginny, he could not force her into marriage. Her fear of the institution ran deep, and he had to respect that fear. He loved her too much to push her into something that genuinely terrified her.

But he loved her too much to be content for long with having her for a live-in lover. A primitive part of him had surrendered to an ancient need. He needed to know that the woman he loved belonged to him in every way possible. He sensed that as long as she feared marriage to him, she was, on some level, fearing a complete relationship with him. And that knowledge scared Ryerson.

There was a part of her that still did not belong to him.

The problem was going to eat him alive, night and day. Ryerson took another swallow of cognac and wondered how long he would be able to tolerate the torment. Perhaps he could learn to live with it. After all, he would have Ginny in his bed and in his life. What more could a man want?

A lot more, Ryerson knew. He swore softly. The truth was, he would never be certain of her until she was ready to take the risk of marrying him. The fact that she could still resist marriage left him with a queasy, sinking feeling.

Ryerson swirled the cognac in his glass and narrowed his eyes as he absently watched the small boat in the cove.

"Ryerson?"

Virginia's soft, questioning voice brought him out of his reverie. He turned his head and smiled slightly. She looked soft and sexy and infinitely desirable standing there in the shadows in her prim terry-cloth robe. He had removed the teddy a long time ago, and she had never put it back on. Her hair was tousled and her feet were bare. She had forgotten to take off the bracelet, he saw. Her arm moved and the gems danced in the shadows.

"What are you doing up?" Ryerson asked, holding out his hand.

She came toward him, stepping into the circle of his embrace. "I woke up and you were gone."

"And that bothered you?"

"Yes."

He tightened his arm around her. "You should know by now that I'm never going to be very far away."

She was silent for a moment. "I know."

"I love you, Ginny. I'll try not to push you anymore. I won't drag you to the altar. I don't want to force you into something that scares you as much as marriage does. We'll do things your way."

She put her arms around his neck and softly kissed his throat. "Thank you, Ryerson. Thank you for everything."

"Don't thank me. I don't have any choice in the matter," he muttered, inhaling the scent of her hair. "I want you to be happy with me, Ginny. I don't want you climbing walls, looking for a way out or living in fear of being trapped."

"I am happy."

"That's all that matters for now." He caught her hair in his fingers and made a fist. Gently he used the grip to arch her head back so that he could kiss her. He heard her gentle sigh and felt the firm curves of her breasts beneath the robe. The terry cloth parted of its own accord, and Ryerson found himself gazing down into deep, sensual shadows.

He was about to slip his hand inside the open robe and explore the mysteries he knew awaited him when he saw another kind of shadow out of the corner of his eye. This one was moving down in the cove near the boat. Ryerson froze.

"What's wrong?" Instantly Virginia sensed the change in him. She looked up anxiously.

"Something moved down by the boat."

"An animal?"

"Possibly. But I think it's one with two feet instead of four." He released her and moved closer to the window, trying to peer through the darkness. The shadow flickered again, moving onto the dock and heading toward the boat. Ryerson swung around, grasping Virginia roughly by her forearms.

"Listen to me. I want you to stay right here and keep everything locked up tight. I'm going down to the boat."

"I'll go with you," she said immediately.

"No you will not." He released her and moved quickly down the hall to the bedroom. He thrust his feet into sneakers and reached under the bed for the .38.

Virginia was waiting for him in the other room, her expression taut and anxious. She looked at the weapon in his hand and her mouth tightened. "Ryerson, I don't think you should go down there."

"I don't have much choice. I can hardly call the cops. There aren't any on the island. Dammit, I thought we'd be safe here." He was already at the back door, letting himself out into the soft rain. He paused only to glance back briefly. "Remember what I said, Ginny. Stay inside and keep everything locked up tight."

"Ryerson, please..."

He gave her no further chance to argue. Closing the door softly behind him, he waited only until he heard her slide the bolt in place. Then he made his way around the corner of the cabin, heading for the cover of the trees.

His main advantage, Ryerson decided, was that he knew his way around the island. He did not need to follow the path from the cabin to the dock.

The rain silenced his movements through the woods. Ryerson avoided the impregnable blackberry thickets and made his way around the larger depressions in the ground, which he knew would be holding rainwater.

He could keep an eye on the path from his position in the trees, and so far no one was moving toward the cabin. That meant whoever was messing around with the boat was still busy at the dock. He tried to imagine who would be attempting to steal the small cruiser and came up with no viable prospects. Then he started wondering who might want to wreck the boat. That led to more interesting speculation.

Dan Ferris's name came to mind.

Somehow, Ryerson knew, this was all connected to that damned bracelet. Every instinct he possessed was convinced of that.

A stand of pine provided concealment near the dock. Ryerson used the trees and the darkness for cover as he moved toward the boathouse. In another moment, he would have to step out into the open. He hoped the rain would continue to obliterate any noise he might make. He was no *ninja* warrior, that was for sure—just a man who knew motors and power systems inside out. Hardly the kind of background needed for this type of thing. The gun weighed a ton in his hand. He hadn't used one after the night his father had accidentally shot Jeremy, except for his brief stint in the army.

Ryerson was about to take his chances in the open when the shadow inside the cruiser moved abruptly. A man stepped out onto the dock. Ryerson held his breath and tried to relax his grip on the gun. If this was going to work, he had to look cool and in command. No worse than facing a board of directors or an angry client, he told himself reassuringly.

But before he could move, the man on the dock opened the metal door of the boathouse and went inside. The door stayed open. Ryerson released the breath he had been hold-

ing and moved silently across wet pine needles to the side
of the small building.

This was a chance he couldn't pass up. If he could reach
the door in time he could slam it shut and lock it from the
outside, effectively trapping the intruder in the boathouse.

He raised the gun and leaped lightly onto the dock. He
was only a foot from the open door when the man inside
the boathouse decided to step back outside. Bad timing.

Ryerson hurled himself at the metal door. There was a
howl of muffled rage as the intruder ran straight into the
slamming door. The gun and a flashlight that had been in
the man's hands clattered to the deck as he took the shock
of the metal door on his right arm. The weapon skittered
across the boards and plopped into the black water. The
flashlight followed. The intruder reeled back inside the dark
boathouse, clutching his injured arm.

"Don't move," Ryerson said softly. He stepped into the
doorway, straining to see his victim in the darkness. He held
the gun steady in his hand. "Not one inch."

The stranger stared at him for an instant, his face impossible to see in the shadows. Then he disappeared, leaping
sideways out of the pale light seeping in through the open
door.

"Damn."

So much for the Rambo approach. Ryerson jumped
through the doorway. He had to move fast.

The stranger shot forward to meet him, and the two men
collided in the shadows. They both landed with a solid thud
on the wooden planking.

Ryerson thought about the possibility of a knife as he and
the intruder rolled across the floor. Brigman had been killed
with a knife, and the Toralina cops had said the job had
been done by a man who knew what he was doing.

Both Ryerson and his assailant were fighting blind. Ryerson tried to slam his gun against the side of the man's head
and struck a coil of rope, instead. Disgusted, he let go of

the gun and concentrated on using his hands to win the silent, deadly struggle.

It didn't take good night-vision, merely proximity and desperation, to land several thudding blows. Ryerson absorbed two—one in the chest and one in the shoulder—before he got in a decent swing of his own. When he did manage it, he had the satisfaction of hearing something crack. His opponent grunted and heaved violently, trying to dislodge Ryerson.

The man was big. Big enough to shove Ryerson aside for an instant. Before Ryerson could grab him, he rolled clear. There was a scrambling sound on the wooden planking. Ryerson went still, fighting to control his breathing. He could see nothing and knew that his only advantage lay in the fact that the other man was equally blind.

He heard the heavy, gasping breaths in the darkness and followed the sounds closely, praying he was not giving away his own position with the same kind of breathing. Water lapped softly at the planking.

A board squeaked, and Ryerson felt the dock give slightly. The intruder was trying to find him in the darkness. Ryerson stayed where he was, striving to pinpoint his own location. Cautiously he put out a hand and found a metal toolbox. He knew where he was now, and he remembered the fishing net he had stored on the shelf next to the toolbox.

Silently he swept his fingers around in a short arc, seeking the net. Wood squeaked again, and the heavy breathing came closer.

Ryerson's fingers closed around the net. He moved slowly to a kneeling position, aware that the small sounds he was making were probably giving away his location. He had no choice. He couldn't get the leverage he needed while lying on his side.

"Got you, you bastard," the intruder hissed and closed in on the source of the small noise he had heard. Something heavy arced through the air not far from Ryerson's head.

The man had probably snagged a hammer or wrench from a shelf.

He felt the man move in the darkness.

At the last instant, Ryerson slung the fishing net. It fanned out silently, enveloping its target in a mass of soft nylon.

The intruder swore furiously as the net settled around him. He yelled his rage and stumbled wildly about as he tried to shake himself free. The more he struggled, Ryerson knew, the more tangled he became.

Ryerson surged to his feet and stepped backward, once more seeking the shelving where he had found the net. This time his fingers closed around a large flashlight he kept there.

He grabbed the light and snapped on the beam. The intruder was flopping around on the dock, looking very much like a large fish caught in the net. He swore again and ceased his struggles as the light played over him.

Ryerson aimed the beam at the intruder's face. "Well, hell," he finally murmured. "You're not Ferris."

The stranger's eyes narrowed fractionally for a few seconds, and Ryerson knew he had recognized the name. It was not a reassuring thought. For the first time, he realized there might be more than one intruder on the island.

And Ginny was alone back at the cabin.

Ryerson picked up the rope on the shelf and went toward his victim with grim determination. He needed some information, and he needed it quickly.

"Is Ferris here with you?" he demanded with seeming casualness as he methodically went about the task of tying the intruder's hands and feet. One thing you learned when you owned a boat was how to tie good knots.

"Go to hell."

Ryerson spotted the gun he had brought down from the cabin. It was lying near a clam-digging bucket. He finished tying several strong, tight knots and then went to pick up the heavy weapon.

The intruder glared at him derisively, clearly not impressed by the gun. Maybe he sensed it wasn't loaded, Ryerson thought with an inner sigh. Or maybe he just figured Ryerson wasn't the kind to pull the trigger on a bound man. Either way, the fool was right.

But there were other threats available.

Ryerson planted one sneakered foot solidly against his victim's shoulder and started to push.

"Hey, what the hell...?" The man gasped as he was rolled to within an inch of the dock. The cold, dark waters of the sound sloshed with lazy menace.

"The water's not that deep here yet," Ryerson said pleasantly. "The tide's only partway in. If you find your feet, you should be just barely able to stand with your chin above the surface. Until the tide comes in completely, that is. We have some really dramatic tides around here. In another half hour or so, the water will be a foot higher. That will be about seven inches too high for you."

"You can't do this!"

"I don't see why not." Ryerson nudged him a little closer to the edge of the dock. "If it's any comfort, you probably won't have to worry about drowning. This water's so cold that you'll be lucky to survive for more than thirty minutes in it. Hypothermia is the real threat here. Either way, if I'm not back fairly soon, you're in trouble."

"Damn you!"

"If you want to make sure I get back in time to do you any good, you'd better give me an idea of what I'm facing out there." Ryerson used his foot to edge the man's bound legs toward the water.

"Stop it, you bastard. You can't kill me and you know it."

"I'm not going to kill you. The water will do it. And you've got an option, don't you? All you have to do is tell me what's waiting for me out there."

The man's eyes blazed in impotent fury. "Ferris is on the

island,'' he snarled. ''We came ashore in two different places. My job was to take care of the boat so you couldn't use it to get away. Ferris went to check out the cabin. He was supposed to wait for me. We were going to go in together.''

Ryerson switched off the flashlight and headed for the door.

''What about me?'' the bound man demanded furiously.

Ryerson didn't bother to answer. He shut the door of the boathouse on his way out.

VIRGINIA STOOD AT THE WINDOW for long moments after Ryerson had left. She knew there was little she could do, but she hated the helpless feeling of being the one who had to wait.

After several agonizing minutes, she saw a figure emerge from the cruiser and go into the building. Her palms were damp. Perspiration trickled down her side under the robe. She leaned forward intently. An instant later, she saw another large, solid shadow step out of the trees. Ryerson. He was leaping for the metal door.

And then, without any warning, both men disappeared inside the boathouse. Ryerson had gone in after the intruder.

Virginia jerked free of the temporary paralysis that gripped her. She had to help Ryerson.

Racing for the bedroom, she found her jeans and a shirt. She pulled the clothes on, not bothering with more than one or two buttons on the shirt. The long sleeves dangled around her wrists. She fumbled with her shoes, and then she let herself out the front door, heading for the path that led to the boathouse.

She stumbled in the darkness, barely able to discern the narrow path in front of her. Frantically she grabbed for a pine branch to steady herself before she lost her balance.

She had just managed to catch herself when a man

loomed up out of the shadows behind her and jerked her to
a halt with an arm around her throat.

"Well, well, well," Dan Ferris murmured in her ear. "If
it isn't the lady with the sexy wardrobe. The water around
here is a little colder than it is down on Toralina, isn't it,
Miss Middlebrook?"

"Ferris," she whispered, barely able to speak because of
the muscular arm holding her still. She was pressed back
against his body. She could smell the sweat on him.

"That's right. Dan Ferris. You and Ryerson have given
me nothing but trouble, lady. You know that? I nearly lost
you both after you left Toralina. Took me a week to find
you. Then I had to bribe the guy who owns the marina on
that other island to find out where you were. I've had it with
both of you. Come on. Since you're out here running around
in the darkness, I have to assume Ryerson is, too. Let's go
find him."

"He's not...he isn't..." The arm tightened around her
throat and Virginia felt something cold and sharp touch the
side of her neck. She trembled, remembering that Harry
Brigman had been killed with a knife. "What do you want
from us?"

"The bracelet, for starters. After that, Miss Middlebrook,
the most important thing I want from you and your lover is
silence." He half dragged, half shoved her down the uneven
path.

She knew then that Ferris meant to kill her and Ryerson.
The bracelet burned on her wrist under the long sleeve of
her shirt. She wondered what Ferris would do if he knew
she was wearing it.

Ferris dragged Virginia to the clearing in front of the
boathouse and then, holding the knife to her throat, he called
out loudly.

"Seldon? You in there? What's going on? I've got the
woman."

There was silence for a long moment. Virginia felt the

dangerous tension in her captor. The knife tip pressed against her throat. She closed her eyes briefly and prayed that Ryerson was safe.

"Seldon!"

There was a groan from inside the boathouse. "I'm in here. Tied up. Ryerson's out there somewhere. Watch out for him, Ferris. The bastard's fast."

Ferris swore viciously and started to yank Virginia back into the safety of the trees.

"That's far enough, Ferris. Let her go." Ryerson stepped out from the shadows on the far side of the boathouse. Moonlight gleamed on the gun in his fist.

The rain had stopped. There was enough moonlight now for Virginia to see her lover's face, and what she saw stunned her. There was nothing in his expression of the indulgent, home-and-hearth, Mozart-loving man she had come to know so intimately during the past few weeks.

Violence vibrated in the air, and the knife dug a little more deeply into Virginia's throat.

"Let her go?" Ferris scoffed coldly. "Now why should I do that? Miss Middlebrook is my insurance policy. If you think you're good enough to shoot me without hitting her, you're welcome to try. There are very few men who are that good with a gun, though, Ryerson. Odds are you'll kill her, and you know it. Put down the gun."

Virginia looked at Ryerson and shook her head. "He's going to kill us both, anyway," she said with a calm that amazed her. "So take a chance."

Ryerson ignored her. "What do you want, Ferris?"

"I already told your woman what I want. The bracelet and your silence."

"We'll give you both if you let her go."

"Sure you will," Ferris said scornfully. "You're a businessman. You'll understand my wanting a little more insurance than just your Boy Scout word of honor. Now put down that gun before I put this knife into her throat."

Ryerson slowly lowered the nose of the weapon and took a couple of steps forward.

"I said, put it down!" Ferris snapped shrilly. He dragged Virginia farther out of reach, edging back toward the dock.

"As soon as you let her go." Ryerson continued moving forward cautiously.

"I'm not going to let her go, but I'll be glad to start showing you how serious I am."

Ferris pressed the knife deeper into Virginia's throat. She shuddered. The bracelet seemed hotter than ever on her wrist, and she wondered why she was so aware of it. Unconsciously she moved one hand to the arm on which she wore the bracelet.

"Stop it," Ryerson said calmly. "I'll give you the gun." He held it out.

"Just put it down on the ground."

Ryerson tossed it onto the wet pine needles. "The gun's yours. Now let her go."

"Not a chance." Ferris started pushing his captive forward, apparently intent on getting his hands on the gun. He kept the knife at Virginia's throat.

The bracelet was practically setting fire to Virginia's wrist. Surreptitiously she unsnapped the catch, only half-aware of what she was doing. She caught the glittering thing as it slipped into her palm.

"Is this what you want, Ferris?" she asked softly. Emeralds and gold and the white fire of diamonds gleamed in the pale moonlight.

"The bracelet," Ferris breathed, astounded. "Give it to me, you *bitch*."

But Virginia's arm was already in motion. She hurled the bracelet toward the water. It shimmered for an instant in midair and then it sank beneath the cold waves.

"No, damn you, no! You *bitch*!" Ferris lashed out savagely with the knife, but Virginia was already throwing herself to one side. For once her size and build were a distinct advantage. She was big enough to pull Ferris off balance. The shifting pine needles underfoot aided her effort. Her violent action changed the direction of the knife stroke.

Virginia felt cold, slicing pain in her shoulder instead of her throat and then a thudding impact as Ryerson hit both Ferris and her with the full force of his weight.

She rolled free of the violent battle on the ground, sitting up to clasp shaking fingers around her injured shoulder. She squeezed the wound tightly, trying to ignore the pain as she watched Ryerson and Ferris struggling on the ground. She felt dizzy. When she shook her head, trying to clear it, she realized Ferris was almost on top of Ryerson's gun. Belatedly she staggered to her feet.

"No!" she screamed, launching herself toward the weapon. Horror struck her as she realized she was too late.

Ferris's fingers closed around the gun. He raised it quickly, aiming at Ryerson, who ignored the threat of the weapon. Ferris pulled the trigger.

There was a faint click, and nothing happened.

Before Ferris could recover, Ryerson had slammed a fist, his full weight behind it, into Ferris's jaw. Ferris slumped on the ground. The gun fell from his fingers.

Virginia stared first at the gun and then at Ryerson. Ryerson just looked at her as he staggered to his feet.

Virginia gazed back at him in numb disbelief. "It wasn't loaded?"

"I'm a businessman," Ryerson said dryly as he walked toward her. "I believe in statistics. A loaded gun is more likely to be used against its owner than it is against an intruder. Of course it was unloaded. I'm not a complete idiot."

"Why did you buy it in the first place?"

Ryerson exhaled heavily. "Because you seemed so determined to get a gun of your own. And because I didn't know what we were up against, and it looked as if the cops weren't going to be much help. And because I couldn't think of anything else practical to do to protect you. There. Satisfied? As you can see, it was a totally wasted exercise in machismo. The gun didn't do me any good at all.''

Virginia's grin was a bit shaky. "Some guys are so macho they don't even need to use guns, Ryerson. Guess you're one of those." Then the dizziness overwhelmed her, and she crumpled forward into his waiting arms.

Ryerson caught her. "My God, he got you. The bastard stuck that knife into you. Why didn't you tell me you were hurt?''

"I was going to mention it," Virginia said apologetically.

CHAPTER ELEVEN

"ARE YOU SURE you're all right?" Ryerson asked for what must have been the hundredth time since the emergency clinic had turned Virginia loose with a few stitches and some pain pills. He was busy docking the boat as he spoke. "We could have gone straight home to Seattle. We didn't have to come back here this morning."

Virginia shook her head as she prepared to step out of the boat. She was still wearing the clothes she'd had on in the middle of the night. The sleeve of her shirt was blood-stained, and there was a small, neat white bandage on her arm. "I feel fine. My arm hardly hurts at all. Just a flesh wound, as they say in the thrillers. The important thing is to find the bracelet."

"We'll never find it, Ginny," Ryerson said patiently. "Face it, honey, it's long gone. No telling where it landed when you tossed it into the water last night. And the tide's gone out since then."

"It's too heavy to float out on the tide."

"Maybe. But it could easily have been covered up with sand or debris or seaweed. Don't count on finding it."

"You've got to have faith, Ryerson." She jumped off the boat and strode along the dock, studying the terrain revealed by the retreating tide. "That bracelet is ours. I know it is. We'll find it. We were meant to have it. It helped save our lives last night."

Ryerson finished securing the boat and walked toward her with wryly lifted eyebrows. "I'll admit your tossing it

into the water made an interesting diversion. Ferris panicked.''

''And you were ready to take advantage of his panic,''
Virginia concluded with a rush of feeling. ''You were magnificent last night, Ryerson. Absolutely magnificent.''

''You weren't so bad yourself,'' he told her dryly. ''The
bit with the bracelet was a real inspiration.'' The rueful
amusement faded from his silver eyes. ''Ginny, you'll
never know how scared I was when I tried to make Ferris
exchange the knife for my unloaded gun.''

''Nonsense. You didn't look scared at all. You looked
big and ruthless and very dangerous.'' She shivered. ''Ferris was the one who was scared. I could feel it.''

''Don't argue with me, Ginny,'' Ryerson retorted
harshly. ''I know what I was feeling, and the feeling was
one of pure terror. It would have been too easy for him to
have put that knife into your throat and then made a grab
for the gun. When you got his attention with the bracelet
and then pushed him off balance, you saved your own life
and mine, too.''

''Yours, too?'' Virginia glanced at him curiously. ''Oh,
you mean because you would have tried to rush him at the
last minute and he would still have had the knife.''

''He could have gotten both of us with that knife. He
was an expert, don't forget. The cops said so. I would have
been an easy target because if I thought he'd killed you, I
would have been insane. I wouldn't have been able to think
clearly enough to do anything but get my hands around his
neck. Which is probably not the best way to attack a man
who's holding a knife,'' Ryerson concluded pointedly.
''Do you know what it would have done to me to see you
get your throat slit?''

She looked back at him and saw the raw emotion in his
face. ''Oh, Ryerson,'' she whispered, running lightly back
down the dock to wrap her arms around him. ''Don't think

about it. We saved each other last night, and it's all over now. I love you so.''

He held her tightly for a long moment, his face buried in her hair, his palms moving warmly on her back. "I love you, too, Ginny. More than anything else on this earth.''

Virginia raised her head from his shoulder and smiled. "We did all right for an information retrieval manager and a diesel motor man, didn't we? Wait until my family hears the whole story." She glanced over the edge of the dock. "Oh, my gosh—*there it is*! There's the bracelet, Ryerson!"

Ryerson watched with gleaming eyes as she raced back along the dock and jumped down onto the sand.

Virginia kicked off her shoes and took two steps into the shallows. The bracelet was lying on a rock barely an inch below the surface.

"It's just been sitting here all night waiting for us to come back and find it, Ryerson!" she exclaimed triumphantly. There was no way she could have missed it. The morning sun was releasing the fire in the stones, and they shone up at her like small, glowing green and white suns. She reached down and scooped the old bracelet out of the water.

It dangled from her fingers, shimmering and glittering, and sparkling with drops of water. She laughed up at Ryerson. "It's ours again. We've found it. The thing belongs to us. I know it does.''

Ryerson crouched on the dock and studied the links of emeralds and gold and diamonds in her palm. He said nothing for a moment, and then his eyes met Virginia's. "*Is* it ours?" he asked softly. "Now that we know Brigman, Ferris and Seldon stole it?"

Virginia's triumph disintegrated into disappointment as reality took over. She looked down at the bracelet and sighed. "You're right, of course. I don't know what got into me. Ever since you won it in that poker game, I've had the strangest conviction that this bracelet really does belong to us. It's as if we were meant to have it. Things have been going so well for us since then. We've fallen in love since we came into possession of this bracelet. It even helped save our lives last night. I can't bear to give it up.''

"I know how you feel." Ryerson stood up and stepped off the dock onto the sand. He waited for Virginia to wade out of the water. As she came to stand in front of him, he smiled quizzically. "But do you really think things will change for us if the bracelet goes back to its rightful owner? I love you, Ginny. Nothing could change that.''

Virginia closed her eyes briefly as a sense of deep serenity welled up inside her. The bracelet was beautiful, and she would always feel a sense of possession toward it, but the love she had found with Ryerson was far more important than any piece of jewelry could ever be.

She opened her eyes and smiled. "I love you, Ryerson. And you're absolutely right, as usual. Nothing could change the way I feel about you.''

"Then we'll see if we can track down the rightful owner through that certificate of appraisal that we found in the box.''

He put out his hand and Virginia slipped her fingers trustingly into his. The bracelet shimmered in Virginia's fingers as she walked up the path toward the cabin with Ryerson.

"I WANT TO HEAR every detail," Debby Middlebrook announced two days later as she met Virginia and Ryerson for lunch. "I got most of the story from Mom and Dad, but I want to have it firsthand. Tell me everything, and start with how Brigman got the bracelet in the first place.''

Virginia chuckled as she buttered a chunk of sourdough bread. She glanced at Ryerson, who was examining his salmon with grave interest.

"You tell her," Ryerson said. "I'm hungry." He picked up his fork.

"Ferris, Brigman and Seldon operated a theft ring that preyed on wealthy tourists who stayed in out-of-the-way locations in the Caribbean—places such as Toralina Island. It generally worked this way, according to the cops. Brigman was a professional poker player who usually engaged the male victims in a series of high-stakes games. Ferris entertained the ladies while their men were busy playing cards. Seldon stayed out of sight and did the dirty work. The three of them were careful not to be seen together so no one would make any connections after the thefts."

"Got it," Debby said enthusiastically.

"But the three men were basically business associates, not friends. Eventually there was, as they say, a falling-out among thieves. Ferris and Seldon began to suspect that Brigman was cheating them somehow, perhaps because he was in charge of fencing the jewelry. They were no longer sure he was splitting the take evenly."

"As it turned out, they were right to be suspicious," Ryerson put in around a mouthful of salmon. "Brigman had stolen the bracelet on his own. He didn't let his partners know about it."

"But Ferris and Seldon discovered the truth when they confronted him on the last night of our stay on Toralina. There was a violent quarrel, and Brigman wound up dead. Ferris used his knife on him, and Ferris is very good with a knife, as it happens. In fact, he apparently enjoys using it, according to the police." Virginia shuddered.

Ryerson picked up the tale. "Before Brigman died, however, he told his pals he'd lost the bracelet in the poker game with me. After Brigman's death, Ferris came looking for the bracelet in our room. Seldon wasn't so bold. He was nervous because of the murder. He decided to lie low."

"But Ryerson scared Ferris off that night in the hotel

room?'' Debby asked. ''Even though Ferris had that knife and was apparently not afraid to use it?''

Ryerson grinned. ''Ferris told the police that when he saw me come through the doorway with Ginny's travel-size hair dryer in my hand he thought I was holding a gun.''

Virginia beamed proudly at him. ''Ryerson was wonderful that night.''

''Right. I covered myself in glory and a pink napkin,'' Ryerson agreed dryly.

''A pink napkin?'' Debby glanced from one to the other with a puzzled expression.

''It's a long story,'' Virginia said hurriedly.

''I can imagine. You know, this whole thing is incredibly bizarre. I can't envision either one of you going through all these adventures. Neither of you seem the type, if you want to know the truth,'' Debby remarked with sisterly bluntness.

''Love does strange things to its victims,'' Ryerson murmured. ''I personally am looking forward to returning to my nice, normal, sedate existence. Ginny provides more than enough adventure in my life.''

''So what happens now?'' Debby demanded.

''Well,'' Virginia said slowly, ''the police are not overly concerned with the bracelet. There's no record of it being reported missing on St. Thomas, which was where Ferris said it was stolen. In fact, the cops think Brigman might not have stolen it at all. They think he probably won it in a poker game, and that's why he decided he didn't have to share it with his pals. Whatever the truth is, the bracelet is ours now. But Ryerson is making some inquiries, which I'm hoping won't pan out. I love that bracelet.''

Ryerson cleared his throat. ''I was going to tell you, Ginny. I think I've located the owner. I got a message from the jeweler who did the appraisal this morning. I'm afraid it belongs to a Mr. and Mrs. George Grantworth of San Francisco. I'm going to phone them this afternoon.''

Virginia exhaled regretfully. "Easy come, easy go, I guess. It was nice owning it for a while." She brightened. "You know, I'm rather curious about the Grantworths."

Debby wrinkled her nose. "Why?"

"Because that bracelet is very special. I want to see what the owners are like."

"It's just a piece of jewelry," Debby remarked. "A beautiful piece, I'll grant you, but still—"

"It's not just a piece of jewelry," Virginia said forcefully. She looked at Ryerson. He smiled at her with his eyes.

"No," he said quietly. "It's not just a piece of jewelry. We'll go together to return it to the Grantworths in person. I'm curious about them, too."

GEORGE AND HENRIETTA GRANTWORTH were thrilled to learn that the bracelet had been found, and they were eager to meet the couple into whose possession it had fallen. Virginia and Ryerson took the morning flight to San Francisco on the following Saturday. A cab delivered them to an elegant old Victorian house in the expensive Pacific Heights area of the city.

"It does look like the sort of place where this bracelet would be right at home doesn't it?" Virginia noted wistfully as she walked up the steps beside Ryerson. She had a growing conviction that Ryerson was right. They had located the legal owners of the bracelet. Until now she had been hoping against hope that it was all a mistake.

"I'm afraid so," Ryerson murmured. He leaned on the doorbell. "Look at it this way. We'll feel virtuous about this for weeks to come."

"How dull." Virginia smiled wickedly. "One of the things I've been enjoying lately is feeling a little unvirtuous."

"Hussy."

"I packed the red teddy for tonight," she whispered.

Ryerson's eyes gleamed. He was about to comment when the door was opened by a neat, friendly woman in a housedress and an apron. She looked at them inquiringly.

"Yes?"

"Virginia Middlebrook and A. C. Ryerson. We're here to see the Grantworths. They're expecting us." Ryerson gave her his most sedately reassuring smile.

"Oh, yes. They're waiting for you in the living room. Come right in."

Two people rose in greeting as Virginia and Ryerson entered the beautifully restored Victorian room. Virginia liked them both on sight. If the bracelet had to be returned to anyone, then it might as well go back to these two, she decided. She studied them carefully as introductions were made.

Henrietta Grantworth was probably in her seventies, but there was an elegance about her that was ageless. It was obvious that she had been a beautiful woman all her life. Her silvery hair was done in a regal chignon, and her blue eyes were full of charm and intelligence.

Her husband was a distinguished-looking man a few years older than his wife. Virginia knew he must have been nearly eighty, but he carried himself with the confidence and energy of a much younger man. His thinning hair had once been black, and his dark eyes were alert and assessing. He extended his hand to Ryerson with obvious pleasure.

"Please sit down," Henrietta said. "I can't tell you how much we appreciate all the trouble you've taken to bring us the bracelet. It disappeared from our hotel room on St. Thomas several weeks ago. We notified the police on the island, but they let the matter drop once we left. When we checked again last week to see if there had been any progress, there wasn't even a record of our report. George and I assumed we'd probably never see the bracelet again.''

"We've owned it for years," George said, glancing fondly at his wife. "Henrietta came into possession of it at about the time I first met her. She always liked to think it had something to do with our finding each other. She was very upset when it was lost.''

Henrietta smiled warmly at Virginia. "I was just sick to think that it might have wound up in the hands of criminals. It wasn't meant for that kind of fate. But I should have known better than to worry. The bracelet always finds its way into the proper hands.''

"What do you mean?" Virginia asked as she slowly withdrew the jewelry box from her purse.

George chuckled and looked at Ryerson. "Henrietta has always been convinced that the bracelet is rather special. Not just because of its intrinsic value but because it has enjoyed a very romantic history. It always seems to end up belonging to people who are very much in love. My wife inherited it from a cousin who fell in love with her husband shortly after she had inherited the thing from her grandmother, who claimed the bracelet was responsible for her own happy marriage. And so on.''

"The stories go back for several generations," Henrietta said firmly. "And I'm sure they're all true. There's a legend attached to the bracelet. Supposedly it belonged to an aristocratic French family by the name of Montclair. It was part of a set that was broken up during the French Revolution. I don't know what happened to the other pieces, but I do know that whoever has come into possession of the bracelet has enjoyed a great deal of love and happiness.''

Virginia was enthralled. "The bracelet has always been owned by lovers?''

Henrietta nodded quickly. "Sooner or later, it's always turned up in the possession of two people who fall in love and marry. George laughs when I tell the story, but the truth is, I think he believes just a little in the legend himself, don't you, dear?''

George smiled lovingly at his wife. "A smart man does not argue with good fortune, my sweet." He picked up her delicately boned hand and kissed her fingers. "And there is no doubt but that I have been a very fortunate man.''

Virginia watched the elderly couple, aware of a deep longing in her own heart. This was the way it should be, she thought with sudden clarity. This was what she wanted with Ryerson: a lifetime of shared love and happiness.

She glanced at Ryerson and saw that he was watching her with an unreadable gaze. She turned back to Henrietta Grantworth. "I'm glad the bracelet belongs to you," she said in a small rush of emotion.

"Thank you, my dear." Henrietta opened the box and gazed down at the bracelet. She was silent for a long moment, and no one broke the silence as she studied the contents of the box. When she looked up at last, she looked straight at Ryerson. There was a suspicious dampness in her clear blue eyes. "The bracelet has always been associated with love and marriage," she whispered.

Ryerson reached out and caught Virginia's fingers. He smiled down at her. "We may not have had it in our possession for long, Mrs. Grantworth, but I can assure you, it was very definitely associated with love while it was ours.''

"Yes," Henrietta said. She closed the box with a decisive movement. "I can see that." Her eyes twinkled as she flicked a quick glance at her husband. "It definitely seems to have been associated with love. But what about marriage? I must warn you, Mr. Ryerson, the men who come into contact with the bracelet inevitably wind up offering marriage.''

Virginia's fingers were nearly crushed in Ryerson's large palm as he smiled at Henrietta. "All the men in the legends have wound up offering marriage?''

"Oh, yes," Henrietta assured him. "All of them. Of course, up until recently there wasn't much option for an honorable man who found himself in love. He did the right thing by his lady. Not like today when a man thinks he can have his cake and eat it, too."

Virginia blushed at the familiar words. It was not so long ago that Ryerson had said something very similar to her.

"A lot of things have changed in the past couple of hundred years, Mrs. Grantworth," Ryerson said smoothly. "Today it isn't always the man who tries to wriggle out of marriage."

The grandfather clock in the corner chimed in the silence that followed his comment. Virginia suddenly found herself the focus of three pairs of interested eyes. She looked first at George Grantworth, who was watching her with indulgent humor and a curious understanding. Then her gaze slipped to Henrietta, who was studying her with an expectant expression.

Virginia turned to Ryerson. He was contemplating her with that same unreadable look she'd noticed on his face earlier. She swallowed cautiously and made her decision.

"Well, Ryerson," she said briskly, "when are you going to do the honorable thing and make an honest woman of me?"

Ryerson grinned, relief and happiness heating the silver in his eyes. He pulled Virginia into his arms, hugging her fiercely. "Just as soon as we can get a license, honey."

George Grantworth chuckled. "I know how you feel, Ryerson."

"You must allow my husband and me to give you your first wedding gift," Henrietta Grantworth said with quiet certainty. She smiled and held out the jewelry box to Virginia.

Virginia turned in Ryerson's arms, totally astounded. "The bracelet? Oh, no, Mrs. Grantworth. We couldn't possibly accept it. It belongs to you."

"The bracelet has a way of choosing its proper owners. I'm convinced that it was destined to belong to you. George and I have everything we need or want. Nothing will ever alter our love for each other. Something tells me that it's time the bracelet went on to another couple, and I believe you and Mr. Ryerson are the lovers it was meant for this time around."

"But, Mrs. Grantworth," Virginia began rather feebly. "It's too valuable to just give to strangers."

"The true value of the bracelet cannot be expressed in monetary terms. I think you know that as well as I do. I give it to you with my blessing and the hope that you will be as happy as George and I have been."

Ryerson tightened his grip on Virginia. "It's all right," he said softly. "We can accept it. It's ours."

Virginia heard the certainty in his voice and knew that he was right. Her fingers closed around the box. It seemed to her she could feel the warmth radiating from within. "I don't know how to thank you, Mrs. Grantworth," she whispered.

Henrietta laughed. "Don't thank me. The bracelet has a will of its own. I'll tell you the truth, my dear. I knew the minute I opened the box and looked at it that it was no longer mine. It belongs to you now. I'm sure of it. Far be it from me to interfere with destiny."

"You know," George Grantworth said easily as he rose to pour a glass of sherry for his guests, "I've always thought it might be interesting to track down some more of the history of that bracelet. Never got around to it myself, but you two might want to give it a whirl. Should be interesting."

"Where would you start?" Ryerson asked curiously as he accepted his glass.

"Why, France, of course," Grantworth said thoughtfully. "I had that crest traced once out of curiosity. The Montclair family has an ancient history in France. Apparently there was once a castle. Probably nothing left of it by now, but you never know.''

A WEEK LATER Virginia tumbled an armful of travel brochures down onto the turned-back bed in Ryerson's condo and stretched out beside them. She was wearing the scandalous red teddy, the bracelet and a plain gold ring.

''A castle,'' she breathed. ''A real castle. It's still there after all these years. What a perfect spot for a honeymoon. The brochure says, and I quote, 'The famous Montclair castle has been turned into a first-class luxury hotel catering to those who seek relaxation as well as fine accommodations in the French countryside.' Just think, Ryerson—French wine, French food and French clothes.''

Ryerson folded his arms behind his head. ''Don't tell me you're going to spend our honeymoon shopping for clothes.''

''The French,'' Virginia informed him gravely as she looked up at him from beneath her lashes, ''are famous for designing the world's sexiest lingerie.''

Ryerson grinned. ''Is that right?''

''I have it on the best authority.''

''Ah. Well, in that case,'' he said as he pulled her down across his chest, ''I think we can include a shopping expedition on this trip to France. You were born to wear sexy underwear.''

''What about you?'' Virginia asked with a soft laugh.

''Me? I was born to take it off you, of course.'' He slipped the satin straps of the red teddy off her shoulders. He paused as she nestled closer. ''Ginny?''

''Hmm?'' She was toying with the crisp, curling hair on his bare chest.

''No second thoughts or regrets?''

She knew he was referring to the simple wedding ceremony they had gone through that afternoon. ''No second thoughts and no regrets,'' she whispered, very sure of her answer. She lifted one hand to touch the side of his hard face. "I've been waiting all my life for you, A.C. It just took me a while to realize what I'd been waiting for."

Ryerson saw the love and certainty in her eyes, and his own gaze blazed with satisfaction. "The waiting is over. For both of us." He reached out to turn off the bedside lamp. Then he found Virginia's mouth and took full possession.

The Montclair bracelet glowed in the shadows, promising a lifetime of love and happiness.

IMPULSE

Vicki Lewis Thompson

CHAPTER ONE

The "William Tell Overture" blared from the speakers inside the henhouse as April wielded her paintbrush in the early-morning light. She didn't realize Ida Mae Lowdermilk was standing at the bottom of the extension ladder until her old friend resorted to her hog-calling voice to override the music.

"Lavender?" Ida Mae shouted. "You're painting the henhouse lavender?"

"This side," April called down without pausing in her work. She'd known Ida Mae since third grade, and they didn't stand on formalities with each other. "The rest will be apple green, daffodil and robin's-egg blue, in that order."

"I don't know if Booneville is ready for this." Ida Mae sidestepped a large glob of paint that plopped to the ground and lay like an iris petal in the dust. "Couldn't you at least stick with one color?"

"Not with the cans on sale at Bender's Hardware," April shouted back. "Besides, Irene would have loved the effect of it." She continued sweeping the brush across the weathered boards.

"Maybe she would have, God rest her soul," Ida Mae conceded, "but what will your folks think of such a thing?"

"They told me the place was mine to do with as I wanted, provided I kept the money coming in." April moved down a rung and slapped another lavender swath

across the henhouse. The fresh paint smelled like beginnings, not endings, and that suited April just fine. Irene
would have wanted her to look ahead, not back.

"Your music's invigorating this morning."

"The chickens asked me to turn it up. They're feeling
funky today."

"I hate to think what kind of eggs they're laying with
this racket. Listen, I'm getting a stiff neck and laryngitis
from our conversation," Ida Mae said. "Suppose you
could come down?"

"I suppose." April hung the paint bucket on the ladder
and laid the brush across the top. Slowly she descended
the ladder and faced Ida Mae. Her childhood friend looked
the way she always did—pert and scrubbed, blond hair
short and disciplined, checked blouse tucked neatly into
her jeans. "Where'd you stash the kids?"

"My mother's. I thought you'd be a little upset today,
and I didn't want my three little potato bugs adding to your
problems."

"You could have brought them, Idie. Children would be
nice to have around this morning." April realized her
glasses were speckled with lavender paint, and she shoved
them on top of her head. Better to have the fall landscape
blurred than polka-dotted.

Ida Mae assessed April's appearance with a glance.
"You look terrible."

"These are my painting clothes."

"That's not what I mean, and you know it. Your hair
looks as if you tied it in a knot, and your eyes are like two
burned holes in a blanket."

April shrugged. "So?"

"So come inside and I'll fix you a cup of tea." Ida Mae
put an arm around April's waist and guided her toward the
white farmhouse. "I guess even I didn't realize how much
you loved that old woman. You're taking it mighty hard,
aren't you?"

"I'm okay." April felt the tears threaten again. How stupid. She wasn't even related to Irene, although she had come close to being a granddaughter-in-law, if there was such a thing. "Mom spent the day here yesterday. She arrived soon after the news was out. She would have slept here last night, too, but I made her go home. I'm a big girl, after all."

"Who's lost a dear friend," Ida Mae added.

"I miss her already," April confessed as she walked with Ida Mae up the wooden steps and through the squeaking screen door. "I think she knew this was about to happen. She'd drop little hints, trying to prepare me. But I wouldn't pay attention, didn't want to pay attention."

"I know, I know," Ida Mae crooned.

"She had such a spark, such a neat way of looking at life. She would have been at home anywhere in the world—Paris, London, New York...."

"But she stayed right here in Booneville." Ida Mae bustled around the kitchen making a pot of tea on the old enameled stove. "That should make us all feel good about our hometown."

"Yeah, that's something she taught me, all right—to appreciate this place." April sank down on a kitchen chair and let Ida Mae fuss over her. Her friend was good at caretaking, and at the moment April was grateful that she didn't have to put up a front for this person she'd known for eighteen years.

Ida Mae set cups and napkins in front of them. "Prettiest little town in all of central Illinois, if you ask me."

"I don't know about that, Idie. But we've made progress with the square."

"We have." Ida Mae poured the tea. "I noticed today that the frost has nipped the mums a little, but they're still blooming."

"And painting the gazebo sure helped. Remember how Irene got out there and worked right along with the rest of us, as if the summer heat were only a minor nuisance? We were all drenched in sweat, and she kept whistling and painting.''

''After seeing your henhouse, I'm surprised we ended up with white for the gazebo.''

''Irene and I considered other colors, but we decided the sculpture, when we finally got it, would be change enough for everyone. Damn! I wish Irene had stuck around long enough to get that sculpture project through. I don't know how we'll manage without her. I kept asking her how we'd raise the money to commission an artist, but she kept telling me not to worry. Now what are we supposed to do?''

Ida Mae poured the tea and sat down. ''You sound a little put out.''

''Maybe I am. Irene left us in the lurch.''

''But the beautification committee was your idea, April. You can continue without Irene.''

''I don't have her clout in Booneville. Who will listen to me?''

''I will, and so will the others on the committee.''

''That's not exactly the whole town, Idie.''

''No, but don't forget Mabel's married to the president of the bank.''

''Yeah.'' April's laugh contained no humor. ''Can't you just see Henry Goodpasture loaning us money for a sculpture?'' The warm tea soothed her throat, easing the lump that had stuck there ever since yesterday morning when she'd heard about Irene. ''I guess the sculpture isn't so important.''

''Of course it is! Stop talking like that. Irene wouldn't have tolerated a hangdog attitude from you, April Marie, so stop it this minute! Where's your hairbrush?''

April lifted an eyebrow. ''Going to give me a paddling, Idie?''

''That's a thought, but I had in mind straightening out

that mane of yours." She got up and walked to the back bedroom. "Never mind. I'll find it."

April gazed after her friend, bemused by the offer to brush her hair. Was she really such a wreck? Maybe so, in contrast to Ida Mae. But Idie always looked perfect, even when she was slopping hogs or riding a tractor.

"Here we go." Ida Mae stood behind April's chair and began to work. "You *did* tie this in a knot! All this beautiful chestnut hair, and you treat it like dead cornstalks."

"It's plain old brown hair, Idie. Heroines in novels have chestnut hair. Mine's brown."

"Have it your way. But you shouldn't tie it in knots."

"Couldn't find any rubber bands this morning."

"Sake's alive, woman." Ida Mae untangled the strands of hair and reached for the glasses on top of April's head. "Here, hold these."

As Ida Mae stroked the brush across April's scalp and down to her shoulders in an efficient rhythm, April began to relax. "Remember when we used to spend all night doing each other's hair and gossiping about boys, Idie?"

"I gossiped about boys, plural. You only had eyes for Dan."

April was silent for a moment. "Is he in town yet?"

"Yes. The will was read this morning, and although I don't know all that was in it, I drove out here this morning to tell you the most interesting part."

April sat up straighter in her chair. A will. April would have liked hearing it, those last requests of Irene's. But of course April wasn't privileged to hear the will because she wasn't part of Irene's family. To accomplish that she would have had to marry Dan. "And what's so interesting?" April prompted. Ida Mae loved to withhold dramatic information until the last possible moment.

"There's not going to be a funeral."

April twisted around to look at Ida Mae. "What do you mean, no funeral?"

"There'll be a private grave-side service for the immediate family, and I guess that's only Dan and his mother."

"That's all." April thought again that if she had married Dan, she would have been part of the immediate family and allowed to stand next to the grave with Dan and his mother. But she'd married wild Jimmy Foster, to everyone's dismay and eventually to her own.

"Anyway, after the burial the whole town is invited to a giant hot-dog roast on the square, all paid for by Irene. It's in the will."

"A hot-dog roast?" Gradually the confused frown cleared from April's brow, and she began to laugh. "A hot-dog roast?"

Ida Mae nodded. "With entertainment by the Booneville High School Marching Band, in uniform."

April pounded on the back of her chair with delight. "I knew she wouldn't go out just like everyone else! I knew it!"

DAN BUTLER WANDERED through his grandmother's house, touching all the things that she'd loved—shelves of books on every imaginable subject, her favorite armchair, the herb garden on the kitchen windowsill, her upright piano. He and his mother would choose the few things that they wanted, and the rest would be sold with the house. Neither his Chicago apartment nor his mother's town home in Indianapolis could hold furniture that filled a two-story house.

He tried not to think of strangers living here. Why did people have to die? Why couldn't things stay the same? Many years ago, when his father had been killed and Dan had moved into this house with his mother, he'd asked the same questions. Today he had adult logic to guide him, but he discovered logic didn't ease the pain of losing someone you loved.

"Dan."

He looked up at his mother, who stood at the head of the stairs. "I was hoping you could take a nap, Mom. Has my prowling around kept you awake?"

"No." She shook her head, and her soft blond hair ruffled with the movement. "I've been lying up there in your old bedroom thinking about you."

"Me? Why?"

His mother came down the stairs slowly. Both of them had been moving slowly the past few days, as if their hurt were physical rather than mental and quickness would sharpen the pain. "Because you're alone," she said, coming to the foot of the stairs and laying her hand on his arm. "That's not right."

"I'm not alone. I have friends. I date. I came damn close to getting married last year."

"That's just it. You've come close, but you always back away. For some reason there's no…magic."

"Mom, for crying out loud. Magic is for kids. I'm fast approaching thirty."

His mother shook her head again. "Magic is not just for kids. Your father and I had it."

Dan covered his mother's hand with his own and felt the familiar outlines of her heirloom ring, the one his father had given her, the same one his grandmother had received from his grandfather. "I guess you and Dad were lucky."

"Yes, we were, in spite of what happened. I know you think I'm crazy, but I believe some of our luck had to do with this ring." She pulled her hand from under his and slipped the ring from her finger. "I'm giving it to you."

"Hey." Dan stepped back and shook his head. "There's no way I'll take that from you. We may have talked about my giving it to my fiancée, but I don't have one. Even if I did, I've decided that you should keep the ring. It reminds you of Dad."

"These days it reminds me that you haven't found that

special love you need. Maybe if you have the ring, something magic will happen for you.''

"That's crazy."

"Dan, Irene expected this ring to be passed down. Now
that she's gone, I feel a great responsibility to do so. Please
take it. Humor me. Knowing that you have the ring fills
me with hope for the future, and I need that right now,
with so much sadness around us."

Dan hesitated a moment longer before taking the emerald-and-diamond heirloom from her outstretched palm.
"This doesn't feel right."

"It will, Dan. Give it time."

ON THE DAY of the funeral and hot-dog roast the air was
as crisp as a fresh apple. The streets of Booneville were
lined with the vehicles of those who, like April, lived too
far from town to walk. April struggled to find a parking
space near the square and finally ended up two blocks
away. As she got out of her pickup truck, she could hear
the band strike up its fight song. April smiled. Irene had
been exactly right in her plans. "The Booneville High
Fight Song" was far more appropriate for Irene than a
funeral dirge.

The leaves on the giant oaks lining the town square had
turned the color of butter, and the red maples beside the
gazebo blushed from the first cold caress of fall. The vivid
red was repeated in the band uniforms and the yards of
crepe-paper streamers twirled around the gazebo posts in
barber-pole fashion. April thought how much Irene would
have appreciated the whole display.

The aroma of hot dogs drifted from the immense barbecue grill that had been brought over from the Baptist
Church, and April decided that the Methodists and Pres-
byterians had emptied their church basements to provide
enough long tables and folding chairs. The square was

jammed with adults and children, and April wondered if any of Booneville's 1,042 residents had stayed home.

She'd intended to wait awhile before searching the crowd for Dan, but instead, her gaze went directly to him as if she had no free will. Besides, he did stand out, she argued with herself. His navy-blue suit in this year's style marked his transformation into a city boy, despite his rural roots. His dark hair showed the deft hand of a stylist instead of the utilitarian clippers used by Jake, the local barber. And Dan's face wasn't harvest-season tan as were the faces of his old high-school buddies who surrounded him.

April hated to admit what she was really looking for and dreading to find—a woman by his side, a Chicago woman with obvious claims to him. After April and Irene had become friends, Irene had confided that Dan had been involved in two serious relationships, neither of which had progressed to the engagement stage. The last thing April had heard, however, was that Dan's mother still wore the heirloom ring that had been her token of engagement and would serve the same purpose when Dan chose a bride. At one time April thought the ring might belong to her, but those days were over.

At the moment Dan appeared to be flanked only by Booneville people. If he'd brought a woman down from Chicago with him, April would know it soon enough. Anyone from the city would stand out, just as he did, and most of the people milling around on the square would be discussing Dan's new girlfriend within minutes of her arrival.

April decided to mingle and tackle the problem of speaking to Dan later. Now that Irene was gone, common decency dictated that April seek him out and express her condolences. She wished now that she hadn't avoided him quite so carefully all these years. If they had bridged the painful gap of their estrangement earlier and fallen into distant friendship, her contact with him today would have been easier.

Instead, her palms were clammy with sweat after only this brief glimpse of him. April feared that her emotional attachment to Dan still existed, but she doubted seriously that he felt the same. Not after what she'd done.

April found her mother and father in the line of people waiting for food. "May I cut in?" she teased, jostling herself between them.

"Why, the nerve of some people," her mother said with a smile. Then she turned and hugged her daughter. "You're looking much better."

April's father put his hand on her shoulder. "I'm sorry about this, honey. You were closer to Irene than most."

"I'll miss her, that's for sure."

"But you're not wearing your heart on your sleeve today," her mother said approvingly. "I like that new fall coat, and I think gold is definitely your color. Makes your eyes look like brown velvet. Especially with your contacts in instead of the glasses."

"My goodness, Mom."

"Can't I be proud of my only child?"

"But you're embarrassing me." She looked around for something to divert attention from herself. "Not everybody could give up the idea of wearing black, I see."

"Tradition dies hard, sweetheart. I reached for my black church dress three times before I finally grabbed this orange one and put it on. A lot of people are shocked by the way Irene wanted things. They expected a viewing last night at the funeral home, but of course there was none of that. I think we will have a prayer in a little bit, though. I saw Henry Goodpasture rigging a microphone up at the gazebo. By the way, have you seen Dan yet?"

"Sort of."

"I just commented to your father that Dan's even more handsome now than he was as a boy, isn't he, Pete?"

April's father snorted. "Thelma Jane, you have the subtlety of a sledgehammer."

"April knows what I mean."

"Yes, Mom, I'm afraid I do. I'm sure Dan is no longer interested in me, and unless he's changed a lot, I'm not interested in Dan."

"People forgive other people, April. Jimmy Foster was a youthful mistake on your part. Dan's a big enough person to understand that."

"Mom, please don't try to play matchmaker, okay? Irene used to drop hints all the time, too, and that was one thing about her that irritated me. Dan has known for two years that Jimmy and I were divorced, and I haven't noticed him hightailing it down from Chicago to throw himself at my feet, have you?"

"Well, he'd need some indication from you that—"

"Enough, Mom. I broke up with Dan eight years ago for a reason, and I have no proof that he's changed. The fact that he hasn't risked contacting me proves that he hasn't—that he's still careful, practical, unromantic Dan. Lovely to look at, but boring to hold."

"April!"

"Sorry, but it's the truth." Well, almost, April amended to herself. The steamy scenes in the back of Dan's Chevy still created a remembered zing of sexual excitement, even after all these years. Then there was the night of the senior prom, when Dan had driven up from Blackburn College so he could be her date.

She'd bragged to all her friends that Dan would certainly propose that night and slip the heirloom ring on her finger. Instead, he'd made his stuffy speech about waiting until he'd finished college and had a good job before they became "involved."

April had understood that his attitude was reasonable. That was the trouble. She had wanted him to love her beyond all reason, to need her so much that nothing else mattered except being together. She'd told him—cruelly—

that she might not be able to wait that long. A month later she was married to Jimmy.

"April, honey, you're holding up the line." Her father's gentle nudge brought her back to the present.

Ahead of her, her mother was filling her plate and exclaiming over the variety of salads weighing down the table.

April tried to take an interest, although food was at the bottom of her priorities. "This potato salad looks like yours, Mom," she said, putting a spoonful on her plate.

"It is."

"But I thought everything was to be provided."

"It was, but we all knew that Jesse's Café wasn't up to this kind of order. Besides, most of the women wanted to bring something. We always do, when someone passes on. The family can take home the leftovers."

"I hate to say this, but I can't picture Dan loading food into his car for the drive back to Chicago, and his mother certainly won't drag it back to Indianapolis, either."

"They might decide to stay a few days, and they'll have to eat, won't they?"

April knew there was no arguing with her mother on this topic. The need to bring food for a grieving family was completely ingrained, even if the gesture was sometimes inappropriate. April hoped the townspeople would eat every last morsel so that Dan and his mother wouldn't have to deal with three-bean salad and coleslaw at the end of the day.

Across the square, Dan took advantage of a few moments alone to scan the crowd for April. He finally saw her wandering through the serving line and putting very little on her plate. He felt a tug at his heart. She didn't feel like eating, either. Perhaps she, more than anyone else here, was experiencing the same sense of desolation that his grandmother's death gave him.

An older couple came up to offer condolences, and Dan

acknowledged their sympathy with half his attention as he strained to keep track of April in the crowd. The gold of her coat beckoned to him like a nugget winking from a streambed filled with more ordinary stones. The coat was belted, showing off the small waist he probably could span with his hands, even now.

He realized that all the women he'd dated in the past eight years had looked a lot like her—slim build, long legs, brown hair that shone like burnished wood in the sunshine. He'd been to bed with two and almost married one, but that had ended when he'd called her April in the midst of a passionate moment. He thought of all the times since April's divorce that his grandmother had urged him to contact his former love, but pride and the fear of a second rejection had stood in his way.

Now, in death, his grandmother had found a way around his reluctance, had managed to have the last word on whether or not he'd see April again. The terms of the will guaranteed that he and April would work together, unless she declined the board appointment. Knowing April, Dan didn't expect that. His mouth was dry at the prospect of talking to her again, and his grief made him feel exposed and vulnerable. He wanted somebody to hold, but that person couldn't be April, not so soon, anyway, and maybe not ever.

For some reason he thought of the ring tucked into the breast pocket of his suit. Ever since his mother had given it to him, he'd worried about losing it, and carrying the heirloom around in his pocket seemed the safest course. He'd forgotten that he had it there until now, when he caught sight of April. Briefly he recalled his mother's speech about the ring's magic and then dismissed her words as sentimental nonsense. Thinking of April and then the ring was just a coincidence.

Gerald Sloan, his grandmother's lawyer, appeared at his

elbow with a plateful of food. "I stood in a long line to get this for you, so you'd better eat it," he said.

Dan looked at the heaped plate and shook his head. "Sorry, Gerry. You eat it."

"Hey, son, your grandmother wouldn't want you to waste away. She'd want you to take advantage of this spread."

"Did she put that in the will, too? That her grandson is required to consume so many hot dogs and so much potato salad at this crazy party?"

"Maybe she did, at that."

"Come on, Gerry. Give me a break."

"Okay. Will it bother you if I eat, then?"

"I wish you would. Maybe if your mouth's full, you'll stop hounding me about my nutrition. You sound just like Grandma. Nag, nag, nag."

"And you loved her for it."

"Yeah, Gerry, I did."

"How's your mom doing?"

"Pretty well, I think. She once told me that losing my dad was so awful that anything else that happened in her life would be duck soup in comparison."

"That's probably true. They were so much in love it was kind of like a storybook romance. Of course, some say that ring had an effect on their devotion, but I don't believe that kind of superstition."

"The way Grandma used to tell it, their relationship changed the day he gave her that ring, but I find that theory hard to believe, too. Sure, it's a valuable piece of jewelry, but so are most engagement rings."

Gerry shrugged. "Who can say? Although there *is* something about this one, maybe because of its age. It seems to have a timeless quality."

"Getting pretty philosophical, aren't you?" Dan considered telling the lawyer that the ring was now in his pocket but decided not to. Gerry would speculate about why, and

Dan would have to admit that his mother was trying to marry him off.

"Yeah, well…I'll blame my philosophical thoughts on your grandmother." Gerry finished the food on his plate. "Speaking of that fine lady, I think we ought to make the announcement before people start heading home. Wouldn't want anyone to miss the big news."

"I guess you're right. Most everyone seems to have gotten their meal."

"Then I'll head on up to the microphone. Each of the ministers has asked to say a little prayer first. Considering that Irene liked to rotate her attendance, they all appear to have some claim on her."

Dan smiled. "And nobody has an exclusive claim. She used to drive them all crazy, playing musical churches, with me trailing right along behind her. I swear if there had been a Buddhist temple in Booneville, she'd have gone there, too."

Gerry chuckled. "No doubt. Well, I'm off. When did you say the first board meeting should be?"

"I can make it down by ten next Saturday morning."

"Fine. Chin up."

"I'm trying."

April had stood about ten feet away and out of Dan's peripheral vision while she waited for him to finish talking with Irene's lawyer. She didn't want her first conversation with Dan in eight years to be an interruption of someone else's discourse. When Gerald Sloan left, April stepped forward so that Dan could see her coming. She noticed the widening of his pupils; he was caught off guard, ill-prepared for her unexpected appearance.

She held out her hand. "I'm sorry about your grandmother, Dan." She sounded much calmer than she felt.

"I'm sorry, too, April." He took her hand and held it for a moment as he looked into her eyes. "How have you been?"

Instantly April regretted offering to shake hands with him. His firm grip was too familiar, even after all the years since she'd felt the texture of his skin. "Fine," she mumbled, aware of each of his fingers, of the creases in his palm.

She wanted to jerk her hand back as if from a hot stove, but that would give away too much. It was incredible how his touch brought back all the longing and unsatisfied passion of those nights they'd spent parked on lonely farm roads. They hadn't made love, not quite, and April remembered only too well that Dan had always been the one to call a halt. Practical Dan. She extricated her hand as gracefully as possible.

They stood for a moment in silence before he spoke. "I, uh, heard about the divorce," he said at last.

"Yes, well…" April couldn't look into the blue of his eyes any longer for fear she'd find accusations there. "Jimmy wasn't cut out for running a chicken farm, I'm afraid."

"I hear you're doing quite well, though."

"I make ends meet."

"That's saying a lot these days, with farmers declaring bankruptcy right and left." He shook his head. "I don't know why anyone would want to farm these days."

"It's an independent life, for one thing." April remembered this argument. They'd had it before. She'd always suspected Dan's aversion to farming had a lot to do with his father's death. Dan knew that farming could kill someone you loved. A tractor going up an embankment could tip over and crush the life from a man before anyone realized he was late coming home from the fields. Such a death had the power to change a little boy's life forever.

"Sure, you've got independence," Dan countered. "You're free to put in a crop and pray for the right amount of rain at the right time. If you're lucky, you harvest something, and if you're a real miracle worker, you sell your product for a decent price. That's a hell of a way to live, if you ask me.''

"I suppose. I happen to like it.''

"You've always been a risk-taker.''

April searched for any malice in his tone and could find none. "Thank you,'' she said, deciding to accept his statement as a compliment.

"Besides, your farm is diversified, with the beehives and the pick-your-own produce to supplement the eggs you sell.'' He grinned. "I've heard you've renamed the place, too.''

"Corny, huh? Ida Mae suggested it as a joke, and I decided it might bring in more business.''

"I bet it does. But how many people show up expecting lectures on sex? If I saw a sign advertising The Birds and the Bees, that's what I'd think.''

April laughed. "That's because you've always had your mind on—'' She stopped and glanced up quickly into his eyes. The old spark was there, and the sexual excitement was zinging between them as if eight years hadn't come and gone. April was aghast that the attraction could bloom again so fast. She cleared her throat. "But I'll admit farming's still chancy, compared to your job. How do you like the big city?'' she asked more formally.

He took his cue from her tone. "Lake Michigan's nice. Business is good.''

"But do you like it?''

"Chicago's very noisy, April. The sirens get to me the most, but...'' He sighed. "Yeah, I like it okay.''

"Dan, you don't sound—''

Static from the loudspeakers interrupted their discussion, and Dan laid a hand automatically on her arm. "Listen, April. Perhaps I should warn you about something.''

"Let us pray,'' boomed a voice from the speakers.

Dan dropped his hand from her arm, and they both ducked their heads obediently. The prayers offered were for a woman they both loved, and they concentrated on the comforting words with a closeness of spirit they hadn't known for many years.

When April heard a choked sound from Dan, she knew he was fighting to keep from giving way to his emotions, and she reached out and laced her fingers through his. He gripped her hand tightly until the last of the solemn prayers was over, and then with a shaky sigh he released his pressure on her fingers. She didn't look at him. Her eyes were brimming, and she was certain his were, too. He wouldn't want her to notice.

At the end of the prayers for Irene, Gerald Sloan went up to the microphone and adjusted it for his shorter height. He took a piece of paper from his coat pocket, as if he'd written a small speech.

The lawyer cleared his throat. "Citizens of Booneville, your late friend and neighbor, Irene Butler, greets you. She hopes you had a wonderful time this afternoon, and that this celebration will serve as a model to improve other such usually dreary occasions."

April leaned over to whisper to Dan. "I bet she wrote that!"

"Yep, she did."

Gerald Sloan continued to read. "Most of you know me as a simple country woman, which I am, but I've been able, through investments, to amass an embarrassingly large estate. I hereby bequeath the income of the estate, which will amount to approximately two hundred and fifty thousand dollars a year, to the town of Booneville."

April gasped.

"The distribution of the money will be supervised by my grandson, Daniel Butler, with the aid of a board of directors that I have personally selected from the townspeople. Those directors, if they are willing to serve, will be Henry Goodpasture, Gerald Sloan, M.G. Tucker, Bill Lowdermilk and April Foster."

April's mouth dropped open, and she looked at Dan in bewilderment. Irene had put her on the board with all those men? And with Dan?

He answered her unspoken questions with an uneasy smile. "You know, April, she always did like to make things interesting."

CHAPTER TWO

APRIL STOOD IN A DAZE as Gerry Sloan finished his speech with the information that the first board meeting would be the following Saturday, and anyone unable to serve on the board should contact him immediately.

"Will you do it?" Dan asked gently.

"I...I don't know. I guess so. That's what she wanted." Gradually April recovered her equilibrium. "How long have you known about this?"

"Just since the reading of her will. I had no idea she had so much money. Nobody did."

"But you could have been rich," April said, blurting out the first thing that came to her mind. Then she blushed at having spoken aloud a truth that must be embarrassing to Dan.

Dan didn't seem embarrassed. "She wouldn't plunk two million dollars down and say, 'Here, Dan.' That wasn't her style. She wants me to earn my money, just as she earned hers. You should know that, as close as you were to her."

"We couldn't have been too close, for her to have two million dollars I didn't know about."

"But, April, nobody knew, not until Gerald Sloan opened the safe-deposit box and found all the deeds and stock certificates."

"I still can't believe it. If she was a millionaire, why did she drive that old Plymouth? Why did she buy paper napkins on sale, like the rest of us? She could have afforded linen ones and thrown them away after each meal!"

"And what if she had? Would your relationship with her have been exactly the same?"

April paused to consider his question. It was an interesting thought. She started to answer just as the high-school band launched into a spirited version of "Stars and Stripes Forever."

Dan leaned closer to her. "Could we go somewhere and talk?"

"I don't think so," April said, glancing behind him. "Here comes Henry Goodpasture bringing half the town to express their gratitude, no doubt."

"Damn. There are some things that we—"

"Later," April murmured as Henry came up and placed a fatherly arm around Dan's shoulders. Following close behind were various townspeople, including the Lowdermilk clan, Ida Mae among them.

"I'm bowled over," Henry said. "Just bowled over by all this, Daniel."

"I was a little surprised myself when I heard the will read on Wednesday, Mr. Goodpasture."

"Call me Henry, son." The banker smoothed his mustache. "After all, we'll be working together now to manage this generous bequest of your grandmother's. I can see it now...." And he swept one arm toward the horizon to indicate the scope of his dreams.

April looked away, unable to deal with Henry's grandiose gestures. He'd always been far too officious for her tastes.

"First we can repave a few streets," Henry proclaimed royally, as if everyone would naturally accord him command of the projects. "Then we'll fix the 4-H building's roof, maybe even get a *new* 4-H building. And then the streetlights are looking pitiful. We could use some better ones out on Terrell Road. And we can't forget the cemetery. That fence around the perimeter is practically falling down thanks to termites."

Ida Mae touched April's elbow. "Come on over here a minute," she said close to April's ear.

April turned with relief from Henry's dissertation and followed Ida Mae to a spot away from the crowd gathering around Dan.

"Can you *believe* this?" Ida Mae exclaimed.

"Not really." April shook her head. "Two million smackers. Whew!"

"All that time she struggled along with us while we ran bake sales and bazaars for the beautification committee, and she could have ended our misery with one stroke of her pen. Why, April?"

"I asked Dan the same thing, and he asked if we'd have treated her the same way, if we'd known."

"Maybe we'd have treated her better!"

"I think that's what he meant, Idie. She wouldn't have been one of us anymore. Her wealth would have set her apart from the simple joys we all share in Booneville."

"You mean the simple joys of struggling through a winter because the price of hogs went down again? Or repairing a tractor so many times that you think you could have built your own more easily? To think that whenever I complained to her about our problems, I imagined she understood."

"She did, Idie. Don't be hard on her. I'm beginning to see why she kept quiet about her investments, although I admit the news was pretty shocking at first."

"Why did she do it, if she wasn't planning to tell anyone or spend the money?"

April thought for a moment. "Maybe for the challenge. She loved an interesting challenge."

"That's true. Maybe you're right. Well, at least you'll get your sculpture now."

"My sculpture?" April stared at her in confusion. "Why would you think that?"

"You're on the board that will decide where this money

goes, so just allot some for the sculpture you wanted. And make it expensive.''

"I doubt I'd get it approved." April glanced at the knot of people surrounding Dan, with Henry Goodpasture still holding court concerning all the wonderful projects he had in mind. "Did you hear what Henry was talking about? He's interested in roads and roofs and streetlights, all very practical things. I'm only one board member, and the only woman at that. What chance will I have of wangling money for a piece of sculpture? Henry's already assuming leadership, as he usually does.''

"You've got a good chance. I'll get Bill to vote for it, and M.G. can be persuaded, I'll bet. Irene always liked him. And then there's Dan.''

"Yes, and then there's Dan." She gazed across at his strong profile as he waited for Henry to run down.

"After what you two once were to each other, I can't believe he wouldn't go along with your ideas about the sculpture.''

"Oh, I can, Idie." April thought about the night of the prom, when she'd expected moonlight and extravagant promises of love everlasting. Instead, she'd got a speech that even included statistics about how few married students finish college. "I can believe that Dan would think something like a sculpture would be a complete waste of his grandmother's money.''

"But you'll try, won't you? You will serve on the board, I hope.''

"Yes, I'll serve on the board. It's the least I can do for Irene.''

"You know why she named you, April. She knew the men wouldn't have the imagination to appropriate money for things like artwork and other so-called 'useless' projects. She's counting on you to fight for beauty, as well as practicality.''

"Maybe." April looked over at Dan. What Ida Mae had

said made sense, but April couldn't shake the thought that Irene had been up to something far more personal when she put April on the board with Dan. April wondered if Dan suspected it, too. "Well, Idie, I need to pay my respects to Dan's mother, although I kind of dread seeing her. She's not terribly fond of me."

"That was a long time ago. Don't worry about it. She must still be friends with your folks, at any rate. I saw her talking to them over by the barbecue grill."

"I wouldn't expect her to blame them for the actions of their daughter. But I'm a different story."

Ida Mae gazed at her friend. "How do you feel, now that you've talked to him again?"

"Oh, I don't know." April didn't have to ask which "him" Ida Mae meant. "It's hard to tell about a person in a few short minutes after you haven't seen him for eight years." April wasn't quite ready to confess the disturbing heat that had invaded her when Dan's hand closed around hers. "I imagine he's the same old Dan."

"Now that you're on this board, you should be able to tell soon enough. I'll say this—he hasn't gotten any uglier over the years."

"No," April agreed, "he hasn't." She glanced in his direction once more and found him looking at her. April turned her head away. "Where did you say his mother was?"

"Over by the barbecue grill," Ida Mae replied patiently.

"Ida Mae, get that little smile off your face. I don't plan for anything to start up again between Dan and me. Too much water has gone under the bridge."

"Of course. I was just admiring how well he's kept himself in shape."

"Uh-huh. You don't fool me, Idie."

"You don't fool me, either, April."

"I'll call you next week."

"You do that."

As she walked away from Ida Mae, April sighed. One drawback, or maybe an advantage, of knowing someone forever was being transparent to them. She wouldn't be able to fool Ida Mae into thinking she no longer cared about Dan Butler.

Well, shoot, she'd always cared about him. Just because you cared about someone didn't mean everything was hunky-dory between the two of you, April thought morosely. She wondered if there was any chance that Dan had become more impulsive and creative in his approach to life. Or was he still the careful boy who had smashed her dreams? His reaction to her sculpture project would reveal a lot. Once again April considered how much of this little drama Irene had envisioned when she drew up the terms of her will.

April spotted her parents and Dan's mother exactly where Ida Mae had indicated they would be. April had always had trouble imagining that Dan and this woman were related. Dan's large, athletic build and dark hair must be an echo of his late father rather than the slight blond person who had given birth to him.

April's mother waved as April drew near. "Here she is, now. We were just discussing how well both of our children are doing, weren't we, Jeanne?"

"Yes, we were. How are you, April?"

"Okay, considering." April remembered as she gazed at Jeanne Butler that mother and son shared one trait: they both had the same deep blue eyes. Jeanne's were fringed with blond lashes, however, and Dan's with black. Jeanne didn't use mascara, and the result was a look of vulnerability, made more poignant by her tragic story of lost love. Today those vulnerable eyes, dull from weeping, gave April an idea of how much Jeanne grieved for the loss of another loved one.

"I understand you've made a success with the farm," the blond woman continued.

April suspected that Dan's mother hadn't forgotten that

this was the person who had broken her son's heart, but she was trying to be gracious under the circumstances. April had to admire her for that effort. "Did they tell you about the new name and painting the henhouse?"

Dan's mother smiled. "Oh, I heard about that soon after I hit town. Everyone's gotten quite a kick out of your innovations. I told your parents that they reminded me of things Irene would have done."

April was pleased. "She thought The Birds and the Bees was a little cutesy, but she was all in favor of the painting project. I've been threatening to do it for months."

"How did you ever think of such an idea?"

"It's not original. When I was in Canada with—" She stopped herself before saying "with Jimmy." "When I traveled through the Canadian Maritimes, I noticed the farm buildings were often painted wild colors, although not necessarily several on one building. That was my embellishment after I discovered a paint sale at Bender's. Anyway, Irene liked my plan of bringing a touch of Canada here. I wish she could have seen my henhouse."

"So do I." Jeanne's blue eyes grew more friendly. "I owe her a great deal. Did you know that she paid for my secretarial training?"

April shook her head.

"I tried to repay her later, but she wouldn't hear of it."

Jeanne gestured as she talked, and April watched her intently. Something was different about this woman, April thought. Something was missing. What was it?

"After I got that great job offer in Indianapolis," Dan's mother continued, "when Dan was fifteen and balked at leaving Booneville High—" At this point Jeanne paused and looked pointedly at April. Everyone in the little circle knew that April had been one of the main reasons Dan protested the move to Indianapolis.

April smiled in a self-deprecating way. She'd been only thirteen when Dan made his rebellious stand. She'd foolishly expected him to continue making such dramatic gestures on her behalf. Only later had she realized that leaving Booneville right before his junior year must have seemed riskier to Dan than staying, despite his mother's absence. Even without his interest in April, he wouldn't have wanted to go.

"Anyway, Irene was the one who insisted I take the job and let Dan stay with her to finish out high school. She was very wise to see how much I needed that job to get a new lease on life, and Dan had pretty much outgrown his dependence on me, anyway. He was always so responsible."

April's parents murmured their assent without looking at April. All three of them had been over this ground a million times, as her mother and father struggled to understand why Dan's sense of responsibility had driven April away from him and into the arms of a wild boy like Jimmy Foster. April was afraid they blamed most of it on April's being an only child and willful. She hoped the reasons ran deeper than that.

Jeanne sighed. "I'm really going to miss Irene." She glanced around at the festive gathering. "This is so like her, to turn a funeral into a celebration. And to give her money to the town she loved so much."

"It's unusual, that's for sure," April's father said, glancing at Jeanne uneasily.

"I certainly wouldn't have wanted that money." Jeanne answered his unspoken concern. "I like my life the way it is. And I'm not sure I'd want Dan to suddenly come into two million dollars, either. He's dependable now, but what would that kind of wealth do to him?"

"It didn't seem to ruin Irene." April was a little impatient with Jeanne's attitude. She figured that Dan would be too conservative, if anything, with large sums of money. He might never consider an around-the-world cruise, for example, or a custom-tailored silk suit.

"Irene was one of a kind," Jeanne replied. "We'll feel her influence for a long time to come."

"I'm sure we will," April agreed as she keyed in on the movement of Jeanne's hands. Then April knew what was different about Jeanne Butler, and the knowledge made her cold with apprehension. The emerald-and-diamond heirloom ring, the valuable piece of jewelry that had graced the blond woman's left hand for as long as April could remember, was no longer there.

THE FOLLOWING WEEK was a long one for April. She couldn't seem to get her mind off the subject of Dan and the heirloom ring. She hadn't had the courage to mention the ring to Jeanne Butler, for fear the news would be bad. If Dan had given it to someone, if he had found the love of his life, April didn't want to find out from his mother, who might not be willing to spare April much pain in the telling.

Saturday was the first board meeting, and the prospect of being in close contact with Dan again so soon knotted her stomach with dread. The same sexual attraction existed between them, and yet Dan might already be planning his wedding to someone else.

The decision to marry would have had to be a recent one because Irene would have told her otherwise. Maybe he'd decided this very week. Perhaps in this time of grieving he'd reached out to someone. With one of the anchors in his life gone, he might have wished to establish another close bond. April vowed to find out somehow on Saturday so she would know exactly how things were before she and Dan had to spend any more time together.

April missed Irene with a sharpness that surprised her. She hadn't realized how often she used to pick up the phone and call Irene to discuss ideas for the square, or just to chat. Twice during the last week April had dialed the first few digits of Irene's number before she remembered that no one would answer.

Sometimes April wondered if she'd been a bother to the older woman. In the last two months Irene hadn't felt well, yet she'd never indicated to April that she lacked the energy for their frequent brainstorming sessions. April liked to think that she helped keep Irene active and interested in life, right up to the end. Irene certainly had been an inspiration for her.

On April's infrequent trips to town, she looked, out of long habit, for Irene's Plymouth in the driveway of the house on Irving Street. But of course the Plymouth had already been sold, to someone from Decatur, and the house was up for sale, as well. The proceeds would be added to the estate, thus providing even more money for the town of Booneville.

April's days were busy, as usual. She insulated the beehives against the approaching cold weather and attacked her vegetable garden with the Rototiller. In the late afternoons she supervised the crew of high-school students who picked apples from her small orchard and bagged them for sale.

Painting the henhouse had increased her egg business. People now drove out "just to see that doggone rainbow building" and bought a few dozen eggs "as long as they'd made the trip." Many also took home a jar of honey, some squash and a pumpkin or two. April anticipated her usual brisk pumpkin sales as Halloween approached.

Each evening after chores and a light supper, she sat at the kitchen table to jot down ideas for presenting the sculpture project to the board on Saturday morning. At these moments April longed for Irene's wit and wisdom all the more. April wanted her presentation to be convincing, and Irene would have known just what to say. More important, she would have known what *not* to say.

After April's vagabond days with Jimmy, in which they'd traveled through most of North America and all of Europe, she had an expanded idea of what a sculpture on the square might look like. She especially liked the free-flowing work of modern artists such as Picasso, who were content to suggest a form rather than deliberately define one.

She was aware, however, that Booneville residents might take some time getting used to such an idea. Irene had been the only member of the beautification committee who knew the type of sculpture April had in mind. Irene had thought the contrast of old and new, the Victorian gazebo versus the ultramodern piece of art, would work well. Irene also had envisioned something designed so that children might play on it, just as they played around the gazebo. April could see nothing wrong with that, either. But how much should she say about all this to conservative people such as Henry Goodpasture and Dan Butler?

By Saturday morning, as she drove her pickup truck to the bank for the meeting, a pile of scribbled notes by her side, April was a jumble of nerves. She'd worn her glasses instead of her contacts in the interest of appearing more serious-minded, and she had on a dress for the second time that month—surely a record for her.

Once she'd chosen the dress route instead of jeans, she had felt committed to go the whole nine yards, with nylons and her best brown heels. The offerings of her jewelry box were scant, but she'd unearthed some gold hoops for her ears and a gold-link bracelet that went well with her forest-green dress. Thank goodness she'd bought a new fall coat this year, she thought, parking the truck in front of the bank. Otherwise, she'd be wearing the ratty parka she'd bummed all over Europe in, and Henry Goodpasture would mentally label her a hippie when she walked in the door.

She glanced at the vehicles already lined up at the curb. She recognized them all except one, a sporty little red Honda Civic CRX. That must be Dan's car, she thought, trying to get a fix on his choice of transportation. The color wasn't conservative. Hadn't he once told her that red cars got more speeding tickets than any other color? But April also knew that Hondas were famous for good gas mileage, which sounded exactly like the old Dan. Maybe his fiancée had picked the color.

"Hey, April, ready for the first meeting?"

At the sound of Bill Lowdermilk's voice, she turned with a grateful smile. Bill was fair-haired, like his wife, but unlike her he always looked a little mussed. His face was perpetually sunburned, and his hair was beginning to thin on top. April gazed at him fondly. He was her only guaranteed friend on this board. "I don't know, Bill. I'm really nervous."

Bill put an arm around her shoulders as they walked into the bank. "Don't worry. Idie made me promise during breakfast this morning that I'd back you, no matter what crazy scheme you have."

April laughed. She could picture Ida Mae waving a spatula under Bill's nose and extracting his promise before she served him his sausage and eggs. "I really appreciate your support, Bill. But you don't want to make Henry mad. After all, he does hold the note on your farm."

"Henry doesn't scare me none," Bill drawled, lapsing into the country-boy accent he used whenever he joked around.

"Well, he scares *me*," April admitted. "Now hush, Bill, before you get us both in trouble. I assume we're meeting in the back room."

"Seeing as how nobody's out here in the lobby, I think you're right. Ready?"

"I'm a lot readier than I was before you showed up. Let's go."

They walked through the lobby toward a dark wooden door marked Private, and April's heart began to pound. Dan was on the other side of that door, and the knowledge gave her goose bumps. She also realized that showing her feelings at this point could land her in a mess, especially if Dan was engaged. As Bill opened the door for her, she composed her face into a neutral mask.

The bank's windowless conference room was nearly filled by a long heavy table surrounded by matching chairs upholstered in green leather. At April's entrance, the four men seated around one end of the table stood up. April smiled nervously at their show of manners. Being the only woman in the group wouldn't be easy.

"Please sit down," she said, unconsciously looking to Dan for help. Today he wore slacks and a blue velour pullover that echoed the color of his eyes. He looked so good that she wondered if she could keep from staring at him throughout the meeting. "Under the circumstances, I think I should be treated like any other board member."

Dan caught her pleading glance. "April's right," he said, sitting down. "We're all equals here. That was my grandmother's intent, as you'll see in a moment." He gave April and Bill a friendly smile. "Glad you're both here. It's not quite ten yet, but we may as well start. I guess everyone was eager to discuss spending money this morning."

"Money is my business," Henry said, leaning back in his chair and smoothing his mustache.

April figured the statement was meant to underline Henry's position in the group. He had no intention of being "equal" as Dan had put it, but April understood why Irene had named him to the board. Had he been overlooked, he would have caused all kinds of problems out of hurt pride. April and Irene had discussed the same situation when they formed the beautification committee and finally had included Henry's wife, Mabel, in order not to create a powerful enemy.

As for the other members of the board, Gerald Sloan's appointment wasn't surprising. If Irene had trusted him with her legal affairs, she'd trust him in this. Bill Lowdermilk had assumed a leadership position among the younger farmers in the area, so he was a logical choice, and M.G. Tucker was one of the kindest men April had ever known. She'd always wondered if his interest in Irene went beyond neighborliness, but the older woman had never openly encouraged him in all her years of widowhood.

"Before we begin discussing possible projects, I'd like to explain how my grandmother wanted this board to operate," Dan said, opening a folder in front of him and taking out some papers to pass around the table. "I've made copies of the provisions so each of you can read them, but I'd still like to talk about the structure of the group so there will be no misunderstandings."

April felt encouraged by the strength and determination in Dan's voice. For one thing, he had mastered his grief well enough to conduct this meeting with authority, and he also didn't sound ready to turn the decisions over to Henry Goodpasture.

"As you'll see by the sheet in front of you," Dan continued, "my grandmother appointed six members on purpose. Although I'll run the meetings and eventually write the checks, each of us has an equally weighted vote when it comes to project approval. That means that with an even number on the board, we could have a tie. My grandmother meant that as a test of our ability to work together. Five members would have made the decisions too easy."

"This looks like Irene's handiwork, all right," M.G. said, adjusting his wire-rimmed glasses. "She liked to keep the pot boiling."

Henry shook his head. "Almost all governing boards are uneven numbers. We could end up in a stalemate this way. Then what?"

"That's what the last paragraph is about," Dan said. "If the board ties on a vote, we have ten days to reconsider. If we are still unable to agree, all the money reverts to the state. Oh, and if all six of us can't agree to work under these conditions, the same thing will happen."

"That's ridiculous!" Henry peered at the offending paragraph.

M.G. laughed out loud. "That's Irene. In order to keep

the money for Booneville, we'll have to work as a team. I think it's a beautiful plan. I agree to it.''

"So do I," Bill said, tossing his copy of the provisions on the table.

Dan looked around the room. "Gerry?"

"You've got my vote."

Henry glared at the paper for another few seconds. "Mine, too, I suppose," he mumbled, "although I don't know why she couldn't have appointed five or seven of us."

At last Dan focused on April, who had been sitting silently at the end of the table. "How about you, April? Are you in?"

She stared at him, trying to make sense of Irene's provisions. Then the puzzle pieces fell into place. Irene envisioned Bill, M.G. and April as the liberal influences on the board. Henry Goodpasture and Gerald Sloan were on the conservative side of the fence. If Dan sided with them, they'd have a certain tie over issues such as her sculpture project. Irene had planned her strategy carefully.

April realized that she was expected to work with Dan, win him over to her side on the more creative projects. Irene might have hoped that in the process April and Dan would rediscover their old love. But obviously Irene hadn't counted on Dan's becoming engaged between the time she wrote her will and the first meeting of this board.

"April?" Dan said again.

She felt a stab of pain at what might have been if Irene's plan had worked. Instead, Irene may have bequeathed April the disturbing task of working closely with Dan while she watched him marry someone else. But did she have a choice? "I'm in," she replied.

CHAPTER THREE

WARMTH FLICKERED in Dan's blue eyes. "Good."

April wondered how much of Irene's strategy Dan had figured out. He must have guessed that Irene wanted to throw the two of them together, but did it make any difference now? Of course, April realized that the complex structure of this endowment had many objectives other than matchmaking.

In order for the town to continue receiving its legacy, these six people would have to work in harmony. What a challenge Irene had given them on that one! Not only were April and Dan obligated to get along, but Henry Goodpasture and M.G. Tucker, a volatile combination if April ever saw one, had to, as well.

She glanced at the other two men sitting at the table. Gerald Sloan was easygoing but conservative, and Bill Lowdermilk had the liberal ideas of the younger farmers in the area. Given the makeup of the group, keeping the money in Booneville would be a small miracle, but Irene had loved working miracles.

And so do I, thought April, looking straight at Dan. *Let the action begin.*

As if in answer to her thoughts, Dan flipped open a steno pad and picked up a black pen. "I suggest we establish a list of projects as our first step. As you make suggestions, give an estimate as to how much money you think the work would require. Then we'll vote on which ones to do this year."

April cringed. An outstanding sculpture would cost thousands of dollars. What chance would such a request have when these men could imagine using those thousands in some less nebulous way? She decided to wait awhile before giving her suggestion.

Henry leaned forward immediately. "Streetlights," he intoned. "The best crime deterrent in the world is good lighting, which Booneville is sadly lacking. That should be number one."

"Crime?" M.G. looked amused. "What crime, Henry?"

"Just last week Hazel Fitzsimmons had a pumpkin pie stolen from her back porch, not ten minutes after she set it out to cool."

M.G. winked at April. "My, that's serious. Would a streetlight have prevented that, do you think? I thought they usually went along the street, which wouldn't do anybody's back porch much good."

"That's not the point," Henry flushed. "In fact, the pie was stolen in the afternoon. The point is that it was a pie last week, but it could be a television set next, or the cookie jar you keep your cash in, M.G.."

"Come on, Henry. You're just sore because I haven't got every penny in this bank of yours so you can fool with it."

Dan cleared his throat. "Uh, gentlemen, let's continue. How much would streetlights cost, Henry?"

Henry named an approximate figure, and Dan wrote it down. Bill spoke next, pointing out, as Henry had the week before, that the 4-H building could use a new roof and a good coat of paint. Gerald Sloan reported that the basketball court in the gym was in pathetic shape, and M.G. brought up the matter of new high-school band uniforms. Henry said they had looked fine to him last Saturday, and Dan steered them away from yet another argument.

As he wrote on the legal pad, Dan wondered if his grandmother had held some long-hidden grudge against him, to put him in charge of this mess she'd carefully concocted.

These people would never get along, if the first interchange was any example. Of course, if they couldn't agree, the money would simply go to the state and his job would end. Dan glanced at April and realized he didn't want that to happen.

Part of the problem was meeting in this bank, where Henry felt comfortable and in command. Dan realized he'd accepted Henry's offer of the room last week because he'd been too muddled with grief to realize the implications of meeting here, where Henry's power over the community was so evident. Next time they'd find another spot, a more neutral gathering place. That is, they would if they met a second time.

Dan took another suggestion from Bill Lowdermilk and two more from Henry, but he was watching April, who hadn't said much of anything yet. He'd noticed the glasses when she first came in. She was doing her female version of a Clark Kent disguise again.

In high school she'd worn them, a similar large round pair, when she wanted to impress someone with her scholarly attitude. The glasses made her appear quiet and unassuming, but Dan knew better. Did he ever! April became a different sort of woman when she took off those glasses.

He felt the dull beginning ache of desire as he recalled the night she lost a contact lens during a heavy petting session in the backseat of his Chevy. They'd both been pretty worked up, but he'd decided they should turn on the overhead light to look for the damn thing, which was expensive. Afterward she'd insisted the mood was ruined and had made him take her home. She would rather have lost the contact, she said. He remembered that she'd almost lost something else that night.

Dan cleared his throat. "April, how about you? Any ideas for spending this money?"

A faint pink spread over her cheeks. Her blush, combined with the owlish glasses, made her look much younger than twenty-seven. "Yes, I do." She picked up the papers in front of her and glanced at them before folding the whole batch and shoving them to one side. "I think we need a sculpture on the town square," she announced.

Henry stared at her. "Haven't I heard something about this before? Sounds like what Mabel was gabbing about with the beautification committee you two are on together."

"Yes, we have discussed the possibility, but we had no idea how to pay for it." April met Henry's stare. "Irene Butler was on the committee, as well."

"All right," Dan said, turning to his notepad. "Let's put the sculpture on the list. How much?"

"Wait a danged minute," Henry objected. "A statue is all well and good, but what does it do for the town? Just provides an outdoor facility for pigeons, if you ask me." He leaned back and grinned at his own humor.

April noticed that Henry had used the word "statue" instead of "sculpture," but she didn't bother to correct him. If he had an image of some soldier on a horse, that was probably better than if he fully understood her intentions. "I realize all the other suggestions are important," April said, "but so is beauty. People need something to look at that will interest them, intrigue them, lift their spirits."

Gerald Sloan gave her a kindly look. "Don't you think leaky roofs and rutted streets ought to come first, April? It's difficult to have high spirits if the rain's coming in on you."

"No, I won't fall into that trap," April replied. "If we accomplish all the practical tasks first, we'll never get around to spending money on something just because it's beautiful. I say money should be allotted to the project this year, even if some of the other things have to wait."

M.G.'s tone was placating. "I understand your enthusiasm, April, but people around here are having hard times. They might not appreciate money being spent on something with no demonstrable value."

April sat up straighter. "I disagree. A stunning piece of

art on the square is exactly what Booneville needs, perhaps more than any of these other improvements, just *because* times are tough. People need to be reminded that life shouldn't be reduced to profits and losses. We're all still dreamers, aren't we?''

You certainly still are, Dan thought. *Oh, lady, you haven't changed at all.* ''Give me a figure, April.''

She closed her eyes for a moment before naming a generous amount. She heard the quick intake of breath around the table. All of them, including Bill, thought the estimate was foolishly extravagant.

''I think it's time to vote,'' Dan said. ''Remember we've got approximately two hundred and fifty thousand to spend. I'd advise each of you to total your choices on a piece of paper before we vote. Obviously we can't do everything this year.''

April sighed. If M.G. wouldn't support her, she had little chance, unless maybe Dan…but no, she didn't expect that. From the murmurs around the table as they prepared to vote, she knew the sculpture project wouldn't take place this year—probably not any year. It would be disregarded each time as more ''worthy'' ideas came up.

Dan conducted the vote democratically, she had to admit, taking projects in order of how many considered them important. Quickly the big money was decided and only a few thousand were left. Not enough for the sculpture, in April's estimation.

''Well, what about this project of April's?'' M.G. asked. ''I've got it on my list. Anybody else?''

''I do,'' Bill said.

April gave him a grateful smile. Ida Mae would hear about this. Bill was a true friend. ''So do I, of course,'' she said.

''Me, too,'' Dan said.

April tried to conceal her shock, apparently without success.

"I think April's a little surprised that some of us consider culture an important element," Dan added with a lopsided smile.

"That's not true." April ducked her head and studied the sheet in front of her. "Anyway, there's not enough money left to cover my estimate for the sculpture."

"Take less," M.G. suggested.

"Less?" She studied M.G.'s face. He was telling her that this was her chance. She could have a smaller amount now, or possibly nothing in the future. April believed he'd assessed the situation well.

"All right," she said, turning to Dan. "Let's vote on this amount for the sculpture."

Dan looked around at the group. "Objections?"

"Yes." Henry leaned his forearms on the table. "Each of you should realize that if you vote this money for some statue, we won't get the new fence around the cemetery. Simple as that. Lots of us have loved ones buried in there, and we'd like to see them properly fenced in."

A muffled sound came from M.G. Then he cleared his throat. "Henry, they aren't going anywhere."

"Let's take that vote," Dan said quickly, biting down on his lower lip. "Bill?"

"In favor of the sculpture," Bill said.

April wasn't surprised that M.G. also voted for the sculpture and that Henry and Gerald voted against. When Dan voted in favor, giving her the money, she restrained her first flash of excitement. After all, if he'd voted against her, there would have been a tie. If it had held, all their work today would have been wasted. Dan's vote was practical, after all.

"So you have something, at least," M.G. said after the vote was complete.

"I hope it's enough to find a good sculptor," April replied.

"Where were you planning to look?"

"I'd hoped to tour the galleries in Chicago and find some-one there."

Henry sat back, nursing his first defeat. "Chicago, huh? There's some weird stuff up there. Like that Picasso, for example. You ever seen that, Gerry?" He turned to the only person who had supported him in the negative vote.

"It's different, all right," the lawyer agreed. "What you got in mind, April?"

"Well, I—"

"Tell you what would make me feel a whole lot better about this," Henry interrupted. "Dan lives in Chicago. How about if he goes around to the galleries with April and sort of supervises?"

April bristled. "Supervises?"

"Might be a good plan," Gerry said. "More than one member of the board should be in on the choice of the artist, anyway."

"Yeah, April," Bill added. He'd looked increasingly un-comfortable after Henry's mention of the Picasso. "Why not have Dan tag along? He's got good taste."

"I'd be glad to," Dan said, pretending to ignore the re-bellious jut of April's chin. "Does everyone agree on that, then?"

M.G.'s eyes twinkled. "Sure."

April clenched her hands in frustration. "But I don't need—"

"We'd all feel better about it, April," Henry said, smoothing his mustache.

April wanted to rip out that neatly trimmed mustache, hair by hair. "In that case, of course we'll do it that way," she said with a gracious smile.

"As long as we're going to have this statue," Henry con-tinued, "I'll tell you what I think would look real good. I'd like to see old U. S. Grant in full uniform, riding his horse into battle against the Rebels. Wouldn't that be something to be proud of?"

April looked up at the ceiling to keep from laughing. In her imagination she'd predicted that Henry would suggest exactly this sort of statue. She'd figured he'd want either Grant or Abraham Lincoln.

"Grant would be nice," Gerry agreed. "Or Lincoln. Maybe Honest Abe splitting rails. That would look good in bronze. Don't you agree, April?"

"Well, actually, I think Lincoln and Grant have been a little overdone in Illinois," she began cautiously.

"But everybody knows who they are," Henry said. "You don't want to go putting up a statue of some fellow that nobody knows."

April couldn't resist. "Why does it have to be a man?"

The room was completely silent.

"Now wait a minute," Gerry said finally. "We don't want any *Venus de Milo* type thing right on the square, where the kids will play, and everything…" His face turned the dull red of an old barn.

April covered her mouth with her hand and bent her head. Bless their hearts, these men thought sculptures were either men doing noble deeds or naked women. Booneville definitely needed this work of art, which would be neither one, if she got her way.

"I'm sure April wasn't planning something like that," Dan said without much conviction.

She glanced at him. He was giving her a look of warning, and she longed to throw them all into a tizzy by suggesting that the sculpture might be of a nude woman *and* man. But she'd only be defeating her purpose by keeping them stirred up. "No, I wasn't planning anything like that," she said, and watched them all sink back with relief.

"Of course you weren't," Henry said. "Besides, Dan wouldn't go along with that sort of foolishness. He's a sensible young man, and I know we can trust him in this. When will you go to Chicago, do you think?"

April thought quickly. "Soon. Right after Halloween,

perhaps, if my parents will take care of the farm for a few days." Belatedly she remembered that Dan was supposed to be a part of all this. "Of course, I can work around your schedule, Dan, if that's not convenient," she added with exaggerated courtesy. And what about his fiancée, if indeed he had one? April's presence in Chicago might be awkward for him. She secretly hoped it would be.

"The first week in November is fine." Dan rested his chin in his hands and gazed at her thoughtfully. "Just fine."

April wasn't quite sure what to make of that look. He seemed to be assessing her in some way, and her skin prickled in sensual response. Was he engaged or wasn't he? Rude or not, she'd ask him after the meeting. She had a right to know before she skipped blithely up to Chicago and then came face-to-face with the woman.

The meeting ended with Dan asking the others to take various responsibilities for the other projects. April admired the way he handled the delicate matter of directing the three men who were all old enough to be his father, and Bill, who had played football with him and was a friend. April had never noticed Dan's leadership abilities before, and she recognized Irene's influence in the careful way Dan motivated the group to work together. It seemed that Dan's grandmother had known what she was doing when she put him in charge.

At last everyone began pushing back chairs and gathering notes. As the men switched from talk of the endowment to a discussion of the previous night's high-school football game, April edged around the table and touched Dan's arm. "Could I see you for a moment before you head back to Chicago?"

His glance was cheerful. "Sure. I'm not leaving right this minute, anyway. Henry and Mabel have asked me over for lunch."

Figures, April thought. "That's nice," she said aloud. "Then maybe you'd like to drop by the farm on your way out of town? I'll give you a pumpkin to take back to the big city.''

He smiled. "We don't have too many trick-or-treaters in my apartment building."

"I didn't mean— Oh, well. It was a stupid idea."

"No. I shouldn't have teased you. I'd love a pumpkin. Maybe I'll even carve it, for old time's sake. Expect me by two, okay?"

She gazed into his eyes. "Okay." Was he remembering that Halloween, so long ago, when he'd come out to the farm with his grandmother to pick out a pumpkin? He'd been fifteen, she thirteen. The two of them had been put in charge of finding the perfect jack-o'-lantern for his grandmother's front porch, and then Irene had suggested they carve it right there, together. The boy and girl, still so young, had laughed and teased each other all the way through the task.

Then the moment had arrived when the laughter stopped and both she and Dan had sensed the first dim awareness of the man and woman they were becoming, sampled the first taste of wanting. Looking at him now, April knew that she'd never completely lost that yearning for Dan. Perhaps she never would.

APRIL NEEDED all the produce business she could get, but she wished everyone had stayed away that afternoon. Unfortunately for her privacy, the Saturday before Halloween was the perfect time for families to drive into the country in search of the perfect jack-o'-lantern and a sack of apples for dunking in caramel.

Knowing that she'd no doubt have to work that afternoon, April had changed out of her dress and into jeans and a red sweatshirt. She couldn't wear her contacts, either, although the urge was strong to look a little sexier for Dan. But with her glasses on she could see the customers, and with them off she could read the scale when weighing the pumpkins.

The contacts were lousy for close work. So much for glamour—as if it mattered. Dan was engaged.

When he arrived a little after two, April's driveway was a busy thoroughfare. She stood in the front yard behind a wooden picnic table that served as a counter for the scale and the cash box. Business was so steady that she scarcely had time to nod hello to Dan as he parked the red Honda and sauntered over.

"Looks like you could use a hand," he said, glancing at the line forming beside the scale. "Let me weigh and you collect the money."

"Don't be silly, Dan." April took a pumpkin the size of a basketball from a little girl and placed it on the scale. "Go on in the kitchen and have some hot cider," she suggested, sliding her glasses down her nose to read the scale. "It's on the stove." She handed the pumpkin back to the little girl and readjusted her glasses before making change from a twenty-dollar bill the girl's father took from his wallet. "The rush should be over in a sec."

"Doesn't look like it. Two more cars just turned in the drive. Besides, if I weigh, you don't have to go through that routine with your glasses. Here." Without asking he took a giant pumpkin from her arms and lowered it to the scale.

"But I didn't ask you out here so that you could work."

He flashed her a smile. "For a city boy this isn't work. Let's see, this one's thirty-two pounds. Now be quiet and take this nice lady's money."

"Good advice," the woman said, handing over the amount April asked for. "And be grateful for the help. Some men of my acquaintance wouldn't even offer, especially if it's a good afternoon for fishing."

April laughed. "True." She thought immediately of her fun-loving Jimmy, who had always seemed to disappear when the time came for chores. Because life on the farm was a constant series of chores, one day he had simply disappeared, period.

She and Dan worked side by side for the next hour without a break. She wondered if he had any reaction at all when they accidentally brushed against each other in the course of waiting on customers. She was acutely aware each time it happened, and her heart raced for several seconds afterward.

Relax, she warned herself. *The guy's engaged.* She wondered if she could be the sort of perverse person who didn't want a man until someone else showed an interest. But no, she'd wanted Dan plenty in high school. He just hadn't shared her fervor. If he had, she'd be married to him now.

Married to Dan. April knew the experience would have been totally different from being Jimmy's wife. Partway into their six-year marriage, she'd admitted to herself that Jimmy no longer excited her sexually. It wasn't his fault—unless she counted lack of maturity his fault. She'd tried to change her response. Nothing had worked.

Secretly she believed that had she been a more enthusiastic lover, Jimmy might not have left. Therefore she couldn't blame him for the divorce, although most people in Booneville did. Jimmy's reputation was ruined here; no wonder he'd headed for Oregon.

And today all the passion she hadn't been able to manufacture for poor Jimmy was being whipped into life by the slight friction of Dan's arm against hers, the occasional bump of a thigh. Life wasn't fair.

"April? Sixteen pounds, kiddo."

She blushed and turned away. How many times had Dan repeated himself while the line of customers watched her staring off into space? "Right. Sixteen."

Dan put his head close to hers. "Where were you?"

Thinking about you. About sex. "Daydreaming. I'm sorry."

"Never mind. Don't look now, but we haven't had another car pull up for about five minutes. Maybe the deluge is over for a while." He weighed another pumpkin. "Twenty-one pounds."

"I hope so. The money's nice, but I really wanted to talk with you."

"That's nice. I really wanted to talk with you, too."

She glanced at him. Was he going to discuss his engagement, just to get things straight between them? Maybe he'd noticed something; maybe he knew her well enough to pick up signals she was unwillingly giving off, and he didn't want her to embarrass herself. What a depressing thought.

April waited impatiently for the last customer to pay for his pumpkin while Dan carried two wooden lawn chairs from the front porch and placed them facing each other behind the picnic table.

When they sat down, April felt a moment of panic. Now he would tell her, and she didn't want to know. She waved her hand toward the diminished mound of pumpkins. "I had planned to give you one," she said, staving off his announcement for a little longer. "But the best may be taken."

"Then I'll choose one with character, as my grandmother used to say."

"That's right. She never liked the perfectly round pumpkins, did she?" April smiled at Dan as they shared another memory of the woman they would miss for a long time. When Dan opened his mouth as if to speak again, she hopped to her feet. "Why don't you pick the one you want, while I get us that hot cider I promised you earlier?"

"Bring a knife and a spoon and some newspaper. I've gotten in the mood to carve the face, after all this."

"You're just humoring me."

"No, I'm not. I have to keep in practice, don't I?"

April looked back over her shoulder. "In practice? What for?"

"So I can teach my kids someday."

His statement caught her like a blow to the stomach. She wasn't going to accept the news of this engagement gracefully. "Oh. I suppose so," she mumbled, turning away to walk quickly into the house. He'd probably present his fiancée with the carved pumpkin, and she'd be charmed with this rustic gift, a symbol of the quaint traditions of rural living. Nuts.

When she returned with mugs of cider, and a newspaper tucked under one arm, Dan was drawing a face on a tall skinny pumpkin that sat on the table in front of him.

"I borrowed your pencil from the cash box. What do you think?"

"Looks like M.G. Tucker." April had given herself a talking-to in the kitchen and had vowed to be breezy and unconcerned with Dan. His love life was out of her jurisdiction, and her attraction to him was irrelevant.

"Yeah, especially if I bend some wire to look like glasses. I always thought he was sweet on Grandma. Did you bring the knife?"

April reached into the back pocket of her jeans and pulled out a paring knife and a large spoon. "This should be quite a pumpkin."

"Good therapy." Dan plunged the knife into the orange rind and cut a circle for the top. "I haven't hollowed out a pumpkin since..." He glanced at April and then returned to his task. "In years," he finished, twisting off the top and scraping the pearly seeds and stringy pulp onto the newspaper at his feet.

"I've carved one every Halloween." April sat down and picked up her mug of cider. "Except of course when I was out of the country."

For a while the only sound was the scraping of the spoon against the inside of the pumpkin. "Don't you miss it?" Dan said at last while he continued to scrape. "All that traveling?"

"Actually, no."

"Being stuck in one very small town is okay with you?"

"Sure. I finally learned that I'm a small-town girl at heart.

I'll take other trips someday, but never for so long at one time. I like Booneville and my life here.''

Dan continued to scrape, although the inside of the pumpkin yielded no more seeds or pulp. ''You're not lonely?''

April recoiled from the intimate question. What gave him the right to ask it? ''Not especially,'' she lied. Before she'd wanted to postpone talking about his engagement. Now she wished he'd get it over with. ''Listen, Dan, I've been thinking about my tour of the galleries in Chicago. Under the circumstances, shouldn't I do that alone? I'll check with you before I make a final selection of sculptors, but you don't have to baby-sit me while I'm investigating the possibilities.''

Dan stopped scraping and looked at her. ''Under what circumstances? And what makes you think I'd consider it baby-sitting?''

''I'm sure you have more important responsibilities than squiring me around. You have your work, and your set of friends there. I don't want to intrude.'' *Say it, please. Don't make me drag it out of you.*

His laughter was bemused. ''You wouldn't be an intrusion. What is it, April?''

''Dan, I know your mother isn't wearing the ring anymore, so you may as well be frank with me.''

''I'd rather be Dan.''

''Do you have to make stupid jokes at a time like this? I assume you're getting married, and I...don't want to bother you when you're in the midst of wedding plans. Now do you understand?''

''Yes, but you don't.''

''What?''

''As a matter of fact, I do have the ring, but I'm not marrying anyone. My mother gave me the ring because...''

''Because why?'' April's heart beat faster.

He gave her a quizzical smile. ''Never mind. Just because. Anyway, I'm perfectly free to 'squire you around,' as you put it. Would you like to stay at the Palmer House? I can get you a discount through my company's corporate account there.''

''I...I don't know what to say.''

''That's a first.''

''Dan, stop it. I've had a severe jolt here, thinking you were engaged, and I don't need your smart-aleck remarks.''

''Oh?''

April saw an assessing look on his face again and realized how much she'd just given away. She couldn't think of any words with which to call back what she'd said, and she could tell by his searching expression that he wasn't going to leave the subject alone.

He put down the spoon and leaned forward, his blue eyes focusing on her with an intensity that made her tremble with desire. She had never wanted him so much, and she feared that he knew it.

His tone was quiet and controlled. ''What *do* you need from me, April?''

CHAPTER FOUR

APRIL SWALLOWED. "I don't know what you mean."

"The hell you don't."

"A lot—" Her vocal cords wouldn't work smoothly. She tried again. "A lot has happened between us, Dan."

"And a lot hasn't."

Her pulse thundered in her ears. His meaning was all too clear. "I'm not the same girl you dated in high school."

"I should hope not. I'm hardly the same man, either."

"And...and I thought you were getting married."

"You thought wrong."

"Yes." She studied his face, so familiar and yet unknown, too. Eight years of experiences that she hadn't shared were hidden behind those blue eyes. Of course there had been women. Knowing Dan, April imagined the relationships had been serious, passionate...and consummated.

How well did he remember those nights after high-school dances when they'd parked along moonlit farm roads and tempted each other, veering away from forbidden pleasure at the last moment? They were adults now. Nothing was forbidden anymore.

Considering the direction of her thoughts, she wasn't surprised when he reached for her, guiding her out of the chair until they were standing, staring silently at each other.

Carefully he took off her glasses and laid them on the picnic table. Then he framed her face with his hands. "Tell me what you need."

"Maybe I don't know," she murmured, trembling.

"Maybe we can find out."

As he lowered his head, she closed her eyes. At the soft caress of his mouth on hers she was catapulted back in time to those long-ago days of loving Dan, of welcoming the scent of him, the urgent press of his lips, the whisper of his breath against her cheek.

At first his touch was agonizingly familiar, and she could have been fifteen again, sharing their first kiss, declaring the first words of undying love. But his embrace soon became less tentative, the exploration of his tongue more demanding. As mature emotions pumped through her, April realized that innocence was gone forever, for both of them. Their virginal high-school-sweetheart days were over, and they knew it.

With some effort at self-control, she pulled away. "Dan, we're in the middle of my front yard in broad daylight."

"Then let's go inside." He was breathing hard.

April shook her head. "This is too fast."

"Too fast?" He stared at her. Then he began to laugh. "That's true, I guess. I've only known you for about thirteen years."

"We've been apart, Dan. We have some catching up to do."

"Could have fooled me. I think we just caught up."

"Dan, I don't want to make any…mistakes."

His expression grew more cautious. "Neither do I, now that you mention it."

"Maybe my trip to Chicago will give us a chance to get to know each other again."

He nodded slowly. "Could be."

"Dan, I can't help the way I respond to you. I've always—" She waved her hand in the air, unwilling or unable to explain further. "But other things are important, too, don't you agree?"

"You're asking me? Somehow the lines seem to be reversed from a discussion we had a few years ago. Yes, I agree, dammit. But a few things have changed, as you pointed out. I was pretty good at restraint back in those days. I can't guarantee that kind of control now.''

April felt a flash of white-hot desire. Hadn't that been what she had wanted eight years ago, a man driven beyond reason by his passion? Yes, by his passion, but also by his love. That was it. She had no idea how much love figured into all this. And she needed to know.

"I think the Chicago visit will give us a chance to find out a lot of things, Dan.''

"I guess you're right. We really haven't spent any time together in the past few years.'' He regarded her thoughtfully. "What about the hotel? You don't have to stay there, April.''

Her body quivered as she imagined heading for Chicago and rushing straight into his arms, into his bed. "Yes, I do.''

He nodded. "Then I'll make the reservation. Is a week from Monday what you want?''

She smiled. What she wanted was to be back in his arms right this minute. "That's fine.''

He gazed at her without speaking. Then he took a deep breath. "I think I'd be wise to hit the road,'' he said, picking up his jack-o'-lantern.

"Yes,'' she said with a fond look. "That's best.'' She watched him drive away and wondered if she was a damn fool. He would have stayed the weekend if she'd asked. They could be lovers by now. But she'd made one terrible mistake eight years ago. Falling into Dan's arms now would be like a driver who sees danger, overcorrects and smashes into a different obstacle. As much as she hated to admit it, April was learning caution.

THE BEAUTIFY BOONEVILLE committee ordinarily met each Wednesday afternoon in the library, but it hadn't convened since Irene's death. April decided that a meeting was in order, however, before she went to Chicago. She wanted to be sure the committee was behind her.

First she called Ida Mae, who agreed that the women should gather on Wednesday afternoon, as usual. Irene would have expected them to carry on without undue sentimentality, Ida Mae said. She promised to notify Bess Easley if April would get in touch with Mabel Goodpasture.

On Wednesday a storm blew in, stripping the multicolored leaves from the trees and pelting the town with a heavy rain. April parked the truck in front of the library and stepped over the gutter clogged with soggy brown remnants of fall's splendor. She wasn't fond of this cold, wet prelude to winter and often wished the seasons would go directly from the brightness of autumn leaves to the pristine beauty of the snow.

She skirted puddles on the sidewalk as she hurried through the rain to the library's front door. The snow probably wouldn't arrive for another month, she thought, and then the weather might affect her sculpture plans if the artist wanted to do some of the work on the site. Perhaps she'd have to wait until spring to see the culmination of her dream for the square.

Mabel Goodpasture, a well-endowed woman nearing fifty, was already inside shaking the rain from her black umbrella. "Hello, April. I bet I know what we'll be talking about today. Henry said something about money for a statue, and I knew right away you were behind that."

"I think Irene would have wanted us to continue the beautification program for the square, don't you, Mabel?"

"Oh, absolutely. Although Henry isn't very excited about a statue, I can tell you."

"I know."

"But don't let that worry you," Mabel said over her shoulder as she led the way back toward the periodical section of the library where the committee usually met. "We'll bring him around."

"If you say so." April was awed by the change in Mabel since the beautification committee was formed two years ago. Irene's influence could be seen in that, too. Mabel never used to oppose her husband in anything, but Henry's autocratic days were numbered. Rumor had it that they'd already fought over how the house was to be redecorated and where their oldest child would attend college. Would the sculpture be the next topic of dissension?

As April and Mabel approached the reading area, they were greeted by the steady ping of rain falling into several buckets positioned on the floor and both couches.

Myra Gibbons, Booneville's librarian, hurried forward with another pan. "Oh, ladies, the roof in this section has finally given away. You'll have to move to the children's area for your meeting."

Mabel glanced around at the drips. "I'm not surprised. The roof must be at least forty years old."

"It should be replaced," Myra said, positioning her pan under another leak. "I asked M.G. Tucker to put in for that from the Butler money, but I guess we won't get the roof this year. Too many other projects, M.G. said."

April felt her first stab of guilt over the sculpture. Vaguely she remembered M.G. discussing the library's roof, but when the money was nearly all spoken for, he'd suggested that the sculpture receive the last amount. Of course, it hadn't been raining then, and the roof hadn't started to leak.

By the time Ida Mae arrived with tiny, birdlike Bess in tow, April had worked herself into a lather of indecision. She looked at the four of them, sitting in a circle on tiny chairs with their knees almost to their chins. A leaky roof was more important than art, wasn't it?

Ida Mae finished her discussion with Bess about their two oldest boys, who were in the same grade at school. Then she turned toward April. "Ready to start?"

"Why, yes, of course." April realized she'd been waiting because Irene had always opened the discussions. They had no officers, but Irene had been the one who had taken charge of the meetings. Now the three other committee members were looking to her instead.

"Tell Bess about the statue," Mabel prompted. "Bill's already told Ida Mae, I'm sure."

"Well..." April twisted her hands together. "As you remember, Irene and I had talked about a sculpture for the square, something for the northeast corner that would balance the gazebo on the southwest corner. We didn't have any money for it, but on Saturday the board that is handling Irene's estate income voted an amount for that purpose."

"Terrific!" Bess clapped her hands.

"But now I wonder if we should take it," April added. "You all saw the buckets when you came in. The new library roof wasn't approved for this year, but the sculpture was."

Mabel sat up straighter in her tiny chair. "Oh, we have to have the statue. Let one of Henry's projects wait if we need a new library roof."

April almost laughed but knew she didn't dare. Mabel was absolutely serious about her rebellion. If Henry said the sky was blue, she'd claim it was purple with a completely straight face.

"I have a thought," Ida Mae said. "Bill told me which projects were approved, and I bet if each one of the amounts, including the money for the sculpture, were shaved by, say, ten percent, the library roof could be replaced, too."

"Sure, that sounds good," Bess said immediately. "What do you think, April?"

"I think it will be difficult to find a good sculptor with the money we have now, let alone a smaller amount."

"In all of Chicago?" Ida Mae protested. "Come on, now. I know you and Dan will find someone, even for less money."

Bess looked confused. "What's this about April and Dan in Chicago?"

What indeed? April thought, but she quickly composed her features and explained the plan for selecting a sculptor to Bess, the only one without a connection to the board. "I wanted this meeting," April added, "to make sure the committee trusts me to choose someone."

"Of course we trust you," Bess said. "You've been all over Europe, which is more than the rest of us can say."

"But I'm going next year," Mabel said, squaring her shoulders. "I've tagged along on my last Michigan hunting vacation. Henry can come with me to Europe, or he can go to Michigan alone and shoot things."

Bess stared at Mabel. "You'd go to Europe all by yourself?"

"If I have to."

"My goodness." Bess looked as if she couldn't imagine such independence. Bess was sweet, but not terribly bright, in April's opinion. Irene's brand of spunk hadn't transferred itself to Bess.

"I still wonder if we shouldn't give the whole amount to the library," April said, leaning her chin on her hands. "What do you think Irene would have wanted?"

"Everything," Ida Mae said. "The whole ball of wax."

"Probably," April agreed. "Okay, I'll propose this ten-percent cut to the other members of the board. Somebody will have to call Dan."

"You can do that," Ida Mae said with a wave of her hand.

April lifted an eyebrow in Ida Mae's direction. Her friend was pretty quick to suggest that April be the go-between. "Is there any more business we have to discuss?" she said, changing the subject.

"I think we're out of commission until spring, don't you, April?" asked Mabel. "Except for mulching the flower beds before the first snow and hiring some kids to rake leaves, the statue is about all we can do during the winter. Next spring we can start a campaign for all the businesses on the square to spruce up. I've already told Henry that the bank needs new awnings, and in some other color besides that putrid green.''

"Shall we still meet every week?" April glanced around the group.

"Absolutely," Mabel said. "Even if we can't physically do things, we can plan for warmer weather. Besides, I like getting together."

"So do I," added Bess. "I enjoy the feeling of doing something for Booneville. Let's keep meeting."

"That's fine with me," April said. "Of course next week I'll be in Chicago, but the week after that I'll be anxious to tell you about the trip."

"And we'll want to hear everything," said Bess with a smile. "I think it sounds exciting."

A sudden churning sensation in April's stomach reminded her that Chicago would indeed be exciting. She also doubted that she'd be telling the Beautify Booneville committee everything about her trip.

THE COOL AUTUMN WEATHER seemed to sharpen the edges of the landscape as April merged her old pickup truck with the hundreds of other vehicles funneling into Chicago on Interstate Fifty-seven. After driving the farm roads around Booneville for the past two years, April felt inadequate to the task of navigating the multilaned expressway choked with vehicles, but she was determined to take the Outer Drive and see the water. Lake Michigan was the best thing about Chicago, as far as April was concerned.

She didn't dare take more than occasional glances at the white-capped blue water on her right as she was propelled along with the traffic, but she knew it was there, just the same. The freshness of the lake and the breeze that blew almost continuously from it seemed to sweep Chicago clean of the grime that hung over many other big cities she'd visited.

On her left towered the gray giants of the Chicago sky-line, the man-made peaks from which financial wizards viewed their kingdom. April always got vertigo when she walked down Michigan Avenue and looked up to the top of the tall buildings. Through an optical illusion they appered to lean precariously over the street as if ready to crash down on her at any moment.

She realized that the same illusion made straight rows of corn seem to fan out on the near side of the field and gather to a point on the other. It was called perspective. April preferred the perspective of the fields. Only the expanse of Lake Michigan provided her with the serenity she felt when gazing across acres of farmland punctuated only by tele-phone poles, occasional windbreaks of trees and an isolated grain elevator.

April watched for the first left turn that would take her over to Wabash Avenue and the Palmer House. She'd timed her arrival so that she could check right in, and then she was supposed to call Dan. Her hands trembled as she shifted the truck into a lower gear to take the turn. Somewhere in Chicago was Dan Butler, at home here, not awed by the big city as April still was, even after all her travels abroad. Dan's presence nearby was both reassuring and unsettling. How would her life be changed when she drove away from the city five days from now? Certainly it would not be the same.

The valet at the entrance accepted the keys to her battered truck without a trace of a smile, and a bellhop appeared immediately to take her suitcase, scarred from her vagabond existence with Jimmy. For a brief moment April longed for Booneville's unpretentious way of life, where what she wore and how much she tipped had no relevance.

As she stepped into the lobby, she was glad for the quick shopping trip to Springfield that had yielded the calf-length wool skirt she wore with a very fashionable pair of boots and a soft angora sweater. A few other clothing purchases nestled in the old suitcase that the bellhop carried toward the check-in counter for her. April was determined not to be a hick, not in front of the sculptors she would interview and certainly not in front of Dan. She had forsaken her glasses in favor of her contact lenses for the occasion.

The room was five floors up and had a view of the street below, an amenity not lost on April. Some of the hotel's windows, she knew, looked out on the buildings at either side. Dan had wanted her to have something nicer than that. She realized that she'd missed his brand of thoughtfulness, had almost forgotten what it was like to be cared for in this way.

The room exuded understated elegance through muted colors and dark woods glowing from years of careful polishing. The heavy drapes and thickly carpeted floors hushed the sound within and without so that April could close her eyes and almost forget she was in the middle of a city.

Except she couldn't because the room had the scent of the city, not the farm. Even up here, five stories above the street, she caught the acrid smell of car exhaust. Gone was the fragrance of wet earth turned by a plow, of mown hay in late summer and wood fires in the winter. She couldn't live here, not ever. How did Dan manage?

"Will that be all?" the bellhop asked, placing her suitcase gingerly on the floor as if he feared it might come apart.

"Yes, thank you." April was proud of the way she handed him the tip she had ready in her hand, although she hated the whole process of shoving money at people. Mentally she recorded another strike against city living, where tipping was a way of life. But she was here for five days only, and she could play the game for that long.

When the bellhop left, she rummaged through her purse for Dan's number at work and picked up the receiver of the bedside telephone. This was the third time in a week she'd talked to him on the phone. Last Wednesday night she'd called about shaving ten percent of the funding from the other town projects. After some communication back and forth among the other board members, Dan called her to say everyone was in agreement.

Their conversations had been lean, indicating that neither was willing to wander from the subject of business into the murky waters of their personal lives. There was so much to say, and the telephone didn't seem the way to say it.

A receptionist came on the line at Adonis Sporting Goods and switched April to Dan's office. April tried to picture him there, sitting behind a desk, working with sales reports. Her Dan. *Her Dan?* Where had that come from?

"Dan Butler speaking. May I help you?"

"It's me, Dan. I'm here."

His tone changed from efficient courtesy to genuine warmth. "I thought it might be you. I've been watching the clock. How was the drive?"

After their straightforward conversations last week she hadn't expected this intimate kind of greeting. "Fine," she stammered. "No, not fine, crazy. I should have driven a tractor up here so that I could intimidate some of those kamikaze nuts on the Outer Drive."

Dan laughed. "Is the truck parked now?"

"And for the next five days, thank you. I placed the keys in the gloved hand of the valet. I doubt he's ever driven such a vintage model into the parking garage of the Palmer House."

"Probably not."

"Anyway, it's shoe leather and taxis for me."

"Or my Honda. In fact, I'd hoped to chauffeur you to some galleries this afternoon, but the boss called a sales meeting."

"That's okay. I'll walk to the ones close to the hotel. No problem." She hoped her disappointment wasn't evident in her voice. Of course he had a job, and she shouldn't have expected that he'd pop over here the minute she picked up the phone.

"Dinner, then? Let me take you out somewhere."

"That would be nice but certainly not necessary if you—"

"I thought we were going to get to know each other while you're here?"

"Uh, yes, I suppose we did say that."

"Changed your mind?"

"No. I'd…I'd love to have dinner."

"I'll be there at seven."

"Great." She hung up the phone and immediately ran for her suitcase. This was definitely the night for the black slinky thing she'd found at the last minute during her Springfield shopping spree. She'd shown her mother everything she'd picked out except that dress. One look at that black number and her mother would have wondered what April had in mind for this Chicago trip. Until April had decided about Dan, she didn't want her mother getting funny ideas.

She checked the black dress for wrinkles before hanging it and everything else on the attached wooden hangers in the closet. No wire for this place. Then she checked her watch and discovered she still had several hours to kill before seven o'clock. She might as well spend them doing what she'd told Dan she'd be doing—touring the nearby art galleries. She grabbed her purse and room key and left.

THREE HOURS LATER, as she limped along in the deep shadows of Michigan Avenue in the late afternoon, she cursed herself for hiking around in her new boots before they'd been broken in. By the time she'd realized her problem, it was too late. She debated taking a cab for the last six blocks and decided that was a foolish waste of money.

Back in her room, as she eased the boots from her battered feet and peeled off her nylons, she wished she'd taken the cab. Maybe then the blisters wouldn't have broken.

The bathwater stung her feet, but she hoped somehow to salvage the situation enough to put on the black high heels that went with her dress. Fresh from her bath and feeling a little better, she dressed in black panties and bra and applied her makeup. Then, as a last test before putting on her dress, she gathered the left leg of a pair of black patterned panty hose and tried to ease the material over her foot.

April wasn't a real fan of physical pain. With a yelp she removed the intrument of torture from her foot. If she couldn't stand the stockings, what hope was there for three-inch sling pumps? None, that's what. She couldn't go to dinner tonight, unless Dan favored places that allowed the patrons to dine in bare feet. And she had been so determined not be a hayseed here in the big city. She was willing to bet that a Chicago woman wouldn't march twenty-five blocks in a new pair of boots.

She tried to call Dan at his apartment, but he'd apparently already left. She could do nothing but tell him when he arrived that she'd take a rain check on his offer. Should she admit the truth or invent some excuse about a headache? She was debating the issue when the telephone rang.

"April?"

"Hi, Dan. I was trying to call you."

"I'm in the lobby. Should I come up, or would you rather meet me down here?"

She'd intended to put him off with the headache excuse, but the sound of his voice filled her with yearning. Dammit, she wanted to be with him, blisters or no blisters. "Well, to tell you the truth…" She stalled, searching for a way out of her dilemma. Then her gaze fell upon the leather-bound menu on the walnut writing desk.

"To tell you the truth, Dan," she said, making her decision, "I think it might be more fun to order room service tonight, don't you?"

CHAPTER FIVE

DAN HESITATED only a fraction of a second. "Sure, why not? I can cancel our reservations from your room."

That fraction of a second proved long enough for April to understand what her suggestion must mean to him. She'd invited him to spend the evening in the privacy of her room. Her room had a bed in it.

Well, was making love to him what she wanted tonight? And if so, what about all that talk about "getting to know each other" before taking this precipitous step?

April admitted to herself that she had no idea what she was doing. Maybe the room-service idea had sprung from a natural urge to conceal her stupidity about her new boots. Then again, maybe her subconscious desire to make love to Dan had thrown the suggestion forward, masked as a clever ploy to save her pride.

What now? Dan was on his way up, and she was dressed in her underwear. If she didn't put on some clothes, her decision about the tone of the evening would be made pretty quickly by the man ascending in the hotel elevator.

Until she knew her own mind better, she'd forget the slinky black dress. That would have been fine in a crowded restaurant, but not under the present circumstances. She debated quickly, expecting his knock on the door at any minute.

After rummaging through her limited choices, she finally grabbed a pair of brown wool slacks and a tailored apricot-colored blouse of a material that imitated silk. She pulled the clothes quickly over her black underwear. The elevators must be busy, she thought, when Dan hadn't yet arrived. She took the extra time to brush her hair and check her makeup.

For her tortured feet she chose her comfortable fluffy slippers. Then, when Dan still wasn't at the door, she added the last touch. Racing into the bathroom, she took out her contacts and replaced them with her glasses. There. She looked casual yet conservative, sweet instead of sexy.

The knock came at last, and she gulped with nervousness. What did one say to reverse the thoughts of a man who thought he'd been subtly propositioned? April elected to say nothing and let her appearance speak for her.

From his shocked expression when she opened the door, April figured that her appearance must have spoken volumes. She almost laughed as he stared in disbelief at her slacks, blouse and fluffy slippers. She wondered if his fantasy had been a revealing negligee, sexy loungewear, or perhaps Saran Wrap and a smile.

He, on the other hand, had worn the perfect counterpart to her black dress. A topcoat was folded over one arm, and April noticed that he looked even better in a tux now than the first and only time she'd seen him wear one—at the senior prom when they broke up.

"I stopped at the bar and ordered a bottle of wine to be sent up," he began uncertainly. "Should I cancel the order?"

"Why?"

"Well, I—" He stopped speaking, apparently unable to admit that the wine had been part of a seduction scene that he now doubted would take place.

His discomfort bothered her. He was, after all, an old friend and deserved to know exactly why she'd suggested this intimate dinner. "Oh, Dan, come in and sit down. I'll explain everything. Let me take your coat. In fact, both your coats. I've caused you to dress up for no reason, all because of my own stupidity.''

"What stupidity?'' He handed her his tux jacket and his topcoat.

"I'll tell you when we're settled.'' She wondered what it was about a white pleated shirt and a black satin cummerbund that were so compelling. Maybe she hadn't seen enough men dressed up like this, and the novelty of formal clothes attracted her. To avoid acting like a hayseed, she'd better not stand around staring, either. She walked to the closet and hung both coats on hangers.

"Shall I ditch the tie, too?''

April turned around. "That's the kind you have to tie yourself, isn't it?'' she asked with a grimace. "I'll bet you spent ten minutes getting it right.''

"Twelve.''

"I feel like a jerk.''

"Don't.'' Dan pulled the tie until the two ends dangled on either side of the row of pearly studs down the middle of the shirt. Then he unfastened the collar button and took out the first stud and put it in his pocket. "But I'd sure like to know what's going on. What's the matter?''

Nothing, April thought, watching him take the studs from his cuffs and roll the shirtsleeves back over his muscular forearms. Talk about making lemonade from lemons. If Dan looked handsome in the tux, he looked sexy as hell half out of it. She wasn't sure what she was doing, but she liked the way it was turning out.

"Well, I did something dumb,'' April began, crossing to the small table and two chairs positioned by the window. "I'll show you.'' She sat down and eased off one of her slippers. "Look at this.''

Dan crossed to the chair and glanced down at her foot. "Ouch.'' He knelt in front of her and took the blistered foot in both hands. "You'll never make it to the ball this way, Cinderella.''

She repressed a shiver of delight as he cradled her foot
in his palm and examined the broken skin on her heel and
her little toe. "I knew I should have turned one of those
pumpkins into a coach before I left the farm."

He glanced up from his appraisal. "New shoes?"

April nodded. "Boots. You'd think I was a kid on the
first day of school. Remember how we used to suffer after
a barefoot summer? The first day we'd wear our new shoes
and then limp around slathered in Band-Aids for days afterward."

He rubbed his thumb tenderly along her instep. "I hope
you had some luck at the art galleries, considering how you
sacrificed your feet this afternoon."

"Not really." She tried to keep her tone light, although
it wasn't easy while he was stroking her foot like that. "I've
learned that finding a sculptor willing to work for the
amount we have to spend won't be easy."

"You didn't come up with any names at all?"

"Not this time out."

"Poor April." Without warning, he bent and placed his
lips against the vein that ran across the top of her foot.

"Dan!" The touch of his mouth on such an unexpected
part of her body brought a rush of desire that embarrassed
her. "Don't be silly," she protested with faint conviction,
pulling her foot away.

He placed both hands on his knees and gazed at her
steadily, his blue eyes smoldering. "Are you afraid of me,
April?"

"Why would you think such a ridiculous thing?" She
smoothed the fur of the slipper with her hands to stop them
from trembling. "I've known you practically forever."

"That's not what you said when I saw you last, after the
big pumpkin sale. You said a lot of time had gone by, and
we didn't know each other well at all. You acted afraid then,
too."

"That wasn't afraid, that was cautious."

He lifted a dark eyebrow. "Cautious? You?"

"Yes, sometimes. I told you I'm not the same person I was eight years ago."

"Is that why you're dressed like a schoolteacher tonight?"

April straightened in the chair. "I'm sorry if you're disappointed. I have a limited supply of clothes, and this happens to be—"

"The least provocative thing you could find on short notice. I'm glad you didn't have more time before I arrived. You might have spread cream on your face and put your hair up in rollers."

"You're exaggerating."

"And the glasses, April. The glasses are a dead giveaway. We may have been apart for eight years, but there are some things I remember very well. One is that you hide behind those glasses when you don't want anybody to think of you as a sexy woman. It may work for the general public, but as for—"

A knock at the door interrupted him.

"The wine. What timing." Dan sighed and got to his feet. "Maybe it's good timing, at that. The situation seems to call for it."

"What situation?"

Dan half turned on his way to the door. "Getting to know you, Mrs. Foster."

Mrs. Foster. In point of fact that's who she was, although hearing it from Dan, spoken in that tone, made her cringe. She wished now that she'd asked the judge to reinstate her maiden name, but she hadn't thought of it at the time of her divorce.

While Dan answered the door, April looked down at her feet, one bare and one clad in a fluffy slipper. She took the other slipper off. Why was everything so complicated all of a sudden, just because she'd got blisters on her feet and couldn't go out? But things *were* complicated, and signals were getting mixed, partly because she had no clear idea of where she wanted to go from here.

The waiter entered the room bearing the wine and two glasses on a tray balanced head-high. He placed the tray with a flourish on the table next to April. She felt slightly uncomfortable with this stranger in the room. Was he wondering what the arrangement was here, with the room in her name and a man keeping her company in it? Probably not. He was paid not to wonder anything. This was the big city, not Booneville, she reminded herself. People's private lives belonged to them alone.

Still, she stood and padded over to the desk containing the room-service menu. "We may as well order now, don't you think?" she asked Dan in a tone meant to convey casual friendship instead of rampant passion.

"If you like," he replied, watching her carefully.

April looked at the waiter. "Can you take our order for dinner?"

"Certainly, ma'am."

"Then I'll have this." She pointed absently to an item under the entrées before handing the menu to Dan.

"I'll have the same," he said, closing the leather cover and tossing the menu back on the desk.

"Very good, sir." The waiter handed Dan a glass with a small amount of wine in the bottom.

"You'd better let her taste it." Dan motioned to April. "She's been to Europe, and she knows more about this than I do."

April glanced at him. One thing was becoming clear to her. They'd have to discuss her marriage to Jimmy. She waved the glass away. "I'm sure it's fine."

"Very well." The waiter poured their glasses half-full and set the bottle on the tray. As he headed for the door, Dan followed him, murmuring a few things April couldn't hear while he handed over the tip.

After closing the door, Dan returned to the table and picked up his glass. "To Auld Lang Syne."

April touched her glass to his. "To new discoveries."

"You can't make discoveries if you're afraid," he reminded her gently.

"Cautious."

"Right. Cautious." He sipped his wine.

"I'd...I'd like to tell you about him, Dan. About Jimmy."

He looked away. "I'm not sure I want to hear."

"Yes, you do. Some of this must be said, or it will fester between us forever. Can't we sit here at this table and bring each other up-to-date like normal friends who've been separated?"

"Is that what we were, normal friends? Funny, but I thought we were more than that to each other, once upon a time, before the clock struck midnight and the coachman turned into a rat."

April saw the hurt still lingering behind his offhand response. After eight years her defection still had the power to bring pain to his eyes. Well, if that weren't so, would they have any basis for building something again? Hurt and anger were better than indifference, weren't they?

She put her hand on his arm and felt the tenseness there. "We were more than just friends," she said softly. "That's why we have to talk about it, about what happened, if we're ever to be more than friends again."

"Okay." Dan sighed and sat down, curling his spine against the rigid lines of the chair. "Tell me about Jimmy Foster. Tell me why I shouldn't hate his guts."

"If you're going to hate anyone, you should hate me," April said, pacing in front of him. "I encouraged Jimmy."

His question, the one that must have burned in him for eight years, came roaring forth like thunder. "Why, dammit?"

"Because I thought you didn't want me."

"Good God."

"Or didn't want me enough," she amended. "Enough to ask me to marry you right then so that we could be together. Oh, Dan, I'd had enough of waiting, of wanting and not having."

"And you thought I hadn't? You thought you were the only one fighting your hormones in the backseat of that old Chevy? When I think of all the times that I almost—"

"But you didn't because you always maintained your control. I both admired and hated that quality in you."

"Me, too. Especially after all that waiting and Jimmy Foster stepped in."

There it was, spelled out. She supposed Dan had a right to be bitter, when after all his nights of stern resolve, Jimmy Foster became her first lover. She poured herself another glass of wine while she debated whether to tell him the most important part of all. "Would it matter to know that my...relationship...with him wasn't very satisfying?"

His glare was chilling. "No." Silence. "Yes, dammit, I suppose so. If I were a nobler sort, I'd be sorry that you had a rotten time with him, but I'm not that noble. I'm glad that Jimmy Foster wasn't all that you'd hoped when you rode off with him on that ridiculous tractor covered with crepe paper."

"You heard about that?"

"You hear about everything in Booneville. Except what you just told me about your private life with him. I have to assume I'm the first person you've ever told, or I'd probably have heard that, too."

"You are the first person. I'm a little ashamed—no, a lot ashamed—that I wasn't a better wife to Jimmy. He had reason to leave, Dan."

He shook his head. "I can't imagine how he could leave, once he had you. I couldn't imagine anyone being that kind of fool."

"That's because you don't know how I was. After the

first year or so, when the infatuation had worn off, I dreaded having him touch me. My parents wondered why we didn't have any kids. They didn't know that we seldom had sex, and when we did, I insisted on birth control. I didn't want his children. I kept telling myself that things would get better, but they didn't. He finally left.''

Dan closed his eyes, masking his own pain and the sympathy he didn't want to feel for another man. "Poor bastard," he said at last.

"Yes." April sank to the chair opposite him. "There isn't much more to tell about me. The strange thing is, I think your story may be happier than mine, although you took the greater blow eight years ago."

"Maybe you're right." Dan stared into his wineglass, not speaking for several minutes. "I didn't have your problem, anyway. I went beyond the infatuation point at least twice, but..." He swallowed the last of his wine and gazed at her.

"What?"

"Never mind." He set his glass on the table. "So marrying Jimmy was only a maneuver to get back at me because I didn't want you enough, or so you thought. If I had swept you off your feet, if I had lost control just once in the backseat of that Chevy..."

"The story would have been different," April said softly.

"Are you telling me that my care and consideration for our future landed us in this mess?"

"At eighteen I wanted impetuosity, Dan." April smiled ruefully and looked away. "Perhaps I still do, a little, even at twenty-seven."

Dan rose from his chair. "All right, dammit, I can be just as—" Another knock sounded at the door and Dan paused. "Our dinner just arrived."

"Yes, I think so."

"I guess we should let the man in."

"I guess we should." April gazed at his retreating back with a stab of disappointment. Had she expected that he'd send the waiter back to the kitchen and throw her on the bed after her declared need for spontaneity? Maybe. But he hadn't exactly done that, although for a minute she thought he might have been close.

The waiter carefully created a romantic setting by turning down lamps and lighting candles on the table he wheeled into the room. After he left, April glanced at Dan in appreciation. "This is really lovely. I've never had a candlelit dinner in my own hotel room before. You arranged this with him, didn't you?"

"Yes, but I have the strangest feeling that you might have wanted me to do something else a minute ago."

"Nonsense. This is wonderful."

Dan held her chair. "I guess it's a little more impressive than Jesse's Café."

"Just a little."

For a moment, as Dan hesitated with his hands still resting on the back of her chair, April wondered if he was still thinking about whether to forget dinner. Then he removed his hands and walked to his side of the linen-covered table.

Her sigh of disappointment was so faint that he couldn't have heard, yet he gave her a piercing glance as he sat down and unfolded his napkin. She followed suit, smoothing the soft cloth into her lap before picking up her fork. Then she began to laugh.

"What's funny?"

"I just realized that I ordered chicken."

"You didn't know what we were getting?"

"I wasn't paying much attention. I sort of closed my eyes and chose something. Apparently I chose chicken, of all things, although this is the most exotic-looking chicken dish I've ever seen."

"At these prices, I should hope so."

"Don't worry. I'm paying for this as part of my room bill."

He looked at her. "Who said you were paying for the room?"

"Now wait a minute, Dan."

"No, *you* wait a minute. These five days are on me."

"I'm not sure I like that. I'd feel too much like a kept woman if I accepted such generosity."

"How you feel is entirely up to you."

"Is it?"

"That's right. This is your room, not mine. I, uh, think maybe I owe you a few days at the Palmer House."

"Owe me? What on earth do you mean?"

"Don't you remember?" he asked softly.

She frowned, searching for the meaning of his tender look. Then she found it. "Oh, Lord. Of course." So many years ago, when they were both still in high school, two young lovers had planned the distant prospect of their honeymoon and picked the most elegant place they had ever heard of—the Palmer House in Chicago. In the turbulent times that followed, April had forgotten about the honeymoon, especially when Dan hadn't proposed on the night of the prom.

She gazed at the mature man sitting across from her. In another year he'd be thirty. Already faint lines crinkled at the corners of his eyes, and his smile lines were deepening, too. "We were so young, Dan."

"I guess we were." He laid down his fork and folded his napkin. "And I loved you more than anything in life."

His statement hit her like a blow. He had loved her more than anything in life, and she had thrown that love back in his face when she married another. Her appetite for the gourmet dinner was gone, and obviously so was his. Her words came out almost as a whisper. "I...I don't suppose there's any forgiving what I did, is there?"

"Yes, there is." He pushed back his chair and stood up. "But I think we've raked each other over the coals enough for one night."

She wasn't sure what to expect until he turned from her and walked toward the closet. Then she realized he was leaving. Leaving? She sat there, churning with indecision. Hadn't she wanted some time for just what had happened tonight, for some communication, some understanding between them before they made a decision whether to become closer than friends?

"I'll call you tomorrow. Maybe I'll be able to get the afternoon off, and we can tour some galleries together. And take a taxi if you go out, will you? Those feet are a mess."

With that he was gone. She stared at the closed door, stunned that he would disappear so quickly, so irrevocably. The candles still flickered on the table. More than half their meal remained on their plates, uneaten. Gradually she became aware of an aching sense of loss and realized that she had made a decision about how this evening would end, and it wasn't like this.

Throwing her napkin down, she bolted from the table and raced across the plush carpet to the door. Flinging it open, she dashed down the hall to the elevator and punched the button. Could she possibly catch him?

The elevator next to her slid open, but the arrows indicated it was going up, not down. She turned back impatiently to the one in front of her. "Come on, dammit," she muttered.

"Going somewhere?"

She spun at the sound of his voice. "Dan!"

"You crazy, barefoot woman."

She hurtled across the space between them, and he crushed her in his arms.

CHAPTER SIX

THEY CLUNG TO EACH OTHER, laughing between kisses, working around the impediment of her glasses until Dan took them off with a growl of frustration.

"You might as well not use these with me, April," he said, tucking them in the pocket of his topcoat before gathering her close once more. "They don't work."

"What? I can see perfectly well with—"

"You know what I mean," he said, nuzzling behind her ear.

"Yes." His caresses made her breathless. "I never wanted them to work, anyway. But I didn't know that until you left."

"As you notice, I haven't left. I couldn't." Dan gazed into her flushed face. "I should. I should go this minute. Oh, April—"

"Come back to the room." She caught his hand and tugged. "Your dinner's getting cold."

"To hell with my dinner." He slipped his arm around her waist and held her against his side as they walked down the hall.

"That's what I wanted you to say the first time."

"I know it. Don't you think I know it?" He tilted his head back in frustration. "Butler, will you ever learn?"

"You came back, Dan. That counts for something."

"I hope so. I need all the points I can get."

They stepped through the door that April had left open when she ran to the elevator. She glanced at him sheepishly.

"I didn't even close and lock the door. Pretty irresponsible, huh?"

Dan nudged the door shut with his foot and tipped her face up to his. "Do you honestly expect me to complain because you wanted me so much that you raced out of here without locking up?"

"I did want you so much," she admitted, losing all false pride as she witnessed the unchecked desire blazing in his eyes.

He touched her cheek with his open palm, and she realized he was trembling. "You need to know something because I don't always have the sense to tell you. I want you just as much, April. Every bit as much." He took a deep, steadying breath. "And now let's lock that door." He released her long enough to hang the Do Not Disturb sign on the front knob. Then he closed and locked the door.

Taking off his coat and tux jacket, he dropped them across the desk chair. Then he eliminated the distance between them and drew her close. "Let's start over."

She gazed up at him, questioning.

"Just for tonight," he said with a smile. "I'm not asking either of us to go back eight years. I doubt if we could."

"Probably not. But sometimes…"

"Yeah, me, too." He traced the line of her eyebrow. "God, but you're beautiful."

"I don't…think you've ever told me that."

"I haven't?"

April shook her head.

His lips hovered above hers, and his breath was warm and sweet on her face. "Then forgive me for being an idiot. A very young idiot."

"Perhaps we both can forgive, Dan."

He lowered his head. "I can't think of a better way to start than this."

She met the open hunger of his lips with her own. Greedily they tasted each other, tongues exploring in patterns established long ago, patterns now vested with new urgency and meaning. This time, at last, there would be no stopping.

April splayed her fingers across the pleated front of Dan's white shirt and stroked the muscled breadth of his chest. He groaned in response, reaching for the hem of her blouse to tug it from the waistband of her slacks. As he slipped both hands beneath the fabric and gripped her waist to mold her against his body, April gasped at the wild surging of a desire that she'd almost forgotten could exist.

Fitting her pelvis to his, she brushed against his aroused manhood. Long ago this pulsing hardness beneath the material of his trousers had frightened her a little, but now she ached for the completion promised by his fullness pressing against her.

"All those nights in the Chevy," Dan murmured, working down the buttons of her blouse. "Do you remember? I lived for those few moments when I could touch your breasts and love you that much, at least. Even though I knew the agony I'd face, trying to hold back from doing more, I was crazy for those magic times."

"So was I. You made me a little crazy, too. Your hands felt so good."

"You remember?" He pushed her blouse off her shoulders and away from her and unfastened the front clasp of her bra.

"I've never forgotten. Oh, Dan…" She moaned as he cupped one of her breasts in his palm and stroked the tip with his thumb.

He kissed her lips and tasted the salt of her tears. "Don't cry," he murmured.

"I've…I've missed you."

"I hope so."

"All those wasted years…"

"Don't think of that now. Don't think at all." He unfastened her slacks, and they slid to the floor. She stepped out of them and kicked them away. Then with a quick shrug she discarded her bra.

He stood back, needing to see her, for the first time, in the light. He sucked in his breath. Women like April were the reason artists painted nudes, he thought. The round perfection of her breasts was something he'd only guessed at in the dim interior of the Chevy. She was a study in symmetry, with her narrow waist and gently flared hips.

He gazed at the triangle of black lace that mapped the last uncharted territory, the place he'd never dared to go during those nights when they'd steamed up the car windows with their youthful passion. Black lace. What had she been imagining when she chose to wear it tonight? His voice was hoarse. "You're...magnificent."

His words seemed to startle her into shyness. "I'm not eighteen anymore. I'm afraid that I'm not as—"

"Yes, you are," he said unsteadily, fighting the urge to rip the last barrier away. Instead, he gathered her close until her breasts pushed against the crisp white of his shirt. "You're more. You're not a fragile young girl now."

"I was never fragile," she murmured, kissing the cleft in his chin. "You just thought so. Sometimes you treated me like a china doll."

With a groan he kissed her hard, plunging his tongue into her mouth, as if to tell her that time was over. His hand swept downward, pulling the lower half of her body tight against the ache that was becoming unbearable. The texture of the material stretching across her silken skin was an affront to his touch, but he knew it would soon be gone.

His kiss slid down the arch of her throat to her collarbone. They were both gasping for breath. "Whatever you were before, you're all woman now."

"Yes." She shuddered and closed her eyes when he bent his head and took her nipple in his mouth. The love games they'd played as teenagers seemed insignificant compared to the heat he was building in her now with the pressure of his teeth and lips. All woman. His woman. She couldn't change that, even if she tried. Tonight he was claiming her body with the natural assurance he'd lacked eight years ago, and she had no defenses against him. But then, she'd probably never had any where Dan was concerned.

When he slid his hands beneath the elastic of her panties, the sensation was the same as if she'd touched a live wire. This was the border beyond which they'd never crossed. They were crossing it now, as Dan knelt before her, drawing the black garment down as his lips and tongue caressed the flat plane of her belly.

Had it been any other man, she would have pulled away in embarrassment as he kissed the damp curls that he slowly uncovered, but she could deny him nothing. Soon any reluctance she felt vanished. He'd found the center of her need for him, and she was aware of nothing but the dizzying pleasure he provided.

When her knees threatened to buckle, he wrapped her in his arms, steadying her while he loved her in a way she'd never known, never allowed before. The hollow ache inside became mind-shattering. She tossed her head from side to side and moaned his name. "Please," she cried. "I want to have...all of you."

In answer he swung her into his arms and carried her to the bed. He put her down on top of the spread, not bothering to turn back the covers. She didn't care.

"Love me," she begged, pulling his head down and fitting her mouth to his. She tasted the exotic flavor of her own desire on his lips, and she whimpered with her desperate passion. She fumbled with the studs of his shirt.

Changing their deep kiss to quick, nipping forays, he gradually drew away from her. "Let me take care of that," he said, stilling the frantic movements of her hands. His breathing was rapid and shallow as he worked with the studs, having only slightly better success than she. At last he got them out and wrenched the shirt away. Then he pulled off his shoes and socks and the black satin cummerbund.

When he stood up and stepped out of the dark tuxedo pants, April gazed at him without shame. He was clad only in a pair of tight navy briefs that made his arousal nearly as evident as if he'd had nothing on. "I want you," she whispered. "Come here."

His glance flicked over her, lying naked on the red-and-gold patterned spread, and he shook with the force of his desire. She was so ready for him, skin pink from the friction of his hands and his mouth, and there, where he would sink into the depths of her, the dark curls were damp with passion.

He wanted to strip the briefs from his heated body and bury himself in her now, without waiting. He knew she wouldn't question him if he did. She'd said she wanted impetuosity. Yet he couldn't completely forget his responsibilities. His training ran too deep. "Just a minute," he said softly. "There's something I have to get." He went to the desk and reached into the pocket of his coat.

"Dan?"

He returned to her and leaned down to kiss her swollen lips. "Some things can't be impulsive, April," he murmured. "God, I wish they could."

She reached up and cradled his face in her hands as his meaning became clear. "You're talking about birth control."

"Yes."

"But when..."

"It didn't take me that long just to order wine."

Her eyes filled with tears of chagrin. "Here I blame you for not being spontaneous, and then you save us from... from—"

"Hush, April. Just kiss me."

She did, using every inch of her body, caressing his bare skin as she welcomed the pressure of his hair-sprinkled chest, the hard-muscled leanness of his thighs separating hers. He cupped her bottom in both hands and lifted her to meet his first thrust.

At the moment he entered her, he whispered her name, and she knew she would never forget that urgent, breathless cry. It told her, more than a million spoken words would have, what she needed to know. Whether he admitted the truth or chose to keep silent didn't really matter. He still loved her.

The thought brought her immense joy, followed soon after by a deep, abiding guilt. He still loved her, after all she'd done to make his life miserable. Her frantic desire abated as those eight long years played themselves out in her mind. The memories came between April and her pleasure, draining away the promise of fulfillment.

But Dan deserved more. She wrapped her arms around his sweat-soaked body and moved with him, wanting him to have the completion she couldn't find. When it was over, he might be angry, but for now he'd have the satisfaction he'd waited so long for.

"April," he groaned, "not so…wait, I can't—" He tried to hold her still with the weight of his body.

"It's okay," she whispered, urging him on.

"No. I want—"

"Let go, Dan. Let go."

With a moan that spoke of both ecstasy and despair he gave up his fight for control in an explosive climax. Slowly he sank against her, his body trembling with the aftershock. She held him close and savored her own elation that he'd had this, at least. Now he'd probably leave her, and that would be the end. Men didn't care for women who couldn't respond instantly. Jimmy had taught her that. She waited sadly for his first words.

His labored breathing gradually returned to normal. "Oh, April," he murmured, nuzzling behind her ear. "Next time will be better, especially if you can hold still once in a while. Don't give up on me.''

"What do you mean? It's not your fault. I was the one who—''

"Yes, but if I'd had more control, everything might have been different. I was afraid this would happen, after all these years, but have patience. We'll get it right.''

"But…how do you know? Maybe that's just the way I am. Maybe I'm not any good at this.''

His soft laughter rocked them both.

"What's so funny?''

He raised himself on one elbow and gazed down at her with a broad smile. "You. I realize what probably happened. Somewhere along the way you started thinking again, that's all. I warned you about that.''

April began to relax. Here was a man who was so secure that he wasn't going to blame her if the experience wasn't everything it could be. What a miracle. He didn't consider her a disappointment. He even seemed to understand. "I did start to think,'' she admitted. "About how I'd loused things up and never gave us a chance.''

Dan's voice and gaze caressed her. "We have that chance now. Unless you're going to spend all your time thinking, that is.'' He stroked the hair back from her forehead and kissed her there. Then he began lightly rubbing her shoulder and arm in an almost nonsexual way, making no attempt to touch the more sensitive area of her breasts.

As her nervous tension over their first encounter subsided, April felt the warmth of renewed desire prickle her skin. She caught her lip between her teeth and glanced up at him.

"Oh, April, I like the look in those big brown eyes.''

"Dan, I—''

"Keep that thought.'' Gently he levered himself away from her. "I'll be right back.''

While he was gone, April recalled the rhythmic excitement as he had moved within her, the urgent force of his thrusting body and the beautiful moment of his climax. This time she vowed to experience that with him, to be a total participant in their lovemaking instead of an observer.

Swinging her legs over the side of the bed, she stood up. Then she threw back the covers and stretched out on the cool white sheets. She moved her hips restlessly and enjoyed the heat created by the friction of the sheet against her skin. Her nipples tightened into hard buds as she remembered the sensation of Dan's lips and teeth closing around them. Yes, he knew how to love her, if she'd let him. And she would let him.

She turned her head on the goose-down pillow and found him standing beside the bed gazing at her. Silently she held out her hand. Grasping it, he lay down beside her, his blue eyes intent on her face.

April licked her dry lips. "I think this time will be different."

"That's nice."

"I want to touch you."

"That would be even nicer."

Slowly she moved her hand downward over his belly until her fingers closed over the velvet shaft that could give her such pleasure if she put aside her guilt and regret over what was past. She closed her eyes and caressed him. His skin was so smooth there, so tight with desire, desire for her. The drenching force of her own passion built as she stroked him.

He moaned and she opened her eyes. She watched with growing excitement as his eyes glazed with passion and his jaw clenched with the force of his attempt at restraint. His need fueled hers, and she began to shake.

"Now," she whispered.

He nodded, unable to speak. He turned away for a moment and then was back, hovering above her. She grasped his hips and pulled him down, down into the moist depths of her innermost self. She was centered there, waiting for him. All else had disappeared. Nothing remained but this joining; nothing mattered but the jolt of feeling every time he pushed forward, the spiraling tension that once had led nowhere and now had a destination.

Inarticulate cries splintered the silence as he brought her closer, ever closer to release. Their bodies became slippery with desire, their muscles as tight as coiled springs. They surged together again and again, each time shuddering in reaction.

With April's last rational moment she called his name before the world became a whirling carnival ride ablaze with lights and color such as she'd never known before. Dimly through the turmoil buffeting her she felt his strong arms around her and his whispered words of love before he joined her in a wild jubilation of fulfillment.

She had no idea how long they lay together in total abandonment. It could have been minutes or hours before Dan left the bed briefly and then returned to lie beside her.

She touched his cheek. "Thank you."

"You did it, not me."

"I'm not so sure. Anyway, you gave me a second chance."

"What fool wouldn't?"

"Dan, all men aren't as sensitive as you are. I learned that lesson the hard way."

He gazed at her thoughtfully. "I'd say old Jimmy has a lot to answer for, after all."

"He was young, too." April traced the fullness of Dan's bottom lip. "Maybe this has all worked out for the best."

"At this particular moment you won't get any arguments from me on that."

"Maybe we weren't ready for each other eight years ago."

"And now?"

She realized how quickly the conversation had turned to the subject of commitment, and this was only the first day of her Chicago visit. Was she in any shape to comment on their relationship, after he'd just given her the most wonderful lovemaking experience of her life? If he asked her to marry him, she'd probably say yes. If he asked her to jump from the top of the John Hancock Center, she'd probably do that, too.

"Let's enjoy this week," she said, smiling to take the sting out of her words, "without thinking about the future just yet. Do you mind?"

A shadow darkened his blue eyes. "Of course not," he said, but his tone betrayed the lie in his words.

"Dan, I've hurt your feelings."

"No." He sighed. "Well, a little. But you're right. I guess now that I've found you again, I want to wrap everything up in a neat little package. That's my personality, you know."

"I know." She tried to laugh but didn't quite make it. The sound was more like a cough. Practical Dan. What she really wanted, she realized, was a romantic courtship in which he wooed her as if he had some doubt about the outcome. As Jimmy had done, perhaps? But that had been such a mess. Still, she wanted more than an easy slipping into the old ways, in which he took their pairing for granted.

Yet she loved the tender way Dan cared for her, and that was part of his personality, too. Was she asking too much to have both in one man, this man?

CHAPTER SEVEN

DAN LEFT APRIL'S BED in the early hours of the morning and fumbled with his clothes.

Sleepily she rolled to one side and watched him dress. "I wish you didn't have to go."

"Me, too." He bent to give her a quick kiss before tucking in his shirt. "But hardly anyone wears a tux to work at Adonis Sporting Goods."

"Will you have to put in a whole day?"

"Not if I can help it. With any luck I can take the afternoon off, buy you lunch and tour some art galleries afterward."

"That's not necessary. You should probably sleep instead. I'm lousing up your schedule, Dan." She remembered how scrupulous he'd been about keeping training hours when he was a football player.

"Are you kidding?" He sat beside her on the bed and smoothed her hair.

"No. I remember how you used to be about getting your eight hours. I'd stay up all night studying for some test, but not you. You always said sleep was the most important thing, that you couldn't function without it."

He looked down at her and shook his head. "That sounds like me, all right. I even thought about those wonderful sleep requirements of mine when I knew you would be here for five days."

"See? And now it's—" she raised herself on one elbow and looked at the red numbers glowing from the digital clock by the bed "—three-twenty. You'll be lucky to get four hours now."

He smiled. "Three. Unless I skip my morning workout."

"I feel terrible."

"You should." As he leaned down and nuzzled her earlobe, he breathed in the shampoo-fresh scent of her hair. In high school the smell of her hair used to drive him wild. Used to? At this very moment he was wondering if he might be able to stay another hour and still make it to work in some sort of shape.

He couldn't remember ever being this obsessive about a woman. Besides, of all the women in the world this was the one he should avoid. Her track record was terrible with regard to stomping all over his feelings. Yet his appetite for her was insatiable, and he wanted to make the most of every minute she was in Chicago.

"Dan." She grasped his head in both hands and forced him to look at her. "Go home."

"I don't want to. For some reason, sleep has lost all its appeal."

"You'll hate me today while you're propped in your desk chair trying to stay awake, or worse, calling on some client and dozing off in the middle of your sales pitch."

"I doubt I'll hate you, April. Maybe I should just quit my job. It's getting in the way."

She laughed. "Such talk."

"I'm half-serious. Anyway, let's organize this whole thing better."

"Now that's the Dan I know."

"Move to my apartment for the rest of your stay."

She raised both eyebrows.

"Don't worry. Nobody from Booneville has to know about it. You've seen the inside of the Palmer House, so you can describe the room perfectly to Mabel Goodpasture or Bess Easley."

"How did you know what I was thinking? Or that I'd have to describe anything to those two?"

"I also grew up in Booneville, don't forget."

"Well, you're right that I must be able to discuss the decor of my fabulous room, as much to give them a vicarious experience as to prove I stayed here and not with you. But, Dan, I really didn't intend for us to—"

"Live together?"

"I guess that's the expression."

"We're talking about four days, April, not a lifetime." He realized as he said the words that he wasn't talking about four days at all. But he'd settle for that right now. He'd settle for a diet of bread and water and rags to wear if he could have her in his own bed for one more night, let alone four.

"I...when would you want me to check out of here? I don't think three-thirty in the morning is exactly—"

His heart began to pound with excitement. She was considering his offer. "Of course it isn't. I'm the only one who has to go rushing off into the night. You can leave later today, say around noon, the normal checkout time. Sleep in this morning. Order breakfast, and pack. I'll pick you up for lunch and the gallery tour, and then we'll head back to my place. How's that?"

"Unfair. You'll be slaving away all morning and squiring me around all afternoon while I play the Queen of Sheba."

"You can make it up to me later."

"I doubt it. You'll be too exhausted."

He gazed into the limitless depths of her brown eyes. "Somehow I don't think so. Have we got a deal?"

"What if you can't get the afternoon off? I'll be checked out with nowhere to go, and I hardly think I'll traipse over to your apartment by myself."

He decided the fencing was over and spoke with firm authority. "I'll get the afternoon off. I'll be in the lobby at twelve to pick you up."

Her capitulation was immediate. "Okay."

Dan took a deep breath. She was his for the next four days.

APRIL WAS SITTING in the lobby, her well-worn suitcase by her side, when Dan walked through the revolving door precisely at noon. The sight of him infected her with the same excitement she used to feel as a child each time she came downstairs on Christmas morning. The expression on his face reflected the same sort of emotion, and April wondered if they were goners, both of them.

She'd stayed awake thinking of him long after he'd left this morning, and even when she'd closed her eyes, his blue gaze had haunted her fretful dreams. It occurred to her that she might be falling in love, but she didn't quite trust her judgment on that score.

She loved how he loved her, but what about the rest, the daily routine of living? April wasn't sure how they'd get along, considering his basically conservative nature. The next four days should be very interesting.

But the next four nights would be more than interesting, she thought as he strode toward her. How typical of him to remember birth control last night, when she'd forgotten completely about that little detail. It wasn't such a little detail, either. Neither of them were in a position to deal with an unplanned pregnancy.

She stood up, wondering what to say as he drew near. Everything was so different between them now. As he approached and she looked into his eyes, her nipples tightened and she felt a fluttering awareness at the apex of her thighs. No one had ever affected her that way with a mere glance, not even Dan eight years ago. But he wasn't quite the same man, and after last night she wasn't at all the same woman. Words of greeting lodged in her throat.

For a moment he didn't speak, either, as they silently assessed each other in the light of day, with all their clothes

on and only a few short hours separating them from their
last passionate embrace.

Dan cleared his throat. "How're your feet?"

"My feet? Oh—" She looked down at them in surprise.
Her feet weren't the part of her clamoring for attention right
now, and she'd forgotten about their pivotal role in last
night's chain of events. "They're fine as long as I have on
these flat shoes, but that's all I can stand to wear."

He coughed into his fist. "Don't I wish."

She looked up at him, startled, and then they both started
to laugh. "Lecher," she said under her breath so that only
he could hear. It excited her to know he was thinking the
same thoughts as she.

"So I'm discovering."

"At least you're a punctual one. It's exactly twelve.
You're right on time, as usual."

"So are you, I might point out," he said, gathering her
close against his unbuttoned coat. "I've missed you."

He carried the scent of the cold, fresh wind blowing in
from the lake, and when she stood on tiptoe to kiss his
cheek, his skin was cool. "I've missed you, too."

He drew back with a wry grin. "Not much, judging from
that sisterly peck on the cheek. Although I have taken note
of the fact you're wearing your contacts, and we all know
what that means. Come on, can't you give me a better welcome?"

"Dan, we're in the middle of a hotel lobby."

"That's right. I keep forgetting that you're not used to
this big anonymous city. Believe me, April, you won't start
any gossip if you give me a decent kiss."

She needed no more encouragement, with his lips so in-
triguingly close and the memory of last night as fresh as
morning coffee. Winding her arms around his neck, she
kissed him fully on the mouth.

With a muffled groan he tightened his grip around her
waist, and she could feel his heart thudding as they pressed

together in full view of hotel clerks and bellhops. Within seconds April forgot everything except the erotic thrust of Dan's tongue as he reminded her eloquently of their last encounter.

Slowly he released her. "Much better," he said, struggling to bring his breathing back to normal. "Too good, in fact. Maybe you knew what you were doing with that peck on the cheek."

April flushed. "Everything's taken care of at the desk. Let's get out of here."

"That means you paid," Dan said, helping her on with her coat. "I had planned to do that. Should have gotten here early, I guess."

"I settled the bill at eleven, in case you tried to. No, Dan. I can manage the expense, especially considering you'll be putting me up for the next four nights."

Dan grinned at her. "That sounds so platonic after the way you just kissed me." He circled her shoulders with one arm and picked up her suitcase. "Let's go."

"By the way, we didn't discuss my truck. Should I follow you this afternoon?" She winced at the idea of trying to drive in tandem through downtown traffic.

He glanced at her. "That wouldn't be much fun. Wait here a second." He put down her suitcase and crossed the lobby.

April watched him talking with the people at the registration desk. When he reached into his back pocket for his wallet, she realized he must be paying for her parking spot for the extra days, and she decided to let him do it. Driving in Chicago wasn't her idea of a good time, and she'd be just as happy to leave the truck parked here until she left town on Friday. Friday. At this moment she didn't want the day ever to arrive.

"Now we can go," Dan said as he returned and hoisted her suitcase once more. "The truck will be fine here until you go home.'' He took her hand and started toward the revolving door.

"Thank you. I just cost you some money, but I appreciate not having to deal with the traffic.''

"It wouldn't have made sense. This is easier, and besides, I want you with me.'' He proved his point by crowding both of them and the suitcase into one glassed-in section of the revolving door.

April was laughing by the time the spinning door thrust them both outside next to the uniformed doorman. Dan certainly surprised her with these little moments of craziness. Had he been like that before? She didn't think so. Hope rose in her that maybe she and Dan might have a future, after all.

The parking valet arrived with Dan's red Honda and helped April inside while Dan took care of the tip. She admitted reluctantly to herself that she liked being taken care of every once in a while. In her bitterness over Dan's practical handling of their young love eight years ago, she'd shoved aside her memories of his kind consideration and efficient management of details. Now, after the years with Jimmy, she understood how abrasive life could be when a man lacked those skills.

Dan veered into the stream of cars and delivery vans with the ease of a practiced big-city dweller. "We'll eat at a little German place I know—not too fancy but excellent food.''

"I'm glad it's not fancy, with me in my sensible shoes.'' April relaxed as she watched him move deftly around other vehicles. "I haven't asked you anything about where you live. I hope I won't be crowding you.''

He gave her a meaningful glance. "No, April, you won't be crowding me.''

"How do you know? Have you ever...that is, did you have anyone living with you before?''

"No, I never quite trusted anyone enough for that.''

She was taken aback. "Because of me?'' she ventured.

"Maybe."

"Then why are you having anything to do with me now? Aren't you afraid I'll hurt you all over again?" April herself was afraid of that very thing.

He kept his eyes on the bumper-to-bumper line of cars. "I'm petrified, but I can't stop myself. I should probably have my head examined for getting involved with you, but here I am, delirious with happiness because we'll be together for a few days."

"You are? Deliriously happy?"

"Yes." He stopped at a red light and muttered something she couldn't quite hear.

"What did you say?"

"Oh, nothing. Silly superstition. My mother predicted that having the ring would change my life."

"You mean the heirloom?"

"That's the one."

"Then you don't believe what your mother says about the ring." She felt a familiar twinge of disappointment. He was rejecting a romantic notion once more.

"If it has such power, why didn't it save my father so my mother could grow old with the man she loved?"

"I heard the ring was supposed to bring love to its owners, not guarantee long life. Your parents were very much in love, according to everyone in Booneville."

"And now she's alone."

"With some beautiful memories," April added.

Dan glanced at her. "Maybe that's all the ring is good for, then, beautiful memories."

She knew he was testing her, taunting her to suggest that their relationship might become more than this short interlude, this handful of beautiful memories. Dan liked a sure thing. He always had. But she knew their future together was a long way from a sure thing. She didn't respond to his statement.

She was becoming more and more curious about the ring,

however. She couldn't credit it with bringing her and Dan together after eight years. Irene had done that with her clever bequest to the town tied with all sorts of strings designed to snare April and Dan, as well as challenge the townspeople to earn their legacy.

Yet Dan could have resisted the idea of spending time with April and foiled Irene's attempts at matchmaking. Instead, he was pursuing the woman who had hurt him before, and for reasons that seemed to elude him he was risking more heartbreak. Was the ring responsible for that?

Dan stopped for another light, and she gazed at the row of display windows on her side of the street. The tide of lunchtime pedestrians, whipped by the November wind, ebbed and flowed in front of glassed-in mannequins dressed in furs and elegant evening wear. April figured that if she rounded up all the people in this square-block area, she'd have approximately the population of Booneville.

As Dan eased the Honda forward again, April clutched his sleeve. "There! I just saw it!"

"What?"

She craned her neck to keep the small sculpture in view as the current of traffic took them away. "Can you stop?"

"Not here. I'd have to find a parking garage. What did you see?"

"The most beautiful sculpture. I have to know the artist. Please, let's park the car and go back."

"That's a tall order. Besides, what about your feet?"

"Never mind my feet. Look, the next light just turned red. If you can't find a parking garage, drive around the block and pick me up in front of the gallery. I think it had a name like Anderson's or something." Without waiting for an answer she opened the car door and stepped out.

"April…"

She glanced back briefly and noticed his exasperated expression. Well, too bad. Chicago was a big city, and she wasn't sure about the name of the gallery. They might not

find it again, or if they did, the sculpture might be gone.
Besides, excitement drove her to act immediately. She had
seen material proof that someone would understand her vision of the sculpture to be placed on the Booneville square.

She dodged honking cars and trucks as she hurried to the
safety of the sidewalk. The blisters on her feet hurt, but she
ignored the pain and walked quickly down the block. The
gallery was somewhere in the middle of the next one, and
she had to be in and out with her information before Dan
circled back to pick her up. Something about his expression
had told her that he wouldn't park the car.

On the second block April moved closer to the stores
lining the sidewalk. She caught a glimpse of herself in the
reflecting glass and decided she looked a little wild, with
her hair blown into disarray and her almost running gait.
Dan probably preferred his women to be more sedate. Too
bad, again.

The sculpture appeared almost as a surprise in the very
next window, and she'd been right about the name of the
place, she noticed with satisfaction. She stood very close to
the window and looked.

The sculpture stood about two feet high and was the color
of dry earth. April cocked her head to each side, trying to
determine if the shape was anything recognizable, but she
finally decided it was not, unless it mimicked something as
free-form as a piece of driftwood. All the movement of the
piece as it undulated and intertwined was upward, reaching,
stretching toward some indefinable goal.

The title of the sculpture was printed on a small card
propped next to it. April laughed when she read the title.
How appropriate to everything that had happened to her and
was still happening. The name of the sculptor was Erica
Jorgenson, and the piece cost three hundred and fifty dollars.

April opened the wooden gallery door and stepped inside.
She was the only person in the small area except for a blond
man who approached eagerly at her entrance.

"Can I help you?"

"Yes. I need two things," April said, surveying the paint-
ings and sculpture arranged around the room. She liked the
simple, fresh quality evidenced in everything on display, but
nothing moved her like the piece in the window. "First of
all, I must contact Erica Jorgenson about commissioning her
for some work."

The man nodded. "That can be arranged. I'll need a
phone number for you."

April found her wallet and extracted the card that Dan
had given her with both of his telephone numbers on it. She
gave out the one for his apartment and hoped he wouldn't
object. Anyway, hadn't her move there been his idea?

"And what is your second request?" the man asked as
he wrote down Dan's number on a pad of paper.

"I'd like to buy that piece of Ms Jorgenson's that you
have in the window."

"Of course."

Of course. April smiled at his nonchalance while she
wrote out the check. This gallery owner had no idea that
she didn't do this every day, or that she'd have to sell a
heck of a lot of eggs to pay for something that wouldn't
feed the chickens or harvest the apples or weed the vegetable garden. But she believed what she'd told the board
members, that the human spirit sometimes needs to view
something that has no other purpose except beauty.

He wrapped the sculpture in bubbled plastic and boxed it
while April watched out the window for Dan's red Honda.
She hated to see the sculpture disappear because she wanted
to show it to him right away. Now she would have to wait
until later, probably until they got to his apartment, before
she could unwrap it.

The red Honda appeared from the left and pulled up next
to the curb in a no-parking zone. April figured Dan hated
doing that, and she fidgeted impatiently while the gallery

owner taped the box shut. Then she mumbled her thanks and headed quickly out the door.

Dan leaned over and swung the car door open for her. "I thought you went in for information," he said, eyeing the box.

"I bought the sculpture." Horns honked all around them, but April took the time to settle the box in the back of the Honda before climbing in so that Dan could pull away from the curb.

"You bought it? Isn't that a little small for the town square?"

April laughed. "I bought it for me. I sure hope Erica Jorgenson will do the sculpture for the square, though. Her work is everything I dreamed of. I can imagine something very similar to this, although perhaps in a different medium, maybe bronze."

"What's it of?"

"Well, um…" April thought of how to describe her purchase and how Dan might react to her vague description. "Maybe I should wait and let you see it rather than trying to picture it for you."

He shrugged. "Okay. Ready to eat?"

"Sure."

Throughout their hearty lunch in a little basement restaurant famous for good German food and imported beer, April tried to put aside her thoughts about the sculpture she'd bought and the woman who had created it. By now the gallery owner might have relayed April's message, and Dan's phone could be ringing.

"Do you have an answering machine at your apartment?" she asked Dan abruptly as they finished off their apple strudel.

"Yes. Why?"

"I hope you don't mind, but the gallery owner asked for a number where the sculptor could call me, and I gave him yours. I'm glad you have an answering machine so that I won't miss her call."

"*Her* call?"

"Erica Jorgenson, the sculptor."

"Oh. A woman, huh?"

"Women sculpt, too, you know."

"I'm aware of that, but don't you think hiring a woman might be asking for trouble in Booneville? You've already got an uphill battle with people like Henry Goodpasture."

"Who is sexist. I hope you're not, Dan."

"I do my damnedest to avoid it, but I wasn't exactly raised in the bosom of liberal thinking. If my grandmother hadn't been around, I'd be worse off than I am."

"Dan, I have a special feeling about this sculptor. I wouldn't care if the piece I bought was created by an orangutan. I'd still want that artist to design something for the town square."

"Does that mean we can forget the gallery tour this afternoon? Maybe this situation has merit, after all."

April taunted him with a smile. "Getting tired? And you were the one who insisted that wouldn't happen."

"I said I wouldn't be tired. I didn't say I wouldn't want to go to bed," Dan said, leaning his chin on one hand to gaze at her.

"Dan, my goodness."

"Your goodness is right. And your sweetness, and your loveliness, and your sexiness. I want all of those things. Let's skip the galleries."

Her pulse quickened at the light in his eyes. "I'm worried that the board might not think I've checked enough places."

"But from the way you're talking, your mind is made up."

"I think it is, yes. Except that you're supposed to be—what was the word?—supervising me."

A lazy smile spread across his lips. "Yeah. I plan to do that a lot."

"Dan, be serious. What will we tell the board?"

"As little as possible," he replied with a grin.

"I know how we'll do this. I'll unwrap—"

"Good beginning."

She glared at him. "I'll unwrap the sculpture when we get home, and if you approve, I'll pursue hiring Erica Jorgenson, assuming she'll work for the paltry sum we have to offer. If you don't approve, I'll look for some other possibilities in the next three days." April mentally crossed her fingers. What if he didn't like the piece she had just bought? Then she'd deal with that when it happened, she told herself sternly. Irene used to warn her not to buy trouble.

"That means we can head home right now, doesn't it?"

"I guess so, unless you want me to get the sculpture out of the car and unwrap it here."

"Not on your life. I prefer my unveiling ceremonies to take place in private."

He whisked her out of the restaurant and back to the car in record time, and within minutes they entered the underground garage beneath his apartment building. An elevator took them, along with her suitcase and the boxed sculpture, to the fourth floor.

"I wish I could dazzle you with the penthouse," he said as they stepped into a carpeted hallway, "but the rent goes up with every floor."

Now that they were in his apartment building, April was taut with the anticipation of being in his arms once more. "Who cares about a view?" she said, casting him a provocative look.

"There's only one view *I'm* interested in right now." He took his keys from his pocket as they approached his door.

"My sculpture," she teased, lifting the box she carried.

"Right." He turned the key in the lock. "Hey, do we have to look at this thing right now?"

"Yes. I really want you to see it."

"Damn, that's too bad." He shook his head and ushered her inside.

His apartment, she could tell in that first instant when she stepped into the living room, was immaculate. And although the color scheme in shades of brown didn't show much imagination, the furniture had the sort of free-flowing, Scandinavian elegance she'd always admired. With a touch of bright color here and there the room could be saved from its present air of sterility. He even had a small fireplace, although it looked as if it had never seen a burning log.

"Very nice, Dan." April set the box containing the sculpture on the coffee table and turned to him with a smile.

He put down her suitcase and gazed at her with his hands shoved into the pockets of his coat.

"Dan? Is something wrong?"

"No. I just…never thought you'd be standing here, that's all. I'm— It takes some getting used to."

She gazed back at him. "I never thought I'd be standing here, either. I figured after all that had happened, there was no way we'd ever be together again. I'm glad we are."

"Me, too."

They stood silently for a moment longer, each of them absorbing the emotions flowing between them. At last April spoke softly. "I'll unpack the sculpture, and then…"

Dan snapped out of his reverie. "By all means, unpack that sculpture if we have to take care of that first. I'll hang up our coats and see if I can find us a bottle of wine in the refrigerator."

"Would you please check your phone messages, too?"

"Sure thing."

After he left with their coats, April stripped the tape from the box and lifted out the wrapped sculpture. By the time he returned with a chilled green bottle and two wineglasses, she had positioned the smooth piece of art in the center of the coffee table and was standing back to admire it.

Dan stopped and stared. "*That's* what you plan to erect on the Booneville town square?"

"Yes." She was so lost in contemplation of her new acquisition that she didn't notice the dismay in his tone. "Or something close. It will be spectacular, don't you think?"

Dan closed his eyes. "I think," he began slowly, opening his eyes again, "that it will be a disaster."

"What?" Stung by his reaction, she whirled to face him.

"It won't work."

"Don't say that! I don't want to hear that, especially from you!"

"Okay, I won't say it." He walked toward the coffee table. "Does this have a name?"

"Yes." She folded her arms and glared at him through sudden tears. Dammit. Dammit to hell.

"What's it called?"

She hurled the answer like a javelin. "*Impulse.*"

CHAPTER EIGHT

DAN'S TONE BECAME SOFT, careful, as if he were in the presence of a ticking bomb. "What are you trying to do, April?"

"Bring some beauty to the Booneville square." She fought her tears. She would convince him that the sculpture was a good idea, and not by sobbing on his shoulder, either.

"That's too simple an answer, and you know it. How can you imagine something like this, maybe a ten- or fifteen-foot version, in Booneville? Henry Goodpasture expects somebody on a horse."

"I didn't promise Henry that."

"But you didn't mention what you really wanted, either."

"They wouldn't have reacted well to some garbled description of mine. They'll have to see something, something like this."

"And when they do, I predict the whole project will be canned before it gets started."

"No! I'll bet M.G. Tucker will like the sculpture, and I do, and Bill might be persuaded. That's three out of six. So if you..." She didn't finish the sentence. Judging from the expression on his face, he was way ahead of her.

"I'm the swing vote."

"Dan, let me explain what I—"

"That's okay. I think I get it now. You zeroed in on this sculpture in the gallery window, knew it was the type of stuff you wanted, and without further discussion you want rubber-stamp approval from me. That would help you convince M.G. and Bill to go along, wouldn't it?"

"I thought you'd agree that the sculpture is beautiful, Dan. It's graceful, imaginative, unique—"

"That's a good word—unique."

"What about your Scandinavian decor in here?" she continued, flinging out her arms. "I would have said you'd love something like this after seeing the furniture you've chosen."

"Wait a minute. I never said I wouldn't consider it for this room. Maybe I would. But we're talking about the town square, not my apartment."

"And everything must have its appropriate time and place." April glared at him. "I've heard that somewhere before. About eight years ago, to be exact."

"April, dammit!" He crossed to her and took her by the shoulders. "Do you enjoy being unreasonable? Why must you always go against the grain?"

She gasped in surprise at his aggressive tone and the forceful grip that brought them into close contact. Years before he would have retreated into injured silence at her taunts, but now he was challenging her, physically and mentally. Both anger and passion flared in his blue eyes.

April fought her attraction to that potent combination. She was determined to hold her ground. "Maybe I go against the grain because that's the only way to keep life from stagnating."

"Then what the hell are you doing in Booneville? You're not making sense. If your biggest worry is stagnation, I can't imagine why you'd choose to live in a conservative Midwestern town where you run the greatest risk of doing the very thing you fear most."

"Maybe that's part of the challenge." Her heart was beating as if she'd run up a flight of stairs. She wanted to win this argument, but she also wanted his lips on hers. He was so close she could smell the clean scent of his skin mixed with the musty fragrance of arousal.

"And to think I believed your little speech about being a small-town girl at heart."

"But I am. Don't you see?"

"No, I don't." His gaze dropped to her mouth for a brief moment. Then with an impatient shake of his head he looked into her eyes once more. "Explain it to me."

April took a steadying breath. "Small towns are warm, cozy places to live in. They're also in danger of sinking into a rut. But I can fix that."

"With this sculpture?"

"Yes."

He stared at her in frustration. "You're asking for trouble."

"Maybe."

He gripped her more tightly. "I think you *are* trouble."

Her body was quivering with need for him, but she lifted her chin defiantly. "What do you plan to do about that, Dan?"

His voice was low. "Right now?" He slid one hand behind her head to hold it still. "What I should have done when we walked into this apartment."

She trembled as he brought his mouth deliberately closer, and when their lips met, she moaned softly. He kissed her with firm mastery, draining away her anger and his, replacing it with churning need.

At last he lifted his head and spoke with difficulty. "We'll...work everything out later."

Dazed with the force of his kiss, she nodded.

"Come here." He led her toward the couch and drew her down, facing him. Slowly he traced a line with his finger from the hollow of her throat to the top button of her blouse. "Undress for me, April."

She gazed at him and knew that she had no business being here. But last night wasn't easily forgotten. She wanted more, no matter how unwise her longing might be. "All right." In the afternoon light she studied the face that had hovered over her during their spiraling moments of passion. The faint shadow of his dark beard was beginning to show along his jawline and upper lip and in the hard-to-shave cleft of his chin. She was filled with excitement at the thought of loving him here in the full light of day, surrounded by the order of his neat-as-a-pin living room.

Dan leaned against the back of the sofa and rested his arm along the top of the cushions. He didn't touch her, but his blue eyes burned with intensity.

She crossed her legs at the knee, and her nylons slid against each other with a faint whispering sound. The ache for him grew inside her, blocking out rational thought and inspiring her to tease him, tempt him into disrupting this proper setting with their wild need for each other.

Dan stared at the spot where her skirt fell gracefully over her knee but had crept up on one side to reveal a sleek strip of thigh. April adjusted her skirt a little higher yet. With calm purpose she unfastened the first button of her blouse. He swallowed as she moved to the next button.

"Am I doing this right?" she murmured, unfastening another button.

"There's no doing it wrong."

When all the buttons were undone, she slipped the blouse from her shoulders and reached one hand behind her back to unhook her bra. As she let it fall away, baring herself to his gaze, his face contorted with desire. With a moan he reached for her and pressed his face against her breasts.

She held his head as he nipped and nibbled at her heated flesh in a near frenzy to taste her, to suck the hard buds she thrust toward him. "I'm…not finished," she said, gasping.

He pressed her back onto the soft cushions. "I don't care." His breath was hot against her breasts. "I've got to have you now."

She arched against the pressure of his mouth as he stoked the fire within her. Sliding his hand up her thigh, he found the waistband of her panty hose. With her help he tugged that garment and her panties away and tossed them to the floor.

Pushing aside her skirt, he pressed the palm of his hand against her. "God, you're so wet," he whispered, stroking her.

She moaned in response. How glorious to be aroused like this, to want someone so much that she had no shame. She lifted her hips toward the magic he was working and begged him to love her.

Dimly she realized there must be one more step before that could happen, but he had taken care of everything before. When he fumbled with the catch of his slacks, she realized, even through the dizzying haze of passion, that he wouldn't take care of everything this time. For perhaps the first moment in his life he'd abandoned reason, just as she'd once wished he would do. Did that make reason her task? "Dan, wait."

"No."

"Get something first. You really don't want..."

His chest heaved as he struggled for the breath to speak. "That's not quite right. *You* don't want."

"*We* don't want."

"Wrong." He kissed her almost savagely and lurched to his feet. "But I'm a good guy. I'll be right back."

When he returned, some of the frenzy was gone. She knew it was wrong to regret that it was. When he entered her, he was in control again, moving skillfully inside her, turning the tables and bringing her to heights of mindless ecstasy. Deliberately he wrung from her the cries of release before he allowed his own needs to carry him beyond the bounds of his control.

They lay sprawled on the sofa as daylight seeped from the room.

"Now we should go to bed," Dan finally murmured against her ear. "To sleep."

"Probably should." She shifted slightly under his weight.

"Dan, I'm sorry that I kept you from the…full enjoyment of…" She was floundering, trying to find the right words.

"I enjoyed myself."

"Yes, but—"

"You did the right thing, April. For one crazy minute there I wanted to make you pregnant. Wasn't that stupid?"

She began to tremble. "You did?" The idea of carrying Dan's baby made her heart swell for a moment.

"Sure. When we were fighting about the sculpture, I wondered if you were about to leave me again. I thought of a desperate and foolish way to keep you around."

"So you weren't beyond reason at all. You knew what you were doing."

"Yes. But I've never had such a wild impulse in my life before, believe me."

She smiled back. "Impulse?"

"Yeah." He smiled back.

"Maybe my sculpture had some effect."

"Maybe. Or that crazy ring. Something's messing with my head."

"Seems like it, Dan." She hesitated to tell him how much his impulse to give her a child thrilled her. "What makes you think my being pregnant would make any difference between us? This is the eighties, you know."

"Instinct, I guess. Would it?"

"Yes, and that's why we're not going to let it happen. If we decide to…go on together, in some fashion, there mustn't be anything affecting our decision except ourselves."

"You're right. And that's why we need to get this sculpture business settled and out of the way."

"The sculpture! I completely forgot to ask if you had any calls on your answering machine."

"Just one from Erica Jorgenson, asking you to call as soon as possible," he said lightly.

"What? You should have told me sooner." April struggled to sit up, forcing Dan to roll away from her onto the floor, where he landed with a thump.

"Hey!"

"Gee, I'm sorry." She peered down at him in the dim light. "Are you okay?"

"I think I've just been dumped for a piece of sculpture."

"You're so witty." She ruffled his hair and picked up her discarded blouse as she stepped over his prone body. "Where's the answering machine?"

"In the bedroom," he said, "right down that hall. On the table where the drawer is still pulled out, as I recall. Some guy was in a hurry, and the woman seemed to be in a bit of a hurry herself. Remember that?"

"Oh."

"Yeah, *oh*. Would you rather have made your call first?"

"Don't be silly. Why don't you pour us some wine while I'm gone?"

He watched her go, buttoning her blouse as she left. "I hope I'm not being silly," he said softly to himself.

ERICA WAS DELIGHTED to hear from April, and they agreed to meet at Dan's apartment. After conferring with Dan, April set the time for ten in the morning, following his suggestion that she meet with the sculptor while he was at work. April welcomed the chance to talk with Erica alone, considering Dan's less-than-enthusiastic attitude toward the project.

To his credit, he was attempting to compromise. Although his judgment remained the same, he'd agreed not to block April's attempt to win over the rest of the board. He would remain noncommittal, neither endorsing nor denigrating the modernistic concept, thus giving her time to get a reaction from the other four members and the town in general.

All of this was predicated on Erica's acceptance of the commission, and April had doubts about that, considering the small amount of money the town had to offer. She kept

her reservations to herself, however, as she and Dan enjoyed
their first breakfast together and discovered the joys of a
romp in bed when they were both fresh from a good night's
sleep.

After Dan left for work, late for the first time since taking
the job, April prepared for Erica's visit by making coffee
and setting out a plateful of chocolate-and-marshmallow
cookies she found in Dan's cupboard. She chided herself for
her down-home preparations. If Erica Jorgenson turned out
to be anything like her work, she wouldn't be swayed by
coffee and cookies into creating a masterpiece for a pittance.
Still, April hoped the sculptor turned out to be exactly like
her work.

She wasn't disappointed. Erica arrived in a swirl of royal
purple that partially hooded her abundant blond hair and
draped in imaginative folds from her lithe body. April es-
timated that Erica might be close to six feet tall.

"I'm Erica Jorgenson," she said immediately when April
opened the door. Then she swept inside without waiting for
an invitation.

April became aware that her mouth was open and closed
it before she turned around to greet her visitor. Erica had
thrown back the purple hood and was standing with her
hands on her hips and her legs braced apart while she surveyed the sculpture in the middle of the coffee table. Too
late April realized she shouldn't have set the plate of marsh-
mallow cookies and the coffee cups on the same table. The
sculpture deserved its own space free of clutter.

"I'll create a pedestal for you," Erica said, unhooking
her cape and flinging it onto the couch. "This will never
do." Underneath the cape she was dressed in an expensive-
looking jumpsuit in winter white that was belted at her hips
with an oversize gold chain.

"The sculpture won't stay in this room," April said, and
immediately tried to picture where it would fit in her Victorian farmhouse. But wasn't the point to jolt people with a

few surprises, a few things out of place? ''I'm taking it back to Booneville.''

"Where?" Erica focused her gray eyes on April as if seeing her for the first time.

"Booneville, Illinois. It's a very small town, so I'm not surprised you haven't been there."

"I take it you live in Booneville, then?"

"Yes."

"Small towns can be very nice. What do you do there?"

April recognized that Erica was accustomed to making judgments about everything, and she smiled to herself as she answered the question. "I run a poultry and produce farm called The Birds and the Bees." What would Erica say if April suggested the sculpture was purchased to help her hens lay better? Maybe the artist would snatch her work and leave.

To April's surprise, Erica chuckled and gave her a warm look. "Cute name."

"It's not a big farm, but I like it there."

"I can relate to that."

"You can?"

"Sure. I've often thought about moving to the country. The peace and quiet would be heavenly for my work, but I'd have a hell of a time marketing my sculpture in Booneville, Illinois. For that I need the big city."

April grabbed the opportunity to plug Booneville. "I think you'd love spending time downstate, Erica—as a change of pace, of course. Sit down, please, and I'll tell you my plan. Would you care for coffee?"

"Regular or decaf?"

"Regular." April had found both in the cupboard and had chosen the full-strength brew, figuring a cosmopolitan creature like Erica wouldn't mess around with anything less.

"Then I'll pass, thanks." Erica sat down on the sofa as if she owned it. "I have to keep a steady hand for my work."

"Of course." To avoid appearing too chummy, April chose a chair at right angles to the couch. After Erica's response to her offer of coffee, she didn't mention the cookies and wished fervently that she knew a magic trick to make them disappear. Fruit and cheese might have worked, and maybe a glass of Perrier.

To April's dismay, Erica looked directly at the marsh-mallow-and-chocolate mound squatting pathetically beside her glorious work of art. "These look sinful."

"You're right. I shouldn't have put them out."

"No, you shouldn't have. Here goes my diet." Erica picked up a cookie with obvious relish and bit into it.

April stared at her.

"Well, don't just sit there making me feel guilty. You have to eat them, too."

April grinned. "Would you like some milk?"

"Please."

Within minutes they were both munching away, and Erica was dipping her cookies into her milk. "Now that we're reduced to our real selves," Erica announced as she took a third cookie, "I should probably tell you my real name, which is Bertha Crabapple."

April choked on her milk.

"Please don't spread this information around, April."

"But you look so...so *Swedish*."

"I think so, too. Maybe in another life I was Swedish. I've been thinking of changing my name formally, but I haven't done it yet, so occasionally somebody like Rolf Anderson, the gallery owner, will slip and call me Bertha. I thought you should know, if we'll be working together."

"But you don't even know what I want you to do."

"No, but I like your taste." Erica tipped her head toward the sculpture. "And your decisiveness. Rolf mentioned that you barreled into the gallery and bought this in less than five minutes."

"Well, I—"

"Don't explain. You might ruin my fantasy. I love to imagine people are that excited about my work."

"Oh, I absolutely am."

"What is it you want me to create for you, then?"

April outlined her project for the town square and included a description of the gazebo as the counterpoint to a large sculpture created by Erica, a sculpture similar to the one resting in front of them.

Erica nodded, a faraway look in her eyes. "Bringing modern art to the hinterlands. I like it." Then she glanced at April. "Although frankly I'm surprised that your farm is prosperous enough for you to donate such a generous gift to the town. You must have super chickens down there in Booneville."

"Oh, it's not my money. A dear old lady died and left the income from her estate to the town. That's where the funds are coming from."

Some of the enthusiasm left Erica's expression. "Ah. And how much are we talking about?"

April paused. The amount she had to offer seemed to shrink in her mind until it was laughably inadequate. Finally she worked up enough courage to say the figure out loud.

Sure enough, Erica laughed. Then she stood up and reached for her cape. "The cookies were marvelous, and I'll be glad to make you a pedestal for this piece." She gestured toward the sculpture. "But as for the town square, I think we're wasting each other's time."

CHAPTER NINE

"ERICA, WAIT!" April caught up with her before she reached the door. "Isn't there any way? Perhaps you could use less expensive materials, or make the sculpture a little smaller. And we wouldn't have to have it right away. We could wait until you have spare time."

Erica shook her head as she tossed her cape around her shoulders. "You're talking about compromising the integrity of the project, and you don't want that. Better to have nothing than something less than what you envisioned." She gazed with sympathy at April. "Maybe you can find another sculptor who would be willing to do this for the exposure without making anything on it. The amount you're talking about would barely cover the cost of materials."

"I don't want another sculptor. The minute I saw your work in the gallery window I knew you were the one who could create exactly what I had in mind. Now I'll compare every other artist's sculpture with yours and find it wanting."

"I love to hear all of that, of course, but I have to earn a living, too. And besides the materials, I'd have expenses when I came down there to erect the sculpture because I'd have it shipped in pieces. I'd have hotel bills, meals—"

"No, you'd stay with me in the peace and quiet of the country. You could stay as long as you liked, Erica, and work on other things, too. Didn't you mention that you'd enjoy that? Here's your chance."

"Yes, but—"

"You also mentioned exposure, and that wouldn't hurt, either. I'm sure a project like this would merit all sorts of media coverage, and I'd make sure that you got it." April tried not to think of how the residents of Booneville would react to television cameras on the town square.

"You have a point there, I'll admit. None of us in the art world is successful enough to ignore publicity opportunities, but this would cost me a bundle, and I'm inclined to let someone else have the limelight this time."

April took a deep breath and played her ace. It could be the high card that won the hand or the low one that solidified Erica's refusal. "One thing I didn't mention before was that I expect some resistance to the project from a conservative faction in the town."

"Oh?" Erica raised an eyebrow.

"Some people in Booneville want to keep things exactly as they've always been, no matter how boring that might be. One man in particular, the president of the bank, didn't want a sculpture at all. Finally he agreed that we might have one if it could be a soldier on a horse or something like that."

"I see." The light of battle crept into Erica's gray eyes.

The subtle transformation registered with April and she continued talking. "The woman who died and left money to the town was a good friend of mine and a very creative person. In her will she appointed me, the only woman, to the board that administers the funds. I think she intended that I keep the town moving forward, and this sculpture is my way of striking a blow for progress."

"What about this resistance? Is it strong enough to thwart your plan for my sculpture?"

"I don't know," April answered honestly. She noticed that Erica had said "my sculpture." She was considering the idea. "But I'd put everything into the fight to guarantee that you get the commission and not somebody who's willing to create a soldier on a horse."

Erica faced April for the first time since starting out the door. "I think we have enough military statues in Illinois, don't you?"

"I certainly do."

Erica extended her hand. "You get that bank president to come around, and I'll put up your sculpture."

April felt like shouting but decided to wait until Erica was gone. "Thank you." She accepted Erica's firm hand-shake with as much dignity as she could muster. "Thank you very much."

Once Erica was out the door and safely down the hall, April let loose with a triumphant yell. Had she been in Booneville, the volume would have summoned every hog for miles around.

HER MISSION COMPLETED, April could have cut her visit short and returned to Booneville. Instead, she ignored logic and chose to stay with Dan until her scheduled departure on Friday morning.

"We organized this wrong," Dan said Thursday night as they lay side by side, hips and shoulders touching, fingers intertwined as they basked in the warm glow of their love-making.

April smiled. Dan would probably always think in terms of good or poor organization. That part of him would never change, and that was okay with her. His imaginative and impassioned loving more than made up for a tendency to organize most everything else in his life.

"We should have had you come up over a weekend in-stead of during the workweek," Dan continued. "Any chance you can stay through Monday morning?"

She turned her head on the pillow and gazed at him. "That sounds nice, but I don't think so."

He rolled to his side and slid his hand around her waist to draw her nearer. "We could sleep in Saturday morning. We'd have all the time in the world for a change, instead of having to watch the clock. I'd even serve you breakfast in bed." He placed a kiss on her breast. "Have you ever had breakfast in bed?"

She turned to mold her body against his. "Depends on your definition of breakfast."

"If you stay with me this weekend, we'll create a whole page of definitions."

"Oh, Dan," she said with a sigh. "I can't." She brushed her lips against the smooth cleft in his chin. Typical of his caring behavior, he'd shaved before he took her to bed. "Mom and Dad have been kind enough to mind the farm and do the chores for five days, but I can't impose on them any longer. They've built quite a little social life for themselves in town, and I know staying out there for the weekend would be a bother. That's one reason I set things up this way."

"That farm really ties you down, April."

She stiffened. "So does your job." She'd been wondering if they'd get to this, and if he'd assume she'd give up the life she'd made for herself to be with him in Chicago. "Do you really enjoy selling sporting goods?"

"Beats farming."

"How about living in Chicago? I asked you once before, and you evaded the question."

"Adonis doesn't have an office in Booneville, and something tells me they aren't likely to open one soon. In fact, the next promotion I'm in line for would mean moving to Cincinnati."

"I see."

"That doesn't mean I'll take it, April. A lot depends on...what happens."

"Between us," she clarified.

He lifted his head to gaze down at her. "Does this mean anything to you, what we've found together in the past few days?"

"Of course it does."

"Would you like it to continue?"

She regarded him steadily. "On what terms?"

"No terms. Not for now. With what we've just said I realize that it's too soon for either of us to be suggesting major changes in our lives to accommodate this...feeling between us."

"You're not ready to put a name to it, are you?"

"Are you?"

She stared at him as the tense silence grew. "No," she said softly. "We said those words to each other once before, but I don't think either of us knew what they meant."

"No, we didn't."

"What I felt for you then seems shallow compared to what I feel now, but I don't know if I'm driven by plain old ordinary lust or something more."

He smiled at her. "I wouldn't classify this lust as 'plain old ordinary.' I'd at least give it a rating of colossally wonderful."

She traced the bow of his upper lip. "So would I, come to think of it."

"You know, I do have one term."

"What's that?"

"I want you to keep the ring for a while."

"The ring? Oh, Dan, I don't think—"

"Not to wear. I understand what that would mean to the entire town if they saw it on your finger. But I— Lord, I can't believe what I'm about to say."

"Now I'm really curious."

Dan took a deep breath. "All my life I've heard stories about this ring and how it affects people. I've refused to believe any of it, but..."

"You're weakening," she prompted.

"I think so. Ever since my mother gave me the damn thing, you've been an obsession with me. Then this sculpture project came up, and the board asked me to work with you on it. We haven't agreed on that subject, but at least it brought you up here and we've...found other areas of agreement."

She lifted her head and kissed him gently. "I'd say so."

"April, I..." He gazed into her eyes. "This sounds crazy, but I want to try an experiment. You keep the ring for a few weeks, and let's see what happens."

His seriousness confused her. It wasn't what she expected from Dan, and a vague urge to return to the status quo prompted her to tease him. "If you want a real experiment, you could give it to the cleaning lady and see what happens."

"I don't want the cleaning lady to become obsessed with me."

His response flooded her with surprise followed by tingling warmth. "But you want me to?" she murmured.

"Yes."

APRIL TOOK THE RING HOME on Friday morning. After making love to Dan again in the early light of dawn, she doubted the ring was necessary to keep him uppermost in her thoughts. Still, the very fact that he wanted her to have it was exciting. Whether the ring had special powers or not, Dan was willing to consider the possibility. His new attitude fed April's fantasy that he might possess the romantic streak she longed for in a man.

The ring was to be their secret, so April didn't mention it to her parents when she recounted the details of her trip that afternoon. She also minimized the amount of time she'd spent with Dan and eliminated entirely the information that she'd stayed at his apartment.

She did unearth her sculpture, however, and her parents were speechless for several seconds. At last they mumbled something about the piece being "interesting" and left quickly for their home in town.

April returned to her routine of evening chores and realized that the familiar jobs gave her plenty of time to think about Dan while she worked. As she gathered eggs and tossed scratch corn to her cackling brood, April was astonished to encounter loneliness for the first time in years. She missed Dan.

When darkness covered the farm and the chickens were settled for the night, April wandered back to the house for a solitary meal and an empty evening. Tonight she would not lie in Dan's arms, nor enjoy the gentle caress that transformed her into the passionate woman she was meant to be. The peaceful serenity of a night in the country had become intolerably quiet without the sound of Dan's key in the lock, his eager greeting, his murmured words of pleasure as she held him close after the long hours of separation.

Turning on lights as she went, she walked into her bedroom and took the ring out of her top dresser drawer. The gold setting was the deep yellow of very old jewelry, and for the first time April examined the faint crest etched inside the ring behind the setting.

The crest was divided down the middle and engraved with a jagged mountain peak on the left and three stars on the right. Something was written in tiny script beneath the crest. April adjusted her glasses and held the ring to the light. Just under the crest was a French-sounding name, Montclair, and centered below that was some sort of inscription.

When April realized the words were French and not English, she figured them out. The inscription read:

A.

avec amour,

C.

A thrill of romantic pleasure ran through her. The woman originally given this ring had the same first initial as April's. She wondered if the woman and her lover had indeed lived in France and had once been part of the French nobility.

She felt a sense of privilege in having the ring, even tem-

porarily. Hesitantly she slipped it on her finger. It fit. She
turned it to catch the rainbow of light that sparkled from the
diamonds ringing the teardrop-shaped emerald.

Stretching her hand in front of her, she wondered how
such an elegant ring could feel so natural on the finger of
an Illinois farm girl. As the cool metal warmed to the temperature of her skin, April's thoughts strayed to Dan. She
pictured him putting the ring on her finger in front of a
congregation of friends and family. With a shiver of delight
she imagined his deep voice pledging to love her forever.

The telephone jangled in the next room, one long and one
short ring—her line. Without taking the heirloom jewelry
from her finger April went to the kitchen and picked up the
receiver.

"I miss you so much I'm going crazy."

"Dan! I can't believe it's you. The ring—I put it on a
few minutes ago, and here you are calling me."

"If it was working the way I'd hoped, you'd be calling
me."

"Another few minutes and I might have."

"What were you thinking about?"

"You. I said that."

"I want details."

"Dan, this is a party line. Someone could pick up the
phone at any minute and—"

"Okay, then talk in code. I'll understand."

April cleared her throat. "That's not necessary. They
were general thoughts, really. I miss you, too."

"You're evading the issue, but I won't push it. And I
hope to hell you miss me."

"I do, and watch your language. If someone picks up the
phone, I want you to start talking about your grandmother's
will or something, okay?"

"Okay." He paused. "How are you doing, really?"

"Not great. Once you asked me if I was lonely on the

farm all by myself, and I said no. But tonight, for the first time, I am.''

"Damn, I want to be with you. Whoops, sorry. Anyway, I've tried to figure out an excuse to come down and see you that wouldn't set everyone's tongue wagging.''

"It wouldn't work. They're already speculating about how well we got along in Chicago, I imagine. I told my mother and father an edited version of my visit that they didn't seem to swallow completely. They're at a potluck supper this very minute, and I'm sure you and I are the major topic of conversation.''

"Did you show them the sculpture?''

"Uh-huh.''

"And?''

"They were struck dumb.''

"Hmm.''

"And then they said it was 'interesting.' I don't think they loved it, but then, I didn't expect them to. They weren't wild about my multicolored henhouse, either.''

"I could mention a few things of yours that I'm wild about.''

"Dan, cut it out. Besides, you'll only make this worse. Maybe it's good for us to have some time apart. We'll be able to think about our situation without…well, you know.''

His voice was low and sexy as he teased her. "Without what?''

"You know I can't think straight when we're…when you're…''

"Kissing you all over?'' Dan supplied helpfully.

"That's enough.''

"It's never been enough. How I love touching those sweet, secret—''

"Dan!''

"Places that make you quiver while you beg me to—''

The line clicked.

"And no matter how much you beg me to consider the

cemetery fence, I know that my grandmother would definitely have wanted the library roof repaired," Dan finished in a businesslike tone.

"April, are you using the telephone, honey?"

"Yes, Mrs. Ordway, but I'll be through in a few minutes."

"Don't rush, honey. Sounds like long distance."

Dan spoke. "Yes, this is Dan Butler, Mrs. Ordway."

"Why, Dan, how nice to hear from you."

"Actually I was calling April."

"Well, of course you were. I'll get right off the phone and let you two young people chat."

April jumped in before she could hang up. "Just some board business, Mrs. Ordway. Nothing important."

"Board business on a Friday night? My, but you two are really dedicated."

"You don't know how much," Dan said fervently. "Good night, Mrs. Ordway."

"Good night, dear."

April was torn between laughter and fury. Laughter won out. "You are going to land us both in a pile of manure," she said when she could talk again.

"This is ridiculous. In Chicago we can be lovers and nobody cares. Now that you're in Booneville, I can't even talk to you on the telephone."

"That's the way it works."

"When are you going to spring your sculpture on Henry Goodpasture?"

"Next week. I'm setting up a combined meeting of the beautification committee and the board here at my house on Tuesday night. Would you like to be here?"

"You don't even have to ask, but under the circumstances I'd better stay away. I really don't want to influence this decision one way or the other, April. Right now my feelings for you are playing havoc with my better judgment."

"Good."

"Maybe not so good for the town. Booneville needs a cool head running this board."

"You've always been very good at that sort of thing."

"That was before I made love to you."

April savored his statement for a moment. "I wish you were here," she said gently.

"That makes two of us. Try to manufacture some reason that makes my presence in Booneville necessary, will you?"

"You might not approve of my methods."

Dan groaned. "Probably not. Just get this sculpture thing over with, okay? Once that's settled, one way or the other, we can concentrate on our own situation."

"Did it ever occur to you that the sculpture *is* part of our situation?"

Dan was silent on the other end of the line. "I was afraid of that," he said finally. "April, will you do me a favor?"

"What?"

"Wear that darn ring to bed tonight."

PUTTING ON the emerald-and-diamond ring each night became a sweet ritual for April. When she slipped it on her finger and turned out the light, she felt Dan's presence draw nearer. Her need for him was stronger, it seemed, while she wore the ring, but she welcomed the emotional pull toward the man who made her feel so alive.

On Tuesday night she finished her chores early so she could prepare for the evening ahead. She wore her forest-green dress and her glasses and even went so far as to pull her hair back into a bun. Earlier in the day she'd baked three pumpkin pies, Henry's favorite dessert, and dusted off the silver tea service that Bess Easley and her husband had given as a wedding present when April married Jimmy.

Positioning the sculpture in the living room had taken the better part of Monday. No matter where she put it, the sweeping modern design shouted its presence amid the comfortable but uninspired furniture April had inherited from her parents when they moved out. Years ago she'd begged her mother to take everything to their new home, but her mother understandably had wanted to start over and had saved April a large amount of money in the process.

But now, because she didn't yet have the pedestal Erica had promised, April longed for some sort of stand that would support the sculpture with a trace of style. At last she draped an end table with a white linen tablecloth and set the sculpture on that. It would have to do. Then, as a touch of drama, she placed a second tablecloth over the sculpture so she could have an unveiling.

Bill and Ida Mae Lowdermilk arrived first, and Bill insisted on peeking under the tablecloth.

"I can't tell what it is," he complained. "Can't we take this thing off?"

"I thought everyone should see it at once," April said, steering him away from the corner containing the sculpture. "Besides, you'll love it."

"I will?"

Ida Mae stuck her head in from the kitchen where she was brewing coffee. "You certainly will, darling."

"How do you know, Idie? You haven't seen it, either."

"I know, but I believe in April's choice. And Dan was in on this, too, don't forget."

"Not exactly," April said. "He's not really for or against having this type of sculpture on the square."

Bill glanced at her. "Diplomatic of him, isn't it?"

"He wants to give the rest of you a chance to decide without his opinion."

"He doesn't like it," Bill concluded.

"No, I didn't say that. He—" The doorbell saved April from further explanation, and she went to welcome the next arrivals.

Within ten minutes her living room was filled with people. Gerald Sloan and M.G. Tucker, the two bachelors, had elected to come together; despite their differences in philosophy, they maintained a cordial relationship. Bess Easley had asked if her husband, George, could come along because she hated to drive alone at night, so George was the only member of the group who wasn't actively involved in the project. Mabel and Henry Goodpasture arrived late and argued all the way in the door.

With Ida Mae's help April settled everyone with pie and coffee before mentioning the tablecloth-draped sculpture in the corner. She noticed everyone glancing uneasily toward the ghostly object, but the conversation turned to other subjects, including the Booneville High Bulldogs' chances to take a state title in football and how much the rain had affected the fall harvest.

When the plates were clean and everyone but Henry had declined seconds, April took charge of the gathering. She liked the idea of doing so while Henry still had his mouth full of pumpkin pie.

"As you all know, I spent a few days in Chicago last week looking for a sculptor to design something for the square," she began.

"I hear Chicago was pretty cold last week," George Easley volunteered.

"I guess so." April remembered it as being quite warm indeed, but that had little to do with the weather. She hoped she wasn't blushing. "As all of you also know, I didn't have a great deal of money to offer someone. Nevertheless, I've found a talented sculptor who is willing to work for little more than the materials involved. That's a fantastic deal, and we're lucky to find someone so dedicated to art."

"What's under the sheet?" Henry asked, finally voicing the question that had hung in the air all evening. "Did he make us a miniature or something?"

"In a way, yes." April started to correct Henry's statement and announce that the sculptor was a woman, but then she quickly reconsidered. The gender of the artist shouldn't matter, but to someone like Henry, and maybe even Gerald Sloan, it might. She'd keep that secret for a while.

"He must be a fast worker," M.G. commented.

"The sculpture I'm about to show you wasn't created for us," April said. "I saw it in a gallery window and bought it. Then I asked for the name of the artist and we made our deal—contingent, of course, on the approval of this group."

"But Dan's not here," Gerald Sloan said. "Are we to assume he approves of this choice?"

April took a deep breath. "Dan wanted to withhold his judgment until each of you had a chance to form an opinion."

"I thought he was supervising all of this," Henry said.

April glanced at the banker. How she would love to take the rest of the pie from the kitchen and smash it into his face. "That's true, but when Dan realized that I had a definite idea of what I wanted, he stepped back and allowed me to work somewhat independently. I take full responsibility for this decision."

"Well, let's see this thing in the corner, then," Henry said with a sigh.

April crossed to the sculpture and paused. Her palms were damp with anxiety. "The work for the square won't be exactly like this, but the style will be similar. Just imagine this one about fifteen feet tall instead of two, and you'll get a mental picture of what it will look like." She grasped the tablecloth and whipped it away from the sculpture.

The gasp of surprise came almost in unison. April had expected that. The sculpture was breathtaking. But as she turned toward her seated guests, she gulped. The look on everyone's face, including that of her dear friend Ida Mae, was of unmitigated horror.

CHAPTER TEN

HENRY WAS THE FIRST to bellow his response. "A fifteen-foot dead tree stump? Not with my money!"

"But it's not your money," April countered.

"I beg to differ, young lady. The money belongs to all of us, all the people of Booneville. And I'd like to emphasize—" he paused to point a finger at her "—it's not *your* money."

Mabel Goodpasture stood up. Her initial shocked expression had been replaced with one of defiance as she peered down at her husband over the jut of her ample bosom. "I love this piece of art," she announced. "I think something like this will look lovely on the square."

April closed her eyes. She wanted support, not an extension of a family feud.

"You can't be serious, Mabel," Henry retorted. "Bill can take his tractor down by the river and drag something like this back here for free."

"April has been to Europe, Henry, which you certainly have not. She has a great deal more cultural experience than some people I could mention."

April groaned. "Please, Mabel, I—"

Bess Easley, the peacemaker, intervened. "April, does this piece of sculpture have a name or something? I think it looks a bit like a figure, there, with the hands, no...maybe the whole thing is one hand, sort of—"

"Sort of like our kids make with clay in nursery school,"

Bill Lowdermilk finished, ignoring Ida Mae's urgent tug on his sleeve.

"The sculpture is called *Impulse*, Bess," April said.

Gerald Sloan laughed. "And an unfortunate impulse it was, too. Of course, if a guy can get good money for this kind of junk, I suppose he's a genius, after all."

"That's for sure," Henry added with a chuckle. "Maybe I should start hacking out things like this and give up banking. Must not take more than ten minutes to do one, wouldn't you say, M.G.?"

"Oh, I wouldn't be that hasty about the amount of work that went into this, Henry. There's a certain elegance there. I'd like a little while to think this one over before we decide anything."

Ida Mae applauded. "What an excellent idea. Let's all go home and think before we make any final decisions." She jabbed Bill in the ribs when he looked as if he might object.

"A few days won't change my mind," Henry said, crossing his arms and leaning back in his chair. "How about you, Gerry?"

"I doubt it. This is a far cry from Grant on his horse, which was a darn good suggestion, in my opinion."

"I'm beginning to like it more and more," Bess said, cocking her head to one side. "It does look like impulse, now that I study the shape more. Don't you think so, George?"

Her husband shook his head. "I'm staying out of this."

Mabel walked over and placed her hand on the sculpture as if to give it her blessing. "I'm in favor of April's choice, and that's that."

"And I'm not, and that's that," Henry said.

"And I say let's all sleep on it," Ida Mae said, standing.

"If we're going to do that, I want Dan in on the next meeting," Henry announced. "He can't hide up there in Chicago while we battle everything out down here. I'm calling him tonight. Maybe he can be here this weekend."

April stared at Henry. Dan's wish would come true. He'd have a valid reason to visit Booneville. But when he heard what it was, he might not be so eager for the trip.

Dan's late-night phone call to April confirmed her fear that he wasn't happy with this turn of events.

"I thought after tonight it would be settled," he said. "Who supported you?"

"You expected me to be shot down immediately, didn't you?"

"Frankly, yes."

"Thanks a lot."

"April, this sculpture is folly. You may convince a few of your loyal followers that it isn't, but the townspeople will not like this project, believe me."

"So come down and vote against me. You have Henry and Gerry on your side right off the bat. Bill may vote against the sculpture, too, so your negative vote would finish me off."

"That may be exactly what happens. Can you handle that?"

"Sure."

"And then what about us?"

"I don't know."

"I do, and you were right about this sculpture being part of our situation. You're going to blame me if this project doesn't go through."

"You could make a big difference if you wanted to."

"Listen, I can't imagine this thing on the town square. What's more, I'm afraid erecting it with my grandmother's money will set the town against the whole concept of her legacy."

"No, that won't happen."

"It might. April, you can't force your concept of art down the townspeople's throats and expect them to swallow it."

"I wouldn't force, I would educate. It could be done. You should have seen Bess Easley. At first she reacted against the sculpture, but gradually she began to appreciate it, and before she left, she really liked the concept.''

"Bess admires you. You won't get that kind of cooperation from everyone else in town."

"And certainly not from you."

"April, I— Oh, hell. I'll see you Saturday."

"Are we meeting in the bank again?"

"No. That was a bad idea last time, and whether you think I side with Henry or not, I don't want him to have an unfair advantage. He does in that building."

"I'm glad you realize that."

"We'll meet at Jesse's café."

"That's nice and private. Only half the county comes in for a cup of coffee every morning."

"Jesse's agreed to close down for a half hour, from ten to ten-thirty. It shouldn't take much longer than that."

"Not if everyone's mind is made up."

Dan sighed. "By the way, are you still wearing the ring to bed?"

"I'm not telling."

"I don't know why I asked. I don't believe in the damn thing anyway. Good night, April."

"Good night, Dan." April replaced the receiver in its cradle and gazed into the green depths of the ring on her finger. Dan might believe in its powers if he knew that he'd become her obsession, just as he'd said he wanted to be.

No matter what inauspicious circumstances were bringing him to her, she wanted desperately to see him again. Even his rejection of the sculpture and the harsh words they'd exchanged couldn't blunt the razor-sharp edge of her passion. Whether lust or love ruled her heart she wasn't sure. She only knew she had to have him back in her arms once more, no matter what the cost.

JESSE HARDCASTLE WAS one of the few women in Booneville besides April who ran her own business. Unlike April, however, she declined to take part in community projects, claiming that she and her café were the Switzerland of their little world, an oasis of neutrality in a hotbed of strong allegiances.

April respected her stand and realized the wisdom of it, considering that Jesse would find herself defending her chosen opinions every day of the week and might very well lose customers who didn't agree with her. For April, controversy wasn't nearly as dangerous because her customers seldom lingered to converse over a cup of coffee the way Jesse's did.

Jesse's Café, on the northwest corner of the square and catty-corner from Henry's bank, was the obvious location to hold the board meeting, provided Jesse agreed to hang her Closed sign on the door for the duration of the meeting. When April drove past the café just before ten on Saturday morning, the sign was already in place.

April could see her breath in the bitterly cold morning air as she parked the truck on the square and walked toward the café. During her round of chores before daylight, April could have sworn that a few snowflakes touched her face, and the leaden clouds that now covered the sun indicated that winter would come early to Booneville this year.

The café's windows gleamed a bright welcome. Anxious to get out of the cold but even more anxious to see Dan, April hurried toward the door. Then she deliberately slowed her step. The other members of the board must not suspect that she and Dan had become lovers while she was in Chicago. Her entrance had to be sedate, her greeting to Dan nonchalant. Only he would attribute significance to her choice of contacts over glasses this morning.

Through the clear panes of the door April noticed that the men had pushed two tables together to provide enough room, and Jesse was plying everyone with steaming mugs of coffee and her morning's delivery of Danish. Dan was facing the door and laughing about something.

He hadn't seen her, and for a moment April stood outside the café and savored the sight of him. Like everyone else at the table, he'd dressed for the cold. April was pleased that he still owned a plaid flannel shirt and could slip back into the country atmosphere of Jesse's Café without seeming out of place. In that instant she knew she wanted Dan to come home again for good. Yet he'd told her how he felt about farming. He'd no more be satisfied with chickens than Jimmy had been.

With a sigh April opened the door. The tiny silver bell attached to the inside jingled, and the men stopped talking and turned toward her. "Hi," she said with what she hoped was a jaunty smile. "Any Danish left for me?"

"You bet," Bill said, starting to rise. The others followed suit.

"Nobody gets up, remember?"

"Right," they all chorused and sat down again.

The only empty seat was next to Dan. April took off her old quilted jacket and draped it over the chair. She'd had to go for warmth instead of looks today, including jeans instead of a dress and a yellow cable-knit sweater. While sitting down she allowed herself the merest glance at Dan's face. April looked away quickly. Could everyone else see the emotion shining in those blue eyes? If so, the lovers' secret would be out in seconds.

Jesse bustled in from the kitchen with another mug and a fresh pot of coffee. "Here you are, April," she said, placing the mug on the table and filling it from the pot in her hand. "And I heard that remark about the Danish. You know I wouldn't let these characters devour everything. I saved one of your favorites, strawberry. Want me to heat it up with a pat of butter?"

"Jesse, you know my weaknesses." Instantly April regretted her choice of words as Dan nudged her under the table with his knee.

"She certainly knows mine," M.G. said as he bit into his

pastry. "I hate to tell you, Henry, but this beats all heck out of meeting in the bank. You didn't offer us so much as a toothpick and water."

"Pay me for the service and I will, M.G. Jesse's not donating the refreshments, last I heard."

"Not on your life," Jesse said, returning with April's warm Danish. "I should charge you double this morning. Cold Saturday like this, all the farmers come in for miles around, and I'm losing their business."

"We'll be gone by ten-thirty. I promise, Jesse," Dan said. "And we appreciate your letting us have the place at all."

Jesse grinned. "I'll probably do a landslide business when you clear out. Everyone will want to know what you talked about."

"And you're free to tell them," Dan said, "as long as you get the facts straight. Everyone agreed?"

The rest of the board members nodded.

"We don't want to have secrets," M.G. commented. "Just a little peace and quiet while we work things out."

"Then I'll sit right over here and listen." Jesse chose a table nearby and sat down expectantly.

"And I guess we'd better get started," Dan said. "I understand all of you have seen April's sculpture."

"Have we ever!" Henry exclaimed. "Did she even show it to you while she was in Chicago? I can't believe you let her get by with that monstrosity."

M.G. cleared his throat. "Let's eliminate name-calling from this discussion, shall we? To many people the sculpture is a fine work of art, not a monstrosity."

"Oh, Lord." Henry slapped his forehead. "M.G.'s turning cultural on us."

"We'll proceed with this in an orderly fashion," Dan said firmly. "But first let me straighten one thing out, Henry. I saw my role as April's advisor, not some sort of tyrant who would dictate her choice."

April thrilled to his tone of command and his defense of

her actions. Maybe, just maybe, he'd come through for her after all.

Gerald Sloan put down his coffee mug. "And what, as her advisor, did you say when you saw the sculpture and learned that she intended something very much like it to rise on yon town square?" The lawyer gestured toward the door of the café.

"I said I thought it was inappropriate."

April cringed. Dan's knee pressed hard against hers under the table, and she knew he was trying to tell her he cared, despite what he felt obliged to say.

"That's my boy," Henry said with an approving nod.

"However, she disagreed with me. Had we voted between the two of us, we would have had a tie, so I decided perhaps she should present the idea to the rest of you. Frankly I expected all four of you to reject it. That would have settled the matter."

M.G. shifted in his chair and adjusted his wire-rimmed glasses. "I'd like to say something. When April first pulled the tablecloth off the statue, or sculpture, or whatever, I reacted like everyone else in the room. But the thing grows on you, maybe because you can look at it a million times and see something different each time. A soldier on a horse is a soldier on a horse, period. But this...we might never get tired of it."

April smiled at him. "Thanks, M.G."

"And another thing. I wouldn't be surprised if Irene would have loved it."

"You're right, M.G.," April said quickly. "In fact—"

Gerald Sloan cut her off. "That's speculation."

"I'm glad I have a lawyer on my side," Henry said with a chuckle.

Dan turned to Bill. "You've been pretty quiet through all of this. What's your opinion?"

"Well, it keeps changing, Dan, according to whether I feel like being in the doghouse with my wife or not."

Everyone laughed, including April. Ida Mae was loyal to the end, and she was insisting that her husband be, too.

"But seriously," Bill continued, "I was put on this board, not my wife, and I will make an independent decision." With that remark he looked directly at Henry. "The strange thing is that every day that goes by, I become more intrigued with April's idea. That sculpture on the square would show people around here that Booneville is a progressive town. I like that."

"We'll show them that we're idiots who will spend thousands of dollars on nothing," Henry said with a sneer.

Emboldened by M.G. and Bill's support, April spoke. "Thousands of dollars on a thing of beauty, Henry. And here's something you should appreciate. We'll be getting a real bargain. The amount of money we're offering is only enough to cover materials for a large sculpture like that, which would be true of a soldier on a horse, too, I suppose. Anyway, the artist has agreed to do the work and make nothing on it."

"I can understand that," Henry said, obviously unswayed by her argument. "There's not much work to be done in the first place. Give me the money, and I'll make you something just as good. Maybe better."

April clenched her coffee cup. "Henry Goodpasture, your ego is—"

"April." Dan's hand covered hers.

His gentle touch silenced her as nothing else could have. Instead of dwelling on Henry's obnoxious behavior, she was busy dealing with the warmth of Dan's fingers and the memory of how expertly he had stroked her naked body.

He left his hand on hers for just a moment, not enough to rouse the suspicions of the people around the table. "I would call for a vote at this point, but I'm reluctant to do that. We could have a tie, and if we can't break it, we'll lose the entire legacy. I'd rather not risk voting now when we might end up with an unbreakable stalemate."

April looked at him. A tie. If M.G., Bill and she were on one side, that meant Dan considered himself on the other side. She could only guess how much it was costing him emotionally to deny her what she wanted: Despite her disappointment that he couldn't imagine the sculpture on the square, she grudgingly admired him for sticking with his beliefs and risking her displeasure.

"I think we could do with some input, some public opinion, before we vote," M.G. suggested.

Dan shook his head. "The townspeople couldn't have much of an opinion until they see April's sculpture and have some idea of what we're talking about. She can't have a parade through her living room. She'd never get any work done."

Jesse stood up. "I've been trying to figure this out. How could something you're considering for the square fit in April's living room?"

"It's a smaller sculpture, Jesse," April explained, "and it will only give people an idea of what to expect for the larger one. As to turning my living room into an art gallery, I don't mind if that's what it takes."

"Why not put your sculpture in the café?" Jesse suggested. "You'll have the exposure, and I'll attract more customers."

April smiled. "You're a true businesswoman, Jesse."

"I think that's a great idea," M.G. said. "If April doesn't mind. After all, the sculpture is her property."

"I don't mind. I know Jesse will take good care of it."

Dan glanced around the table again. "Does this suit everyone?"

Henry frowned. "Well, we can't have a vote now, that's for sure, or we'll put all the projects on the line. But I say we leave the statue in here for a week and then vote. We'll know what public opinion is by then, although I can already tell you nobody will want that thing."

"I'd prefer two weeks," April said, thinking quickly.

"Next Saturday night I'd like to invite the sculptor down to give a talk somewhere, maybe in the 4-H building, about the work. Then we can vote the following weekend."

"That might be interesting," M.G. said.

Henry snorted. "We're just dragging out the inevitable, but I can see some of you want to turn this into a circus. I can't save you from your foolishness, so go ahead and take your two weeks."

"All agreed?" Dan asked once more and received a chorus of affirmative answers. "Then let's leave so that Jesse can open for the thriving business she expects once we're gone."

As they stood and bundled up in their heavy coats and all the men except Dan pulled on caps, April wondered how to speak to Dan alone. Surely he wouldn't drive back to Chicago today without stopping by her house on the way out of town. Last time he'd done that, she'd sent him away before their emotions could overwhelm them. This time she wouldn't be so prudish—if he arrived on her doorstep at all.

"Bet I surprised you, huh?" Bill took her elbow as the crowd headed for the door.

"A pleasant surprise," April answered, smiling up at him. "Thanks, Bill. Idie should bake you a whole batch of frosted brownies for that."

"She's tried to bribe me with food all week, but I really did make up my own mind."

"I know. That's what makes it more special. You really believe in what I'm trying to do."

"And so do I," M.G. added, coming to her other side. "We'll get support for the idea. Have faith, April."

"With you two on my side, how can I help it? I wish Irene could be here to be a part of all this."

M.G. looked wistful. "Yeah. But of course if she were still alive, you'd be having bake sales forever just to pay for the sculpture. She wasn't about to tell us she was rich."

"No, and I've decided that was very wise of her," April

8

said. She watched Dan go through the door ahead of them, and she began to panic. What if he left, certain that she was angry enough not to want to see him? She thought quickly. "If you'll excuse me, I'm going to ask Dan to contact the sculptor when he gets back to Chicago. That'll save me a long-distance call."

"Good idea," M.G. said. "And I'm glad you're asking him down. I'd like to meet the guy who created *Impulse*."

April hurried forward and reached Dan just as he was starting the Honda's engine. He rolled down the window at her approach.

"About the sculptor," she said in a voice loud enough for the departing board members to hear. "Could you make the contact for me so I don't have to call long distance?"

Dan lifted an eyebrow questioningly, but his answer was casual. "Sure."

April rested her hands on the open window of the car and lowered her voice. "Driving back today?"

He gazed at her intently. "Why, are you anxious for me to call Erica this afternoon?"

"Not necessarily. I was wondering if you'd care to drop by on your way out of town. It seems a shame to travel all the way down and all the way back without picking up a dozen fresh eggs. They wouldn't spoil between here and Chicago. You could have them with your Sunday breakfast."

"I seldom eat breakfast when I'm alone."

"What a shame."

"That I seldom eat breakfast?"

"No, that you're planning to be alone tomorrow morning." The others were gone by now, and she leaned a little closer. "When was the last time you watched a sunrise over a multicolored henhouse?"

He looked at her in disbelief. "I just shot you down in there."

"I know."

"Yet you're issuing me an invitation."

"That's right. Care to accept?"

His hands tightened on the steering wheel, and passion flared in his eyes. "I may be slow, but I'm no fool."

"Then I'll meet you there."

"Just a minute. What about parking the car outside? Red is a very visible color."

"I think there's room in the old barn."

He gazed at her for a long moment. "If we're going to do this, there's something you should know."

"What's that?"

"I...the games are over for me, April."

"What do you mean?"

"I'm in love with you."

CHAPTER ELEVEN

APRIL CLUTCHED THE CAR DOOR for support. "Why are you telling me that here? Why now?"

"In case you want to change your mind about that invitation. In case you thought going to bed with me will be a carefree experience with no strings attached. It won't."

"Dan, you may be sure about your feelings, but I'm not. What if I hurt you again? What if—"

"It's too late, April. If I lose you again, it will be agony, but I don't intend to lose you. I made up my mind when you walked into the café this morning that whatever happens with the sculpture isn't going to keep us apart. Temporarily it might be a problem, like this morning. I thought you'd be angry about all this and wouldn't want much to do with me for a while."

She averted her gaze. Making this overture to him, after what had taken place in the café, revealed a lot about her state of mind concerning Dan. She glanced at his strong hands as they rested on the steering wheel. No matter what had happened, she wanted him to touch her again, love her again. "Maybe I'm not strong enough to stand on principle right now." She looked into his eyes. "Or maybe it's that crazy emerald."

"You've been wearing it."

"At night. Yes."

"I may become a believer yet." Slowly he stroked the length of her bare ring finger and his voice grew husky.

"Why don't you drive home, and I'll be there in a little while."

"Henry and Mabel's again?"

He shook his head. "M.G. He wants to see me about something."

April turned her hand over and squeezed his. "Don't stay long."

"No way. And you drive safely."

"I will." April gave his hand one more squeeze and hurried away to her truck. He loved her. Even though she'd sensed it before, hearing it confirmed really shook her. He had the courage to say the words out loud while she'd avoided even thinking them.

Twice in her life she'd spoken words of love to a man. The first time, with Dan, had been the product of a young girl's fantasy, a dream destined to be shattered. The second time, with Jimmy, had been infatuation born partially of her disillusionment with Dan. April wondered if the unspoken emotion that gripped her now might be the real thing. She wanted to be sure before blurting out words that contained such power.

The inside of the truck was cold, and she turned on the heater. Raindrops splashed against the windshield as she drove down the two-lane country road away from town. Shaky with excitement, she began making plans for their next few hours together. The weather should keep away visitors and customers. With a little luck, they could have the night to themselves. All to themselves.

BY THE TIME she heard a car in the lane leading to the house, she'd set the scene. He'd admitted loving her, but she wanted more. She wanted him to love this haven in the country, too. He'd grown up in a house like this; the sweet memories were there for her to draw from, and instinct told her Dan wasn't yet a confirmed city boy.

It was raining in earnest now, and she pulled on boots

and a yellow slicker and hat before hurrying out to open the barn door for him. Long ago the barn had been used for a few cows and one horse, but the large livestock had been sold years ago, and the barn was only for storage now. Someday April planned to paint it different colors, too.

When he saw her, he started to get out of the car, but she waved him back in and sloshed through the rain to the barn. He drove behind her but got out again when she struggled with the heavy sliding door.

"I can do it. You'll be soaked," she protested as he came to her side.

He grinned at her and reached for the heavy door. "I guess that means I'll have to take my clothes off and get dry."

"I hadn't thought of that."

"Obviously. You wore a raincoat."

April laughed as together they pushed the door aside. She stepped into the dim interior of the barn while Dan returned to the car and drove it inside. The Honda fit into the center aisle of the barn with ease.

"I saw your Eggs Sold Out sign by the road," Dan said as he climbed out of the car and walked back to her. "Does that mean I don't get my dozen?"

"Do you believe everything you read?"

"Ah, subterfuge." He smiled and touched her damp cheek with the palm of his hand. "I was wondering if any of your customers would be out in this weather."

"No point in taking chances." She turned her head and kissed his palm.

"No," he said with a smile. He framed her face with both hands and tilted it up to his. "You look like an ad for Morton Salt. I especially like the rain hat."

"You could have done with a hat," she replied, reaching up to wipe a drop of water from his cheek. "Your hair is dripping."

"I don't care. It's been a long time since I've gotten

soaked in a rainstorm.'' He studied her lovingly. "You
know, I like the smell of this old barn. It reminds me of a
certain rainy afternoon a long time ago, about this time of
year. Two kids got trapped during a downpour and scurried
in here to keep dry. Then they huddled together to keep
warm. And then… Do you remember?''

"I'm surprised that you do," April said in a voice as soft
as the rain on the old barn roof. "I thought only girls remembered a first kiss.''

He slipped his hand under her damp hair and caressed
the nape of her neck. "I have a memory like an elephant
when it comes to you.'' Gently he urged her closer and took
off her hat with his other hand. "For old time's sake,'' he
murmured, tilting her head back and brushing her lips with
his.

At her small, nearly inaudible moan he lifted his head
and looked into her eyes. The raw hunger reflected there
took his breath away. Dropping her hat to the barn floor he
hauled her, heavy slicker and all, into his arms and kissed
her hard. She was ready for him, her lips yielding and warm,
her mouth open to receive the thrust of his tongue.

The taste of her inflamed him after long nights without
her. Immediately he felt the primitive beat of arousal pounding through his veins, and he fought with the metal clasps
of her rain-slick coat.

At last the coat was open, her softness accessible. He held
her tightly and rubbed the lower half of his body against
her in a vain attempt to ease the pulsing heat she evoked
with only a kiss. He had to love her, had to bury himself
deep within her. But not here. They didn't have to settle for
a blanket on a cold barn floor. Not now.

He left the invitation of her lips reluctantly and refastened
her coat. "Come on," he said, steering her toward the door.
"This old barn was great for a couple of kids, but we're
not kids anymore. I'm taking you to bed.''

They raced through the rain holding hands and dodging

puddles. On the front porch April took off her boots and rain gear and advised Dan to kick off his muddy shoes.

"We can dry the rest inside," she said, tossing her coat on the porch swing and opening the front door.

Dan followed her into the warmth of the living room and felt as if he'd come home. A fire in the hearth dispelled all the gloom of the rainy day and turned the house into a cozy refuge. He remembered the furniture from their dating days. Many times he'd sat on the couch's floral-print cushions talking to her mother and father while April got ready for a movie or a school dance.

The last time he'd sat there, he'd been wearing a tux and feeling like a big man on campus after nearly two years at Blackburn. And then April had come down the stairs, looking like a vision in a pale yellow chiffon dress. His April... Yet in the end she hadn't been his, had she? This house was where she'd lived with someone else, where they'd— He glanced toward the downstairs bedroom.

"Dan?"

He turned to see her standing in her sock feet with her hand out.

"I asked if I could take your jacket, but you didn't seem to hear me."

He unzipped the damp jacket and peeled it away from his flannel shirt. "Sorry."

"Dan—"

"I guess reminiscing comes easily in Booneville. This room...I remember the last time we... Oh, April!" He swept her into his arms and buried his face against her neck. "I'm going to love you until you forget there ever was another man."

April became completely still in his arms. She'd seen him glance toward the bedroom and had assumed he was imagining their lovemaking there. Until this moment she'd forgotten about Jimmy, and that she'd shared that room with him until their divorce. After two years without him she'd come to think of the master bedroom downstairs as hers, not theirs. But for Dan that passage of time had little meaning, especially when he had just relived a last date that had taken place eight years ago.

"Dan." She eased away from him and cradled his face in her hands. "Forgive me. I didn't think. We can go upstairs."

"No." He drew her back against him. "I want to banish him from there. I want to replace his memory with mine."

Tears misted her eyes. "I never really loved him."

His tone was gentle. "You never really loved me, either, did you?"

"Not enough, Dan. Not nearly enough. But I was just a silly girl."

"Silly, maybe, and beautiful and headstrong." He took a deep breath. "I thought I loved you then, but it was nothing like this."

"No." Eyes brimming, she shook her head. "Not for me, either." She took his hand. "And I'm going to make love to you until you forget everything but this moment."

He realized later that she kept her promise. When they stepped inside the bedroom, he stood in the doorway and watched her undress. With her deliberate, seductive motions the past faded from his mind, and the future lost its power to threaten. Her body gleamed in the soft light from the casement window. Piece by piece her clothing fell to the floor.

When the last of it was gone, she remained there for a moment and let him look at her. Shadows from the raindrops coursing down the windowpane traced liquid patterns on her creamy skin. He became mesmerized by the rain shadows as he followed their sliding path down the slope of her breasts to the nippled peaks and beyond, to the curve of her ribs, her smooth belly and the dark curls below.

The chill air seeping in around the window frame smelled of the rain, damp and fertile. The room was cool, yet she didn't seem to feel the cold. Slowly she walked across the hardwood floor to her nightstand and picked up an object lying there. Only when she placed it on her finger did he realize what it was.

Then, wearing only the ring, she came to him. The ancient creak of the wood mingled with the patter of the rain were the only sounds in the room, sounds that would never be the same for him again. He closed his eyes as she began unbuttoning his flannel shirt.

She took her time. When he murmured his impatience and tried to help her with the various fastenings, she moved his hand away with a tiny shake of her head.

"You're in the country now," she said, her voice rhythmic and musical, blending with the rain. "Life moves slower here."

She tortured him with her butterfly touch while she took away the last of his clothing and revealed the full extent of his arousal. With superhuman effort he restrained his impulse to crush her in his arms and take what he needed. Instead, he followed her lead as they stretched out on the brass bedstead.

His senses had never been more alive to his surroundings...the floral scent of the sheets, the sound of the bedsprings under them, the moist press of April's lips on his eyelids, his cheeks, his chin and at last his mouth. Her fragrant hair swung down against his cheek, and her nipples brushed lazily against his chest as she ran her tongue over the sensitive inside of his mouth. He thought he would come apart.

Yet as her kisses moved down the column of his neck, he knew she wasn't through with him. His breathing accelerated with the downward progress she made, and when she reached her destination, he cried out in response to the sweet agony of her tongue and lips teasing his throbbing flesh. When he thought he could stand no more, he wove his fingers through her hair.

"Enough," he said, panting. "April, I can't—"

She retraced her path and kissed him on the mouth. "You're doing fine," she whispered, moving over him, "just fine."

"Wait. I haven't done anything about—"

"It was my responsibility this time. Don't worry." Gently she lowered herself, taking him gradually deep inside as she watched the pleasure sweep over him. His pleasure was hers; his joy filled her with happiness. April knew the truth at last. "I love you, too," she murmured.

He gripped her shoulders, and twin flames sprang to life in his eyes. His words came out in a hoarse croak. "What did you say?"

"I love you, Dan."

"You're sure?"

"Yes."

"Then nothing else matters."

"Nothing but this." She rotated her hips in a slow circle and then reversed the motion.

Dan moaned and looked at her through glazed eyes. "You're driving me crazy."

"That's the idea." She began to rock back and forth, and he picked up her rhythm, pressing upward to increase the friction that was fanning the blaze of their desire into a bonfire of passion.

April writhed against him, and the bedsprings sang with their movements. She had never given so much, nor received so much in return. With every motion of her body she told him of her love, and he answered in kind. The sound of the rain accompanied the soft sounds that grew to exultant cries of release as the lovers shuddered together in a drenching climax.

For a long while Dan lay still, holding her tight and listening to the rain. Finally he reached for her hand as it lay limply on the pillow beside his head. The ring that had felt cold each time he took it from his dresser drawer was warm now from her heat, her unbridled response to him. He wanted to ask her to keep it forever, but he hesitated. She'd admitted her love. Maybe that was enough for now.

She lifted her head, and her brown eyes were warm as she gazed down at him. "Now do you believe?"

"At this very moment you could convince me of anything."

Immediately April thought of the sculpture. Perhaps she could ask him now to support her wishes, and he would agree. Yet she wouldn't do that. Trading on what they had just shared to get her way would diminish their newfound love for each other.

She smiled. "How about if I try to convince you that evening chores on a chicken farm are exciting and fun?" she asked instead.

"Do we have to leave this bed to find out?"

"I'm afraid so."

"Somehow I knew that. Can we come back afterward?"

"I was counting on it."

He ruffled her hair. "Then let's get going. But don't think you can turn me into a farm boy by promising fringe benefits."

"I won't." Yet she wondered if that was exactly what she was hoping to do. She'd grown up watching her mother and father work together on the farm. It wasn't a bad life. She sympathized with Dan's feelings, especially considering that his father had been killed in a farming accident, but she wished he would open his mind a little more.

Dan was cheerful enough as they tended to the chickens and settled them for the night. Chores were lighter at this time of year, and for that April was glad. How would Dan react to the more arduous seasons of spring and summer?

When they returned to the house, Dan stoked the fire, and April heated up the homemade vegetable soup she'd planned for dinner. She'd made bread earlier in the week, and on a trip to Springfield she'd picked up some of the wine Dan had served her in Chicago. The meal would be simple but good, just as she wanted him to perceive her lifestyle here. How could he possibly resist it?

They ate perched on pillows by the fire. As she served Dan seconds of soup and hot slices of buttered bread, she casually mentioned that she'd made both herself.

"I'm getting the picture, April," Dan said with a wry smile. "My favorite wine, home-cooked food, a cozy fire in a wonderful old farmhouse on a rainy night. I'd be a fool not to prefer all of this to my place in Chicago. And I do. But the price you have to pay is too high."

"Are you talking about your father?"

"Some. But more than that is the insecurity. A really bad heat wave could kill half your chickens. Cold is dangerous, too. Lack of rain or too much at the wrong times could ruin your produce for that season. You're totally dependent upon Mother Nature, and she's a fickle gal."

"Maybe I'm dependent on the weather, like you say, but I'm not tied to a boss. I'm my own boss. I like that."

"I would, too, but not under these circumstances."

She gave him a long look. "I don't want to leave this farm, Dan."

"I know you don't."

"It's a long commute from Chicago."

"I know that, too."

"Then?"

"I'm working on it." He glanced at her. "Sounds as if you've considered extending this relationship."

"Maybe."

"Especially if I'm willing to take up farming?"

"Dan, is it really out of the question?"

"Yes."

She sighed in disappointment and frustration.

"Hey." He lifted her chin with one finger. "Don't give up on us just because I want to hitch my wagon to a star instead of a plow. Give me some time to find a solution."

April smiled uncertainly. "Okay."

"And I'm going to get myself another bowl of that fantastic soup."

She laughed. "I'll have to roll you out of here."

"Just so I can still fit through the bedroom door tonight." He winked and left for the kitchen.

"By the way," April asked when he returned, "can you tell me anything about what M.G. wanted, or was your conversation confidential?"

"I can tell you, and only you, because I think you should know, for a couple of reasons. He tried to convince me to approve the sculpture and break the inevitable tie."

"My goodness, he must be more dedicated to the idea than I thought."

"Maybe, but he's dedicated to the memory of my grandmother even more. They were lovers."

"What?"

"I know. I couldn't believe it, either, but then, she kept the secret of her fortune from all of us, so why not this?"

"The money was one thing, but I've never known a love affair to go unnoticed in Booneville. Too many eyes are watching, too many ears listening." April stared into the fire. "But I'm glad for them."

"You should also be glad for yourself. M.G. thought over his sculpture business and decided my grandmother would have wanted what you've proposed, so he'll be your staunch supporter forever. That's one reason I thought you should know about our conversation."

"But he didn't convince you?"

Dan shook his head. "He's operating from emotion. I'm trying to use logic." He looked at the sculpture sitting on its tablecloth-draped stand in the corner of the living room. "Logically that sort of sculpture doesn't fit on the square."

April started to argue that art wasn't ruled by logic, but she thought better of it. They'd been through this enough times, and Dan didn't seem likely to change his mind. "You said there were two reasons you needed to tell me about M.G."

"There are. At one point I asked him why he and my grandmother didn't make their situation official and get married."

"Good question. They were both free to do that, and the whole town would have given them its blessing."

"Well, M.G. wanted to marry her, and not because he knew anything about the money, either. He was in the dark like everyone else in town."

"I'm amazed. Irene was something else."

"She could keep her secrets when she wanted to. But she was painfully honest with M.G. when it came to her feelings for him. She said that he'd never replace my grandfather in her heart. There had been only one great passion in her life, a union that had been symbolized by an emerald-and-diamond heirloom ring."

April started and instinctively touched the emerald stone on her finger.

He noticed her gesture. "That's right, April. It's powerful medicine. Once it casts a spell, the two people involved will never be completely free of each other. I thought you should be warned."

She gazed into the blue depths of his eyes and remembered all the nights she'd worn the ring and longed to have his arms around her. The ring had worked its magic, and she was irrevocably in love with the man who'd given it to her. "To borrow a phrase from this morning—it's too late."

DAN LEFT SUNDAY AFTERNOON, and after her chores on Monday morning April took the sculpture to Jesse's Café. By the time she got home again, her telephone was already ringing, and the stream of calls kept coming for the next two days. No one's reaction was neutral; people either loved the sculpture or hated it. By Wednesday afternoon, when

the Beautify Booneville committee met in the library, the
entire town was choosing sides.

"I've told Henry he'd better vote for that sculpture or
else," Mabel announced to the women gathered in the reading section of the library.

Bess looked at Mabel with curiosity. "Or else what?"

"He knows," Mabel said, and folded her arms.

April frowned as she guessed Mabel's possible form of
coercion. "I would hate to think this issue was entering into
yours and Henry's, ah, private life, Mabel."

"Can you tell me a faster way to make a man come
around to your way of thinking? It's a time-honored method
used by women."

Bess gasped. "Mabel, do you mean that you won't allow
Henry to exercise his husbandly rights?"

"If you're asking if he's getting any exercise in the bedroom, the answer is no, not until he approves the sculpture."

"But, Mabel," Bess protested, her eyes wide, "what if
he *never* votes for the sculpture?"

Mabel pursed her lips. "I don't think that will happen,
Bess. Henry's a normal man, and you know how men are
about that matter."

Ida Mae could contain herself no longer and began to
laugh. "I can't believe this is happening," she chortled.
"Sexual blackmail in Booneville."

"Well, what would you do, Idie, if your Bill hadn't already decided in favor of the sculpture?"

Ida Mae laughed harder. "My protests usually center
around food," she admitted with a grin. "I can do without
that easier."

"I don't think there should be any blackmail, sexual or
otherwise," April said. "Really, Mabel, I wish you
wouldn't resort to—" She bit the inside of her cheek to
keep from laughing along with Ida Mae.

"It's the only thing that will work," Mabel said matter-
of-factly. "He's the most pigheaded man in the world, and

I have to deal with him as best I can. Now don't you ladies worry about a thing. That sculpture will be approved.''

"Let's hope so," April said. "Now about Saturday night's meeting when the sculptor will speak to the townspeople. I thought the beautification committee might act as hostesses and provide some punch and cookies. Volunteers?" April quickly organized refreshments and cleanup for Saturday, and after some discussion about ordering seeds for next spring's planting on the square, the meeting was dismissed.

On the way out of the library Ida Mae touched April's arm. "Any chance Dan will change his mind and vote for the project?"

April shook her head.

"Too bad." Ida Mae glanced at April. "That's some coercive method of Mabel's."

"Uh-huh."

Ida Mae lowered her voice. "I guess she knows what she's doing, but I wouldn't try that on Dan if I were you."

April stopped walking and stared at her friend. "What makes you think I'd have the opportunity?"

"What makes you think I don't suspect what's going on?"

April smiled sheepishly. "And here I thought I was rivaling Irene's ability to keep secrets."

"I've known you too long, girl. Irene wouldn't have been able to keep secrets from her third-grade pal, either. She was lucky not to have one around."

"No, I think she was unlucky not to have someone like you, Idie. You've been terrific through all of this. I just don't want the whole town to know about Dan and me because we *are* on this board together, and people might think that wasn't proper, two board members—"

"In love?"

"I...yes."

"That's wonderful."

"But, Idie, this sculpture thing isn't making our relationship any easier. Sometimes when we argue about that, I feel as if he's the same old Dan, and I should stay far, far away from him."

"He's not the same old Dan, not from what Bill's told me. And because I'm your best friend, I'm going to give you some unasked-for advice."

"Which is?"

"Don't let this crazy sculpture ruin what could be the best thing that ever happened to you."

CHAPTER TWELVE

TRUE TO HER PROMISE in Chicago, April provided Erica with free lodging at the farm when she came to Booneville on Saturday. That meant Dan had to find a place to stay the night elsewhere, but under the circumstances of April's high visibility these days she thought it wiser, anyway.

Erica arrived late Saturday afternoon in a white Firebird that jolted noisily along April's lane and screeched to a stop in a cloud of dust. Through the car window April could see that Erica wore a red bandanna tied like a headband around her blond hair and an elaborately embroidered denim jacket. April decided this must be Erica's idea of country dress.

"You found the place," April said when Erica turned off the engine.

"Of course I did. Even drove through Booneville. It's a lovely little town, but it definitely needs a creative kick in the rear." She climbed out of the car and glanced around, her gaze lingering on the multicolored henhouse. "Nice place."

April glanced at Erica's skintight designer jeans. More of the sculptor's "country look", April decided. "It's quiet."

"True, except for the music. Why are you playing Beethoven out here?"

"The chickens seem to like it better than Bach."

"Oh." Erica gave April a strange look. "Of course."

April laughed. "A lot of farmers play music for their livestock these days. Experiments have shown that it calms the animals and makes them more productive. I've introduced my chickens to classical music instead of popular, that's all. So you see, I'm not as peculiar as you think.''

"Shucks. I was hoping you were a certified loony, like me. And all the farmers paint their outbuildings rainbow colors for some scientific reason, too?''

"Okay, you've got me there.''

"Aha! You are a fellow eccentric, even if you haven't learned to dress the part.''

April laughed and glanced down at her wool slacks and sweater in neutral shades. "I have to make a few concessions if I want to live in Booneville.''

"I understand. Think I'll get away with this garb? After all, they expect some weirdness, don't they?''

"I guess so,'' April admitted with a rueful smile.

"I'm counting on it. I've been giving this town a lot of thought recently.''

"Have you brought some preliminary ideas to show people tonight?''

"Have I ever.'' Erica strode around to the trunk and inserted the key in the lock.

April followed her and caught sight of the rear bumper for the first time. "That's a rental sticker, Erica. Isn't this your car?''

"Nope. Don't have one. My studio's in my flat, and I take a cab everywhere else.''

"Listen, Erica, I didn't realize you'd have to rent a car to come down here.''

"Ah, don't worry about it.'' Erica waved a gloved hand. "I had fun getting behind the wheel again. Unfortunately the officer who stopped me didn't agree that I should have that kind of fun, but what's a little speeding ticket?''

April groaned.

"Anyway, here's my presentation for tonight.'' Erica gestured toward the boxes in the open trunk. "We're giving them a slide show. I already had pictures of my other work, and I had slides made of the preliminary sketches for this one so that everyone can see them better.''

''You've gone to a lot of trouble and expense, and I'm beginning to feel guilty. At this rate the job could become very costly, and I wonder if it's worth the effort for you.''

''It is.'' Erica braced her booted feet and put both hands on her hips. She looked nearly ten feet tall. ''We're fighting the good fight, April.'' She flung one hand in the air. ''We're dreaming the impossible dream. I love it.''

April grinned. ''I'm glad you came down, then.''

''Me, too. Besides, you were right about the possibility for media attention. I can't measure everything I create in terms of how much money I make. This could be a very important sculpture for me.''

''I'm dying to know what you've come up with.''

''You'll love it.'' Erica picked up a long cardboard tube. ''If we've got some time, I'll show you the sketches before we leave for the meeting.''

''We've got time. I finished the chores early, so all we have to do is get you settled upstairs and eat supper.''

''Great.'' Erica grabbed her overnight bag and slung it over one shoulder. ''I hope you've got some of those cookies for dessert.''

''Better yet, I made pumpkin pie.''

''With whipped cream?''

''Yep.''

''I'm going to love the country.'' Erica pronounced as she slammed the trunk shut.

Later April sat and gazed at the sketches spread out on her kitchen table. ''*Growing Season*,'' she murmured. ''This is fantastic, Erica. I can feel all the excitement of spring with new crops poking out of the ground and all those hopeful beginnings.''

''I wanted to design something that would relate to the people here, to what is most important in their lives.''

"And you've done just that," April said, filled with admiration. "They've got to love this. I certainly do."

"Yes, but you were crazy about *Impulse*, and not everyone else in town is, from what you've said."

"Oh, but there's a world of difference between a sculpture called *Impulse* and one named *Growing Season*. People around here can't allow themselves to be guided by impulse all that much. Money is too tight and traditions too ingrained. But the growth of crops is something everyone in Booneville understands and takes pride in. You've made an inspired choice of subject."

"Let's hope so. And you made an inspired choice for our dinner?"

"Meat loaf?"

"I never get to have it in Chicago."

"And to think I originally figured you for a real gourmet."

"Nope. I love basic dishes, but I can't cook even basic stuff worth anything. With me in the kitchen, simple food becomes simply awful. I can see you're talented in that direction, though. Plus you seem to have a successful business here. You appear to be firmly rooted, and I'm a little jealous of that."

"When I was growing up on this farm, I swore never to spend my life in Booneville, but now that's exactly what I want most to do." April sighed. "At least I think it is."

Erica studied her across the kitchen table. "Meaning you also want to be with someone who happens to live in Chicago?"

"How did you know?"

"It doesn't take a genius. When Dan Butler called me about coming down here, he let something slip about being with you in Booneville last weekend, and I know you were staying in his apartment up there."

"I should warn you that he doesn't approve of the sculpture project, at least not with something modernistic like this.''

"So I gathered when he didn't rave about my work on the telephone.''

April sighed. "I want so much for him to support this idea and show that he's able to take a risk for a change.''

Erica lifted an eyebrow. "Show who?''

"Me, I guess. I don't know, Erica. I'm afraid to commit myself to a man who's so damn cautious, who won't rock the boat once in a while.''

"Is he a coward?''

"No,'' April said immediately, shocked at the sound of the word applied to Dan. "That's not the problem.''

"Then maybe he doesn't believe this is a risk worth taking.''

"But if he'd think more creatively, he would see that it is. If he can't use his imagination more, I wonder if he's really the man for me.''

Erica glanced at her. "Only you would know that. I haven't found a man yet who agreed with me on everything.''

"But this is so important, so *symbolic*, don't you think?''

"For you and me, perhaps, but maybe not for him. Maybe he has other symbols.''

April thought of the ring hidden away in her dresser drawer. His attitude toward the ring had surprised her, she had to admit. Still, his other reactions remained typical. He wouldn't reconsider his old aversion to farming, even if it was a way for them to build a life together. As for the sculpture, he would certainly vote against it unless Erica's presentation somehow changed his mind. As April cleaned up the dishes and Erica went over her notes for the meeting, April prayed that tonight's program would make a favorable impression on Dan.

IF SHE CLOSED HER EYES, April could pretend that the crowded 4-H hall was empty. Only a rare rustle of clothing or a subdued cough indicated that Erica was speaking to approximately four hundred people, or most of the able-bodied adults in the Booneville area.

April knew most of them by name. On the far side of the room her parents sat with Ida Mae's parents, Ed and Bernice Higby, and the Lowdermilk family, which numbered eleven adults. April wondered what all these people who had known her for years thought of this ruckus over a sculpture.

April's job was handling the light switches, and a few moments earlier she'd flipped them all down for the beginning of the slide presentation. Erica was standing to one side of the screen giving a narrative as the carousel automatically projected a series of sculptures, some large works in public places and others small pieces in elegant private homes throughout Chicago.

April was glad for the dim light. The less the crowd focused on Erica and her outfit the better. When she'd first stepped to the microphone, a murmur had rippled through the crowd, and April had noticed several elbows nudging neighboring ribs.

Only part of the stir was caused by the fact that the sculptor was a woman. Her mode of dress and her height also prompted heads to turn and usually reserved townspeople to stare. In her boots Erica was taller than most of the men here. Even Dan stood only barely even with her when they had met just before the presentation began.

As the person in charge of the program, Dan sat at the end of the first row of folding chairs. He'd introduced Erica to the crowd with a smooth diplomacy that gave no indication of his feelings toward her work or its appropriateness to the Booneville square. April was forced to admire his concerted effort not to influence the town's reaction.

At last Erica reached the portion of her talk in which she showed slides of her preliminary drawings. In an animated manner she discussed her idea and announced the title of the work. "I imagine *Growing Season* as a symbol of all you stand for here in Booneville," she said.

For the first time murmurs could be heard from the crowd.

"In addition to its obvious reference to your chief industry in the area, the sculpture will also demonstrate that Booneville is interested in the idea of growth itself, of the positive evolution of its citizens, of expanding the vision of the town to include such a progressive work of art in the very heart of the community."

April began to clap before she realized what she was doing. Tentatively some others in the crowd followed suit as the carousel clicked once more and the screen was blank.

"Thank you for your time," Erica said above the smattering of applause. "If we can have the lights back up, I'll answer questions."

Hands shot up as soon as April flipped the wall switches and illuminated the large room.

"We have a lot of children who play on the square," one woman said. "Would this sculpture be dangerous to them?"

"Not if I consider that when I design the final structure," Erica responded. "We can take into account a certain amount of climbing and playing around the base, and create the higher portions so they can't be scaled. I've done that before for park sculptures in Chicago."

Hiram Perkins stood up. "If you want something to represent Booneville, why not put up a giant cornstalk and be done with it? I could weld that together myself and save us all some time and money." Laughter greeted his statement, and when Hiram sat down again, April noticed Henry Goodpasture on his left. Henry carried a large mortgage on Hiram's farm and no doubt had put Hiram up to that last remark. Mabel's subversive tactics must not be working very well, April decided.

Then, to April's surprise, Bill Lowdermilk got out of his chair. His ruddy face was redder than usual, and he wore a stiff new pair of jeans. He stuck his hands in his back pockets and surveyed the crowd. "I'd like to comment on what Hiram said because I thought the same sort of thing myself once. Only I planned to have my kids make the sculpture at school out of pipe cleaners and modeling clay." More laughter swept the room. "But I've changed my mind, especially after hearing Miss Jorgenson's speech. How many of you grow corn? I mean to sell, not just for the table or your own animals?"

At least thirty hands went up.

"That's not even a majority. We grow lots of things besides corn around here. Soybeans, for instance."

Several others murmured their assent.

"I know most of the folks here," Bill continued, "and what they're raising. Even the ones raising Cain." He paused while people chuckled and winked at each other. "Anyway, I think we need something that represents all of us, and proves, like Miss Jorgenson said, that we're a town dedicated to growing. We're progressive. That's all I have to say on the subject."

As Bill sat down, April restrained herself from running over and hugging him. She couldn't have said it better, and many of the younger farmers, who looked to Bill for leadership, were nodding in agreement.

"And I say we'll be the laughingstock of the state if we put up this crazy thing," Henry Goodpasture remarked, rising from his seat.

Cheers went up from Henry's section of the hall, followed by angry accusations from the people surrounding Bill. A few insults were traded, and some fists waved in the air.

As the argument threatened to throw the meeting into chaos, Dan strode to the microphone and called for order. He'd listened to the presentation and the ensuing discussion with a sense of despair. He'd hoped that somehow tonight's meeting would change his mind, give him a reason to support April's project.

Instead, he discovered that the sculptor had created some

romantic nonsense about growing crops, of all things. Henry was right; Booneville would be the laughingstock of the state if the town spent money on some idyllic monument to farming when so many people were going bankrupt. April and her followers were living in a rosy dream world.

The crowd seemed equally divided on the issue. Henry's derision of the idea had influenced those who feared him to join his camp and those who disliked him to lean the other way. Bill Lowdermilk had gathered some support with his statement. Dan wondered if he'd be able to talk some sense into Bill this week, before the vote.

And April. If he thought about her much at all, he'd forget about sticking with his beliefs. Would she ever forgive him for voting against her next week?

He took a deep breath and spoke into the microphone. "I'm sure that all of us on the board appreciate your input. We have a better idea of what's proposed now, and what your reaction is to it. We'll vote next weekend, so in the meantime feel free to contact any of us with your comments and suggestions."

"What do you think, Dan?" someone called.

Dan winced. They weren't going to leave him alone. He hesitated and shook his head. "I'd rather not continue the discussion at this time."

"But we know Bill's opinion, and Henry's, and of course we know April wants it," someone else said. "You're kind of in charge here. Do you think we should put this thing up or not?"

Dan concluded from the man's deferential tone and the silence with which the crowd awaited an answer that his response could very well make a difference. He wondered why his opinion would hold this sort of weight. Maybe it was because he was Irene's grandson or because he now lived in Chicago and was therefore considered more sophisticated.

Whatever the reason, he had the power to tip the scales either way. And he didn't want it.

He looked toward the back of the room, and his gaze found April's. *Forgive me,* he begged silently. He saw a look of panic cross her features. Did she suspect his decision? "I think this particular sculpture would be a mistake," he said clearly.

April felt as if he'd just delivered a blow to her stomach. How could he do this? The blood rushed to her head and her ears began to ring, but she forced herself to listen as Dan continued.

"Ever since the idea of a sculpture was proposed, I've tried to be open-minded and consider whether it would be worthwhile. Now that I see what Miss Jorgenson would like to create here in Booneville, I'm certain it would be a waste of money."

M.G. stood up for the first time. "Why, Dan?" he asked mildly, although April could see the older man's hands clenching the brim of his felt hat. "I think Miss Jorgenson has come up with something that will mean a great deal to all of us."

"That's part of the problem, M.G. She romanticized farming in this sculpture. That might have been okay fifty years ago, but farming's in a lot of trouble these days. Many of you are in debt. I'd rather take this money and hand it to some family that's having a tough time paying the mortgage than spend it on a sculpture that builds false hopes about how easy it is to grow things for a living."

The entire crowd, including April, was stunned into silence by Dan's assessment. He'd turned the subject of Erica's sculpture against itself, and for a moment April had no answer for him.

"I believe Dan's said it all," Henry proclaimed, rising and spreading his arms wide, "and we may as well go home and not fritter away more time on this. We'll take the vote next week, as he said, but I know what the decision should be, and so do all of you.''

As the crowd began to stir, removing coats from the backs of chairs and purses from under them, April snapped out of her stupor. ''Hold it!'' she called and hurried toward the microphone at the front of the room.

She didn't look at Dan. Her intense anger might distract her from what she wanted to say. She stood on tiptoe and spoke into the microphone. ''I know times are difficult for many of us. That's the very reason we need this sculpture. If we give this money to a family or two, they'd be very grateful, but then what of the many others who could use the same help?''

She paused to take a breath. ''This sculpture is for inspiration, to remind all of us why we live in the country, why we pursue this crazy way of life in spite of the incredible odds. Isn't that sort of inspiration worth more than money? Money can only help a few, but a work of art could stand for centuries and tell the world that we in Booneville still believe in a *Growing Season*.''

''I believe in feeding my family,'' someone said, and a large number of people applauded.

''What about feeding your soul?'' April demanded.

''First we have to keep body and soul together,'' responded someone else.

Tears threatened, and her contact lenses began to hurt. She damned the reason for wearing them—to impress Dan. Now, thanks to him, her project had lost most of the support it had gained in the last week and during Erica's presentation tonight. She could still count on M.G.'s vote, and Bill's, but Gerald Sloan and Henry wouldn't have to change their minds because of public pressure, and neither would Dan. Her shoulders slumped as she realized that she had lost.

She barely noticed that Dan reached over and snapped the off button on the microphone. As she turned away, he spoke to her.

"I'm sorry, April."

She looked into his blue eyes and took pleasure in the agony she saw there. "So am I." She wanted to hurt him. "Why don't you come by on your way out of town?"

Faint hope flickered in his expression. "I thought you had a guest."

"I do. I'd like to return your ring."

Pain flashed across his face. "April, don't do this."

"I'd mail it to you, but that would be taking unnecessary chances with such a valuable item. I know you wouldn't want me to take unnecessary chances with anything."

"The ring is yours now."

"I don't want it. It's broken."

"What?"

"You heard me. It isn't working anymore."

"I don't believe you."

"You will. If you'll excuse me, I have to find Bill and thank him for standing by me." She turned toward Erica. "All packed up?"

"Yep."

"Then as soon as I talk to Bill, we can leave."

Dan reached for the case containing the projector. "I'll help you carry that."

Erica moved quickly and snatched the case before Dan picked it up. "We'll manage, thanks." Ignoring Dan, she glanced at April. "I hope you have something to drink in that farmhouse of yours."

As April walked away with Erica, she spoke loud enough for Dan to hear. "I have some very good wine. An acquaintance recommended it to me."

THE FIRST THING APRIL DID when she got home that night was take out her contacts and replace them with her large round glasses. The second was to open a bottle of Dan's favorite wine and pour two goblets full while Erica built a fire in the fireplace. After April put a tape of Beethoven

sonatas on the stereo, the two women sprawled on the flow-
ered sofa and polished off the bottle of wine. When it failed
to blunt their anger, they opened a second bottle. Halfway
through it the edges of their outrage began to soften.

"So I got you down here for nothing," April said, pouring the wine into Erica's glass with the exaggerated care of
someone who is slightly tipsy.

"Not for nothing," Erica said, holding her glass up to
the light. "This is good wine."

April giggled. "Good wine, bad man."

"Is there a chance he'll show up here to get that ring you
mentioned? Because if we finish this second bottle, I may
lose all restraint and kick his behind around that rainbow
henhouse of yours."

April shook her head. "He won't show up. I was wrong
about him. He's a chicken." She giggled again. "That's
funny. If he's a chicken, you should kick him *into* the henhouse."

"No, my dear, he is not a chicken, and you're getting
blitzed."

"I hope so." She took another swallow. "Why isn't he
a chicken?"

"Because he said what he thought, even if it ruined his
love life."

"It sure as hell did," April muttered. "His love life is
terminal. Okay, he's not a chicken. He's a turkey."

"That I would agree with."

"Erica, do you hear a rapping noise?"

"No."

April crawled over to the stereo and turned down the
music. "Now do you?"

"Yeah. Woodpeckers?"

April lowered her voice to a whisper. "Maybe it's him."

"You think so?"

"Maybe. What'll I do?"

"You could leave him out there."

April brightened. "I sure could." Then she frowned. "But I want to get rid of that stupid ring." She got slowly to her feet.

"If you let him in, I will not be responsible for my actions."

"Erica," April said solemnly as she stood swaying over her new friend, "I do not want bloodshed in this house."

"Then you'd better talk to him outside."

"Right. I'll get the ring." April meandered unsteadily into her bedroom and poked through her dresser drawer. "There you are, you scoundrel," she mumbled, and headed back in the direction of the front door as the pounding grew louder. She flung open the door, and Dan almost rapped on her face. "Shh!" she ordered, her breath creating fog in the night air. "The chickens are asleep."

"April, I can't leave things like this between us. I have to talk to you."

"Not necessary. Here." She thrust the ring at him.

"No. I won't take it." He peered at her. "Are you drunk?"

"Yes, and I want to stay that way. So I must get out of the cold. Here." She shook the ring at him. "Jus' take it and leave."

"April, I love you."

"Ha."

"Okay, so you won't believe me now, but keep the ring. Just—" He reached for her, and she stepped back a pace. "April, won't you let me—"

"No. Will you take this damn ring?"

"No."

"Then I guess I'll sell it."

"Sell the ring?" He stared at her in confusion.

"Sure, why not? What good is it on someone's finger, looking pretty? Why not have money, instead? That's Daniel Butler's philosophy."

His blue gaze grew anguished. "April, that's not what
I—"

"It sure is," she said, trying to focus better. "He doesn't
unnerstan' that people need beauty in their lives. We
couldn't make it together, Dan and me." She laid the ring
on the arm of the wooden porch chair. "If I fin' this here
in the morning, so help me I'll sell it." Then she stepped
inside and slammed the door.

BEFORE DAWN the next morning, her head aching from the
wine consumed the night before, April climbed wearily out
of bed. She had chores to do, but first she had to check the
front porch. She remembered vaguely leaving the ring out
there and telling Dan that if he didn't take it, she'd sell it.
He'd probably left the ring, but of course she wouldn't sell
such a beautiful heirloom.

If he had indeed left the ring, it would be a continued
link between them, and April admitted reluctantly to herself
that she still craved that link, in spite of everything. He was
wrong for her; that much had been proved the night before.
Unfortunately the knowledge hadn't changed her love for
him. If she still had the ring, communication between then
couldn't be permanently over.

A rooster crowed as she opened the door to the cold still-
ness of early morning and flipped on the light. The pale
glow illuminated the arm of the old wooden chair. The ring
was gone.

CHAPTER THIRTEEN

"I'VE SCREWED THINGS UP beyond belief." Dan hunched over the coffee mug Ida Mae placed in front of him and let the steam soothe his unshaven face. He felt physically and mentally ravaged by the hours of soul-searching he'd just been through, and finally he could think of no place to go but the Lowdermilks' warm kitchen.

"I wish I could tell you different," Bill said, accepting another cup of coffee from his wife. "But your statement at the end of the presentation last night changed a lot of people's minds. They won't be swayed back easily."

The ring in his slacks pocket dug against Dan's thigh as he shifted his weight in the kitchen chair. "I feel as if I've personally robbed Booneville of its chance to lay claim to something really special, something that would last through the generations. Why couldn't I have realized that sooner?"

"Your position wasn't wrong, Dan," Ida Mae said gently as she joined them at the round oak table. When Dan had arrived a half hour ago looking as if he'd been run over by a truck, Ida Mae had sent her children to a neighbor's house to play for the afternoon. Dan obviously needed uninterrupted help. "You had me half-convinced myself. Farmers *are* in trouble all over the county, and we would be spending money on something no one could eat or wear or use to pay the mortgage."

"Yes, but does anybody mention that when we talk about Mount Rushmore or the *Statue of Liberty*?"

Ida Mae smiled. "No doubt some people have, Dan, over the years."

"I don't want to be one of them," Dan grumbled. "My mother and father struggled with their farm, and she faced hard financial times when he died, but she never once considered selling her ring, which was her private work of art. I grew up knowing there were some things more important than hard cash. Why couldn't I make better use of that knowledge?"

Ida Mae patted his hand. "Sometimes we don't see the truths that are right in front of our faces. Don't be so hard on yourself."

"Okay, we'll forget about my stupidity. Now how can we have that sculpture for Booneville?"

"Oh, we can have it, all right," Bill said, sipping his coffee. "With your vote we'll win approval four to two. But the townspeople won't understand. Many of them will resent that sculpture after what was said last night. We might even have to worry about vandalism."

"We've got to get that support back, Bill. At this point April probably wants nothing to do with me, but I'd be glad to give her another chance to speak and then explain that my original assessment was wrong."

Ida Mae shook her head. "No good, Dan. People around here suspect that you're sweet on April. They'll think you've changed your mind because of her." Ida Mae couldn't help chuckling. "Especially considering Mabel's stand with Henry."

Dan frowned. "What do you mean, Mabel's stand?"

"Yeah, what do you mean, Idie?"

"You must both swear never to say I told you."

"Okay," they said together, both leaning forward in their curiosity.

"She's waging a bedroom campaign against Henry to get him to vote for the sculpture."

Dan and Bill looked at each other and began to laugh.

Bill's face turned beet red, and Dan laughed until the tears rolled down his beard-stubbled cheeks.

"But," Bill said, gasping, "why do you suppose it isn't working?" He glanced at Dan and shook in silent mirth.

"I can't imagine," Dan said, and they both erupted into another fit of laughter.

Finally Dan dried his eyes and leaned his head in his hands. "I'm getting punchy after a night with no sleep."

"I thought you'd been up all night," Ida Mae scolded. "You were always the one who insisted on your eight hours."

"Yeah, April remembers that, too. Seems I have quite a reputation for being a stick-in-the-mud."

"You're conservative, Dan. That's no crime."

"I wonder. Anyway, I discovered last night that some things are more important than sleep, too, such as straightening out the mess I've caused." He glanced at Bill. "I think we've got to buy some time before the vote. Let's postpone it, for, say, three weeks. Maybe that will give me a chance to think of something."

"Henry won't like a postponement," Bill said. "But M.G. and Gerry Sloan shouldn't mind, and April won't care."

Dan looked across the table at Bill. "Will you call her and let her know? I— She might hang up on me."

"Sure. I'll handle the others, too. We'll get the extra three weeks, but I can't imagine how you can change anyone's mind in such a short time."

"Neither can I," Dan admitted. "Maybe I'll talk to Erica Jorgenson. She's mad at me, too, but somehow I feel safer approaching her."

Bill shook his head in dismay. "Sounds like choosing between a charging bull and a hornet's nest to me. That Erica is some tough lady."

Ida Mae surveyed the two men. "So is April," she said.

Dan considered her statement. He hadn't admitted to any-

one how he felt about April, but the time for hiding feelings
was over. "I guess that's a big reason why I love her," he
said quietly.

THE FIRST HEAVY SNOWSTORM of the season arrived five
days later and left April's farm looking as if it had been
wrapped in cotton batting. Her father drove out to help her
shovel a path to the henhouse and the beehives. She made
certain the hive entrances weren't blocked with snow and
double-checked the heaters in the henhouse. After years in
the country she understood the importance of constant vig-
ilance when the weather changed.

Usually she reveled in the simplicity of line that snow
brought to the Illinois countryside. Often she'd snuggle in
front of her cozy fire with a cup of hot chocolate and a good
book, once she'd taken care of her routine chores, or she'd
put chains on the old truck and drive over to Ida Mae's
house where she'd help Idie's children build a snowwoman
and a snowman.

But what she usually did wasn't applicable to her life
these days. Once her necessary jobs were finished, she
walked for hours along the icy country roads. She wasn't
interested in company, but she loathed inactivity nearly as
much, so she walked, staring at the fields extended along
each side of the road like huge sheets of blank paper.

She was angry with herself for not being able to put Dan
out of her mind. What did it matter that his touch set her
on fire, if he had no sense of beauty in his soul? She ordered
herself to stop loving this man who had smashed her dreams
for the second time, but her rebellious heart wouldn't accept
her command, and the ache for him went on.

The second day after the snowfall she returned to the
farmhouse and was stomping the snow from her boots onto
the front porch when the telephone rang in the kitchen. Each
time she'd received a call in the days since Dan had left,

she'd run to the phone with irrational haste, all the while telling herself that the caller couldn't be Dan.

This time she left her boots on as she hurried to the ringing telephone in spite of the wet tracks that would ruin her clean kitchen floor. She picked up the receiver and tried to control her rapid breathing.

"Hello?"

"Hi, sweetheart," her mother replied.

April stared dismally at puddles on the linoleum. "Hi, Mom. What's up?"

"Quite a bit, as a matter of fact. I think you'd better put the chains on the truck and take a drive into town. After you've seen it, you can come and have supper with us."

"Seen what?"

"I wouldn't dream of spoiling the surprise by telling you. Just make sure you drive past the square on your way over."

"Mom, I don't want to sound ungracious, but putting the chains on is a lot of work. Couldn't we have supper in a few days when the roads are clear?"

"Trust me, April, you'll want to see this. Put the chains on and come over, but drive past the square first."

"It had better be good, whatever it is. And remember I've seen the twelve-foot snowman that the Compton kids built last year. I don't want to go to all this trouble for something like that."

"Just do it, dear. You won't be sorry."

"Okay." April sighed. "See you in about an hour, after I've taken care of the chickens and put on the chains. This had better be good," she said again.

"It is," her mother promised, and hung up.

April suspected her mother of some sort of ruse to snap her daughter out of the doldrums. The whole town knew that April's sculpture project was in trouble, and many also suspected that her rumored romance with Dan had been sidetracked, too.

As April finished her chores and took the snow chains

out of an old cardboard box, she tried to imagine what could
be on the square that her mother thought worth seeing. If
the gazebo had toppled under the weight of the snow, or
one of the stately elms had fallen over, her mother wouldn't
have sounded so cheerful and so...was excited the word?
Yes, April decided, her mother's tone had been definitely
excited.

April drove slowly, allowing the chains time to bite into
the ice-encrusted road. She was the only one chugging along
that afternoon, as lowering clouds brought an early twilight
to the silent white fields. A lone cardinal, a splash of red in
the nearly colorless world, perched on a snowy bush beside
the road. April felt the pang of sadness that always came
when she experienced beauty alone. Lovely sights weren't
nearly as lovely without someone to share them.

Closer to town the traffic increased. Headlights were
turned on against the gathering dusk, and the ice on the road
sparkled. April thought, as she always did with the first
snowstorm, of Christmas. Before the fateful night of the
slide presentation she'd looked forward to the holiday and
fantasized how she would spend it with Dan. Now she
dreaded the enforced gaiety of the season.

A glow seemed to come from the direction of the square,
and April increased the truck's speed a little. Whatever was
there that her mother wanted her to see required light. April
was becoming curious in spite of her best efforts to expect
nothing more than another large snowman erected by the
Compton boys.

As she rounded the corner next to Jesse's Café, April
gasped. The snow-covered square was completely illuminated with several spotlights, and children scampered everywhere. At the center of the activity, on the corner opposite the gazebo, were two large scaffolds beside a tall
ice-and-snow object that made April squint in disbelief. She
must be imagining things, she told herself. But no, she'd

studied those preliminary drawings carefully. Someone was building an ice-sculpture replica of *Growing Season*.

April parked the truck and hurried toward the square. A figure stood on the scaffold putting the finishing touches on the top while children sent more snow up in buckets attached to ropes and pulleys. A man directed the children, and as April approached, she recognized Bill under a knit cap and heavy winter jacket.

The person on the scaffolding wore a lavender ski jacket and matching pants, and even before April saw the blond hair tucked under the jacket's collar, she knew the person had to be Erica.

April walked up to Bill and tapped him on the shoulder. "What in the world is going on?" she asked when he turned around.

He grinned and gestured toward the ice sculpture. "Like it?"

April looked at him with a dazed expression. "I don't understand."

"We're going to have our sculpture, April."

"But this will melt."

"That's the idea."

"Bill, you're not making a lick of sense."

A shout came from above them. "Bill! I need another bucket of snow! Is that you, April?"

"Erica, what are you doing up there? I'm getting nothing out of Bill except double-talk."

"What I want out of him is another bucket of snow," Erica called back. "You two can talk later. I want to finish this so I can sit in front of a nice warm fire. You did promise that, right, Bill?"

"That plus a home-cooked meal and dessert," Bill called back as he motioned one of the children to dump snow in the bucket beside him.

When the bucket was on its way up to Erica, April grabbed Bill's arm. "Okay, let's have it. Otherwise, I'm having you two placed in warm padded cells for the winter. Why would you go to all this work for something that will be gone in a week or less?"

"Simple. We figure that if we show people how beautiful the sculpture will be, they'll come to accept the idea—like it, even. Then when the thing melts, they'll want it back in a more permanent version."

"But we'll have a tie vote on the board."

"Don't count on that."

"Really? You mean Gerry Sloan might change his mind? He's the only one I can imagine doing that."

"Maybe Gerry will change his mind, but I don't expect a tie."

"This demonstration won't change Henry's mind, and Dan is in Chicago and won't even see it, so I think you're working hard for nothing, Bill."

"Maybe."

"Was this your idea or Erica's?"

"I, ah, well, it was—"

"I bet you thought of it, Bill, you crazy, lovable man. Is Erica staying at your house, then?"

"Yeah. We wanted to surprise you, so we snuck her into town."

"Fat chance of that. I'm astounded no one told me until my mother called this afternoon."

"I'm sure a few people tried to tip you off, but it seems you haven't been home much lately to answer the phone."

"That's true," April admitted, thinking of her long, lonely walks. "Anyway, this is fantastic, even if it doesn't work. Can I do anything to help?"

"I think we're about finished, and the kids have loved every minute of it. That was part of the plan, to have the kids help after school so they'd feel a part of the project. I think they'll go home and beg their parents to ask for a permanent sculpture just like this."

April smiled. "They might. They might at that. You may turn out to be a genius, Bill."

"Don't give me all the credit."

"Okay." April called up to the woman on the scaffold. "You're terrific, too, Erica."

"Thanks!"

April turned to Bill. "I'm supposed to have dinner at Mom's, but why don't I come by later? I'd love a chance to talk to all of you."

Bill averted his eyes. "Um, I don't know, April. We'll probably be pretty tired after all this work. I think we'll turn in early."

"Oh. Okay." April tried to hide her disappointment. For some reason they didn't want her to be part of all of this. Yet hadn't the sculpture been her idea in the first place? She felt snubbed. "Guess I'll get on over to Mom's, then."

"Yeah. See you, April."

WITHIN AN HOUR Bill was at home talking long-distance to Chicago. "Why can't I tell her you were behind the whole thing? I'm having a damn hard time keeping it to myself, old buddy. She wanted to stop by this evening, and I had to be rude and tell her not to because I was afraid someone around here would spill the beans. Now she thinks we're shutting her out."

"I won't parade my virtues in front of her like some proud rooster, Bill. Maybe later, after the vote, we can discuss it, but not now. Do you think the plan will work?"

"I don't see why not. Everyone in town is buzzing with news of the sculpture and how beautiful it is. The kids will influence their parents, too. That was a real brainstorm on your part. Damn, I wish I could tell April."

"Please don't, Bill."

"Then I'll have to avoid her like the plague until we vote in two weeks."

"That's okay. The most important thing is getting the

town behind the sculpture and then taking a vote, which should come out four-two in favor."

"I hope these two weeks go fast. And stay cold."

"Me, too. And take a picture for me, will you? I'll never know how it looked otherwise."

"You could come down next weekend."

"No, I couldn't. If I got that close to April, I'd probably go break her door down just to hold her in my arms. Let's get this sculpture business settled first."

"Okay, Dan. We'll do things your way."

"Thanks, buddy."

APRIL FOUND AN EXCUSE to go into town every day until the sculpture began to melt, and then she avoided driving past the square because the sight was so disheartening. She heard fragments of town gossip and realized that support for the sculpture had grown considerably, but what difference would that make if the board had a tie vote?

At the regular meeting of the Beautify Booneville committee April quizzed Mabel Goodpasture and concluded that Henry had not changed his mind, ice sculpture or no ice sculpture. That left Gerald Sloan. Finally, desperate to know if the project had a chance of success, she called him.

"Why, April, what a nice surprise," he said when she identified herself. "I haven't seen much of you lately. I thought you were mad at me because of the sculpture thing."

"No, not really," April said, knowing that she didn't harbor the same antagonistic feelings toward Gerry that she did toward Henry—perhaps because Gerry wasn't as pompous about his conservative opinions and didn't try to run the whole town single-handedly. "But I was curious as to how you felt, now that you've had a chance to see how the sculpture would look on the square."

"That was an interesting experiment, wasn't it?"

"Yes, it was." April held her breath.

"The sculpture looked better than I thought it would."

"I'm glad. Does that mean you've, um, altered your opinion?"

"Well, April, I'll tell you. I did give some thought to changing my mind because the sculpture looked so pretty, especially with the sun on the ice. It reminded me of cut crystal, you know?"

"I know."

"But I thought of all that money and decided that Henry is still right. We ought to look at the practical side of things."

April bit her lip to stifle a groan.

"I hope we can still be friends, April."

"Of course," she heard herself say. "I was just wondering if you'd changed your mind. I'll see you on Saturday for the vote."

April stared at the telephone after she hung up. Bill had made a noble effort all in vain. The vote would still be tied, and April couldn't imagine any of the board members budging. Booneville would lose its entire legacy from Irene unless...

April slumped in her chair. She only had one course of action open to her, and it made her furious to think of having to take it. After the voting was completed, she was resigning from the board. She never wanted to see Dan Butler again.

THE IVORY BEAUTY of the snow was tarnished with car exhaust and mud by the time Saturday arrived. April no longer needed chains to drive into town, and the place where the ice sculpture had once stood was a sloppy mess of ice and mud.

Jesse had agreed to close her café once again for a half hour, and people were gathered all around the square to await the outcome of the vote that would take place inside Jesse's establishment. April walked in with her glasses on and her jaw set. This would not be a pleasant morning, and she refused to smile at anyone, least of all the dark-haired man at the end of the table.

"I guess we're all here now," Dan said gruffly. "And we all know what this vote is about. So let's just go around the table and see what we've got. Bill?"

"I vote for the sculpture."

"Gerry?"

"I'm afraid I have to keep my original stance and vote against it, Dan."

"I understand. Henry?"

"You know good and well how I'm voting."

"Okay. April?"

Somewhere she found the strength to look him right in the eye. "I'm abstaining from the vote."

Dan appeared confused. "Abstaining? Why?"

"Because I can't bring myself to vote against the project, and yet we must avoid a tie. I don't recall anything in Irene's stipulations that covered abstaining, so that's the choice I've made. This way you won't have a stalemate, which could cause Booneville to lose everything."

A murmur of surprise went around the table. Bill opened his mouth to protest April's decision, but Dan shook his head and Bill remained silent.

"That's an admirable stand, April," Dan said, a hint of a smile on his lips.

She saw the smile and glared at him. "I thought you'd be happy with it."

His smile grew broader. "Let's finish the vote. M.G.?"

"I'll go down with the ship. I vote in favor."

Dan nodded. "So we have two in favor and two against and one abstaining."

"Get it over with, Dan," April muttered, staring at the Formica-topped table in front of her.

"Okay. I vote in favor. I guess the sculpture is approved."

April's head snapped up. "Pardon me?"

Henry stood up quickly, and his chair clattered to the floor. "You don't know what you're saying, Daniel. Let's talk this over, have another vote. Look, April even backed away from her own project."

"Only because she was considering the good of the whole town," Dan said quietly. "I wonder if you're doing that, Henry?"

April continued to gaze in bafflement at Dan. "You're voting in favor of the sculpture? But you said—"

"I was wrong. Unfortunately I didn't learn that until after the slide presentation. The damage had been done by then."

Bill cleared his throat. "But you fixed it, Dan. I think April should know that erecting the ice sculpture was entirely your idea."

April looked from Dan to Bill and back to Dan again. "It was?"

Dan shrugged. "I had to come up with some way to show the town how great the sculpture would look. Bill and I even thought of papier-mâché."

"What a mess that would have been," Bill said, shaking his head. "Luckily it snowed before this guy rounded up enough newspaper and paste, and he came up with the brilliant idea of creating the sculpture in ice, like those fancy restaurants do in Chicago. He finally talked Erica into giving it a shot, and here we are."

M.G. beamed at all of them, even the irate Henry. "I couldn't be happier, unless, of course, Irene were here to witness all of this."

"I think she's here in spirit," April said softly, gazing at Dan.

"Well, I won't be a sore loser," Gerry said, extending his hand across the table toward April. "Congratulations."

"I think you're all crazy," Henry said, and stomped out of the café.

Bill watched him go and chuckled. "If he plays his cards

right, he'll go home and tell Mabel that he broke down and voted for the sculpture.''

Dan grinned. "Maybe he likes things the way they are, Bill." The two men exchanged an amused glance.

"I hate to break this up," Jesse said, appearing from the kitchen, "but if what I overheard is correct, you've completed your business, and I've got a horde of customers waiting to come in and buy my coffee and hear my news."

"Sure, Jesse," Dan said, standing. "Let them in."

"I've got a pile of work to do at home," Bill said, heading for the door. "Congratulations, April."

M.G. and Gerry said their goodbyes and left just as the first of the townspeople entered the café.

"Let's get out of here," Dan mumbled and took April's elbow.

"Say, Dan," called one man in overalls. "How'd the vote go?"

"Jesse has the whole story," Dan said, and propelled April out the door.

"Dan," she said as they walked away from the crowd toward his car, "I have a few things I'd—"

"Good. Do you have some free time right now?"

"I...I suppose."

"Then let's go." He opened the passenger door of the red Honda and had her inside before she realized what was happening.

"Dan, where are we going?"

"You'll see. I hope there's still enough snow outside of town."

"Enough snow for what?"

He glanced at her and smiled. "To show you the new Dan Butler."

"The old one was pretty nice, except for a few unmentionable moments."

"Don't remind me. I'd made some progress, but not

enough to count until recently. Thank God you suggested selling the ring.''

''Dan! You didn't!''

He arched an eyebrow at her vehemence. ''What if I have? Will you disown me again?''

''I...'' She paused. ''I never disowned you,'' she said, only now understanding that it was true. ''No matter what you've done, I haven't been able to stop caring for you.''

He reached for her hand. ''That's nice to hear.''

''But, Dan, that ring...it means so much to—''

''You?''

She fell silent, unwilling to admit how much the ring had come to symbolize their love for each other. If it was gone, she would still love him, but some of the magic would be lost.

''Never mind about the ring.'' Dan turned down a rutted lane toward an old farmhouse. ''We have some other business to take care of.''

CHAPTER FOURTEEN

"WHAT ARE WE DOING at the Tennerly place?" April asked as the Honda jounced along the road toward the farm buildings.

"You'll see."

"I can't imagine what you're up to, Dan."

"That's exactly the way I want it. Old Dan has been predictable long enough."

He stopped the car next to Will Tennerly's weathered barn. "Wait here. I'll be right back," he directed, leaving her in the car while he navigated through the ice and mud to the barn door. At his approach Will poked his crinkled face around the heavy door, and Dan followed him inside.

April sat in the car with an unsettled feeling she'd never experienced in connection with Dan Butler. She hadn't the foggiest notion what he'd do next. She was still digesting the information that he'd engineered the creation of the ice sculpture on the square, and that ever since her declaration about selling the ring, he'd planned to vote for the sculpture when the time came.

Had he really sold the ring? She couldn't believe that he'd do it, yet she wasn't prepared to predict what he'd do anymore. He'd always been exciting to her sexually, but now he was exciting her imagination, as well. The feeling was unfamiliar, but she was learning to like it.

Will Tennerly appeared at the barn door once more and laboriously pushed it back. April waited with anticipation. Whatever Dan had planned was about to happen.

First she heard the sound of bells, and then Will's sway-backed plow horse, Ned, who'd been out to pasture for at least five years, plodded out of the barn pulling a sleigh. April grinned at the sight of Ned, looking better than ever in his life, his mane and tail braided with red ribbon and brass bells jingling from his harness.

Dan jumped down from the sleigh to help her out of the car, but April had already opened the door and was crunching across the half-frozen ground toward him. "A one-horse open sleigh!" She laughed with delight. "I didn't know anyone around here still had sleighs."

Will Tennerly drew himself up proudly. "Mine's the only one in the county."

April smiled at him. "Ned looks wonderful, Mr. Tennerly. You've put a lot of work into this."

"You can thank Daniel, here. He made all the arrangements. Course, I did think of the ribbons myself, and the missus provided that lap robe."

Dan reached out and shook the old man's hand. "I appreciate everything you've done, Mr. Tennerly. You still think the back pasture has enough snow to make this thing work?"

"I'd expect so. Just go through that gate yonder and head east until you get to the creek. Then turn around and head back. Should give you a nice ride."

"We'll do that," Dan said. He turned to April. "Are you game?"

"Of course. I've never had a sleigh ride before."

"I was counting on that." He held out his hand to steady her while she climbed into the sleigh. "Especially since the tractor idea's a little shopworn."

She gazed into eyes as clear as the winter-blue sky above them. There was no doubting his purpose with this ride. "It is, isn't it?"

Her heart beat faster at the prospect of what Dan might say to her when they were alone. She wanted this man, wanted him more than almost anything else in the world. What would he ask her to give up for them to be together? How could he take her on a romantic trip through the countryside she loved and ask her to leave it for the city? Dan had made changes in his life, it was true, but April couldn't imagine that he'd decided to become a farmer after all.

As she snuggled under the red plaid lap robe, her feet bumped a paper sack that clinked with the impact. She glanced questioningly at Dan as he swung up beside her. "What have you got on the floor of this contraption?"

"Just ignore it," Dan said with a wink. "You're damn hard to surprise, you know that? Always asking questions." He picked up the reins and clucked to the horse.

"Okay." She'd already figured out that he had his favorite wine and glasses in the bag. His plan must be to take her out to the snowy seclusion of a deserted field and offer to toast their engagement. She loved the plan; she doubted the outcome. Many questions were still unanswered.

They waved to Will Tennerly as they drove out his back gate and into the pasture. The snow was a little thin, and the sleigh scratched more than glided across the ground, but April didn't care. The smoke from the Tennerly's fireplace drifted after them, and Ned's bells jingled cheerfully as he trotted with considerable spirit, considering his advanced age. April pretended she was in a scene from *Dr. Zhivago*.

As Dan shifted the reins to one hand, he reached over to draw her near. "Having fun?"

"You know I am. You're full of surprises these days, Daniel Butler."

He smiled at her. "That's the idea."

"The sculpture was beautiful."

"I know. Bill took pictures for me."

"It would have helped me to know that you planned that," she chided softly.

"I thought of telling you and trying to straighten things out between us earlier, but I changed my mind."

"Why?"

"I opted for the drama of having everything revealed at once. I decided that would appeal to you more."

"What?" April began to laugh. Had he grown to know her so well? "I guess you were right," she admitted sheepishly. "Damn, my glasses are fogging up."

"I figured Bill hadn't blown my cover when I saw those spectacles. You had no desire to impress me this morning."

"But I do now," she said softly.

"I've told you before, April, that you impress me with or without your glasses. I just don't like bumping into them when I kiss you."

"Are you planning to do that?" In spite of the cold she felt increasingly warm.

His arm tightened around her. "It's crossed my mind. We're almost out of sight of Tennerly's."

"Then I'll take them off. I wouldn't want to obstruct your— What's that noise?"

"Probably just the bottle and glasses on the floor. Never mind. Let's turn down here, closer to the creek. Then we'll have some privacy to...talk."

"Dan, I think something's wrong with the sleigh. Something may be coming loose underneath."

"Will Tennerly swore it was in fine shape the last time he drove it."

"Which might have been thirty years ago. Really, Dan, I think—" She was interrupted by a crunching noise, and the sleigh tilted to one side. "Dan!"

"Whoa, Ned, whoa!" Dan pulled back on the reins, and they both scrambled out of the sleigh. He peered underneath the crippled vehicle and swore softly. "The runner's come loose. Probably the bolts are rusted. I doubt if this damn thing will move another thirty feet, and we're well over a mile from the farm. What the hell are we supposed to do now?"

April began to laugh. "Is this the nostalgic version of running out of gas?"

Dan grimaced. "Hardly." He gazed in frustration at her smiling face and eventually began to chuckle. "Talk about typical. I try to be dashing and dramatic and the damn sleigh breaks. Next thing you know old Ned will fall down and die in his traces."

At the sound of his name the horse turned his head and looked at them with solemn tolerance in his big eyes.

"We can unhitch him and ride him back." April suggested.

"Let's unhitch him and tie him to that old stump so he can move around, but let's not go back. Not yet. I still… There's something that I want to—"

"We'll stay," April said gently, putting her hand on his arm. "I'm having a wonderful time, in spite of Will Tennerly's rickety sleigh breaking down."

"Me, too." As he gazed into her eyes, his frustrated expression was replaced with quickening desire. He squeezed her hand. "I'll unhitch Ned."

Within a few minutes they were seated in the sleigh once more with Dan on the lower side so that April slid naturally against his thigh when he helped her climb in.

"This has possibilities," he said, snuggling her against him.

"About that kiss…" She tilted her head and closed her eyes.

His mouth hovered over hers. "But first I think we should talk."

"Mmm."

"Hell. Forget that." He closed the gap between them and claimed the sweetness of her lips with a groan. She answered by opening to him and inviting a more sensual kiss, a stronger pledge of love and passion. He pulled her close and claimed the intimacy she offered, probing the inner recesses of her mouth and gauging the strength of her need by the tiny moan of pleasure that rose from deep in her throat.

With little conscious thought he fumbled with the zipper of her jacket and soon had his hand inside stroking her sweater-covered breast. Not until he found himself calculating whether he could make love to her on this tilted sleigh bench did he come partially to his senses.

"April," he gasped, lifting his head. Her lips were still partly open and red from the pressure of his mouth. Her eyes were closed.

"Don't stop," she murmured. "Love me, Dan."

"So help me I will," he promised fervently. "But not here. I brought you on this ride to talk out a few things."

Lazily her eyelids drifted open. "Could have fooled me."

"I always get like this around you."

She smiled with satisfaction. "No, you used to be much more controlled."

"That was before I knew what it feels like to slip inside you and love you until we both go crazy."

"Dan, I want you."

He took her hand and placed it against his groin. "I'm in the same shape," he said hoarsely. "But help me, April. We have to settle some things first."

She trembled as she felt his arousal and imagined how he could fill the aching void within her. "You're asking me to be the sensible one?"

His smile was lopsided. "One of us has to be, and I seem to be losing the job fast."

Slowly she withdrew her hand and put her head on his shoulder. Then she took a deep breath. "Okay, talk."

"Thank you." His hand shook as he rezipped her jacket. "This obsession I have scares me sometimes. I'm not used to being out of control."

"You don't like it?"

"That's the trouble. I *do* like it. I'm becoming addicted to the feeling of losing myself in you."

"That's not so bad."

"No. Not if you'll marry me."

She grew completely quiet. Here at last was the question that made the blood rush to her head and her hands tremble. Marriage to Dan. Lying beside him every night, waking to his kiss every morning. She ached for that life, but...

"Don't answer yet," he said softly. "That was only my opener."

"Quite an opener," she murmured.

"I wanted to start that way and let you know exactly how I felt, even though I probably have no business asking you to be my wife. Not yet, anyway."

She closed her eyes in fear. "Dan, please, don't start that. We had this conversation eight years ago."

"I know. Look at me, April." His blue eyes searched her face. "But I'm not the same man who held you eight years ago and explained why we couldn't get married. Did you hear what I said first of all? I want you to marry me, and to hell with the problems."

"I heard that, Dan. It gave me goose bumps."

He smiled. "Good. But now you have a right to hear the problems, anyway."

"I...I'll have to live in Chicago."

"Maybe not."

"Dan, you aren't considering farming?"

"No. I realize you'd want that, but I can't be happy as a farmer. I have to have something where more of my control comes into play. I may be able to give up command when I'm loving you, but not when my—our—livelihood is at stake."

"So what would you do?"

"Open a sporting-goods store on the square."

"Oh!" Impressed as she was with his idea, she knew better than to be overly enthusiastic. Booneville was a small town, and businesses didn't automatically survive there.

"Of course that would be the perfect solution, but we both know there's a big risk involved."

"Yep. But I'd rather take that risk than put all of my resources into farming."

"Dan, I believe it will work," she said, excitement creeping into her voice in spite of herself. "There's the high school. I think they buy everything in Springfield now, but with you here that would change. More and more people are getting into fitness, even in Booneville. You'll make it, I just know you will."

"Maybe not, April. That's why you might want to wait and find out before you make any commitment to me. I have to make a living somewhere, and I hope it's in Booneville, but if not, I'll be forced to look elsewhere."

"It doesn't matter."

"What?"

She lifted her head to look directly into his eyes. "You heard me. The answer is yes, Dan. I'll marry you and gladly take that chance. You'll do your best to keep us in Booneville, and that's all I can ask."

Relief erased the tense lines on his face as he absorbed what she'd said. "April, I love you."

"And I love you."

They sat in the white silence and gazed at each other, each unwilling to spoil the moment with the inadequacy of words. A single bird chirped, and April wondered if it could be the cardinal she'd seen before. Now, at long last, she had Dan to share the beauty with her. For always.

He touched her cheek. "This is when we're supposed to drink a toast, but I'd rather go home and make love to you."

"And you went to all the trouble of bringing the bottle and glasses out here."

"Let's take them back. We can drink it later."

Desire quickened her tongue. "Yes, let's."

The journey to April's bedroom became a quest for solitude. After riding Ned back to the Tennerly farm, they quickly tried to extricate themselves from a long discussion of the sleigh's problems. Dan promised to come back the next day and help Will retrieve the vehicle.

Then they made a mad dash into town to pick up April's truck from the square and excused themselves from talking with several people sauntering along the sidewalk. Once away from town, they drove in tandem well over the speed limit to reach the seclusion of April's farm. When they arrived, she hung her Eggs Sold Out sign on the mailbox by the road.

Finally they stood in her bedroom holding each other and kissing as if they were survivors of a shipwreck.

"I thought we'd never make it," Dan said as he tried to kiss April and remove her clothes at the same time.

"First Tennerly and then all those people who stopped us on the square." She peeled off his shirt and kissed his chest. "Can we tolerate a small town, Dan?"

"They'll just have to learn," he replied, sliding her jeans over her hips, "that we require a certain amount of privacy."

She stepped out of the jeans. "A lot of privacy," she breathed as Dan reached beneath her panties and caressed the damp triangle concealed by white lace. "Oh, Dan." She undulated her hips against his probing fingers.

"Tons of privacy." He bent to kiss her gently swaying breasts.

"Come to bed," she murmured, drawing him toward the soft mattress as she worked at the fastening of his pants.

"I thought you'd never ask." He finished her undressing job and tumbled with her onto the bed. "Mmm, the sheets smell of you. Fresh as the country."

"I want them to smell of you." She pulled him on top of her. "That warm, sexy man-scent of yours." She rubbed her nose against his chest. "I love it."

"Tell me what else you love. This?" He kissed her

deeply, taking her breath away before lifting his head and gazing down at her.

"Yes," she whispered.

"This?" He kissed her throat and gradually moved lower until he took her nipple in his mouth and sucked gently.

"Yes, oh, yes." She arched against him.

At last he spread her thighs and touched the throbbing spot with his manhood. His breathing was labored. "This?"

"Yes!" Gripping his hips, she urged him forward.

"April," he said into her ear, "I don't have any protection."

She looked up at him, her voice fierce with love. "I don't care. I want your children. Our children."

A look of primitive joy flared in his eyes. "So do I," he said hoarsely, and plunged into her.

ONLY ONCE THAT DAY, when Dan brought out the bottle of what turned out to be champagne instead of his favorite wine, did April think of the heirloom ring. Dan had not mentioned it again, even when he had proposed to her. She wondered if he had indeed sold it, and if not, where in the world it was.

At dinner that night, which Dan had arranged in a secluded corner of Jesse's Café, she found out. The meal had been interesting. Despite Dan's request for medium-rare steaks, Jesse had cooked them her usual way—fried to a crisp. There had been some trouble in the kitchen removing the cork from the wine bottle, and consequently the wine contained tiny bits of bobbing flotsam. In addition, Dan had forgotten to emphasize that baked potatoes usually accompanied filet mignon, not French fries.

The two lovers chuckled their way through the courses, held hands and stole a kiss whenever no one seemed to be looking.

"Honestly, it's the most romantic dinner I've ever had,"

April said, as Dan tried for the third time to light the candle stuck to a saucer in the middle of their table.

"I think the romantic part will have to come later, after we get back to your bedroom." Dan succeeded in lighting the candle and placed it away from the draft that had been snuffing it out all evening.

Jesse appeared beside their table. "Everything all right over here?"

"Just fine," April said, beaming at her.

"Are you ready for that other item, Dan?"

Dan glanced at April. "Anytime, Jesse."

"I'll be right back."

"Dan, you're doing it again."

"What?"

"Springing stuff on me."

"You bet. I'm really getting the hang of this business now. You'll never know what's coming next."

She smiled uncertainly. "I see."

"Hey, don't worry." He covered her hand with his. "Underneath I'm still the same steady guy. And there's one thing you can count on, no matter how many crazy stunts I pull. I love you, April. I always will."

"I'm so glad, because I need you desperately."

Jesse cleared her throat to alert them of her approach. "Well, here it is. Not exactly perfect, but you get the idea."

April stared at the object Jesse placed on their table.

"If you look at it from a certain angle, it does look like a heart," Jesse offered, cocking her head to one side.

Dan groaned. "What angle—standing on your head? I thought you said you could do an ice sculpture?"

"I thought I could," Jesse said. "It's harder than it looks."

"Oh, well." Dan glanced at April, who seemed to be mesmerized by the dripping chunk of ice. "We tried."

"The…the ring," April whispered. "You didn't sell it."

"Of course not," Dan said, taking her hand as Jesse tactfully retreated. "It belongs to you, to us. It's a symbol of the love we've found."

"I believe that, too." Tears sparkled in her eyes. "It really is a magic ring."

He shook his head and picked up the candle to melt the ice away from the brilliant piece of jewelry. "I'm not sure if the ring has special powers or if you do. Probably a little of both, but I know where this heirloom belongs." His hand trembled slightly as he picked the emerald-and-diamond ring out of the sculpture and slipped it on her finger.

April swallowed. "Dan, the stones seem brighter, more beautiful than before. You'll probably laugh at me for imagining such a thing is possible."

Dan held her hand and gazed into her eyes. "Never. With you in my life, everything has become possible."

"Even magic?"

His gentle smile was for her alone. "Especially magic."

EPILOGUE

ONCE THEY DISCOVERED the impending wedding of Dan and April, the townspeople of Booneville expected no less than a June ceremony on the square followed by a hot-dog roast. The happy couple refused to wait that long, however, and eloped within a week after announcing their engagement.

As a compromise to the disappointed citizens, April and Dan promised a grand reception on the square during the last week in June, after Erica completed the sculpture. They even agreed to repeat their wedding vows and cut a cake fashioned by Jesse Hardcastle in the approximate shape of *Growing Season*.

From Christmas until June Dan worked hard to establish his sporting-goods store. Booneville and neighboring towns responded to his efforts, and business also increased for April at The Birds and the Bees. She joked with Dan that she might need some tutoring in the subject of birds and bees, however, because she still wasn't pregnant.

Dan concluded that they were both too distracted with work to make babies properly. He suggested taking a long-overdue honeymoon following the June ceremony so they could concentrate on the matter for an entire week.

Therefore April's glow of anticipation was genuine on that bright summer afternoon when she and Dan reaffirmed their vows before the assembled residents of Booneville. Her simple summery dress and wide-brimmed straw hat reflected the carefree jubilation she felt at having her man all to herself for seven days.

The square had never looked more lovely, with beds of petunias and pansies planted by the Beautify Booneville committee surrounding the gazebo where the ceremony was held. Across the expanse of lush grass, mowed the day before expressly for the event, rose the graceful work of art called *Growing Season*. Reporters and photographers from as far away as Chicago and St. Louis clustered near the shining flanks of the sculpture and awaited an opportunity to interview the attractive couple pledging their love in the dappled shade of the gazebo.

Even Henry Goodpasture was in a mellow mood because the new sporting-goods store on the square was located next to his bank, and he'd noticed an improvement in his own business. He and Dan talked often, having neighboring businesses, and one day Henry had mentioned all the travel brochures on European vacations that were lying around his house these days.

Dan had asked to borrow a few. Before Henry could talk them out of it, Dan and April had made reservations he thought they could probably ill afford at a newly opened luxury resort in France. Henry gazed up at the couple embracing in the gazebo and shook his head. Dan was turning into a romantic fool if he thought there might be some connection between a resort named Montclair and the chicken scratching inside that emerald ring April wore.

As the lovers drew apart and smiled at each other, Mabel nudged Henry in the ribs. "They're so beautiful, Henry."

"They're nuttier than fruitcakes, Mabel." Henry sighed and glanced over at the sculpture thrusting upward into the blue sky. "I don't get it. Dan Butler used to be such a sensible young man."

TRUST
Rita Clay Estrada

CHAPTER ONE

CLAY REYNOLDS strode into the Hilton Ballroom to assure himself that everything was in readiness for that night. Once a year he gave a cocktail party, mainly to thank his associates for their business, although a few close friends would be there as well. He wasn't fond of occasions that pressured him into inane congeniality, nor was he fond of crowds, but socializing was good for business so he had no choice.

Tonight he felt even more pressured than usual. Tonight the woman he'd decided to marry was going to play hostess. He wanted everything to be perfect. He wanted *her* to be perfect, to reinforce his occasionally shaky decision to marry her.

On the champagne table stood a fountain and glasses, and centered on the hors d'oeuvres table was a large ice sculpture of a playful dolphin. On either side of the room was a bar, each bartender busily stocking it with ice and drinks. The polished dance floor was surrounded by tables covered in spotless white tablecloths. There was an area set aside for a three-piece combo, so the musicians would be screened off from the general hubbub.

Everything was perfect. He nodded approval to one of the men assisting at the hors d'oeuvres table, then turned and walked back down the hall to the elevator. After eight years the annual party was a tradition, and so was his rented suite. He figured if he had to arrive early and be the last one to leave, he might as well stay the night. It worked out very well.

As he entered his suite the telephone was ringing.

"Yes?" He spoke absently while weighing the decision to either change into his tuxedo or have a drink first.

"Hello, darling. I just wanted to hear your voice." Magda's deliberately low-pitched tone filtered over the phone. Though phony, it was also very effective.

"Are you ready for this evening?" He pulled at the knot of his tie, then loosened the top button of his shirt.

"I can't wait. I hope you like my dress. It's just a tiny bit daring."

"As long as no one touches you but me," he answered almost by rote. There were certain things he had learned to say to keep his dates happy. Possessiveness seemed to be a sign they cherished. Sexual arousal was another. He had to remind himself that Magda wasn't just another date—she was his bride-to-be.

"Oh," she chuckled low, "you mean you'd fight for me, darling?" Her voice promised what the reward to him would be for a black eye.

He smiled cynically. "Of course. I just can't guarantee I'll win."

"With your broad shoulders and strong arms?" Her voice was a sexy whisper that irritated him rather than leaving him wanting more. "Besides you never lose at anything."

"There's always a first time, Magda." He shrugged out of his coat and flung it on the bed, impatient now to take a shower, pour a drink and relax before donning his best smile and manners. "The car will pick you up at eight. Right now, I'm headed for the shower, so I'll see you then." It was a statement and a closing.

The line sang with silence for a few seconds, and Clay could almost feel Magda's disappointment that he wouldn't play the game anymore. "I'll see you then, darling," she promised, apparently having recovered quickly.

"I'll be waiting for you." He hung up without even saying goodbye. Suddenly he felt tired.

Sinking to the edge of the bed, he held his head in his hands. A vision of Magda danced in front of his eyes. She was classically beautiful, with bone structure that most models would be envious of. She was slim but well formed in all the right places. Her sense of color and design was impeccable. So why the sudden doubt?

It was ridiculous! Forcing any thoughts away that didn't fit his original plans, he undid his cuffs, shrugged out of his shirt and threw it across the bottom of the bed. He was marrying to have a home and children and a gracious hostess, and he had selected his prospective wife with that specific purpose in mind. The decision concerning who would share his private life and income was just as important as any big business deal, and it deserved as much deliberation as everything else he had done to build himself into a success. There was nothing haphazard about his choice or his requirements in a wife. It would work.

He ignored the niggling doubt in the back of his mind. Magda and Clay had tentatively discussed a premarital contract just last night and he knew she would sign. It would ensure both of them a measure of security. It was that simple. Contracts were a way of life with him, and without them he felt vulnerable.

It was a shame his parents hadn't signed one, but with their outlook, they wouldn't have kept the terms anyway. But they *had* taught him one hell of a lesson: never trust anyone—not even parents—not to aim for the jugular. His parents were certainly past masters at it. They always said they'd fallen in love at first sight, but Clay knew that everything after that had been a fight. His own observation was that most parents left a lot to be desired when it came to raising a child in a loving atmosphere. Even more important, he'd never seen his mother or his father laughing, enjoying each other. They were miserable together. They were miserable—period.

Their form of marriage wasn't for Clay, so he'd chosen

carefully. He didn't care if bells didn't ring or stars didn't shoot. Magda was compatible to his needs, and in time he would grow to trust her enough to relax and enjoy whatever their relationship might grow into.

To wait around for a wife because some fleeting emotion called love hadn't hit him over the head was ridiculous. He doubted there was such a thing. What was disguised as love was really the base instinct to mate and procreate. It evaporated as soon as the deed was done. He'd seen it happen often enough.

Confidently he stepped into the hot shower. His decision to marry Magda was right.

MUCH LATER, showered and dressed in his tuxedo, he stood once more at the door of the banquet room, a smile lifting the corners of his mouth as he and Magda greeted his incoming guests. With only a few exceptions, he was happy to see them. Success was in the air.

After everyone had gone through to the large ballroom, Magda gave him a peck on the cheek and whispered that she'd be right back. He smiled absently and patted her hand, his mind on his guests as he tallied those who weren't there yet.

"You've really got them packed in here." David Childers stood just behind Clay sipping on his Jack Daniels and water. Clay grinned, relieved to see him. David was the one person he could relax with.

"Had to. The list grows. Maybe next year I'll have it at the country club instead," Clay said under his breath. "Glad you got here, though. It's nice to see a friendly face."

"Ah, the price of success." David gave a mocking sigh.

Clay stared at his best friend, his eyes narrowed. He could see what others couldn't. That "Laura ache" was there again. "Where's Laura? You told her to come, didn't you?"

"I don't know where she is. She invited someone else to escort her."

Clay cursed under his breath. "You're really living dangerously, aren't you? You were supposed to bring her."

"I know, Clay. I know." David's voice sounded resigned. He was apparently kicking himself too hard to be able to stand Clay kicking him, too.

Clay didn't say any more. Now wasn't the time to go into it. Ordering a drink from the waiter, he gave David a commiserating squeeze on his shoulder before beginning the long circular path around the room, greeting a few people he had missed at the door and making sure everyone was having a good time.

The band began playing a seductively slow number, and he watched many of the older couples get up to dance, draping their arms around each other in much the same way they had probably done in college. He gave himself a pat on the back for the choice of the band. Just the right blend. Not too old-fashioned, but not too modern, either. Everything was going smoothly.

A streak of brilliant red flashed by the corner of his eye, and he turned in that direction as if drawn. Standing by the hors d'oeuvres table was a petite woman-girl whose long red hair rivaled the brilliance of the dress she wore. A bright emerald-green blouse and full skirt combination in some shiny and questionable fabric, came to just above a pair of very shapely ankles. His eyes moved back up again. Her small plate was piled high with all kinds of goodies, her hands moving almost quicker than the eye as she chose a jumbo boiled shrimp and stuffed it directly into her puckered mouth. Full lips. Wide eyes—he couldn't see the color from here, but he'd bet they were green. Slender to the point of being thin. Trim ankles and high heels that looked as if she was barely able to totter in them. Who was she?

He frowned as he watched her pop another plump shrimp into her mouth. When she tilted her head back he saw the flash of green stones dressing her small earlobes. His gaze narrowed, focusing on the teasing gleam that shone through her mane of red hair. Whether they were great fakes or the real thing he wasn't sure, but he could tell they were perfectly suited to her—even from this distance.

He scanned the room, searching for a possible escort. No one came forth or was paying her the slightest attention.

A guest claimed him, but Clay promised himself that later he would find out who she was. He didn't question why. He didn't have time, as he was swept into a debate on Texas teams by a client who was a football addict.

A half hour later he was ready to leave his own party. Magda had returned to his side and wound her arm through his, lightly clinging to him while graciously discussing the pros and cons of a particular hairdresser with one of his customers' wives.

Terrific. That's exactly why he needed a wife—someone to handle the other half of most couples he had to deal with. She was doing a great job and he said so with his eyes. She smiled back, telling him silently that she expected a reward for her services. He grinned.

She even looked the part. Her dark hair was drawn into a very distinctive roll at the back of her head, showing off her aristocratic bone structure. Her slim body was encased in a smoke-gray dress that molded to her hips and breasts while leaving the impression of long legs. Understated elegance. The doubts he experienced in her absence about his choice of wife disappeared with her next to him.

Excusing himself from both her and the group, he began to circle again, and again a flash of red caught his eye.

The redhead was seated at an inconspicuous table in the back corner of the room, right in front of the kitchen doors. Her crumb-laden plate sat in front of her. One of the young waiters stood by her side holding a glass of champagne, his grin positively lecherous.

Clay angled through the tables, his eyes never leaving her face.

"Really," she explained patiently. "I only wanted a glass

f water. That can't be *too* hard, can it? Even truck stops
erve water with their chili and chicken-fried steak, for
'ete's sake.''

"But—'' the waiter began.

"What's the matter?'' Clay asked quietly.

The waiter seemed to hesitate and Clay could tell that he
vas looking for an excuse for his actions. "The lady asked
or a drink and I brought her champagne. Now she says she
vants water.'' He saw the hard glint in Clay's eye and re-
cted quickly. "I was just going to get it, sir,'' and he scur-
ied off toward the bar.

"My heavens.'' The little redhead's voice held something
kin to awe. "I think he wanted a tip for *water*!''

"Probably,'' Clay said cynically before diverting his at-
ention back to the girl in front of him. "Is everything else
ll right?'' He slipped into the seat next to her. Her eyes
vere green all right, almost exactly matching the color of
he stones that graced her ears. The widest, greenest green
e had ever seen. He could get lost in that brilliant sea-grass
reen....

"I'm fine, thank you.'' Those eyes also held a hint of
umor. Her voice was soft and sweet, the sounds of a Texas
ccent rolling around him. "Nice party, don't you think?''

Her words barely registered. He was wondering why he
vas here at her table, instead of calling someone to quietly
scort her out. She was obviously a party crasher— Then
er comment registered, and Clay tried not to grin too
videly. "Not bad,'' he agreed. "Do you know many of the
uests?''

Her eyes darted away, then came back matched with a
lelightfully impish smile that seemed to hold him in her
pell. "Oh, a few. But there's no use talking to them here.
run into them all the time, you see. We're always attending
he same parties.''

Clay's grin became broad. She was lying through her
eeth, but he was having fun listening. "And do you know

Clay Reynolds?'' he asked softly, unable to keep from bait
ing her.

"The man who's giving the party?'' she guessed. "I see
him occasionally, but he doesn't get out much, does he?''

"He's old, is he?''

Her hand dusted the air. "Oh, sure. But you know how
those guys are. Entertainment is a must. Money buys any
thing.''

"I see.'' Hiding the laugh that wanted to burst out, he
waved to the waiter and signaled for his own drink to be
brought to him. It came quickly, along with the girl's glass
of water.

"Do you live here in San Antonio or are you part of the
Austin bunch?'' Clay asked.

"Oh, I'm from Austin,'' she said, jumping at the clue.
"I'm only in town for the party, you know.''

"What's your name?''

Suddenly the breeziness left her, seeping invisibly into
the air. He watched with fascination as her carefree expres
sion evaporated to be replaced with something that almost
brought tears to his eyes. "Katherine,'' she said quietly.

"Katherine what?''

"Just…Katherine.'' She stared down at the glass of water
in her hand before tilting her chin at him as if he were a
windmill. "And I don't really know anyone here.''

"I know.''

She searched his face. "You're the one giving the party,
aren't you?'' It was a statement more than a question. Her
insight intrigued him.

"Yes.''

"And your money paid for the food.''

"Yes.''

A small smile tugged at her full mouth. "And you're not
an old fossil.''

"Not on the outside.'' His lips mirrored hers.

Then the small smile disappeared. Her vulnerable expres

sion tugged at him. "Class act" was all she said before emptying her glass of water. Clay watched her delve deep inside herself for what shreds of dignity she had left. She looked him square in the eyes, hers as clear and clean as a spring-fed creek. "Thank you for not making a scene. I appreciate it. Really." She braced her hands on the table and began to stand.

"Where are you going?" His voice was sharp, sharper than he meant it to be.

Her brows rose haughtily. She might not be a heavyweight, but she wasn't afraid to take him on. "None of your business. I've eaten and now I'll leave quietly." She stood, then her face went white, highlighting a scattering of freckles beneath the surface. "Oh, lordy, not now," she groaned just before gracelessly crumpling back in her chair and then dropping toward the floor in a faint.

Clay moved quickly. His arms circled her tiny waist and shoulders just fast enough to keep her from hitting her head on the edge of the table. He lifted her to his chest, and, feeling as if he was carrying a feather, he strode toward the kitchen doors, hoping no one at the party would notice anything unusual.

Waiters stood around staring at him, their mouths slack or smiling knowingly. He wanted to punch each one, but wouldn't let go of his grip on the girl to do it. "How do I get the hell out of here?" he growled, holding her even closer to his chest, protecting his small bundle.

One of the waiters pointed toward a back door. "Through there."

Following the direction, he came out in the back hall of the hotel. He hurried directly to the elevators, but the ride up to his room was the longest he had ever taken. He maneuvered his load carefully when he reached his suite door so he could find his key, then fumbled with the lock in his impatience. The girl named Katherine moaned, and he cursed under his breath.

Finally the door opened and he strode in, kicking it closed behind him. He carried her through the living room and into the bedroom, placing her gently on the center of the bed before dialing the hotel desk. "This is Clay Reynolds. Please send a physician to my room immediately." The phone landed in the cradle with a snap.

Leaning over her supine form, he brushed the tangle of red hair away from her brow. He searched for some sign of alertness, but there was none.

Her face was heart-shaped. The bones beneath her fair skin seemed almost too fragile to touch and light purple smudges under the golden-brown dusting of lashes showed extreme exhaustion. His fingers brushed her collar and he could feel the birdlike bones underneath. She looked as delicate as a hothouse flower, yet he knew her to be as nervy as they came. He smiled at the picture of her arguing for her glass of water. Apparently she hadn't eaten lately, if the way she was stuffing hors d'oeuvres down her throat was any indication.

Then he spotted the earrings. No wonder he'd been able to see them from across the room. They were exquisite. From the large, perfect, teardrop-shaped emerald hung five rows of small but perfect diamonds held together with golden thread, which now rested against his finger. Bending his head, he looked closer at the intricate webbing of gold. In today's jewelry making, gold wasn't often used with diamonds. If he wasn't mistaken, these earrings were the real thing, not one of the copies that were so plentiful these days.

He touched one, grazing her neck as he lifted the stone slightly and turned it to catch the light. It was a beautiful, clear green stone, its color matching the emerald of her eyes. A gift? Stolen? His curiosity was piqued. Where would a girl like her get expensive earrings like those? A lover who tired of her, but not before gifting her with these? No. They were too expensive even for that.

When the knock on the door came, he jumped, guiltily pulling his hand away.

The doctor was a guest of the hotel, on vacation with his wife. He was kind, a little harried and very quick in his examination. Clay stood quietly by the bedroom door, waiting for him to finish. He had given the man all the information he had.

Katherine's eyelids fluttered, stopped, fluttered again, then opened. "Who are you?" Her voice was strong. Definite.

"Dr. Grossman," the older man said as he smiled down at the woman, and Clay's stomach tightened. The old man had no right to look at a young girl that way. But the physician was apparently not paying the slightest attention to Clay's silent signals. "How are you feeling right now?"

"Sleepy. But not hungry." She smiled back, warm and friendly as a puppy. She hadn't looked at Clay that way and it irritated him.

"I don't think you've been taking care of yourself very well lately, have you?"

"Not hardly." Katherine's voice was full of dry self-derision.

The older man pinched her arm, then watched closely. "You need rest, good food and lots of water. You're slightly dehydrated." The doctor replaced the stethoscope in his bag.

"Of course," Katherine said with mock subservience. She was becoming more awake with every minute. "I'll take care of it immediately."

Her dry sense of humor flew directly over the doctor's head. He snapped the small black case closed. "Good."

"Are you sure that's all that's wrong with her, Doctor?" Clay asked, stepping into the room. His hands were clenched in his black tuxedo pockets, his eyes boring into hers.

"Pretty certain. But you might have her get a complete

checkup." He stood and straightened his suit coat around his portly frame. "Until then, let's see what rest, water and good food will do."

With golden-brown eyes Clay stared down at Katherine, and she stared back, her eyes widening as she realized that he'd been here all along. Her heartbeat accelerated under his gaze. She glanced around the room. Expensive. His food, his room, his doctor. When would he call *his* police? She sighed in resignation. Whenever it was, she was ready. She was too exhausted to go one step further without help— anybody's help—including the handsome but stern-faced man at the door who seemed to be in complete control as he paid the doctor off. With cash. Deeper in debt.

He turned and left the room to show the doctor out.

She sat up as the outer door softly closed. Brushing her tangled hair away from her face, she waited for him to come around the corner where she could see him. She needed to try to read his expression so she could guess what he was going to do next. The alternatives were as varied as her scattered thoughts.

Then he was there, a frown on his brow barely hidden by the golden-streaked hair that fell forward to be impatiently brushed back by a long lean hand. He was a golden and brown man, made up of all the warm shades in between.

"Who are you?" he asked abruptly.

"I told you. Katherine. Who are you?"

He ignored her question. "Katherine who?"

She shrugged. "I haven't decided yet."

"What does your birth certificate read?"

"O'Malley," she mumbled, her bravado gone in an instant.

"Well, Katherine O'Malley, what am I going to do with you?"

Again she shrugged her shoulders, but her eyes drifted down to the spread that covered the bed. She didn't want to cry. Not yet. Not in front of him. Not in front of anyone.

His next abrupt question brought her gaze back to him. "Do you have a place to stay?"

"No."

"Are you from here?"

"No."

"Where, then?" he persisted.

She sighed wearily. "Does it matter? Just do what you're going to do and get it over with."

"What do you think I'm going to do?"

His tone was almost conversational, and irritation rose in her. He was playing with her. "Either call security and have me thrown out, or call the police and have me picked up."

"Neither, little girl," Clay drawled, just as the phone rang. He muttered an expletive through his clenched teeth and walked to the small nightstand. "Hello," he barked.

Katherine cringed for the person on the other end of the line. She commiserated with the caller, knowing that she was next in line to be on the receiving end of his temper. If he wasn't going to have her kicked out, did that mean that he expected payment? Judging from her clothes and circumstances, he had to know that she didn't have a dime in her pocket. That meant he had to ask for payment by the age-old barter system. But that type of barter wasn't an option for her....

"I'm sorry, but it couldn't be helped. I'll be down in just a few minutes. Meanwhile, keep everyone happy for me, okay?" His voice had changed from angry to cajoling. Katherine recognized the tone. He wanted something and he was going to get it just by asking. "Good girl," he said, his voice laced with satisfaction. "See you soon."

He hung up and golden-brown eyes once again focused on her. She stared back. He was the first one to retreat, turning his gaze to the small hands in her lap. They were well formed, but with broken nails and calluses. Worker's hands. She thought about hiding them, then decided against it; it was too late.

"Where are you from?"

She shrugged again. "Everywhere."

"The name of the town." His voice was crisp, his attitude one of an attorney with a hostile witness.

She cocked her head at him, her green eyes shining brightly. "You don't give up easily, do you?" she asked.

A small smile tugged at the corners of his mouth. "No."

She sighed. "I'm not telling you," she said simply. "It's my business."

"And now it's mine."

"No." She shook her head in contradiction, her eyes showing just a glimpse of the pain she was feeling. "It's still my business. Your business is deciding what you're going to do with me."

The smile he had been holding back finally broke out. So did a deep, dark, wonderful chuckle that flowed through her body. She couldn't help smile back. "All right, Katherine. You win," he said, but the glint in his eyes told her otherwise.

"Where did you get the earrings?"

His change of subject confused her for a moment, but then her eyes hardened. She touched each ear as if confirming her jewelry was still where it belonged—attached to her ears. "None of your business, but I didn't steal them. They were given to me. In love."

He grunted, refusing to admit he didn't like her answer. If he was right and those jewels were real, they were worth a small fortune. It didn't make sense that she'd wear an outfit that came off the rack of the cheaper clothing stores and then wear earrings that were worth the equivalent of the price of a Mercedes. Perhaps she was lying? He didn't think so, but he couldn't be sure....

Picking up the phone, he called room service and ordered soup and a sandwich, a pitcher of iced tea and their best, most fattening, dessert. When he hung up she was still staring at him. "You don't like what I ordered?"

She nodded, reluctant to believe in her good fortune. "It's perfect, but I'm already stuffed. Why are you doing this?"

He stared down at her, his hands back in his pockets, straining the black material across his muscled thighs. Finally he walked toward the door, his voice so low she almost didn't hear it. "Damned if I know." When he reached the door he turned around and cleared his throat. "My shirt's on the bed. Use it for a nightshirt. Take a bath, eat, then get some sleep. We'll talk in the morning. If you need anything, call the desk and they'll get it for you."

"And where are you staying?" Her green eyes were steady as she looked at him. Hundreds of offers of the same kind put this one in its proper perspective. No one ever gave something for nothing. She'd learned that the hard way. She wasn't upset; she wasn't even disappointed. Just curious. What were his plans and what method of payment did he think justified his care?

"I'm sleeping in the living room. Don't worry, little one. You're safe until the morning, when I grill you again. If you need me for anything, give a call down to the desk and they'll find me. Meantime, enjoy yourself, but stay in the suite."

"I will," she promised softly, earning another puzzling look from him. But where else did he expect her to go, she wondered. If she had had a place, she'd have already been there, not crashing parties so she could grub snacks that wouldn't qualify for bird food.

He hesitated another moment, then turned and slapped his hand against the doorjamb. "Good night."

"Good night," she repeated to no one. The door had already closed quietly behind him.

CHAPTER TWO

CLAY GAVE A TUG on his cuff links as he strolled back into the ballroom and glanced around at the guests still having a good time. It seemed that none of them—except Magda—had been worried by his absence.

Magda nodded, her eyes narrowing on him as she stood near the band, apparently in a discussion of hors d'oeuvres with the head waiter. It was part of her job to ensure that the table was never empty of its tidbits. Evidently she was more than capable of handling it. Later he would answer for his absence.

He was making his way toward a group of men engaged in a heated discussion when he spotted Laura, her blue eyes glistening with tears as she watched David's back in retreat. He immediately changed his course to head for her, seeing Laura as the solution to the problem of the girl upstairs. His friendship with Laura went back so long that he couldn't remember a time they weren't friends, and he trusted her implicitly.

"May I have this dance?" he asked quietly, taking in the light traces of her tears.

She turned to face him, her hand clinging to his as she nodded. "Please," she said huskily.

Clay slipped his arms around her and began edging his way toward the center of the dance floor. The band was playing a slow number that was almost as many years old as their friendship—years that had gone by too fast in the past and would probably speed up even more in the future

"David get to you again?"

She nodded, her mouth pressed against his jacket.

"Did you give him a good swift kick in the you-know-what?"

That brought a tremulous smile. "You used to be able to say that word in front of me."

He grinned back, looking down at her with eyes that twinkled, but still showed his concern. "That was when I was young and brash and without taste."

"Ohh." She pretended to be awed at how far he'd come. "And now you're such a man of the world and second only to James Bond in style and panache."

"Something like that," he said, twirling her around. "But occasionally even I don't have all the answers, and have to ask favors from others."

Her smile slipped. "If it has anything to do with David, I'm sorry...."

His arm tightened. "Nothing to do with David, I promise." He could feel her slim body sag with relief, underlining the tenseness that seemed to invade her very skin. "I need help with a dress. Something sedate and too small for you."

Her brows shot up. "What?"

He sighed. "If you promise not to laugh, I'll tell you about it," he said, hoping to distract her enough to smile a little.

"With a teaser like that, how could I resist? Tell all, Clay. I'm hanging on your every word." A smile lit her face.

He explained about Katherine O'Malley, stretched out upstairs in his room, and how she got there, earning more than one chuckle from Laura as he unwound the tale. "And so she needs something that isn't quite so flamboyant if I'm supposed to get her out of here early in the morning and send her on her way. Think you can help?"

She chuckled. "Your problems are solved. Just inside my door is a brown paper bag filled with clothing I was going to drop off at Goodwill. There's bound to be one or two dresses that might fit. Most of them are loose sun dresses that I've had for a hundred years and don't wear anymore.''

He gave a relieved sigh; he'd come to the right woman. ''Thanks. Can I send my car over and pick them up now?''

''Sure. You know where the key is.'' No matter how many times he and David had lectured her during the past two months, she continued to leave an extra key to the front door in a plant hanging on the porch.

The band slid from one slow song into another and Clay continued to dance with Laura, intent on getting everything straightened out. ''Thanks. It shouldn't take more than half an hour.'' He glanced up to find two men glaring at him. ''By the way, who's the tall guy with the Yuppie look who's been hanging around you?''

''You obviously aren't talking about David.''

''Obviously,'' Clay agreed dryly. ''He lives in shorts and knit shirts. It's the other one, over by the table.''

She hesitated just a moment, not bothering to look over her shoulder. ''Bob Hardy. He works with me and I asked him to escort me tonight.''

''Why didn't you ask David? He would have loved to have brought you.''

''No.'' She shook her head, that vulnerable lost look returning to her blue eyes. ''He was supposed to be escorting Petra.''

''I doubt that. He hasn't seen her in weeks.''

''Really?'' She gazed up at him, hope daring to shine in her eyes, and he felt a wave of protectiveness flood through him. She hadn't had it easy these past ten years, and occasionally it showed. Her marriage had been rocky at the best of times and finally ended in divorce just before she returned to San Antonio. The experience had taken its toll, robbing her of self-confidence in personal relationships while allowing her to be a bear in business. ''He was dating her when I returned here. Everyone told me so.''

Clay ignored that. "And when he was dating Petra, he never leaned against a wall and shot daggers at his best friend for dancing with her."

Laura stiffened in his arms. "Is he doing that now?"

"Yes," he chuckled. "So smile and pretend you're having the time of your life."

"It doesn't matter. He's not mad because I'm dancing with you. He's angry with me for dating a man he doesn't like."

Clay hesitated, then decided to plunge in. "How do you know it isn't because he wants to be in Bob's place?"

Laura tilted her head up to look at him, an inexplicable sadness in her eyes. "It's really over, Clay. Best friends can't always fall in love."

He sighed, remembering a long list of regrets that bound both of them to memories better left in the past, and held her closer. "I had that feeling, but I was rooting for you both."

"So was I. I guess we weren't really compatible or ready."

"Ready for what?" Clay asked, a thousand alternative answers springing to his mind.

"Ready to face the fact that lust isn't love."

"Lady, I can imagine a lot of things you two weren't ready for, but those two emotions never came to mind." Love. Lust. Possessiveness. David probably felt all of those for Laura. After all, the man had loved her for almost as long as he'd known her....

The song ended and Laura pulled away. "Walk me to the table, please," she asked quietly, and he nodded, his mind suddenly elsewhere. Upstairs.

"Thanks," he said, grateful to Laura for helping him out on such short notice. Magda might have been closer to the little redhead's size, but he certainly wasn't going to ask her now. He needed her to help keep things oiled, he told himself, seeking an excuse for his behavior.

After making sure Laura was taken care of, he walked across the room toward the hallway doors, wondering if he should check on Katherine one more time before he sent the driver to Laura's. One part of him said yes, but his logic overruled. He'd give the driver the address, and when the bag was delivered, he'd go upstairs just once more, and check on her. After all, the doctor had examined her and he had ordered food. What more could she possibly want?

It took less than two minutes to give the driver instructions and send him on his way. It took another minute to walk back into the party and look as if he'd never left. It took three minutes to spot another flash of red standing at the doorway, trying to gain his attention—and receiving everyone else's.

Her tiny heart-shaped face mirrored worry. Golden-red hair billowing around her shoulders in buoyant curls, she was bent forward as if to reach across the room to him.

He frowned, excused himself from the conversation he hadn't been participating in anyway and made his way toward Katherine. What the hell was wrong now?

Her relief at seeing him was evident in her expressive face. "I'm sorry for bothering you, Mr. Reynolds, but I wanted to thank you for your kindness before I left." She took two steps backward into the hallway as he approached closer.

"Left for where?" he demanded.

She shrugged her shoulders, looking everywhere but at him. "I'm not sure. But I can't accept your hospitality any longer. It's not right."

"You can, and you will."

"You don't know me from Mrs. Astor's horse. How do you know I wouldn't steal you blind?"

When he didn't answer, she began to turn. "See. I really can't stay."

"Katherine." It was an order. She stopped, turned and stared at him, seeing the unspoken command in his eyes.

"No," she began, shaking her head only to have him interrupt.

"I'm responsible for you. If that doctor thought for a moment that you were leaving, he'd blame me." He took her shoulders and turned her around. "So you'll march upstairs and get back in that bed."

She balked, casting a furious glare over her shoulder. "I'm not a child, and don't you dare patronize me!"

"I'm not. I'm just telling you what you're going to do until tomorrow."

"No, you're not! I'll do as I damn well please. And whatever it is, it isn't any of your business!"

"The hell you say!" Clay said through clenched teeth. "You'll do what I say or I'll have an all-points bulletin out on you in thirty seconds. It could take a long time to explain those baubles hanging from your little ears when you're wearing a dress that couldn't have cost more than an average meal." His eyes held hers. "The chief of police is right inside. Is that what you want?"

Her green eyes darted over his face, searching for the truth. It must have been there, because her shoulders drooped. "You'll get in trouble for helping me. Your girlfriend, or fiancée, or wife will be terribly angry."

He grinned at her fishing techniques. She wasn't going to come out and just ask him; she wanted him to volunteer information about Magda. Angry wasn't the word he would have used to describe how Magda would react when she found out about his little stray. She might be jealous, possessive, even slightly offended. But she would have to love him to be angry—and she didn't. No more than he loved her. He was amazed at what he was thinking.

"Let me worry about that." He took her arm and practically marched her toward the elevator. "And you'll have to stay in the room until I get there." He slipped her the key and punched the floor number then stepped outside of the elevator, watching the doors hide her sad, waiflike face from his view. For some inexplicable reason he wanted to take care of her. It must be that her tiny size provoked a protective, fatherly part of him into action. It never dawned on him to delve into the threats he'd uttered to keep her there. He just wanted it. Period.

But her face was imprinted between him and the closed elevator doors. He shook his head and shrugged his shoulders as if ridding himself of the image. It didn't work. He carried the image all the way back to the ballroom. Even pasting on a smile that was necessary to greet a few late stragglers didn't detract from his thoughts of her.

LAURA'S DATE stepped in from the large back veranda. The man didn't stop at the table he had occupied earlier, but headed straight toward the front door. Clay watched him leave with a spurt of satisfaction. That jerk didn't need to be hanging around Laura and upsetting David's apple cart. David could upset his own without any help.

It seemed forever before the party began to break up. Finally couples began to leave in groups, each saying how much they'd enjoyed the party. Magda stood at his side, her manner cool and confident, secure in her position in his life. Once when she leaned over to kiss one of the women on the cheek, the engagement ring he had given her caught the light and glittered like a knowing eye. A flash of dread hit his stomach and he turned his eyes away. What in the hell was the matter with him?

When the last guest had left they quickly checked the room to make certain that no one had left anything, then slowly walked out of the ballroom, her arm entwined in his. "It was nice, wasn't it?" Magda said with a sigh as they walked the long, glass-enclosed corridor.

"Perfect," he said, gently squeezing her arm. "And you were a perfect hostess. Thank you."

She gave him a sensuous smile. "You're welcome. But

I'm sure you'll find some way to reward me, darling. Perhaps a nightcap?''

He halted in front of the large revolving door, shaking his head ruefully. ''Not tonight. I'm beat. If you don't mind I'm going to put you in the car and send you home for your beauty sleep.''

She pouted delightfully, but had the grace to give in without arguing, even though he could see the gleam of battle in her eyes. She'd wait until a more opportune time to fight: a time when she would win the war instead of just the battle. ''Very well, if you insist.''

''I do.'' He grinned, admiring once more his choice of a wife. ''I'll make it up to you,'' he promised.

He walked her to the limo, gave the driver his instructions and kissed her chastely on the cheek. He was not quite ready to admit he was relieved when he saw the car drive away. A quick look at his watch told him it was almost two in the morning. Sleep was next on the list.

THE LIGHT from the living room spilled across the bed, highlighting a spray of golden-red hair on the pillow he was so ready to use. Damn. Somehow during the tail end of the evening he'd forgotten Katherine was in his bed. He backed away into the living room slowly, stumbled over a paper bag of clothing left by the door and cursed softly under his breath.

Because of some misplaced sense of chivalry, he was supposed to fold himself into a comfortable position on the couch and sleep the rest of the night away.

It was either that or kick the redhead out of his bed. Or…share it with her.

He brought himself up short. He didn't need complications in his life. In any form.

The couch didn't look so bad after all.…

MORNING CAME when the bellhop knocked on the door with a tray filled with breakfast and a pot of steaming hot coffee.

Clay had left a breakfast order to serve as a wake-up call, but had forgotten to change the order to include his "guest."

"Give me another order of this in fifteen minutes," he said as he slipped the waiter a twenty-dollar bill.

"Including the coffee?"

"Especially the coffee."

"Yes, sir." The man grinned as he angled out the door. "Right away."

"Thanks." As the front door locked, Clay walked toward the bedroom door, wondering what to do next. His clothes and the bathroom were in there. And so was Katherine O'Malley.

His problem was solved when the woman he had been thinking about—dreaming about—stuck her head around the door and gave a spritely grin. "Good morning." Her voice was husky with sleep.

"Good morning. Are you hungry?"

She shrugged a bare, silken shoulder, and his eyes caught the movement, his imagination taking over to create what was hidden behind the door. Did she have freckles other than the small ones that dotted her pert, uptilted nose? Or was the rest of her skin as creamy golden as that one slim shoulder?

He pulled his glance away from her and firmly focused on the food upon the roll-about table. "You should be. Come eat while I get dressed."

"What about you?"

"I'll eat after I take a shower."

"Oh." Her glance darted from him to the couch and back to the food, the green depths of her eyes lighting with the beginning of impish delight. "Aren't you sorry now that you decided to give me the bed? I could have slept there without any problem. After all, I'm much smaller."

He *had* noticed and was irritated with himself for doing

so. "I had a good night's sleep," he said blandly, ignoring the thought of her, posed in sleep on that brocade-covered couch. Satin against silk… "Put some clothes on and get out here before this food gets cold."

"Then can I take a shower after you?"

"Yes," he said, the thought of her naked and slick with soap creating havoc in his mind. What the hell was the matter with him? He was supposed to be playing the part of a knight in shining armor, not the lech of the party! It was irritating to have such a strong sexual reaction to a woman, without being mentally prepared for it. Normally he chose the time and place of his arousal, not the other way around. "Hurry up," he ordered roughly.

The door closed quietly between them, shutting him in a room that minutes before had been filled with sunshine. He poured himself coffee and drank half the cup before he realized he'd scalded his tongue. Slamming the cup down, he opened the drapes, staring out at the view of San Antonio's skyline.

The bedroom door opened behind him, just as someone knocked on the outer door. With a muttered expletive he answered it, knowing it was the bellhop with the extra breakfast, and also knowing that the same young man would stare at Katherine and jump to all kinds of conclusions. But he couldn't very well ask her to disappear as if she were some hooker finishing a morning's work.

He was right. The bellhop's eyes honed in on Katherine and she gave a sunny smile in return. "Well, hello," he said, and she giggled.

"Here," Clay said, stuffing another five in the young man's hand. "Thanks."

"Anytime," he said as he walked backward to the door, his eyes still glued to Katherine's smiling face. "Anytime at all, Mr. Reynolds."

Clay could hardly contain the irritation he felt as he

slammed the door in the boy's face. Damn! Some jerks in this world actually sat on their brains!

"More coffee?" Katherine asked, pulling up a chair to the table and pouring herself a cup.

"Yes." He watched the tiniest, flirtiest hands tilt the coffee pot to fill his cup. "I take it half-full."

The pot came up at exactly the right spot, without a drop spilling on the tablecloth. "Okay?"

He couldn't help returning her smile. "Okay."

"Why don't you have a seat and eat your breakfast with me, then take a shower?"

He couldn't resist. She was his guest, almost against her will, so the least he could do was be sociable before sending her on her way. Pulling up the desk chair, he sat across from her and uncovered the plate on his side of the table. "Why not?"

Katherine picked up a piece of toast and lavished it with honey butter. "Do you have many parties? Is that dark-haired girl your wife? No, I guess not or I wouldn't be here. Your fiancée? Your sister? No, not your sister. She doesn't look at you the way a girl looks at her brother. She must be your fiancée or girlfriend." She peeked at him through golden-brown lashes. "Girlfriend?"

He bit into a piece of bacon. "Fiancée."

"Mud flaps," her voice was filled with teasing disappointment. "I should have known."

His eyes darted up. "What?"

"I should have known," she repeated patiently.

"Before that."

Her brows rose, making her look like a child playing the role of an adult. Her eyes were guileless and he almost got lost in the green of them. "Mud flaps?"

He nodded, taking another bite of bacon so he'd have a reason to swallow. She had on the same outfit that she'd worn last night, only now the top buttons were undone to show a creamy expanse of throat and just a hint of feminine softness at the rise of her breasts.

"It's just an expression that keeps me from saying what I really want to." She grinned and her whole face lit up. "I might shock somebody if I said what I thought."

"Try me," he ordered, amazed at how low his voice sounded.

"Well…" She leaned forward as if to impart a secret, and she did—there were no freckles on the rise of her breasts. "I was hoping that your fiancée was your girlfriend. That way I'd stand a chance of catching you myself. Then I'd have you and my career and beautiful clothes and live happily ever after!" Her chuckle wrapped around him, enclosing him in its warmth, its promise, its delightful effervescence. He grinned back, the corners of his mind telling him he must look like a besotted fool while the rest of him didn't care.

He answered her teasing with his own. "But wouldn't it be difficult to manage your career and my home and me and all the closets of beautiful clothes? I mean, you've got to be a space scientist or an astronaut. At the very least one of *Fortune 500*'s top executives."

"No." Her smile slipped a little, but determination etched her features. "But some day I'll be a damn good secretary and some up-and-coming young man will be at the top of whatever company because I helped put him there."

He leaned back and stared at her through narrowed eyes. He hadn't known too many women who strived for anything other than the right catch, the right marriage, the right man. Her teasing about money slid over him. It was what he expected from the women he knew. "Are you a good secretary now?"

She bit into a slice of toast, her small teeth tearing it delicately. "Not yet. But I learn fast."

"Then what are you? Right now, that is."

"Up until two weeks ago I was a short-order cook and waitress at my brother's truck stop."

Clay sipped his coffee, not really tasting it. "Then what happened?"

"I quit." It was a simple statement but Clay had a feeling there was an enormous story behind those two words.

"To do what?"

"To come to the big city and see if I could get a job that would train me to be the kind of secretary I want to be."

He dropped the pretense of eating, focusing all his attention on her. "So you go around crashing parties and eating off hors d'oeuvres tables, hoping to meet people who would hire you?" How much was he supposed to believe of this story? "I know this might seem a silly question, but why didn't you ask your brother to send you to secretarial school? It would have been easier."

Her eyes clouded with something that looked like hurt. She tilted her chin in the air. "My father was kind, but not smart. Dad left the truck stop to my brother, believing that men are always able to manage business better than women. And my brother is a sweet love-sick man who believes that girls should be ornaments, or work for their relatives so they can be watched over. After all, most girls don't have the brains God supposedly gave to males." She sighed. "Robbie comes from the same old school as my dad did, only Dad believed that women could become excellent secretaries and it was okay for them to do so. Robbie believes any training for women is a waste of time when they'll probably get married and raise kids anyway." She sighed heavily. "Although I love him dearly, Robbie's really limited in his scope of the world."

"I see," Clay began, still confused. What was wrong with her brother's outlook?

"No, you don't. But it doesn't matter." She ran a hand through her hair, pushing it behind her shoulder to expose one of her earrings. They fascinated him, catching his eye as they swung gently from side to side, caressing her neck. "It took me almost three years to save up five hundred dollars to come here and find work. In fact, it was my father who finally gave me the push I needed to leave. Just before he died, he gave me another hundred dollars and these earrings." She lifted the rest of her hair to give him the full view.

"They're beautiful," he murmured. "And expensive."

She nodded, dropping her hair so that it framed her creamy skin again. "Yes. But the one thing I don't want to do is sell them. My dad found them in a pawn shop in Galveston when he and Mom were on their honeymoon. They had gone down to the harbor and were watching all the ships coming and going. The pawnbroker had told them the jewels were a replica of some earrings that a French nobleman had designed and given to his true love. Later, because of the crest on the back, Dad found out they were the real thing and definitely the most expensive thing he'd ever bought. And for a song, too." She smiled sadly. "Dad used to promise Mom that he'd take her to France one day so she could see where the original owners used to live. She was always fascinated with French history. It seems that some of my ancestors came from France and settled in Ireland during the revolution. When Dad found these earrings he told her they would have to do until he could afford the passage."

"Really?"

She nodded again, her expression sincere in her attempt to explain. "There's a crest on the back of one of the earrings. A mountain peak, beside three stars with a name written below. Montclair. They say you can locate anyone by his crest." She took a sip of coffee. "The other earring holds initials and a few French words. They're very special."

"Just like your parents."

It was a trite remark, but the sadness on her face made

him wish he hadn't reminded her of her loss. "Mom wore them on every special occasion I can remember. She used to laugh and call them her good luck charms, and deep down I think she really believed that." She leaned forward. "Dad used to say he gave them in love and they would always represent his feelings."

"And did your dad ever take your mother to France?"

She leaned back in the chair. "No, they never made it. But it didn't seem to bother Mother that much. She used to laugh and tell me that when I grew up she and Dad would send me to France instead. She used to say she didn't need to see someone else's homeland when she had my father."

"So now you have the earrings. What are you going to do with them?"

She shrugged. "I don't know yet. Dad told me to sell them and use the money for secretarial school, but I can't bring myself to do that."

"What happened to the cash you had?"

Her eyes widened. "This town is expensive! In two weeks the money was gone and no one would give me a chance. The only job they wanted me to take was the one I left. If I did that, I know I'd be stuck there the rest of my life. I'd rather die than do that again." Her voice had grown softer with each word until he could barely hear the last sentence.

But he did hear, and her words slammed into his guts like a fist. "That's ridiculous." His comment was like the snap of a rubber band.

"No. That's life—hard, cruel and true." She stood, her shoulders squared. "But what would you know about that side of life? You look as if you were born with a silver spoon in your mouth and had brains enough to clamp down on it."

"I worked damn hard to get where I am." His eyes grew cold.

"And you made it." She turned and walked toward the

bedroom door. ''I've yet to achieve my goals, and I'm not even sure how I'm going to do it. But I will. I swear I will.''

''Good luck,'' he muttered to the closing door, wondering how in hell he'd slipped into this predicament. Twelve short hours ago, he was planning a party and was satisfied with his life. Now, for some reason he couldn't explain, he was aching for something that was missing. He grimaced. What? Disaster in the form of a redhead? Complications in the form of lust? To hell with it. Nothing was worth reorganizing his orderly life. He was exactly where he wanted to be.

In an hour or so he'd be home, minding his own business. He'd give the girl a hundred and send her back on the highway to happiness. She was a survivor, she'd do okay.

Leaning back he closed his eyes, belatedly wishing for the sleep he hadn't had last night. He quickly opened them again, surprised that when he shut out the room he saw a vision of a redhead with green eyes and a vulnerable mouth. And she had been smiling up at him from his own bed.

He took another gulp of coffee. The mind played strange tricks on people when they were tired, and this was the strangest of all.

He was engaged to Magda, and he would stay that way. Period. The end.

But then he closed his eyes again and propped his head against the chair. He had to wait for Katherine to shower, anyway, he reasoned, so he might as well enjoy it. Didn't doctors say that fantasies were good for the mind? They were certainly playing havoc with his body....

CHAPTER THREE

THAT WAS IT—he would plead temporary insanity. Besides, this whole experience would be all over in a matter of days and his life would neatly slip back into its normal, everyday pattern. All he had to do was wait his craziness out.

Unlocking the front door of his condo town house, he pushed it open. He was probably suffering from something similar to prewedding jitters. After all, any man could be attracted to a woman while engaged to another. And if he hadn't been attracted to Katherine O'Malley, he'd worry that the first signs of rigor mortis had set in. The problems came only when a man followed his attraction through with actions that would betray his fiancée's trust. But anyone could look....

"It's beautiful," Katherine whispered as if she were in church or a library. She stood just behind him in the two-story entryway and craned her neck to see the inside adobe balcony that ran around the second floor game room, then bent forward to view a small section of the living room. "And it's bigger than the truck stop!"

He grinned. "That's saying a lot."

"The decor is so...so..."

"Stark?"

"No. Simple—yet elegant."

"Thank you."

"Did you decorate it or hire someone else?" She looked up at him and he could see the genuine interest.

"I did it. Surprised?"

She shook her head and her hair curled around her shoulders, lightly caressing the small collarbones. But her eyes held the delight of a child. "Not at all. I bet you could do anything if you set your mind to it."

He smiled, suddenly feeling like king of the mountain. "It's all right if you walk into the living room. I promise it won't swallow you whole," he teased, his glance taking in her tiny feet planted to the floor as if they were glued there. She still wore those ridiculously high heels, but at least she had on one of Laura's casual sun dresses. It had no waist and fell in multicolored folds all the way to midcalf. It was becoming, but not sensuous.

Her eyes touched his and he held his breath, taking in the beautiful fern-green clearness of them. They were so sweet, so pure, so very very beautiful. But lurking there was also a sadness that seemed to weigh on her slight frame. She reminded him of a wonderland wood sprite who would disappear as soon as the brilliance of the sun filtered through the forest to illuminate the ground.

"Is it as large as it looks?"

"Yes." He cleared his throat. "The main guest bedroom is upstairs."

"And your bedroom?" she asked quietly.

"Off the living room. Downstairs." Was she propositioning him? For one wild second he certainly hoped so. Then he came to his senses.

Her eyes were still locked with his. He could feel a thousand emotions flashing through her, sorting out a myriad of possibilities. Then she smiled, slowly at first, but the heat of it hit his stomach like a laser beam. "Thank you," she said.

He shrugged. "It's only for a while, until you can get on your feet. Besides, Consuela will be glad to have more help," he said, referring to his executive secretary. "She's always complaining about how much she has to do by herself."

"I wasn't speaking about the job," she admonished softly. "I was thanking you for…everything." With a lightning swiftness that he was beginning to associate with her, she rose on her tiptoes and brushed her lips against his cheek, her hand resting on his shoulder for balance. "Thank you, again." Then her touch and lips were gone, and he was chilled by their absence.

Once Katherine had toured the house, she went upstairs. Clay sat in the living room, looking out at the woods beyond the glass floor-to-ceiling windows that stretched across the back of the house, his whole body tense with expectation as he listened to the soft sound of Katherine's steps as she crossed and recrossed the parquet floor of the guest room.

He didn't know what had made him offer her the use of his home until she was established elsewhere. He didn't even know what he had meant by "elsewhere," but he knew he wanted to help.

Yes, she was beautiful and charming and terribly sexy in her tiny way, but he hadn't offered his support for those reasons. He had helped because, quite frankly, she had touched something deep inside him that he hadn't known he possessed. For lack of a better description he named it a well of compassion for the underdog.

"I'll be collecting stray cats next," he muttered into his can of beer. If David was here he'd know how out of character this action was for Clay. Clay and David and Laura. The three musketeers from the University of Texas. Together they were going to conquer the world.…

Well, David was making it big now creating computer programming for major companies with special needs. Clay even used a few of David's tailor-made programs for his own real-estate business.

Clay was doing better than he had dreamed possible, owning one of the largest real-estate conglomerates in the Southwest. He had honed a talent for choosing land that, because of location, would become part of other company's packages when they wanted to expand.

And Laura was on her way to being indispensable to a business world who realized her talents. Just transferred back to San Antonio and now part of the board of directors for a growing retail clothing chain, she was both beautiful and intelligent—a formidable combination.

None of them seemed to have dreams they couldn't achieve.

Was Katherine the same? Or did she merely have illusions that would break her spirit before they came true? He hoped not. He'd admired her spunk; and her drive to succeed almost equaled his. So what harm was there if he helped her along with it a little? After all, just because she was a female didn't mean she couldn't use a male helping hand.

He gulped down the rest of the can and crushed it in his hand. "Liar," he growled, standing up and going to the refrigerator for another.

KATHERINE PACED the floor in her bedroom. The guest bedroom. Clay's guest bedroom. She stopped in front of the dresser mirror and stared at herself. "Katherine Maureen O'Malley. I don't know how you've done it, but you stepped on a beehive and came up smelling like honey, an' none o' the bees 're stingin' you," she trilled. "And what's more, I believe you're in love."

Her smile disappeared. No. That couldn't be true. She didn't know much about love, but living above the truck stop had certainly taught her about lust. She'd seen it all her life. As a child she would stretch across her small bed and stare out the window at the parking lot below, seeing more than a child her age should.

Oh, a few of the guys were great, talking about their wives and playing pool or sipping a brew, but they were the exception to the rule. The life of a trucker was hard, both on him and on his family. And most of the men who stopped at her father's place seemed to have been divorced and were fancy-free, still seeking the perfect woman. Meanwhile, who would care if they fooled around a little? Or if they never strived to be perfect men?

Her brother was no exception. He'd done his share of boasting and doing. Until Uda came along. Uda was a young German girl who had caught him quick and held him fast. She didn't lift a finger, and that ensured that Robbie would be forever busy at work, with no time for another woman.

And Uda had made Katherine's life miserable.

Only her father had had faith in her dreams. Only her father had realized she hadn't begun to utilize her talents or intelligence and probably never would as long as she stayed where she was. Her dear sweet dad had given her his most precious possession: her mother's earrings. With those beautiful earrings and a hundred dollars he had handed her an opportunity to change her life for the better. Then, two weeks later he died in his sleep, believing Katherine's dreams would now be fulfilled.

Now she had to prove his faith in her. She'd show him. She'd show the world, she hoped. Not as confident right now as she had been when she'd left, Katherine needed a respite from the overwhelming tension of the past two weeks. But things would change. And when she had made it big in the secretarial world, she'd find a way to pay Clay back for his faith in her and his help. In the end Katherine would pay off all her debts and make it in her chosen world.

The dull metallic thud of pots and pans banging around reminded her of where she was. Clay Reynolds was downstairs.

Now *there* was an enigma if ever there was one. He was definitely high society and just a touch gruff and extremely arrogant. But underneath he was a pushover. Knowing that, she'd be damned if she'd take advantage of him, especially realizing that his fiancée was going to have a screaming fit when she found out there was another woman living in his home. No. Katherine couldn't hurt him that way.

She sat cross-legged on the bed and stared out the window at the top of the post oaks that were clustered in the backyard. But what else could she do? She had nowhere to go and no knowledge of how to change the path her life had taken. She was plum out of decisions and tired of trying to make sense of the world outside the truck stop.

All she could manage was to hang on for the ride and see where she wound up. She prayed that it would be close to Clay, who was more the top candidate for the Knight in Shining Armor award than he ever realized....

"AND THEN I told her she could keep my damn clothes and that I hoped she'd have better luck selling them than I did wearing them!" Katherine sat on the dining room chair, gnawing away on the smallest drumsticks she'd ever eaten. They were delicious.

"So you took off, with a landlady holding all your belongings, and decided to head for Austin with a trucker?" Clay asked, fascinated by the story of what had happened before they met. He was also intrigued with her mouth as it moved to form words.

"All except my earrings." She grinned.

"You were wearing them?" he guessed.

She nodded vigorously, choosing another small drumstick from the plate in the middle of the table. "Is this tempura batter?" she asked, and it took him a minute to assimilate the change of topic. He nodded. "It's so tasty." Her small tongue darted out to catch a stray crumb. His eyes followed the movement. "So when I passed the hotel and saw the load of cars, I figured, what did I have to lose by stopping? After all, truckers are always going to Austin, but this hotel might not have the same party next week."

"Weren't you afraid you'd get caught?"

She gave a lithe shrug. "What would they do—kick me out? The good Lord knows, I've been kicked out before."

"What about school?" he asked. "Did you take any business courses or typing classes?"

"Mmm." Nodding, she quickly chewed and swallowed. "I took one year of typing in my freshman year and a general business course that taught the rudiments of filing and office management in my second year." She slipped one dainty finger into her mouth and sucked the juice that shone there.

Clay forced his eyes away from her and took a sip of wine. His stomach tightened at the sight of that small action. It was time to regain control of the conversation and keep his mind on the story at hand. He couldn't remember ever having been so interested in a person before. She was certainly different from anything he was used to. "But if you had this burning desire to be a secretary, why didn't you take more courses?"

She gave a heavy sigh and wiped her hands on a cloth napkin. "Because my father had a stroke and was partially paralyzed, so I dropped out at the end of my sophomore year to care for him while my brother ran the truck stop. My father promised me that as soon as he was able to take care of himself, I could enroll in secretarial school." The sunny smile left her face and was replaced with a terrible sadness. "I didn't know then that he would never recover. After steadily going downhill, he died a month ago."

Silence filled the room as she drifted into memories in which he had no part. He felt sorry for her, knowing that losing both her parents must have been a hard blow to accept. Especially since she seemed close to her family.

"It's too late to worry about it now," she said and sighed. "Now I've got to learn to take care of myself and get the education I need."

"You never finished school?" Clay's brows rose as he placed his glass back on the table.

Her chin tilted. He knew that look—it meant she was going to give him a piece of her mind, right between the eyes. "We are legends. And I did complete high school. I took the GED test and passed. That means that I've got the education equivalent to a high school graduate. I even have a diploma to prove it."

"Legion."

"What?" It was her turn to look confused.

"Not 'We are legends,' like a story, but 'We are legion,' like an army."

She didn't give in easily. "A small point."

He grinned. "Very small," he agreed.

Her green eyes turned stormy. "Well, if it's that damn small, then stop smirking," she snapped.

"I'm not. I'm smiling."

"It looks like a smirk to me." She leaned closer to study his mouth, and his grin widened. He refused to recall how long it had been since he had grinned so much! The fresh scent of her lingered in the air between them, and he sniffed it as if to keep it inside him. "Yes." She nodded. "It's definitely a smirk."

"You're looking for an excuse to argue," he managed to say calmly. "I refuse to do so."

She crossed her arms and he was shocked by his awareness of her breasts. They were outlined against the light cotton fabric—small and pert. A beautiful size and perfectly in proportion to her build....

"And you can quit staring at me. I know I look underdeveloped, especially compared to your...your fiancée," she said, having a hard time getting the hated word out.

His eyes popped open and his head snapped up, a light blush tinging his tanned cheekbones. "That's not exactly polite table conversation."

"Neither is staring polite."

"I wasn't staring."

"And I've got a diploma, whether you think so or not."

She was belligerent. She was beguiling. And he hadn't felt like laughing so much in years. He knew he was rusty, but two could play her game. "And your breasts are beautiful. Just right for you."

Her eyes widened as his comment soaked in. That did it! He was being just as outrageous as she was! Her frown slipped into a smile, the smile into laughter that bubbled from her toes to her throat and echoed lightly in the room.

Then he joined in.

When the laughter died down, their eyes met and held. Silence seemed to slice the room in two, and thoughts tumbled through his head at the speed of light.

"When are you getting married?" she asked softly.

"In six months."

"Oh."

He cleared his throat and sat up straighter. This new relationship had to move to a firmer footing. "I've got an idea about a place you can stay, but I have to check it out. Do you have any clothes that would be suitable in an office environment?"

Katherine sighed. He was back to being aloof again. "No," she admitted. "Unless you count those three sun dresses as suitable."

"What about at that rooming house where the woman is holding your belongings?"

"I have five outfits there, one or two might work, but I don't have the money to bail them out."

"I do," he said, pushing away from the table. "You clean up the kitchen and I'll make a few phone calls." He saw that defiant look wash over her piquant face. She obviously didn't like to be ordered around. "I cooked dinner, remember?"

Reluctantly she nodded.

He left the room as quickly as possible, heading toward his study just off the master bedroom. Breathing space. That's what he needed. Time to get his priorities in order.

Katherine was a nice girl in a bad situation, and he was just helping her out. That was all. He repeated that over and over as he closed the study door and headed for the phone. First he'd get her clothes back and then he'd see about finding her a place to stay. Once that was accomplished, his life would be back to normal and he could give a sigh of relief for completing what he shouldn't have started in the first place.

The rest of the evening passed peacefully. Clay played some tapes on an obviously complicated stereo system that had awed Katherine. He drank another two glasses of wine and read a new spy story that had just hit the bestseller list, but it didn't hold his attention as much as the sprite who was sitting on his couch did.

She was seated in the corner, her legs curled under her. Her eyes were closed and there was a small smile on her parted lips that told him she loved the sound of light jazz almost as much as he did. Where had she acquired the taste for it? Certainly not in a truck stop between San Antonio and the Gulf of Mexico!

Finally he dropped all pretense of reading and watched her openly. If God had made leprechauns, this would be what they had developed into over the centuries.

Her hair billowed around her shoulders like an aureole, her skin was so clear it was almost translucent. Most men he knew would give their eye teeth for a chance to dress her up and parade her in front of others—until they found that they couldn't curb her wayward tongue or her slightly unorthodox attitudes....

Katherine felt the pressure of his gaze, but couldn't gather enough nerve to open her eyes and see his expression. Was he laughing at her or would there be pity in his gaze? She didn't want to know. It was enough to sit here on a couch that cost more than all the furniture in her father's apartment and listen to strange music that had an unusually soothing effect.

He had made a deal with the landlady and was picking up her clothing tomorrow, despite Katherine's protests. Now she not only owed him for his kindness and hospitality, but she owed him money, too. Her smile drooped. But she'd pay him back somehow, if it took her all her life. Katherine Maureen O'Malley would be beholden to no man. It would be an even exchange or there wouldn't be any exchange at all. Except this one time....

The phone rang and jolted her out of her reverie. With the snap of pages slapping together, Clay put the book on the coffee table and headed for his study. Her stomach flipped as his voice changed from a harsh bark to soft chuckles. It must be Magda. His fiancée. That word hurt more than any other she could think of.

It was time to face the fact that she was falling head over heels in love with a man so far out of her sphere that he might as well be on another planet. Try as she might, there didn't seem to be any way to head off the fall she knew was coming. She was all wrong for him, she kept telling herself, but it hadn't stopped her heart from tripping over her head in an effort to love him. Knowing that Cinderella stories had nothing to do with reality didn't seem to help, either.

His voice drifted to her, and even though his words were muffled, the intimacy of his conversation came through loud and clear. He was treating Magda to a lovers' dialogue, and Katherine ached with the unwelcome envy that surged through her body with every vowel spoken.

What was the matter with her? She had no right to infringe upon anyone's life, especially not upon the man who was trying to help her stand on her own two feet! All she would do was hurt herself even more by harboring thoughts that had no place in her life, her situation.

She held herself stiffly against the couch, praying the emotions that flowed through her like an inky dark river would leave quickly. She wanted peace, and with that peace would come contentment. She knew because she'd had it once and had starved for it ever since.

She sighed, leaning her head back on the firm cushion. There hadn't been such a thing as peace in her life since she was a child. At the tender age of ten, she had lost her mother to cancer. She didn't linger and slowly fade away, but was ill one week and gone by the end of the month, leaving a vast and empty hole in all their lives.

Her father had been devastated, barely able to work without being reminded of the large, happy woman who had walked the same linoleum he was walking, cooked the same food he was cooking. She had smiled the same smile he no longer could find in his repertoire of facial features. Oh, her mother hadn't been beautiful or svelte or even outstandingly intelligent. Instead, she was overweight with a face that would have been called Irish-cute in its youth. And she had never understood multiplication. But she had been the very glue with which the family was stuck together. They had all used her as the pivotal point in their lives—the sun they all circled.

When she'd died, their lives and peace and happiness had shattered into a thousand pieces, never to be glued back together again. And since her mother's death, Katherine had been seeking that elusive, comforting security, not knowing exactly what it was, but realizing she would recognize it when she saw it…

Right now, she recognized it in Clay, and that was frightening.

He didn't want her. He didn't want to be any more than a friend in need. It was *her* heart that was crying out, not his.

Her best move would be to repay his thoughtfulness guardedly so she wouldn't interrupt his flow of life. She would be the best friend he ever had.

His voice drifted in and out of her thoughts, a sentence here, a chuckle there. She snuggled deeper into the marshmallow-soft couch and gave a small sigh. It felt nice to make her decisions on life before she slept. That way her mind was cleared of problems.

CLAY STARED down at the woman curled in the corner of his couch. She might be as small as a child, but she was certainly all female. He knew because his libido had shouted at him all evening, despite his dire warnings to himself.

Before he went into a trance staring at her, he decided he might as well send her off to bed and head for his own. Tomorrow was supposed to be a busy day, although for the life of him he couldn't remember anything he wanted to do at work. The only item on his list right now was to wrestle Katherine's clothing back from the landlady. Everything else was secondary.

He sat on the side of the couch and brushed a curl away from her cheek. "Katherine," he murmured, wondering where the force of his voice went. Damn! Her name sounded too much like a verbal caress. He cleared his throat. "Katherine!"

She jumped, and he pulled his hand back quickly. Her green eyes widened as she stared at him seated next to her. He smiled. "I'm sorry, I didn't mean to startle you. I just wanted to point you in the direction of your room so you could sleep in comfort."

"Thanks," she said, relaxing and stretching her arms over her head. "I didn't realize I had dozed off."

"You're entitled to. You've had a busy week."

Her eyelids drooped with tiredness, giving her a sensuous look that tingled through him. "I guess I have," she admitted, uncurling to stand in front of him. "I'll see you in the morning."

"Right." His tone dropped two octaves, his golden-brown eyes glued to her.

But he still wasn't expecting it when she bent down and

dropped a kiss lightly on his lips. "See you in the morning, Clay."

"Yes. Sure." He watched her walk out of the room and toward the stairs. Her fingers hooked the straps of her shoes, her arms drifting sensuously about her as she swayed across the room, her small bottom swinging sweetly from side to side as she glided barefoot across the thick carpeting.

Cursing under his breath, he turned and stared out at the night, attempting to rid himself of the image of Katherine walking across the room. But the vision was indelibly burned into his mind.

It was over two hours before Clay found his own bed. Another two hours before he could close his eyes without seeing a flame-headed sprite whose green eyes glittered with the promise of sensual dreams and whose touch was as light and airy as stardust.

CHAPTER FOUR

MORNING CAME TOO EARLY, but Clay was forced to greet it anyway. After turning off the alarm clock that he'd set for seven, he heard Katherine in the kitchen. The smell of sizzling bacon wafted under the closed door. He sniffed, stretched, then rested his head against folded arms, imagining her puttering around. A small smile tilted his lips as he mentally watched her going through the motions of cooking breakfast.

She would be in a short T-shirt and even shorter shorts, her golden-red hair held back by a bright green ribbon. In her unusually husky voice she would be lightly humming a tune that would soak into his skin and make his body sing along. Her movements would be graceful and quick, as sensuous as a knowledgeable woman's wiles.

The sound of glass breaking shattered his imagery. Or perhaps she would be as clumsy as a child....

He sighed and pulled himself off the bed. He might as well shower and eat. He had a full day ahead of him.

KATHERINE TURNED the bacon over, humming an old country-and-western tune in a kitchen that was the dream of a gourmet cook. Only she wasn't that kind of animal. Bacon, fried potatoes and eggs with toast or flour tortillas would have to do; she had never learned how to make hollandaise sauce for eggs Benedict. She had a sneaking suspicion, though, that the latter was probably more Clay's style.

She glanced down at the multicolored sun dress she had

worn yesterday and had on again this morning. It was faded and not at all flattering, but at least it covered her. Her fingers traced the plait of heavy hair that fell down her back, making certain it was still neatly contained. Wishing had never gotten her anywhere, but once more she wished she had soft, smooth hair, more height and fuller breasts. And not necessarily in that order.

The muffled sound of an alarm clock whispered through the rooms, and she glanced quickly at the large brass-and-glass clock on the far living room wall. He must have set his alarm for seven. It continued to hum for over a minute before it stopped.

She could almost see him, his jaw shadowed with early-morning stubble, his eyes closed, his lashes onyx against his golden-tanned skin. She'd bet he didn't wear pajamas to bed. Light, golden-copper skin would contrast sharply against the white of the sheets. His sun-streaked hair would be ruffled, like a child's, but to her fingers it would feel sensuous. His mouth. His mouth would be slightly parted and warm breath would pass in and out, gliding past his firmly formed lips....

Enough. Her muscles tightened and her nerves sang with tension. She spun around and reached for the fork to take the bacon out of the pan. Instead, she hit the small, half-filled glass of orange juice sitting on the counter. It tilted sideways and, spilling its sticky contents, quickly rolled across the counter and into the sink, breaking with the sharp sound of tinkling glass.

"Mud flaps," she muttered, gingerly picking up the broken pieces and wrapping them in paper towels before dropping them into the trash. This is what she got for daydreaming about impossible quests. Reality wasn't Clay asleep or awake. Reality was a broken glass and sticky counters and floor.

By the time she'd finished cleaning up the mess and salvaging the bacon, water was running in the downstairs bathroom. With fingers that were less than deft, she sliced up the two potatoes she had cleaned earlier, then dumped them into the leftover bacon grease and began frying them. When Clay turned the shower off, the potatoes would be cooked and waiting. Brown eggs sat on the countertop, ready to be broken and cooked to his preference.

She poured another glass of juice and walked to the un-curtained bay window in the small kitchen eating area. There she paused to stare at the forest outside.

It was beautiful in an untamed way. Instead of carefully placed shrubs and immaculately tended beds, there was an abundance of trees crowding all the way up to the deck that ran the full length of the back. The branches created sooth-ing cavelike shadows where mounds of wild fern clustered together for protection. She could see tulips and day lilies gathered here and there in clumps, as if casually dropped rather than carefully planted by someone trying to imitate nature. About halfway back through the yard was a wood and wrought-iron bench that faced the back corner of the woods, inviting someone to sit there and contemplate the wonders of nature.

"Katherine?"

She pivoted, the dress streaking around her calves like a circular rainbow. Her hair flew back to allow a glimpse of richly jeweled earrings gracing small lobes. Her jade-green eyes were wide.

"What is it?" He was standing far enough away from her, yet he knew that if she hadn't been so close to the window, she would have taken two steps back.

"Nothing." She shook her head and the sunlight bounced around her golden-red halo.

"What is it?"

"You startled me."

"What were you thinking?"

Her eyes were wide, unflinching. Honest. "About how wonderful it would be to walk out there in the moonlight. I bet you could catch moonbeams darting through the leafy canopy.''

He took a step closer. ''Would you like to do that to-night?''

''No.''

''Why not?''

She gave the smallest of smiles. ''Because I like the way I think it would be better than the way it really would be.''

''How do you know?''

That sadness in her eyes again. ''I just do.''

The silence stretched between them as Clay watched her, his eyes narrowed. She was honest and...right.

He had often thought fancifully that moonlight was captured by the shady boughs of the trees. He would sit on the deck with the house lights out and watch the black-shadowed trees bend and dance in the softly playing breeze, listen to the light chatter of leaves talking to each other, and wonder if it was magic.

And so had she.

He took two more steps, towering over her, and a wave of that protective emotion she evoked washed over him. Protect her from what? some far-off part of him asked. Only he didn't have the answer.

Fear and tension were still radiating from Katherine as if she were a thundercloud throwing out the beginnings of a lightning storm. She scooted around him, ducking under his raised arm. ''Ready to eat?''

''Eat what?'' His voice was a growl. His brows met over the bridge of his nose.

''Breakfast. Bacon, potatoes and whatever kind of egg you want.''

He wanted none of the above, but couldn't—wouldn't— say so.

''How do you want your eggs?'' she persisted, walking back toward the stove top and reaching for them.

Clay sighed. "Over easy." Eggs would have to take care of the hunger he was barely able to acknowledge himself.

With forced brightness, she smiled. "Over easy it is." But there was still that hint of fear or wariness in her eyes and he wasn't brave enough to pursue the cause.

Clay Settles Reynolds wasn't sure what formed his own fear: how could he help her through hers?

He couldn't say how he had made it through breakfast and then out the door, without uttering more than one or two words. The phone had rung twice and he had let the answering machine pick it up, not wanting to have the outside world intrude upon the silent time before the morning bustle.

Katherine hadn't said much, either, cooking his eggs just right before joining him at the small glass table. When his cup was a quarter empty, she filled it to half full with more hot, steaming coffee. When he ate the last of his toast, she slipped one more piece into the toaster and set a jar of blueberry preserves in front of him. All without asking.

It was uncanny. It was also unsettling, and he reacted by frowning, then glowering at her. He didn't like his mind read so easily, so quickly and so accurately. Instead of making him comfortable, it unnerved him.

He got up, wadding his napkin into a ball, and left, only giving the barest of explanations. "I have some running around to do. I'll be back in an hour or so." And he refused to look back to see if her expression was sad or happy with his leaving. He couldn't have handled the answer, either way.

He drove just south of downtown to one of the old, run-down neighborhoods, checking the street against the address Katherine had given him. When he found it, he stopped the car and stared.

It was a large two-storey clapboard house that had seen better days twenty years ago. Maybe. Now, according to the sign out front, it was divided into rooms for rent. The porch dipped under the weight of a saggy-diapered toddler running barefoot along its length. One window held an air-conditioning unit that obviously wasn't working or it would have been humming. Faded white paint was peeled in spots, flaking like the crust of a pie. The whole structure was a monument to antique engineering. What amazed him most was that it was still standing instead of crumbling in a cloud of dust.

He couldn't believe people actually lived in places like this. And yet this was where Katherine had spent her past two weeks.

He strode up the cracked and broken sidewalk and opened the kicked-in screen door, standing for a moment to let his eyes adjust to the dimness inside.

"You want somethin', mister?"

His eyes narrowed, watching the largest lady he'd ever seen waddle toward him. Her dress was supposed to be shapeless, but it wasn't. It hugged every curve and bulge. "I'm looking for Mrs. Adams."

"That's me. What can I do for you?" She examined him closely, then pursed her lips.

"I came to get Katherine O'Malley's suitcase."

"You got the money?"

He held out an envelope. "I'll give you this as soon as you produce the suitcase."

The large lady shrugged, but her eyes were glued to the envelope. "That's fine. I don't care as long as you pay."

The transaction was over in a minute, then Clay was out the door. It took another minute to swallow the bile that had risen in his throat. Being poor was one thing. Being dirty was a whole different ball game. And that place and its landlady were filthy.

He drove to his office with the car windows down. Grabbing gulps of hot air, he tried to rid his lungs of the putrid stench of the ground-floor apartment he had reluctantly entered.

By the time he pulled into his parking slot, he knew with deep-down determination that no matter what he had to do, he'd never send Katherine out in the world until he was certain she was safe from places like that. No one deserved to live like that. No one.

In the back of his mind was another problem he would have to face—a problem he told himself had nothing to do with Katherine. He had chosen to marry for all the wrong reasons and needed to right the wrong for both his and Magda's sake. It wasn't fair to either of them. It had taken all night to face the fact, but at last he had.

CONSUELA WAS WAITING to pounce on him the minute he walked through the door of his suite of offices. Silently he waited for the Mexican fireworks to explode. Her small stature was deceiving, as were her grandmotherly features. The woman was a miniature dynamo—like Katherine. "I've got three new secretaries to train on the computer this afternoon and no trainer around to do it. Either I call the employment agency for someone to work in here while I train or I'll have to cancel. Which will it be?"

He reached toward the plate of fresh cookies that always sat next to the coffee pot: Consuela brought something different every day. "What has to be done here?"

Her back was still rigid. "Mainly answering the phone, typing a few invoices, some filing."

He chewed on the cookies, tasting coconut and butterscotch. Not bad. "I'll take care of it."

Consuela's brows rose in the air. "You? You've got a business meeting at two o'clock. How are you going to do two things at one time?"

"I think I know someone who can fill in for you for a while. You'll be training her in office work next week anyway. Might as well start now."

"A girl?"

Clay nodded, unable to look at her as he reached for the stack of mail set aside on her desk.

"Someone I know? I interviewed?" Consuela was nothing if she wasn't persistent.

"No. A friend. Katherine O'Malley. She needs a job and I thought of letting her help you out."

"Really? Then why didn't you tell me about her before?"

"Because I just found out," he sighed, wondering why she always sounded like a mother. It must have been conditioning at an early age, since she had seven of her own brood to care for.

"Is she a nice girl?"

Clay's eyes twinkled. He'd never before hired a girl he knew. "She's very nice and needs a job. I offered, knowing that you've got your hands full already and were dying for extra help."

There was only the hum of the air conditioning in the outer office as his secretary digested that fact. Then she sighed heavily. "I'll take the help." Consuela granted her seal of approval as if he'd asked for it.

"Good. I'll bring her here after lunch."

She nodded. "By the way, boss. Those cookies are called spell-breakers."

He raised his brow.

She grinned. "I thought you'd need some."

He should have known. Consuela and Magda had never gotten along.

The mail was handled quickly and efficiently, with Clay jotting notes for some and dictating longer answers for others. He and Consuela worked well together, completely organized and in tune.

He wished the day would continue this way, but he knew better. As long as he kept working and busy, he wouldn't be able to think, to puzzle over the flame-haired woman who had entered his life and brought on more complications as each hour passed. She was a wildflower, and he wasn't a very good gardener.

But if he kicked her out, she might wind up in another dump like the one he had just left. What chance did she have of bettering herself if she was stuck in a place like that?

No. He had to help her. He'd put Katherine back on her feet and consider his Christian duty done. Then he could get on with his life.

With an expression of smug satisfaction on his face, he reached for the phone.

"WHY IN THE HELL didn't you answer the phone if you heard me calling to you?" Clay ran a hand through his hair, his frustration plainly visible as he stood next to his desk at home.

"Because you mentioned that you had the answering machine on and I didn't know if I would mess it up if I stopped a recording," she explained, equally frustrated.

"You don't have to stop the recording. You just pick up the phone and wait until the message is over."

Her hands rode belligerently on her hips. Her toes were almost even with his as she craned her neck up to glare into his face. "And how am I supposed to know that? I've never even *seen* one of those things before!"

The fight left him. "Okay, okay. I didn't realize that. I thought…" He let the rest of his sentence drift off, realizing just how snobbish it sounded.

But she finished it for him, her voice dripping with sarcastic sweetness. "You thought *everyone* knew how to operate such a simple piece of equipment." Anger flashed in her green eyes. "Well, I'm sorry, sir, but truck stops don't have answering machines. Nor do the trucks. But I can work a restaurant gas grill or a citizen's band radio better than you ever dreamed of doing!"

"And if I need help on a CB, I'd call you, but the chances of that happening are slim!"

Her breath was warm on his lips as she reached up on tiptoe, almost touching his nose with hers. "Just teach me, dammit, instead of griping about it!"

He did, explaining the procedure of answering calls and listening to recordings. Katherine's lowered head as she followed the steps almost made him smile, but he didn't want to lose the anger that had so recently boiled through him. Anger between Katherine and himself was a lot safer than other emotions.

By the time they were in the car and driving back to the office, he had cooled down and the only obstacle he could drum up to put between them was silence. He pulled the car into his parking slot and turned off the engine, making no move to leave the confines of the car. Katherine waited expectantly, knowing she was about to receive last-minute instructions and hating it. Did he think she was a complete fool? Obviously.

"My secretary, Consuela, is a wonderful woman, but she has a mothering instinct that began when she was an infant herself. Please bear with her. She'll probably repeat everything a thousand times, but she means well."

Her slow smile lit up her face. "I will."

Clay stared at her for a moment, then nodded his head. He reached for the door handle wondering who would explode first, his secretary or his houseguest. He couldn't imagine.

"Clay?"

He turned reluctantly to the wood sprite beside him when her hand reached out to touch his sleeve. "I'll behave. I promise."

Her touched warmed his skin, and he sighed heavily with regret. Who was he to tell her she wasn't behaving properly? He was the one engaged and entertaining a female houseguest at the same time!

BY THE END of the day he was acting like a bear with his paw in a trap. From the moment Consuela and Katherine had met, his secretary had behaved as if Katherine were one of her wayward children returning home. Every time Consuela glanced at the younger girl, her eyes lit up with something he couldn't put his finger on, but didn't trust. He was as wary as hell and he didn't know why.

Katherine pored over the letters that needed to be filed, her brow knit in consternation.

"Don't worry. The files are set up by company, and you just need to check each company name and place them in the proper files, the latest dated letter first," the plump secretary said, giving Katherine a pat on the shoulder. "Just take your time and you'll catch on."

"You think so?"

"I'm sure so." Consuela was nothing if not an optimist. "What you need to remember is which phone goes to which office. I've written down the codes here. See?" She pointed to a sheet of paper stuck to the side of the phone console. "Just make sure you put the caller on hold before you switch over, or you'll lose them."

"Right," Katherine said, wondering how she would get used to doing all this as efficiently as Consuela seemed to. This was certainly nothing like slinging hash! She straightened her spine. She could do it. She could do anything.

By the time Consuela had left for a training session, Katherine was posted behind the desk and ready to handle anything that came her way.

The calls were dispatched with efficiency, so much so that she was polishing her nails on her shirt with pride. Until almost closing time…

When the phone rang, Katherine answered, her voice clear and secretarial crisp. "Reynolds Corporation."

"Let me speak to Clay, please." The female voice on the other end of the phone definitely had a proprietarial edge.

"May I ask who's calling?"

"Magda, his fiancée. Who's this?"

"This is Miss O'Malley."

"Oh." Distant interest laced the caller's voice. "Are you new there, Miss O'Malley?"

"Yes." Katherine's brightness belied the heaviness in her stomach. "I just began today."

A throaty laugh emitted across the line. "Good luck with Consuela. Would you put me through to Clay now, please?"

"Certainly," Katherine responded in what she hoped was her most businesslike voice. "Please hold."

Then she quietly laid the phone back in the cradle and disconnected the line. A smile curved her lips, genuine but slightly guilty.

"Who was that?"

Jumping at the sound of his voice, Katherine darted a glance toward Clay's door to find him lounging against the jamb. "It was, ah, a woman, but I forgot to push the Hold button. I think I lost her."

His brows knitted together. "That was careless, Miss O'Malley. Very careless."

She tried to look repentant. "Yes, sir."

When the phone rang again, she jumped again. There was nothing wrong with her intuition—it was screaming that the woman she had hung up on was calling back.

Clay strode across the room, picking up the receiver with more energy than was necessary. "Reynolds Corporation."

Katherine's green eyes looked everywhere but at Clay. She fiddled with the papers she had been filing, stacking them in neat, inconsequential piles. She could feel Clay's eyes boring into her, but she refused to glance his way.

"We have a new girl today, and she's just learning the procedures," Clay answered to a barrage of words. She could hear the voice, but couldn't make out what Magda was saying. Her stomach tightened.

"I know. And I'm anxious to see you, too." Clay's voice

had softened and it was like dark liquor running over thick cream.

Standing, she pretended to sort through the letters once more and ready them for filing in the cabinets behind her.

"We need to talk," he said, his voice even more husky, and Katherine's mind went wild imagining what he was referring to. She knew, but couldn't admit it. She just couldn't.

"About eight."

Her hands clenched the letters into a mangled pulp, her eyes finally turning to lock with his. A flash of lightning passed between them, jolting her with its force before he looked away. "See you then."

The silence in the office was almost earsplitting. Neither moved as they waited for the other to act, to say something, to break the spell.

"Don't do that again."

"I'm sorry."

"Just don't do it again."

She shook her head slowly. There was a sheen on her green eyes that made them look like highly polished, very coveted emeralds. "No," she whispered. "I won't."

His mouth moved once, as if he were about to say something. Then he changed his mind, turned and strode back into his office. But not before he'd stolen the last cookie from the plate by the coffeepot. The door shut behind him quietly, but it could have been a shout the way it grated on Katherine's nerve endings.

With a sigh she plopped into the desk chair, her hands still clutching the papers. She had to get a hold on herself before she upset two lives: his and hers.

CHAPTER FIVE

IT WAS AFTER MIDNIGHT when he returned from Magda's house. All the way home, his head had been throbbing. He'd been trying to do too much, push too hard; now exhaustion was setting in. At least that's what he told himself.

He'd worked until minutes before his eight-o'clock date with Magda, then tiptoed his way through a broken engagement. It hadn't been an easy decision to make, but he knew it was the right one. He didn't care for her enough to spend the rest of his life with her. It wasn't her fault. And it wasn't his.

Slipping the key in the door, he stepped into the hallway. The house was in darkness except for one small lamp on the Bombay chest in the living room. He walked in, peering over the back of the couch.

A country-and-western waltz played on the stereo, barely audible. Dim golden light danced over the room as if playing hide-and-seek.

But his eyes were trained on the couch. Katherine was curled up in the corner, her hair cascading over the side like a molten, golden-red waterfall. Her chin rested sweetly against a throw cushion that was pressed against her body and held tightly in her arms. Her golden-brown lashes, unadorned by makeup, rested against the creamiest skin Clay had ever seen. For just an instant, he thought of the rest of her body having that same golden-white tint. His hands curled into fists.

Enough of looking into the jaws of temptation.

"Katherine, it's time to go to sleep," he said loudly. The incongruity of his words hit him at the same time as she raised her eyelids and smiled.

"It makes sense to me," she yawned.

She held out her hand and he pulled her up, then dropped his own arms to his side quickly. Katherine's smile was slow and dreamy—and extremely sexy. That exhausted feeling he'd had just a short time ago disappeared.

"Good night, Clay," she mumbled, waving slowly as she made her way toward the staircase. "Sleep tight."

"Good night," he finally ground out. What a thing to say to a man who was watching the sway of the most delectable derriere he'd ever seen. 'Sleep tight' just about summed it up!

He aimed his steps toward the wet bar in the corner and poured a crystal balloon glass of golden-colored brandy, then sank down in the same spot Katherine had just vacated. The heat of her body still clung to the cushions, warming him more than the brandy. Her scent hovered in the air, lightly invading his senses and making him even more aware of her presence in his home.

Deliberately closing his eyes, he leaned his head back and tried to relax. Instead his body hummed with tension. His eyes popped open, dispelling the fantasies he knew were waiting to claim his sleeping hours.

Katherine was nothing more than a friend in need. She was a friend, and a well-rounded man needed both male and female friends.

He would make himself into a girl's best friend and nothing more. He'd help her as much as he could, then walk away when her need of him was over. He'd be damned if he'd allow that wisp of a girl any more leeway with his emotions. Katherine would not be any more to him than his logic dictated. He would *not* allow her to confuse him any more than he already was.

And to that end, he decided to keep his broken engagement to Magda quiet for a while longer. Besides, Magda had her pride, too, and he had already promised that she could take credit for their estrangement.

He refused to think about Katherine using the information to further their own relationship. And friendship was all there was between them.

Taking a sip of his brandy, he tested the word in his mind. Friend. Yes, that was it.

His body finally began unwinding from the tight coil he'd felt earlier. But it wasn't until the middle of the night that his eyes closed and blocked out the view of the ceiling, which happened to be the floor of Katherine's bedroom.

"KATHERINE! Wake up!" Clay stood in the hall directly outside her door, knocking loudly enough to wake her and all his neighbors. He had bounded up the stairs, having overslept himself. One of his most important clients was due in the office early this morning. Now, here he stood in the hallway, a chocolate velour robe belted at his waist and no time to spare. "Damn," he muttered under his breath, reaching for the handle. Stopping just inside the room, he stared at the view in front of him.

At first glance Katherine looked like a lost child in the middle of the large bed. She was on her back, her head turned toward the window that bled dim light into the room. One hand was outstretched, her fingers lightly curled, while the other rested sweetly on her abdomen.

But a step closer dispelled that first impression. Her red hair spilled across the pillows like streaks of brilliant lightning in the dim room. Rumpled sheets were kicked down toward the bottom of the bed to drape her legs erotically. The skimpy, deep-blue teddy barely covered her; peeping from the top was one dusky red-gold nipple. The breath caught in his throat. The straps were almost invisible, showing more creamy skin than should be legal. That, combined with the plunging neckline proved that if he had thought her complexion was beautiful, it was only because he'd had nothing else to compare it with.

"Katherine, wake up. It's time to go to work." His voice sounded strained even to his own ears.

She turned her head toward him. "No," she said slowly and distinctly.

Anger and frustration filled him. "Dammit, wake up! I'm not your mother!"

Her eyes opened then, and Clay almost fell into the vulnerable, green pools. They stared at each other, heightening tension singing in the air between them. Again she smiled. "I'm sorry. I was dreaming and your voice fit right in."

He watched her sit up, pulling the sheet up to rest on her breasts. He couldn't move, couldn't breathe, and his hands were mangling the ties of his robe. "What were you dreaming?" he finally managed, his imagination going crazy with the possibilities.

"Nothing."

His brows rose. "Nothing? I was in your dream and you call it nothing?" he teased, trying to rid himself of the tension.

"It's none of your business." She pushed her hair back over her shoulder, then glared at him with eyes that were now wide open.

She obviously slept with her jewelry on. The earrings dangled conspicuously from her small lobes, catching the early-morning light and twinkling at him as if they were winking. He forced himself to look back in her eyes.

Suddenly the tension in his body eased. He had the upper hand and it felt great. "I think the least you could do is tell me about my part in your dream." He should have been prepared, but he wasn't.

Pulling away the covers, Katherine scrambled to her feet on the mattress, hands belligerently on her hips, tousled hair like a red halo around her face, her jade-green eyes spitting fire. "You're right. You ought to know what you were doing so that it won't happen in real life! I had been working late and when I walked into the living room, you were making mad passionate love to some big-bosomed woman on the carpet in front of the fireplace.''

Her eyes narrowed. She obviously didn't have his complete attention. Well, she amended, she did, but not by her loud declaration.

His eyes were glued to her breasts. The small pearl buttons at the top of her teddy had come undone and exposed a smooth expanse of skin down to her navel. She sighed heavily, looking down at herself. ''I know, it's terrible, isn't it? When God was giving out bosoms, I must have been reading a comic book.''

''Get dressed,'' he ordered tightly. ''We leave in half an hour.''

Her mouth opened to answer him, but before the words came to mind he was out the door and halfway down the stairs. She wouldn't let the tears fall. If he thought her body was that ugly, he could damn well do without her words of apology!

But all morning the image of him standing over her bed haunted her. The soft brown robe emphasized his build and complemented his golden tan. His streaked hair hadn't been brushed yet and looked as if a wanton woman had trailed her nails through it while making love. Her fingers itched to do the same....

CLAY JERKED the water taps, setting the temperature as cold as he could stand. Damn her! She knew damn well she was beautiful! And her breasts! Small enough to fill his palm, they were perfectly proportioned for her tiny size! But it was the golden-red peek of a nipple that had disturbed him the most. It begged to be touched, caressed. Suckled.

He clenched his hands into fists, only to unclench them and wrestle with the knot of his robe. He slammed into the shower, praying that the cold water would shock his senses and wipe out the picture of her standing there, her breasts high enough for him to lean over and taste. He had been just inches away.

The soap turned to mush in his hand as he held it tightly, squeezing it between his fingers. Damn her hide! He made quick work of the icy shower, rinsing as fast as possible and stepping out to dry and rub the goose bumps away.

The man in the mirror stared back at him, and suddenly his shoulders slumped. "You're a stupid fool, Reynolds." But that wasn't new news. He'd known that ever since he had met Katherine O'Malley.

THEY HAD FINISHED dressing, quickly downed their coffee and driven in silence until Clay stopped at the first red light. He glanced at her, holding out his wallet. "Here. Take some money and buy some clothes."

"No, thank you." Her hands remained primly in her lap.

"Take it." He waved it in her direction again as the light changed and traffic flowed.

"I admit I'm a little unusual, Mr. Reynolds, but I'm not after your money."

"Look. I don't want to insult you, but what you're wearing isn't really suitable for the office. Buy a few skirts and blouses that will mix and match and I'll deduct it from your paycheck."

Her eyes were downcast. He was right about her clothing, and it didn't help that feeling of inadequacy she'd been fighting all morning. A frown marred her brow. "Are you open to a deal, Mr. Reynolds?"

His wary glance almost made her smile. "Is it harmful or illegal?"

Just for a second a smile teased her lips. "No. At least I don't think so. Will you loan me a thousand dollars for clothing and my enrollment fee for college? I have collateral."

"What?"

She reached into her purse and pulled out a small brown velvet bag. Spilling the contents into her palm, she held out her hand. "My earrings."

"Your mother's earrings," he corrected softly. "And if I remember correctly, they were your father's wedding gift to her."

"But they're mine now. To do with as I wish. Will you accept them in exchange for a thousand dollars?"

He pulled into his parking slot and killed the engine, then swiveled toward her. "No."

Her heart plummeted. She lowered her hand to her lap, her eyelids hiding the green depths of her eyes. His hand covered hers. "Katherine, I'll lend you the thousand—no strings attached. And you don't have to use your jewelry for collateral. They're yours and you shouldn't give away such a special heritage. Besides, they're antiques and worth much, much more than that."

"They were given to me to seek what I want. I need an education, Clay."

"I'll lend you the money," he repeated. "You don't need to hock your earrings."

She raised her head, her eyes sheened with tears. She swallowed hard. "Will you take them anyway? As a gift?"

"Katherine, I..."

"Please?"

Her green eyes were wide and round as she waited for his answer. She didn't realize he had no choice. "Yes," he said, holding out his hand.

Very carefully she placed the earrings in his care. A feeling of rightness with this decision flowed through her. He didn't know it but she had given them to him in love. He was the only person she would ever give them to....

Clay gazed down at the sparkling jewels, amazed at the warmth they exuded. The deep green of the emerald was only as bright as the brilliance of the small diamonds that

dangled on intricate gold threads. He stared at them, mesmerized.

"You won't regret it, Clay," she told him softly, breaking
the spell the jewels seemed to have created.

"We'll see," he said cryptically, placing the earrings
back into the velvet bag and stuffing it into his inside suit
pocket. "I'll have Consuela cash a check for you."

"Oh, and Clay?"

"Hmm?"

"May I borrow one of the company cars today? I have
to go to the mall on my lunch hour."

"Right. Yes. Of course."

"Good. I promise I won't be long."

"Do you have a driver's license?"

"Of course." She looked surprised. "I can even drive an
eighteen-wheeler, although I admit the opportunity doesn't
come up that often."

He grinned. He couldn't imagine any man letting an imp
of a girl behind the wheel of all that metal.

As if she read his mind, she answered, "It takes strength,
not length. Just because I'm not tall doesn't mean I can't
do anything anyone else can do."

"Except reach tall shelves."

"Without a little help," she clarified, aware of the smile
hiding in the corners of his mouth.

"Or change light bulbs."

"Without a little help," she repeated. "But there are several things I can do that taller people can't."

"Such as?"

"I can slide down a chimney."

"Like Santa Claus?"

She nodded vigorously. "I can also climb under beds and
hide in cabinets. And I can fix Japanese cars."

His brow furrowed, losing her logic. "What does fixing
Japanese cars have to do with being small?"

"The Japanese workers in the auto factories are all small

with tiny hands, so their engines are built with enough space between the engine parts for hands the size of theirs. Mine are perfect.''

She sounded so smug, he couldn't help the laughter that burst from his throat. Her logic was irrefutable even if it was a little strange. "I'll keep that in mind," he finally managed.

"You do that." She grinned, pleased that she could make him laugh after watching him frown all morning.

CLAY PROMISED himself all day that he would call Laura and ask her to take Katherine as a roomer, sweetening the pot a little by helping with the rent. Laura needed all the money she could get her hands on just to keep that newly acquired prehistoric house of hers standing. It seemed the right thing to do for both Laura and Katherine.

Katherine took a two-hour lunch break, and when she returned she was ecstatic. She'd not only bought a few items to wear at the office, she'd also picked up the summer schedule and enrollment forms for San Antonio College.

By the time the day was over, Clay still hadn't made that call. He would talk to Laura tomorrow, he promised himself, ignoring the fact that he could have found the time that afternoon if he had really wanted to.

He made one stop on the way home, to buy another alarm clock. There was no sense tempting the devil by waking Katherine himself in the morning.

They ate a quiet dinner and watched a new movie on TV, then Clay sat in the study and went over papers from the office.

But that night, lying in bed, he couldn't close his eyes and allow sleep to come. Katherine was just upstairs.

The rest of the week followed the pattern of that first day. They came home, took turns cleaning and cooking, then spent a quiet half hour together before he went to the study and Katherine picked up another book. Katherine, he discovered, was a voracious reader.

Tonight, after cooking a light meal, they were sipping wine and having a lively discussion on the office.

Deep down inside, not even quite put into words yet, was the knowledge that he had to move Katherine into Laura's by tomorrow. It had to be done, he knew that, and yet...

He tasted the wine from the fluted glass sitting next to him. "Are you enjoying your work? Is being a secretary everything you thought it would be?"

"I love it," she said simply. "And when I go home, there's never the smell of liver and onions on my hands and in my hair."

He remembered the night her scent had surrounded him like a heavenly fog as he had sat on the couch and felt her warmth in the cushions. Her hair hadn't smelled of anything but sweet wildflowers then. He chuckled aloud, if only to relieve the discomfort the memory evoked.

They talked about all sorts of things besides the office. And though he knew they were each keeping the bad parts of their lives from the other, that was okay, too. There was never a silence that wasn't relaxed, and never a conversation where one of them couldn't pick up the ball and run with it. It was amazing.

They wound up with Clay sitting on one end of the couch while Katherine was curled on the other, and continued talking until late in the night. He had refilled their glasses occasionally with the wine they had opened at dinner, but neither had had enough to be even slightly drunk.

It was the most relaxing evening Clay had ever spent. She was witty and warm and wonderful, and he found himself relating all kinds of things he never thought he would tell anyone. Her warm, husky laughter ran down his spine like chilled champagne as he regaled her with some of the episodes he and David and Laura had shared.

But when Katherine's beautiful green eyes were closing

and they still hadn't moved toward their beds, he reluctantly held out his hand. "Come on, sleepyhead. It's time to go to bed."

"I know," she said, hiding a yawn. "It's been so nice I just hate to end the evening."

He chuckled. "I think the evening ended itself."

Placing her hand in his, she rose, only to wind up pressed against his body. His breath caught in his throat. Without thinking of the consequences he bent his head, his eyes focusing on her slightly parted lips.

He tried to hold back, he swore he did. But the instant his lips met hers, a craving deeper than his very soul cried out and he lost himself in her touch. His arms encircled her small waist, crushing her to him so he could feel all of her against every inch of his hard body.

His tongue stroked between her teeth, ravishing the inside of her mouth, stealing the softness for himself. His ears rang with the need for her. A groan echoed from deep in his throat, a sound that bared his warring frustration and need to the woman in his arms.

"I knew it would be this way," he growled when he finally broke the kiss. But he couldn't stand it. His mouth craved to touch and taste the rest of her flesh, the curl of her earlobe, the slim side of her neck. Her taste was nectar, her scent a field of mind-drugging poppies.

"Shhh," she whispered in his ear, her tongue riding its rim. "Again, Clay. Kiss me again." Her hands ran through his hair, her fingers teasing him with their butterfly touch.

His arms tightened even more as he claimed her mouth again. He was shaking with the need to have her, to be with her. Never, ever before had he felt so weak and so strong. Never had he craved a woman to the point of crying his needs aloud.

"Katherine," he muttered, his lips branding her eyes, her cheeks, her nose. "Katherine."

"Please, Clay," she whispered pleadingly, sprinkling

kisses on his face and neck. She was so tiny, her head barely came to his chest. "Please."

Her mouth was level with his hard male nipple and her tongue shot out to dampen his shirt before suckling gently through the material. Another groan issued from his throat, and his shaking hand reached for her breast. He had been right. She fit perfectly into the palm of his hand, her nipple pressing against the center as if teasing him with her arousal. "Perfect. Dear Lord, it's just perfect," he muttered hoarsely.

"More," she whispered, bringing her mouth up to his. "I want more, Clay." Her hips swayed with his, her softness accommodating his hardness and almost sending him over the brink to ecstasy.

His hands fit against her buttocks, lifting her up and holding her pinned against him as he buried his mouth in the curve of her neck and inhaled deeply, trying to keep his mind from spinning dizzily out of control. He shouldn't be doing this. There was a reason, but for the life of him, he couldn't remember what it was. His senses were filled with her. No matter what he gave, she gave more, and he wanted it all.

"I promise," she choked, tears streaming down her face as she scattered heated kisses on his neck and chest. Her mouth felt like a white-hot branding iron, and he thought he would burst with the pleasure of it. "I won't ask for more. Just this once, Clay. Just once."

His hands tightened, then stilled. His breathing sounded loud and ragged in the quiet room. And he still couldn't let her go. Not yet.

He wrapped his arms around her and rested his head against the crown of her hair. Then he rocked back and forth, as if giving comfort to a baby. "Shhh, it'll be all right. Shhh," he kept saying, wondering who he was comforting, her or himself.

But he had to release her. He knew it. It hurt like hell to

unwrap his arms from her softness, then take a step back from the one thing he craved most at the moment.

"Go to bed, Katherine."

"But…"

"I said, go to bed!" He turned toward the empty fireplace, unable to look at her eyes and see the pain reflected there.

As she reached down and picked up her shoes he slowly pivoted to watch, something inside him wanting to punish himself. With back rigid and head high, she swayed out of the room, never looking back. He couldn't take his eyes from her retreating form.

It took all night to calm down, but that was okay, because he had all night. Tomorrow he would call Laura and arrange things for Katherine. Then he would pray she would forgive him for losing control.

But he knew that this moment of insanity would cost him dearly. He couldn't hide from his own emotions anymore.

NOTHING WAS SAID the next morning. Not a word. And all day long Clay stayed out of Katherine's way. Consuela sent him looks that pointed to the fact he was acting unnaturally, but he didn't care. He was too busy lashing himself with his own whips of guilt to worry about his secretary adding to it.

At midmorning Consuela stepped inside his office with fresh coffee and coffee-cinnamon cookies. "What's this?" he snapped, not wanting the interruption, nor the advice that was dying to trip off Consuela's tongue.

"Spicy hermits," she snapped back, walking out of the room, her back ramrod straight.

By late afternoon he wasn't fit to talk to anyone. Except Laura. And when he called, he almost sounded natural. Almost. She agreed to see him right away.

He strode from the office toward the outside door. "Consuela, do you think you could drop Katherine at my place after work?''

''Your place? Sure.''

''Good. I'll see you Monday, then.''

He didn't look at Katherine, but all the way to the door he could feel her eyes on him, silently condemning him for his odd behavior. And she had every right in the world to do so.

LAURA LOOKED cool and beautiful, as usual. Clay put on his best, easygoing smile and ignored the cold lump of guilt crouching in the pit of his stomach. ''You look terrific.''

She looked him over carefully, and he knew she spotted the dark circles under his eyes. ''And you, dear friend, look like something the cat wouldn't bother dragging in.''

She led the way into the kitchen and served him iced tea, but he didn't hear a word she said until she mumbled something about her car's air conditioning. Nothing was registering.

He had prepared a speech to convince her of the rightness of his idea, but somehow the words were sticking in his throat. ''Laura, I need a favor,'' he blurted out. His eyes darted around the room, noting for the first time how shabby the old house was. ''And you need extra money.''

She chuckled. ''No joke. The wiring in this monstrosity just cost me several thousand. If I was sane, I would have moved into an apartment instead of buying a house with character to renovate. Character is costly.''

''I have a proposition,'' he began, telling her a little of Katherine's background, pretending he had nothing but a cursory interest in the girl.

But Laura was smarter than that and smelled a story. Her gaze pinned him to his chair. ''And just where does she fit into your life? Aren't you still engaged to Magda?''

''Magda has nothing to do with Katherine,'' he hedged, unwilling to admit his engagement was off in case Laura told Katherine. He wasn't ready for that. Not yet. He knew he was creating one hell of a mess, but he didn't know what else to do. "Katherine's just a kid who needs a break and I'm in a position to help her." *Or hurt her,* his mind echoed. He forced himself to go on. "She'll pay half your mortgage payment a month, with the first payment in advance."

Chuckling, Laura held up her hands. "I'll say yes before you change your mind!" she exclaimed, and relief washed over him like a tidal wave.

An hour later Clay strolled out her door feeling much better about the future. Katherine's future. While feeling so content, Clay fixed Laura's car air conditioner. All it needed was freon, and his fiddling with it delayed the trip home and the confrontation with Katherine. *A coward dies a thousand deaths.*

Wherever he turned, he saw her green eyes shining with tears, and yet he knew that Katherine leaving his home was the best thing for everyone, especially after last night. He was already committed to his choice. Now that Magda was out of the picture and he had taken care of Katherine as any good friend should, he could continue with his path in life as a single man. Besides, he tried to tell himself, wasn't one woman much the same as the other when the newness wore off? Quick of tongue and even quicker of pocket.

Somehow the conviction he usually held wasn't there anymore. It was being replaced by doubts, and doubts brought on an even deeper sense of frustration.

CHAPTER SIX

KATHERINE STOOD in the kitchen, a cola in her hand as she stared out the large bay window. The woodland scene wasn't helping to calm her nerves. She listened to Clay's hollow footsteps as he made his way from the front door to the kitchen. She knew when he reached the doorway, but she couldn't turn around and confront him. Wherever he had disappeared to this afternoon, she didn't want to know about it. Somehow she knew that he was going to say something she didn't want to hear.

"Katherine." His voice was quiet but the echo reverberated in her ears. "I found a place for you to stay."

She cleared her throat to ease the lump that formed there. Her heart plummeted. "I can't stay here?" She would not cry. She would not!

His voice sounded as sad as her soul felt. "We both know that's impossible. A friend of mine, Laura Sheridan, has offered to let you stay with her until you decide what you want to do."

She chose a tree and stared at it, willing it to turn into a club so she could hammer Clay over the head with it. The man was impossible! Didn't he know love when he saw it standing in front of him? "Will I continue working at the office?"

"Yes, of course. Consuela would kill me if you quit." He tried to put a smile in his voice, but he couldn't quite manage it. The office without Katherine? Impossible.

"When am I leaving?"

He allowed his eyes to trail up and down her spine and back again. She was so tiny, so very defenseless. So terribly alive and vibrant. "As soon as possible."

"Now?" She spun around. Her shimmering green eyes were as wide as saucers and as vulnerable as a child's.

An imaginary fist hit his stomach with all the force of a boxer's thrust. She was so beautiful and untamed! And everything he hadn't wanted—until now! He shook his head. "Tomorrow morning."

Katherine placed her glass carefully on the table, her hand drifting away from it to arc in the air. "Is this it, Clay? Are you going to ignore what happened between us and go on with your engagement to Magda knowing you'll *never* have what we almost had last night?"

Her eyes were steady, her face tilted toward him as if asking calmly for an answer to an office problem. Frustration raged within him, but he stifled it. If he tried to reason out his feelings, he wouldn't like what he saw. Taking a deep breath, he answered her woodenly. "What happened last night never should have taken place. I apologize."

"The apology is *not* accepted." Her voice was so firm, he was stunned by the rejection. "You have just taken away a very precious moment for me. I'm not sorry for what happened last night. I'm not ashamed of it."

"I don't feel ashamed," he began, fumbling for the words to make her understand that he had taken advantage of her and felt worse for that.

"Yes, you do." She took a step closer. Then another step. And another. "You feel guilty because of Magda." She placed her hand on his chest, bare inches from his heart. "I know," she said quietly. "Because I do, too."

His voice was a bare whisper. His pumping heart had picked up speed. "Why? What happened wasn't your fault. It was mine."

"We share the blame. I don't know if Magda is really right for you or not. Only you can decide that. But I know

that if you were in love with her, you wouldn't have reacted
to me the way you did—the same way I reacted to you.''

He covered her hand with his, the warmth of her skin
igniting a fire within. "I'm not dead, Katherine. Just engaged.''

"To a woman who *doesn't* light your fire.''

"You don't know what you're talking about.''

She smiled. Slowly and devastatingly she allowed her
eyes to speak her thoughts before she did. "Your heart is
hammering against my palm. Your eyes are telling me that
you still desire me.'' Her head tilted. "Tell me you don't
want to kiss me again.''

A groan emerged from deep inside his chest as the de-
fences he had built crumbled like dust against her onslaught.
Need became everything. He swept her hand from his chest
to his back and enfolded her in a clasp that was as possessive as it was erotic. His lips crushed hers, pressuring her
to open her mouth and receive him.

Katherine's fingers slipped up his back and sought the
solidness of his flesh. Her arms tightened as she opened her
mouth and became the aggressor. She pulled him toward
her, molding every intricate curve of her body to his.

He moaned again. A voracious force was building inside
him and he tried to control it, but his mind was numbed to
everything but the taste of her, the scent of her, the feel of
her.

He pulled away, sprinkling kisses on her cheek and neck.
"I want you. You know that.''

"I know,'' she said, smoothing his hair. "And I want
you.''

He knew this wasn't right, but for the life of him he
couldn't help himself and stop now. Everything fled in the
face of having Katherine in his arms. In his bed. With a
swift movement he scooped her up and carried her to his
bedroom, not halting until she was lying in the middle of
his bed.

Sanity returned for just one moment, then Katherine's hands were busy pulling at his tie and he was lost again in the green depths of her eyes and the promise of fulfillment with the woman he wanted above all else. Soon she'd be gone and he wouldn't be able to touch her like this, watch her smile so sensuously or half close her eyes as if ecstasy were claiming her just because he was near.

His breath was warm and shallow, his touch as exciting as lightning. Katherine watched him reach out to caress her as if she were priceless. She ached for him, craved him so badly nothing else mattered. All those sleepless nights fantasizing about what it would be like to be with him were now being realized—and it was better than she had dreamed.

"You're so very special," she murmured, kissing his bared chest.

"Sweet heaven, so are you." He slipped the dress over her head and let it fall to the floor. All that covered her was a slim pair of black panties that left little to the imagination. "You're beautiful," he whispered, drifting one finger over her creamy bare breasts. "So tiny yet so perfect...."

His touch ignited a fire in the pit of her stomach and she stopped breathing, willing his touch to continue. Her hand covered his cheek, and her eyes tried to tell him what her words could not. She wanted to ask him about his cryptic statement. Another time. Another time. *Now* was too precious to lose with conversation.

"You're so perfect, Katherine. So very perfect." Then his mouth tenderly claimed hers. She knew that they were both lost. Their bodies blending together wasn't enough; it would never be enough for her, but it had to do for now.

Tenderness turned to need and need to urgency. By the time Clay was undressed and sprawled next to her she didn't know anything but the sensual demands of her body. He was as essential as breathing. His caresses were intimate, coaxing, claiming. She could hardly speak with the need that he built inside her. "Clay, please," she finally pleaded against his shoulder, smelling the heady masculine scent of him as he teased her unmercifully.

She followed her verbal invitation by opening to him like a flower. But just before the first plunge, Clay stopped, poised above her. "Do you want me, Katherine? As much as I want you? Do you?" He teased her with his movements, and she felt the craving building into shooting sparks. "Tell me!"

"Yes. Yes!" she cried and his lips captured the sound as he plunged inside her, sending showers of light flowing through her body. Shimmering liquid waves of warmth poured over her, through her, surrounded her. She wanted to cry with the beauty of it.

Desire etched his expression as he rocked her body to an ageless rhythm. He thrust once more, and she was sure his spirit melded with hers, floating, entwined.

From far away she heard Clay call her name and her arms tightened in response, unwilling to relinquish her hold. She never wanted to be free of him. His weight felt secure and warm. His skin was heated, slick with exertion. His quickened breathing in her ear was the most wondrous music in the world.

Loving Clay was even more wonderful than she had thought it would be.

A deep sense of completion filled her every pore. But her smile disappeared. She sensed his withdrawal even before he pulled away. Silently she prayed that he wouldn't leave her, but something in the back of her mind resigned her to that fact.

But instead of reality intruding upon her idyll, he rolled to his side and pulled her with him until she was lying on top of him. He kissed the tip of her nose. "I don't know what to say, little one."

She smiled. "Tell me something positive."

His smile mirrored hers, but there was a sadness in his

eyes. He gently pushed back a tendril of hair, curling it around her ear. "You're wonderful. I've never felt that way before. I'm stunned."

"Care to try for a repeat?"

His golden eyes opened wide, first in shock, then in need. He swelled against her immediately. Apparently his libido was more powerful than his thoughts.

"Yes," he growled, winding her hair in his hand and pulling her face down to his.

His kiss wiped out everything in her mind but him, including the consequences of the past hour. But she knew. Soon the piper would call for his tithe, and she'd be left in the cold. It would be silly to think that these past moments would change the course of their relationship. Had she not purposely seduced him? She didn't want to admit it, but already she was readying herself for the next blow.

The rest of the night was a dream. They made love, slept, made love again. His hunger was deep and his need unquenchable. And each time they came together she knew that the morning would bring the shock of parting.

She knew him well enough to realize that he would still carry through his plans.

And she wasn't wrong.

The following morning he stood in the kitchen, a hard, distant expression on his face.

"We're still going ahead as planned?"

"Yes."

"You're blind, Clay."

"Maybe. Maybe we both need the distance to decide what should be done next."

"Scared of me?" she taunted, not allowing her heart to release the tears that wanted to spill forth like a river.

"Yes."

His honesty surprised her. So did her own frustrated anger. Her hands clenched. "Are you really so blind? I'd make

a better wife for you than Magda ever could. I can't believe
you're willing to throw it away.''

"Katherine, I—"

She ignored his protest. "But you, rigid as you are, are
going to pass me by because I don't have the qualifications
you've decided you require in your spouse." His brown
eyes widened, and she nodded her head. "Oh, yes, I figured
it out. Little ol' me, with my G.E.D. education, finally understood. You think you need someone who moves in the
'right' circles and has the right education—the right friends.
Someone who will let you walk all over her as you lead
your own life. You don't want a wife—you want a beautiful,
handcrafted doormat!''

She came so close that her body brushed his and her scent
filled his nostrils. She tapped her finger lightly against his
chest. "*You* are a coward, Clay Reynolds. I don't understand
why I love you at all. But I do. I only hope you come to
your senses before it's too late." She reached on tiptoes and
placed an airy soft kiss on his open mouth, then stepped
around him, heading for her room and the suitcase she had
to pack.

He wasn't following her, which was a blessing. She didn't
think she could have kept her tears at bay much longer. It
was with wooden movements that she succeeded in packing
and walking back downstairs.

The scene in the car was another matter. She had had
time to pull herself together. But so had Clay.

"You'll be happy at Laura's. She's a lovely lady.''

Was the man dense, or what? "I'll be as happy with her
as you'll be with Magda?" Katherine asked sweetly, but her
voice was laced with arsenic.

"Cut it out," he gritted.

"You're a fool, Clay Reynolds.''

"I won't argue.''

There was nothing she could answer to that. Looking
down at her plain black skirt and white blouse, she had to

realize the truth. Aside from the guilt that weighed heavily on her shoulders for taking an engaged man to her bed and offering more than her heart, she should have seen their relationship from Clay's point of view. Magda came from the same social set as Clay. Maybe he was right. Magda suited him—and Katherine didn't.

Clay heaved a sigh. "Look," he began. "I have a business appointment today, but how about attending a concert with me tonight? As a friend? I have box seat tickets. Somebody ought to get some culture out of it."

She knew she should say no. She should shake him so hard his brains would fall out…"I'd love to. What's playing?"

"Ravel."

She wished she knew what that was. Instead, she said a very knowledgeable, "Oh." But her heart spun a thread of hope to hang on to.

EVEN IN HER MISERY, Katherine liked Laura as soon as she met her. Though Laura seemed preoccupied, that was just as well because so was Katherine.

In fact, ever since Katherine had been shown to her room, she'd been crying. Clay hadn't stayed in the house three minutes. He probably couldn't wait until she was out of his home and he could have his privacy and his life back. Damn him!

The tears started again. Was this hated, wonderful, star-studded, hell-ridden emotion called love *only* felt by her? Didn't Clay feel anything other than a normal sexual drive? While she knew a man didn't have to *like* a woman in order to *lust* after her body, she hadn't thought Clay was that way. He didn't seem to have a line of patter that he fed to a woman as if he were fishing for bass. Nor had he given her those purposely sexy, suggestive looks that were meant to be a come-on.

She sat up, wrapping her arms around her slim body. But

his kiss! That kiss and lovemaking had been made up of spun-sugar clouds, and his eyes had lit with emotions that made her heart sing in response. He *had* to have felt something! All she could do was wait and let him realize just how much they had in common: love and needs and wants.

THE EVENING finally came. Until then, the minutes had been hours, the hours, days.

Katherine wore her best outfit, one she'd bought two years ago for a range dance. It was dark blue shot with pink as pale as an ocean sunset. The neck was high, the skirt draped. She had washed and tamed her hair with a dryer and brush, and it lay in seductive waves and curls on her shoulders. Never one to use much make-up, she didn't have any to use now.

A turn in the full-length mirror in her room confirmed what she already knew. She just wasn't sophisticated enough, beautiful enough, tall enough, to make anyone's heart beat faster. Cute as a button, as some of the truckers used to say, but certainly not a femme fatale.

She thought of pleading a headache, but the selfish part of her wanted to see him too badly to let this opportunity pass. Besides, she had promised Laura she would be out of the house for Laura's at-home dinner date with David. There was nothing she could do—except answer the doorbell.

Clay looked wonderful in a lightweight brown suit that pointed up his golden coloring, sun-kissed hair and beautiful brown eyes.

"Are you ready?" he asked, his voice almost a whisper. Her answering smile gave him his dose of vitamin C for the entire week. He hadn't seen her all day and in that time he'd forgotten just how beautiful she was. Heat unfurled in the pit of his stomach as his legs turned to cement. It dawned on him that making this date was probably his greatest mistake with Katherine yet. Last night was bad enough, but this was tempting fate.

Her words still echoed in his head. *I don't understand why I love you at all, but I do.* Those words were the most frightening words in the English language. He had always steered so far away from that particular emotion. It was synonymous with manipulation....

It was with concerted effort that he led her to the car, then got behind the wheel. Stupid! He had been stupid to see her again! After dropping her at Laura's he had returned home to sit and stare at the empty air for over an hour—all the time clutching the pair of antique earrings that held a fascination as strong as their owner did. Her spirit was everywhere. But her voice was gone. That lilting, wonderful, funny, sexy voice.

He'd spent half the afternoon attempting to explain his feelings to David. It was preferable to being alone in his own home, though he knew he'd get used to it. He'd concluded that their relationship would never have lasted the long haul; he and Katherine didn't have enough in common to help them over the many bumps that all relationships had to endure. Good sex wasn't enough.

Then why had he invited her to this concert? He should have left well enough alone.

As they arrived, the lights were dimmed and the orchestra was warming up. A murmur of voices could still be heard, like the droning of bees around a hive. Then came the tap of the conductor's baton on the podium and the crowd hushed.

The orchestra played their best that night, Clay was sure. Katherine sat straight-backed in her seat, a light flush of excitement tinting her cheeks. He watched her surreptitiously, thinking she was delightful. Although he hadn't asked her, he was sure this was her first concert and was glad that he was the one to introduce her to fine music. He would love to be the first to introduce her to a lot of things.... He shut down those thoughts that had sprung up on their own.

But his body didn't get the message. He shifted in his seat, relaxation replaced by irritation. Dammit! She shouldn't be able to do this to him! He should think of her as a little sister. He sighed resignedly. That didn't work, either.

When intermission was announced by the lights going on, Katherine blinked as if coming out of a trance. She turned toward Clay, her eyes filled with wonder. ''How long is intermission?''

He smiled indulgently. ''Only about twenty minutes. Care for a glass of champagne to while away the time?''

Her tongue darted out to rest on the peak of her upper lip. His eyes followed the movement, then without conscious thought, he imitated the act. ''Last time I had champagne was at my brother's wedding and after one glass I told his new wife what I thought of her.''

''How old were you then?''

''Seventeen.''

''And now?''

''Twenty-six.'' She smiled, her green eyes merrily dancing with mischievous light. ''And my brother's wife isn't here.''

''Let's go.''

He'd never been one for champagne, but he ordered two glasses anyway. They were standing by the side of the bar as Katherine attempted an explanation of the effect the music had on her when Clay's name carried across the lobby.

''Damn, man, fancy meetin' you here!'' A large man with even larger hands patted Clay on the back.

Clay stuck out his hand for a vigorous shake. ''Jim, I seem to be running into you everywhere I go,'' he said before making introductions. Mrs. Butler stood by her husband's side, quiet and, to Katherine, looking slightly cowed.

''You also seem to have a different girl with you every time I see you.'' The large man's eyes narrowed on Katherine, practically undressing her. "My, my, what a pretty little girl."

"Lady," she corrected, looking him straight in the eye.

His brows rose and a rumble erupted from his chest. "Fiesty little thing, isn't she?"

"Lady," she said again, a smile slightly defusing her correction. "I am a female over the age of consent, Mr. Butler. Don't let my size fool you."

"You sure got that right, little one. You're all female, all right." His appreciative gaze began undressing her again, and Clay felt newborn antagonism welling in his chest.

But before he could say a word, Katherine spoke up. "I also have a brain. Female variety. It tells me that if you're not kind to little ladies, you're also not kind to your wife or your dog."

"Well, damn!" he said, attempting a grin but not pulling it off. "Some women don't know a compliment when they hear one."

Katherine gave him a piercing look, then set her empty champagne glass on the edge of the bar. "Excuse me, Mr. Reynolds," she said quietly. "I'll be in my seat when the music begins."

Stunned, Clay watched her walk across the lobby to the door marked Ladies and disappear. He wasn't sure who he was more furious with, Jim Butler for his obnoxious behavior or himself for wanting it to pass. A flash of pride seared through him even as he tried to think of something that would placate his business associate.

"Whew, that little lady's in a twitch. Is she one of them women's libbers? I don't like them too much. Not too much at all."

Once more Clay began to answer, but this time Mrs. Butler beat him to it. "That's obvious, Jim. On top of everything else, don't be so blasted obvious!" The older woman stalked off toward the same door that had swallowed Katherine.

Jim stood next to Clay, muttering as he watched his wife enter the ladies' room. He had no style but he wasn't a bad man, Clay knew, just totally ignorant of human emotions. If it wasn't in black and white, Jim couldn't see it. Clay had worked with him for years and had found him to be scrupulously fair. But he came from the old school of Texans: the one which held there was nothing like a man and nothing better than a Texas man. In Jim Butler's book that placed women as third-class citizens.

The older man had looked at Magda the same way, but Clay hadn't found himself swamped by this feeling of overwhelming protectiveness then. He tried to justify his feelings and his first thought was that he wanted to protect her because she had made herself vulnerable to him by admitting she loved him. That didn't hold water.

Deep down inside he knew it was time to search for some answers, and he had a feeling that he wasn't going to be too pleased with a few of them.

The rest of the evening was a disaster. Katherine came back to the box and sat next to him as the lights dimmed. Her back was stiff and she looked as if her facial muscles had frozen just as she was eating a lemon. Even at that she was darling.

It wasn't until they were pulling up to the front of Laura's house that Katherine spoke to him again. "That's the most obnoxious man I've ever met. Even some of the truckers know better than to approach a woman that way!"

"You didn't handle that whole episode very well, either," he stated quietly. "You purposely tried to provoke him."

Her eyes were large green pools as she turned to him. "You're right. I don't suffer fools in silence, Clay. I never have and I won't start now. At least I'm honest about it."

He ran a hand through his hair. "Sometimes I think honesty is another word for lack of tact. It allows people to voice all kinds of opinions that shouldn't be spoken aloud."

"That hurts." Her words were so simple, so direct.

"Katherine," he began, but her fingers came up to rest on his lips.

"Since we're talking honestly, listen to me a moment. Don't say anything, just listen." He nodded, afraid she would remove her hand and he would lose the warmth of her fingers playing across his mouth. The feeling spread through his body as his eyes followed the nuances of her expression.

"I love you, Clay Reynolds. I'm not supposed to, but I do. I know I wouldn't really make as good a wife for you as Magda could. I'd be possessive of your time, I wouldn't fit in with your friends and business associates and I'd probably say the wrong things at the wrong times, like I did tonight. I'm not dumb, I'm just not as tactful as she probably is. But I'm willing to learn anything you think I need to know. In return, I can give you more love than you ever dreamed of holding. I can give you children and a home that sings with happiness. I can give you all that and more."

"Don't," he protested, his voice hoarse. But before he could speak again she whisked her hand away replacing it with her lips. His world tilted as she sought the inner recesses of his mouth the way he had done to her just nights before. Her hands rested on both sides of his clean-shaven face, touching him as if he were a gift she must return but would relish until then.

As he sought to pull her close, she leaned away. "Not yet. You don't see it yet, Clay. But I'm hoping you will. Soon." She traced the line round his mouth with a fingernail. "Honesty isn't a bad word, really. It's the most important word in the English language—especially when you're talking to yourself." She gave him another fleeting kiss, her lips as soft as butterfly wings. "Good night. Sleep tight."

Then she was out of the car and running up the walk toward the darkened house, swallowed by the night.

He had a lump in his throat from a declaration he knew

came straight from her heart. There was also his own answering declaration that he couldn't put into words. He wasn't sure what love was, and didn't know how to explain himself or his emotions half as eloquently as she did.

"Sleep tight." Those magic words again. He had a fleeting image of her leaning over a crib and saying those same words to a baby, a baby with golden-red hair and big green eyes and a smile that could line the sky with rainbows.

TEARS CASCADED down Katherine's cheeks as she closed the door. She shouldn't have said anything to Clay. He was still attempting to sort out his emotions, look at them logically and deduce an answer. That was fine for a business problem, but it didn't work with personal relationships at all.

She walked into the kitchen, pushing against the swinging door to find the lights on and Laura nursing a cup of hot tea. If it was possible, Laura looked worse than Katherine did. "What's wrong?" Laura said with a sniffle.

What was the sense of pretending, thought Katherine? "I'm miserable. Miserable and frustrated and ready for a fight."

Before Katherine knew it, they were both laughing through their tears. She explained how she felt, but somehow the words weren't as true as when she was sitting in the car next to Clay.

Laura sighed. "What a pair we make. I want David, but in order to get his full attention I'll have to pursue him as if I were a renegade cop after a killer. I'm just not that open. I can't even get him to become a friend, while you've gotten to friendship and can't get to the next step."

"Your date didn't work out, either," Katherine commiserated.

Shrugging, Laura said morosely, "It did for a while. Then, after a kiss that could have set the carpet on fire, he slammed out the door!"

"Same thing here. Only I slammed through the door, instead."

"So far we're not doing too well," Laura said. "I'm just about ready to give up. David will just have to find another best friend and lover—apparently he's not willing to let me fill that role."

Best friends and lovers were Katherine's specialty. She'd seen enough of both at the truck stop. Transient men and even more transient women, long weekends and then on the road again until the next time. It was unusual when there wasn't a woman in the café crying on a Monday over a guy she'd met on Friday.

"We just need to pool our resources, that's all. If you teach me how to be a lady, I'll teach you how to loosen up," Katherine offered, wondering if either was possible. On the other hand, what did she have to lose?

They began immediately, staying up until dawn as they rummaged through magazines, filling scratch pads with crude drawings of dresses and hairstyles and writing lists of things that each needed to explain to the other.

"I'll show you how to set a full table tomorrow. There are a minimum of three forks, three spoons and two knives, and they all have to be in a certain spot. We'll work on the glasses and plates later." Laura yawned.

"Right. Later," Katherine mumbled, her head nodding with exhaustion. "See you then."

Sunday was the same. Each went over everything the other seemed to think important, including walking properly and laughing discreetly.

"I thought all you had to do was get from one side of the room to the other and you were in business." Katherine dropped the book from her head for the hundredth time.

"Wrong. It has to be a glide, as if you're on skates. And the less anatomy that wiggles, the better."

Katherine was honestly glad to see the sun rise on Monday morning. At least she could forget the table-setting procedures emblazoned on the backs of her eyelids! And she had thought that eating peas with a fork instead of a spoon was a step up in the world!

Laura called the office in late afternoon. "Katherine, is Clay very busy?"

"No, but he's like an armadillo without his shell, scurrying into any available hole so he won't have to see me," she declared, angry that she hadn't been able to corner him yet and find out what his reaction to her speech was. On second thought, maybe this *was* his reaction!

Laura's chuckle carried over the line. "Don't worry. Knowing Clay, it's going to get worse before it gets better."

Katherine sighed, running a hand around her neck to ease the tension there. "Thanks for the encouragement. So far he's not too impressed with the new me. But I went shopping at lunch and bought a few new outfits like the ones we discussed. Maybe he'll notice tomorrow."

"I bet he's already noticed," Laura surmised with a chuckle. "If he's gone into hiding then he's already recognized a difference and just doesn't know how to cope with it yet. Clay's a man of habit. He has to think of things a long time before he's ready to accept them."

"Is a century too long to wait?" Katherine asked dryly, earning another chuckle.

"It'll be sooner than that. Oh, by the way, I may not be home tonight. Don't worry about me if I don't show up, okay?"

"David?"

"David," she confirmed.

"Bingo. Good luck!"

"Thanks. Same to you and Clay."

"Fat chance," Katherine muttered, putting Laura through to Clay. Why couldn't she think of any really *good* Irish curses when she needed them? She knew there was one for practically every occasion, but she wanted one to fit Clay's hardheadedness.

Consuela dropped her off at Laura's later that day. Katherine couldn't help grinning as she remembered the note she had left on Clay's desk just before leaving. He had been in the men's room—again.

Mr. Reynolds
Would you please pick me up for work tomorrow?
Laura has plans with David and I have no transportation until my next paycheck.

                                                     Thank you.

She had a small surprise for him when he came to get her, one that would remind him she was definitely a grown-up woman.

NOT BOTHERING to turn on the lights, Clay slipped off his jacket and threw it on the couch, following it with his shirt and socks. His shoes were just inside the door. With tired movements he walked across the room to the bar and poured himself a stiff drink. Then, like a magnet drawn to the source, he walked back to the spot where Katherine used to stand. Sipping the biting liquid, he stared out into the dark night.

Finally his eyes had been pried open to show him that he had made one right decision in this past two weeks of chaos. He'd seen how really lonely he was—a loneliness that Magda wouldn't have been able to assuage no matter how hard she tried.

Magda as a beautiful and charming woman was incomparable. Magda as his wife and the mother of his children, sharing a private day-to-day life, spelled boredom. Lots of it.

He hadn't realized it before. He'd been so damn busy with his *own* list of requirements in a woman that he'd been boring, too.

At breakfast, memories of a red-haired sprite had over-

whelmed him. He recalled how she'd told stories about herself and about life in a truck stop until she had him chuckling all the way to the office. In fact, he didn't remember
ever enjoying himself more. He'd also learned a lot about
Katherine through her anecdotes. All he had to do was read
between the lines. Their conversations had taught him all
about life—and surviving to live and learn another day.

But making one mistake didn't mean he had to make two.
Katherine wasn't the automatic choice for a wife simply
because Magda was the wrong woman for him. Katherine
was fun and witty, but most of the time she was out of his
control. She was the most frustrating woman he had ever
laid eyes on. And the good old-fashioned lust he felt for her
wasn't the answer to boredom. She *made* more complications than she cured.

He ran a hand around his neck, attempting to ease the
tension from his stiff muscles. For a man who'd never had
woman problems before, he sure as hell had his hands full
now! It had been three weeks since he'd met Katherine, and
he hadn't slept a wink since.

He padded to the couch and went through his coat pocket.
Inside, in a scrawled hand that he was beginning to know
as well as his own, was a note from Katherine asking him
to pick her up in the morning.

Clutching it in one hand, he walked into the bedroom and
opened the nightstand drawer. Glittering on top of the choc-
olate-colored velvet bag lay her antique emerald and diamond earrings. Somehow they had woven their own spell
on him. He held them in his hand, no longer amazed at the
warmth they exuded. With a heavy sigh he lay down on top
of the spread. Amazingly, within seconds, he was asleep, a
smile on his lips, the earrings still in his hands.

CHAPTER SEVEN

THE NEXT MORNING he was late. He should have known that once he was finally able to ease Katherine from his mind and find sleep, he'd overdo it.

But she was his first waking thought in the morning, and he was as excited about seeing Katherine as he was reluctant. Her declaration of love, along with his constant need to take her in his arms and make mad passionate love to her one more time, warred with his fear of allowing himself to get emotionally involved. Emotions had never entered his previous relationships, and this was a completely new set of circumstances for him. He'd never felt this way before: wanting to run from a woman as much as he wanted to run *to* her, and he didn't know what to do. Katherine's presence in his life kept him in a constant state of turmoil.

Not seeing Laura's car in the driveway made him wonder how things were going with his friends. Maybe David had finally talked Laura into having the grand affair he had craved from her for so long. Clay hoped so, for both their sakes.

But all those thoughts of goodwill for his friends fled his mind as Katherine opened the door. In fact, he didn't have a thought left to ponder.

Katherine stood in the shadowed hallway, a black, filmy teddy hugging her tiny, perfect figure, leaving just enough to the imagination to be deadly. Even in the heat of the morning, he could see her nipples pushing against the silky fabric, and his breath stopped. Her hair was a riot of soft red curls framing her beautiful face. He swallowed hard, unable to think of a thing to say.

Her long, slim legs were encased in black hose attached to sexy black lace garters that seductively peeked from the hem of her teddy. Tall high heels of the same color graced her feet.

"I'm sorry I'm running late. Could you give me just a moment?" she asked softly, her tone low and seductive, her inflection not hurried at all.

Then he noticed the makeup, a flawless job on already flawless skin. "What the hell…!"

"Please. Just step inside. I'm almost through ironing my dress."

And, like the idiot he was, he did. "Was this planned?" he finally demanded, ignoring the fact that his body responded instantly to the woman in front of him. His mind might be failing, but all his other parts were in excellent working order.

She turned smartly and headed for the kitchen. "Coffee? And yes."

He followed, his eyes never leaving her swaying derriere, until her answer registered. Then he stopped in the kitchen doorway.

"Yes?"

She picked up the iron, daintily stuck out her tongue and licked her finger. With a flick of her wrist, she tested the heat of the iron. It sizzled. So did he. "Yes."

He didn't know how to respond to her honesty, but his body knew what to do. He restrained himself. Barely. Most women weren't fond of the idea of being thrown down on a kitchen floor and ravished by a half-crazed maniac.

He muttered the only word that came to his deranged mind. "Mud flaps." The tinkle of her laughter sent shafts of delightful pain through him to rest heavily in the pit of his stomach—and elsewhere.

He cleared his throat. "Why?"

"When I realized I was running late, I decided welcoming you dressed this way was infinitely better than greeting you naked as the day I was born." She began ironing the skirt of the dress stretched on the board.

"Infinitely," he repeated, pouring himself a cup of coffee and trying in vain to keep his eyes to himself. Suddenly he slammed his cup down on the counter and turned, reached for her arm in frustration. "Do you dress this way when David comes over?" he demanded.

She smiled. A secret smile. "No."

"No?"

Her lips puckered before the soft, slow sound flowed out. "No."

He jerkily turned back to his coffee. Tension seized his body. He was aware of his need, having suffered from it several times before, but never this strongly, this persistently. This hotly. It was as if all the summer day's heat was pouring through him at once, curling around his limbs in anticipation of intense pleasure. Before, he had always taken his pleasures and moved on to another heat, another summer, another woman.

But this woman was different. Instead of the heat lessening, it worsened, crippling him with the force of it. Her lips were parted and slightly pouty, and he wanted to taste them. Her curves tempted his hands to seek them. Her perfume filled his nostrils and senses, making him heady with the scent. And still—stubbornly—he refused himself her pleasure, for her sake even more than his.

She was too vulnerable. He didn't want her to be hurt when boredom set in and the time came for him to walk away. And having an affair, even a long one, wasn't suited to her emotional makeup. She wasn't prepared for the free-and-easy life-style some women enjoyed today. She was the kind who wanted marriage and kids and a backyard swing. He wasn't ready for that.

But the powerful emotions Katherine forced from him

also scared the hell out of him. They were more potent than anything he had experienced before, stronger than he had ever imagined could be possible. He could feel his aching response to her nearness in every pore of his body.

The only thing he had that she could share was his money. Most women he knew wanted that almost as much as he did.

Come to think of it, he wasn't sure what he wanted anymore. Dammit! Katherine represented everything foreign to him, and foreign meant frightening.

"Clay?" Katherine's voice broke into his thoughts and he turned, only to stand, stunned. She was beautiful.

Her black cotton sheath was high-necked, cap-sleeved and demure—and probably the sexiest thing he had ever seen. She held her hair up like a curtain and turned, inviting him to a view of her exposed back. "Could you do the zipper for me? I can't reach."

His hands shook as he grasped the pull tab and brought it up. His knuckles grazed the softness of her neck and he almost groaned with the effort of pulling his hand back. He took a deep breath, commanding his body to do his will.

Katherine turned and smiled, looking serene, confident and just a little mysterious. "Ready?" she asked brightly.

He cleared his throat. "We're flying to Dallas for the day," he announced, amazed at his words and wondering where on earth that decision had come from. He did have an appointment there, but until the moment he'd just spoken, he hadn't known he was taking Katherine along.

"Today?"

"Yes." His voice was curt, but he was lucky he had a voice at all. "I have a business deal to complete and need you along to take notes."

"My shorthand is almost nonexistent," she warned, but her green eyes were alight with excitement. He took credit for that, enjoying her enjoyment.

"It'll do," he muttered gruffly, ushering her out the door, his hand on her arm. "We'll be back before dinner."

"Okay." She smiled, and his heart expanded to fill his whole body.

Without allowing himself to dwell on his decision or to let his gaze linger on her, he drove directly to the airport, gaining entrance to the section where the private planes were kept. Nodding to the man at the gate, he gunned the powerful car engine and traveled down the row of hangars until he pulled in front of his. A small green-and-white plane was being checked over by two workmen in overalls.

"Is it yours?" Katherine asked, her voice so low he could hardly hear.

"Yes." He flipped off the ignition and pocketed the keys. "It's a Bonanza F33A," he said proudly, knowing she probably knew nothing of planes, but having to identify his pride and joy anyway.

She shook her head, slipping out of the car seat and walking slowly toward the plane.

He watched her, mesmerized. When he realized the mechanics were looking at him, he shook his head to rid himself of the spell and walked into the hangar. Before his mind deserted him completely, he had to call Consuela and tell her of his plans to take Katherine.

FIFTEEN MINUTES LATER they were in the air.

"Are you all right?" he asked, leveling the plane and heading for Dallas's Love Field.

"Wonderful! I think I'm in love with flying!" She leaned back in the plush seat and gave a big sigh.

"Is this your first flight?"

"Yes! Isn't this great? Have you flown long? When did you get your first plane? How did you ever learn?"

He gave a deep chuckle, suddenly feeling freer than he had in weeks. Months. Years. "I've been flying since I was twenty-two, when a guy I knew took me up in his plane. I immediately signed up for lessons and I've been flying ever since. I love it, too.''

"If I knew how to fly I doubt if I'd ever come out of the clouds,'' she answered, her eyes glued to the outside window.

He laughed again as he put the plane on automatic pilot. "Clouds are the very things a good pilot stays away from. There's turbulence in there.''

"Really?'' She stared at him with wide eyes, and he couldn't keep from looking at her. "When I was growing up I used to sneak up to the rooftop of our apartment over the truck stop and stare at the clouds, making imaginary animals out of them. Then I'd string together a story and hide in the make-believe world I had created.''

"I can see you doing that,'' he murmured, his hand stretching out to touch the silk of her throat.

"What did you do when you were growing up?''

His eyes grew distant with the memory. "My escape was action. I skateboarded. I lived it, ate it, slept dreaming about it.''

"You mean those things that look like scooters without handles?''

He grinned. "Those things,'' he said, "were my life. I thought I'd be world champion someday.''

She tilted her head and stared at him. "And were you?''

"Alas, no. But I now own a skateboard park for kids, although it hardly breaks even, with the high insurance rates.''

"Then why keep it?''

His face lost its smile as the edge of determination etched his jaw. "Because every kid needs a place to go and dream of making it big, while they're working off all that excess energy they don't know what to do with.''

"You're a nice man, Clay Reynolds,'' she murmured softly. "Outside you're all rough, like lumpy papier-mâché and inside you're all soft, like marshmallows.''

He frowned. "Hardly."

Katherine didn't answer. She just raised her brows as a small knowing smile tugged at the corners of her mouth.

ALMOST TWO HOURS later they landed at Love Field. Clay checked with the ground crew, then slipped Katherine inside the limousine that stood waiting for them. Katherine didn't say a word, but she touched everything from the rich velour upholstery to the buttons on the stereo and the small bottles hidden in the built-in bar.

Clay sat back and watched, enjoying her exploration. It was as if he was experiencing luxury for the first time, the excitement born again. He'd almost forgotten how many perks came with success....

"We're going to a strip shopping center?" Katherine whispered as the driver pulled in front of a small restaurant.

"Yes." He led her toward the brilliant, aqua-colored door. "But wait until you see what's inside," he promised as he led her into the cool, dark depths of one of Dallas's finest bistros. He refused to dwell on the fact that he'd never looked forward to a business lunch as much as this one.

They weren't alone again until Clay was once more piloting the plane back to San Antonio.

He listened to Katherine's remarks about his new client with surprise. She had far more insight into people and their behavior than he'd given her credit for. The owner had had a slight heart problem and wanted to relieve some of his stress. He wasn't averse to selling the strip, but was reluctant to sell the restaurant, which was his real love. Clay felt he could keep the previous owner on as manager of the restaurant and be better off for doing so.

Katherine concurred with his opinion, and he felt good. "And how are you enjoying working with Consuela?" he asked, remembering his conversation with the woman who had almost become his mother over the years.

"I love it. She's a very special lady, even though she sometimes intimidates me."

"Why does she intimidate you?"

"Because she knows so much, and I'm just learning."

"You'll catch on," he assured her, wondering what would happen to Katherine then. His gut tightened.

She grinned, and he tried to grin back. It didn't work. "Consuela is putting me on the computer tomorrow so I can learn more about the real-estate properties," she confided as he began their descent.

"Really? Why?"

"She thought I should know all aspects of the business if I'm going to be working for the office. It would help familiarize me with the entire operation."

"Remember just to observe. Let the salesmen handle the sales. They know what they're doing."

"Right, boss," she teased, only he couldn't crack a smile. He suddenly remembered that three of the salesmen were young, virile and single....

Holding on to a distance he didn't feel, Clay dropped her back at Laura's and drove home, thankful there weren't any meetings to attend.

Morosely he sat in the living room while the sunset put on a spectacular show outside his window. He held Katherine's earrings in his hand, as mesmerized by the twinkling jewels as he was by their real owner. It was strange, but holding her earrings he felt connected to her in some way. He couldn't explain it—he just felt it.

When the doorbell rang, he was irritated at the intrusion until he discovered it was David on his porch.

"Hi! Need some company?" David asked, displaying a six-pack and a rather shaky smile.

"Why not?" Clay muttered, taking the offered beer and stalking back to plop down on the couch. He popped the top of a can. "How'd your date with Laura go?"

"Terrible. I take it yours wasn't that successful, either."

David lounged on the floor, his back propped up by the large leather wing-back chair.

Clay gulped down a few swallows of the cold brew. "We're just friends."

"You're just kidding yourself. I've seen that look before—in the mirror. You're smitten, Clay, and it's bad."

"It'll pass."

"Yup. In about thirty years or so. Give or take a decade."

"Look who's talking," Clay sneered, his frustration topping the scale. "You've been after Laura for years, and once you get close to her, you back off!"

"I know." David sighed, not offended at his friend's accusation. "I'm afraid to press her for more than friendship in case she decides to turn me down and never lets me darken her door again. I'd rather have a small part of Laura forever than force the issue and lose that connection." He stared at his downcast friend. "And you, my friend, are doing the same damn thing. You're just disguising it under other emotions and an engagement you never should have made."

Clay's anger left as quick as it came. "Probably," he finally admitted, feeling better just talking about it. "But I broke up with Magda two weeks ago."

He had David's full attention. "Why? How?"

"I just told her the truth. She and I didn't have what it took to go the distance, and I wasn't ready to commit myself to marriage."

"With her."

He shrugged. "Maybe. I just don't know."

"Katherine gives you a pain in the neck and a bigger one somewhere in the vicinity of the heart?"

"Dammit, yes." His voice was a reluctant growl.

David grinned, but there was sadness in his eyes. "Welcome to my world, friend."

"This is hell."

"You're right," David muttered into his beer can. "And

I think it's time I did something about it. Watching you has made me realize just what a coward I've been."

"Glad to help out," Clay retorted dryly.

David chuckled. "A friend in need..."

"Now if we could only solve my problems as easily."

"Oh, no. You're going to have to fight your way out of your own confusion. You wouldn't listen to me if I gave you the answer on a platter."

"Try me." Clay's voice held a challenge.

"Marry her."

"Marry in haste, repent in leisure."

"Great. Quote clichés all night long, but don't do what I do, do what I say. Marry her."

"As soon as I see miracles happening on your side of the street."

"You're a fool," David muttered.

"I'm in good company."

"I'll drink to that."

Even with a good friend for company, it was a very lonely night.

WHEN SUNSHINE BLAZED through the patio window, warming Clay's skin, it took him several moments to realize he'd slept on the living room floor. With two aspirin and plenty of orange juice in his system, he made the decision to stay home and do his paperwork in the den. It would keep him out of Katherine's way and in his own cocoon to work out his problems.

But he was just as troubled at eight o'clock that night as he had been at eight o'clock that morning.

KATHERINE'S EMOTIONS plummeted when she realized just how much she had wanted her day to end on a different note. Clay was *supposed* to be at work so she could demonstrate her professional ability! He was *supposed* to admire her from afar and wish she were his full-time secretary. His full-time lover. He was *supposed* to wish for her, and then turn wishes into actions....

So much for suppositions.

After a nerve-racking, very lonely day she stepped inside Laura's house and closed the door, leaning against it.

"Katherine?" Laura called from the living room. "Come join us for a glass of wine."

With a sigh she pushed away from the door and walked slowly into the living room. She smiled briefly at David and accepted the fluted, crystal glass Laura handed her. "Hello, you two."

"You look like hell," Laura said, taking in the tiredness Katherine couldn't hide. "What happened?"

"Clay and I flew to Dallas yesterday and closed a real-estate deal he wanted," she said wearily. "And today he didn't even show up so I could show him how much I wasn't impressed by his business acumen."

David chuckled, absently playing with Laura's hair. Apparently all was well with those two. "Normally he won't take anyone with him in that treasured plane of his. It should make you happy, not sad. And Clay seldom takes anyone on business trips. In fact, I'd say you're the first."

Her green eyes widened for a moment, then her shoulders slumped again. "It was great until we landed back here. Then he withdrew, acting as if I had the mumps or something. He didn't even come to work today."

This time David laughed out loud, a deep belly laugh that reverberated off the walls. "He must really be in deep and fighting it all the way."

"Why?" Both Laura and Katherine stared at him as if he'd grown two heads.

"Why?" David looked at both of them as if they couldn't put two and two together. "Because," he said patiently, "yesterday he wanted Katherine with him badly enough to relax his own rules about mixing business with pleasure, and then he obviously got scared."

Katherine groaned and settled into the chair across from them, curling her toes in the plush carpet. "He's feeling guilty, that's all. If he invited anyone, it should have been Magda."

"Why?" David asked, his expression one of surprise. "Magda's been out of the picture for the past two weeks. He certainly wasn't worried about her."

Katherine leaned forward. "What did you say?"

Laura's hazel eyes pinned him to the couch. "What?"

David had the grace to flush. "Damn! I wasn't supposed to say anything. I forgot."

"Well it's too late to remember that now, so spill the rest of the beans," Laura said grimly. "What happened?"

Running a hand through his mink-dark hair, David sighed heavily. "I knew I should have left while I had the chance."

"If you think you can leave all in one piece after dropping that little bombshell, you're sadly mistaken," Katherine stated between clenched teeth. She already had a good idea what had happened, but wanted it confirmed before she allowed her temper free rein.

David realized when he was beaten. "Clay broke his engagement to Magda about two weeks ago."

"Snake," Katherine muttered.

"Trouble," David said grimly.

"You bet," Katherine answered.

"That turkey," Laura exclaimed.

"I'm sorry," David murmured.

"For whom?" Katherine asked.

"For Clay, knowing you two." David unwound his fingers from Laura's hair and stood. "I think I'd better get going before I get in even more trouble."

"David," Katherine said slowly, her mind racing with possibilities. "If you don't tell Clay you spilled the beans, neither will we." She smiled most beguilingly, but the glint of battle in her eyes was enough to warn even the biggest of fools.

David stared at her for a moment, then shook his head. "Amazing."

"Nothing's amazing. He just needs to think this through and see the light. My light." Her voice was filled with conviction.

"I still say he's scared to death of you and I have a hunch you've got your own plans to take advantage of that."

"Clay needs me, David. He just doesn't know it yet," Katherine explained. David's news was the best she'd heard all week, but that didn't mean she wasn't mad at Clay for not telling her himself. The coward!

"I'm sure you'll be the first to tell him," he commented dryly, holding out his hand and pulling Laura up. "Now walk me to the door and hope that I live through this mess. I can see both your minds working overtime already. It's difficult enough to let the other half of the human race win, I don't have to watch the triumph, too."

Laura chuckled. "Poor defenseless guys. None of you stand a chance against the big bad women."

"You said it," Katherine heard him mutter as Laura walked him outside to his car.

She leaned back in the chair and stared up at the ceiling, attempting to leash her Irish temper enough to come up with a sweet form of revenge.

Automatically, her fingers went to her earlobes to caress the jewels that had been there so long. She met flesh instead of stone and dropped her hand. For just a moment she'd forgotten she'd given them to Clay.

All he saw when he looked at them was their monetary worth, but she felt the loss of the gift itself. Perhaps with time—just perhaps—he would grow to realize that anything given in love is worth ten times more because of its emotional value. After all, her most precious possessions were now in his care: her love and her jewels.

Then she smiled. If Irish elves could really conjure up magic, she was hoping her brand of that commodity would work. Now was the time to move into Magda's empty place in Clay's life. One step at a time.

THE NEXT DAY turned out to be the longest day of Clay's life. Every two minutes he was popping his head into the main office. And every time he did so, Katherine was talking to a different client with one of the salesmen standing by her side, nodding his head as though she were reciting everything exactly the way he would have.

Occasionally he would signal her to come to his office, but her sweet smile aimed his way was the only answer. She never took a step toward him.

He felt frustrated by the end of the morning. Was she purposely ignoring him or was she that busy? Then he'd remind himself that he was the boss and could *order* her to come to his office. Then he remembered he was the boss and needed her to earn her wages. It was good logic, but his mind wasn't listening to logic anymore.

As lunchtime came and went and the morning turned to afternoon, frustration turned to anger. His mind kept retreating to the morning he had picked her up when she was dressed in nothing but a sexy teddy and black hose. And every time he saw her with one of the salesmen, he reconstructed the treasures that were hidden under her demure dress, and the blood in his veins would heat and flow like an out-of-control river.

Even dressed as she was, she was too damned attractive to stay in a roomful of men and not cause a stir. And he didn't like the reactions she was causing, if the look in the men's eyes was any indication.

Consuela occasionally gave him a smug I-told-you-so look, but he ignored her, harboring his own anger as if it were gold. He *liked* feeling angry at Katherine—it freed his emotions even if they were the wrong ones.

Leave it to Consuela to rub salt in his wounds. She slipped into his office and closed the door as if she were conspiring, a cup of fresh coffee and a cookie on a napkin as her excuse. He eyed the cookie warily. "All right. What's the name of this one?"

She smiled smugly. "Patience. It has caramel and pecans in it."

"I should have known." He sighed, biting into it and wishing he had more of its namesake.

When he said no more, she waited, but not for long. She finally said the words she had been communicating with looks all day. "I told you so."

Clay leaned back, tossing his pencil on the desk. "Okay, Consuela. Get it over with."

"Katherine is a natural in sales. She just helped land a contract with that framing corporation to turn that old office building downtown into their headquarters. That's almost a half-a-million-dollar sale."

Half of him was thrilled with the sale, but the other half was as frustrated and angry as before. "With whose help? Are you discounting our own, highly trained sales staff?"

She shrugged. "If the customer had thought the salesman was so good he would have bought the darn building the last two times he's been here, or the first three times he saw the building. But he didn't. He bought today, after Katherine talked to him."

There was nothing more smug than Consuela when she knew she had a strong point. Why he put up with her... "He was already presold."

"Huh!" she grunted, her arms crossed to do verbal battle. "Like Oscar Meyer says: 'Bologna.'"

He sighed and pulled himself back up to a straight position. "I'll congratulate her later." Much later, when he could strangle her slender, sexy throat as he politely thanked her for the sale.

"Good. Fair is fair." Consuela uncrossed her arms and reached for the doorknob, silently informing him that she had reached her objective. Now if he could only reach his.

Forget that. If he only knew what his objectives were, he'd be miles ahead of both women!

As the door closed behind Consuela, Clay picked up the pencil he had been using and broke it in half, throwing both pieces across the room.

Damn her hide! Every time he turned around, Katherine O'Malley was taunting him, teasing him, making him feel ten feet tall but twice as dumb. And he didn't understand how one woman could do it!

She didn't weave spells or chant incantations, but she was under his skin like a tick and was twice as much of a pest. If he'd learned anything at all from this mess, he'd learned never to pick up a woman at a party. Ever.

The truth was that Clay knew he'd made a mistake in sending Katherine to Laura's house. He just wasn't sure how to get her to come back to his home—and bed—without groveling.

When the knock came, he growled. "Come in!"

Katherine stood in the doorway, her eyes lit with a thousand fires of triumph, her smile a wreath of unbridled happiness that wrapped around his heart. "Did Consuela tell you the good news?" she asked breathlessly, completely ignoring the scowl on his face.

"What good news?"

"I helped Beau sell a half-a-million-dollar building this afternoon!"

"I heard."

"Isn't it wonderful?" She came toward him, stopping only when she reached the side of his desk. "I think I found my calling. Selling is even more fun than being a secretary, not that I know much about either, yet. But I will!"

He leaned back, his hands clutching the wooden arms of his chair. "And what did you promise to do to help get those sales?"

She perched on the side of the desk like a leprechaun. Obviously she didn't realize that the skirt tugged at her hips and showed more of her legs than he had a right to see. And her hands behind her, pressed on the desk meant that the flimsy silk fabric of her dress was pulled taut against her perfectly formed breasts.... He swallowed hard and prayed his libido would die a quick death.

She frowned. "What do you mean?"

"Are you having drinks with the proud owners? Dinner?"

If she hadn't been so excited, she might have noticed the anger he just barely managed to contain. "No," she chuckled, "although he asked. But I have to study every minute of my spare time for night-school classes."

His eyes narrowed. "Just make sure you know what you're selling, Katherine. Some of these men think a pretty smile is an open invitation."

His hints finally sank in. Her movements stilled, her expression glazed with wariness. "What do you mean?"

He leaned forward, his angry face level with her breasts. "Just what I said. They might take your bright smile for another kind of invitation. You have to watch how you come across. Unless of course, you are inviting...?"

Her face whitened, making the tiny freckles that sprinkled her nose stand out. "You think I'm a hooker in disguise? That I'm selling the world's oldest profession, when most men today can get it for free?"

His jealousy wouldn't let him back down. His anger was too deep for that to happen. "Are you?"

Her green eyes gazed back at him, her look as strong and level as his own. "Think hard, Clay, and be careful what you say. What you answer now will determine how our relationship—friendship—whatever you want to call it, will continue. Do you honestly believe that because I would allow *you* into my bed that I want just anybody there? Do you think I'm only looking for a warm body to snuggle up to? That I make declarations of love to every man I meet?"

His eyes roved the length of her body, right down to the tips of her toes. "I don't know. You've never said."

When he looked into her eyes he saw the hurt he had inflicted. A part of him ached to hold her and retract those ugly accusations. But another part wanted to ravish the softness of her body and never let her go. He needed her: to touch, to ignite, to draw the fever from his body and the jealousy that speared his heart. His needs and his anger warred through him.

She took a deep breath, raised her chin and challenged him with green sparks in her eyes. "What would you say if I agreed? That any man would do?"

He was out of his chair in a second. His hands reached under her arms as he lifted her from the top of his desk and pinned her against the wall. Katherine's feet were off the floor, Clay's body pressing intimately against her. His hands strained against her body as he sought the soft places to torment. His warm breath was sharp in her already-ringing ears. "You think you can flirt and tempt with your seductive little movements and not pay up? Is that it?"

Her fingers trembled as she threaded them through his sun-streaked hair. "Are you going make me pay, Clay? For both of us?" she whispered, her mouth unconsciously pouting the words.

He couldn't help it. His need overpowered his anger and he let go of what little control he had. Groaning, he pressed his mouth against hers, his tongue plundering the tender inside of her mouth. Their breath caught and mingled, creating more heat than he could stand. His body was on fire. He shook with the need to touch her flesh, to feel the softness of her beneath his hands. Beneath his body. His heartbeat raced even more with that thought.

"You're a witch," he muttered roughly, his lips still touching hers, brushing tantalizingly back and forth.

"I love you so much," she murmured softly. "Let me be

with you, Clay. I won't gripe or complain. I understand now.''

Her voice was a whisper, but her words shouted in his ears. ''What do you mean?'' His voice was like a soft rasp as his lips sought the pulse at her throat. But sirens were going off in his head. Warning. Warning.

''I love you and I'm willing to settle for a small part of your life.'' Her wide eyes were the color of forest fern as she stared up at him. ''Any part you're willing to share with me.''

Emotional blackmail, dressed in pretty words. ''You'd settle for being the other woman?''

She nodded her head, her eyes wide.

''What is it that you think I need, Katherine?'' His hands tightened on her ribs, his fingers working magic.

''Someone who cares enough to make you content.'' Her answer was simplicity itself. Damn her. She was absolutely right. And the one thing that would make him feel content also happened to be the same thing he was so afraid of: commitment. Mental, physical, metaphysical commitment.

Katherine needed all that, while he couldn't handle those emotions at all. It didn't make it any easier to know that he couldn't let her go, either. Not yet.

Anger rose like bile in his throat. ''So one hand washes the other, right? In exchange for certain favors from you, I'm supposed to be responsible for your welfare. Is that what you want?''

Again she nodded, but he could see the lack of conviction in her eyes. He took a deep breath and let her down slowly so her toes could finally touch the floor. Taking a step back, he surveyed her. ''It means that you're mine for as long as I say. You can't see anyone else. Not as long as we're together.''

Her chin rose at that defiant angle he was beginning to know so well. ''Of course.'' Her teeth were clamped together. ''And vice versa.''

"Very well," he said distantly, holding her in her place instead of pulling her into his arms again. His eyes focused over her shoulder. He couldn't afford to look at her, to see the hurt in her eyes. "It's four o'clock. I'll be at your place at ten. Meanwhile, get your hair fixed and buy some more sophisticated clothes. I like a sexy woman who is well-groomed. Take my car and get going."

Katherine shook her head as if awakening from a bad dream. Her anger finally bubbled over. She snapped her fingers. "Just like that? Get your hair done and buy sexy clothing, then wait for me to show up?"

"Just like that." His voice was harsh, definite. "Are you still interested?"

Barely banked fury blazed out of eyes that had been soft with passion just moments ago. "Oh, yes, Mr. Reynolds. I'm interested."

"Good." He dropped the Porsche's keys into her palm, careful not to touch her. "Take these."

The heat of her anger continued to seethe through her limbs. She clutched the keys until they bit into her flesh. Without another word, she turned. She needed to get out of there before she took his beautiful antique vase from the side cabinet and slammed him over the head with it!

"Wait." He reached into his desk drawer and pulled out several charge cards, placing them in her hand, also. "Take these, too."

Katherine strode serenely out of the office, but the door crashed back into its frame.

CHAPTER EIGHT

KATHERINE AIMED the gleaming black Porsche toward North Star Mall, her anger apparent in every line of her body.

So he wanted to *pay* for her love, did he? Well, that's what he'd do—that egotistical monster!

Sure, she had offered herself to him. More than once. But she hadn't expected him to take her up on it! He was supposed to confess that Magda wasn't for him, and that Katherine fit him to a tee! He was supposed to apologize to her for wasting all this time, then take her in his arms and confess his love for her. He was supposed to have told her the truth about his aborted engagement!

What had gone wrong?

It didn't matter. The plan had backfired, and now she had to figure out how to open his eyes and see her as the only woman for him. Her eyes narrowed. Clay thought he wanted a kept woman—she'd show him a kept woman.

She remembered something Laura had once quoted and laughed. "Be careful what you wish for—you just might get it."

Laura. As soon as she was in the mall, she'd call her. Laura would know what needed to be done besides spend every dime she could on clothing. There had to be something Katherine could do to make Clay realize just how stupid he was acting! And Laura knew him best.

"Mr. Reynolds," she whispered into the interior as she pulled in front of the Frost Brothers store. "You're gonna get more than you bargained for. I'm worth a lot more than you know. I guar-an-tee.''

CLAY RENTED a two-door Lincoln whose seat could be adjusted to sit as high as Katherine needed it to be and drove home. It would be waiting for her when he took her back to his home tonight.

Opening his front door, he stepped in and felt the blast of chilled air on his face and neck. He needed to relax and sort through some thoughts and problems that were clamoring for release.

After the heat of the outside, the house was almost too cool. It was also empty and quiet as death. He felt as if he were walking into a tomb, which underlined just how lonely he was. Until Katherine came into his life, he had thought he loved and needed this peace, but now it felt as though some vital life-force was gone. He had taunted both of them because of his own basic insecurities, now it was time to come clean and face a few home truths…right after he figured out what those truths were.

At least he'd gotten his wish without groveling. Katherine would be back in his home—and his bed—tonight. But he wasn't too proud of how he'd managed it. Desperation was a strange slave driver.

But before he fixed himself a drink, got a bite to eat or sat down on the couch, he reached for the jeweled earrings kept tucked in the small wall safe in his den. With them clasped securely in his hand, he sat in the wing-back chair and stared at the woodland scene outside his window.

KATHERINE DROPPED DOWN on the couch and leaned her head back. Eyes closed, she allowed the coolness of Laura's house to surround her, finally breathing without feeling as if she were in an oven. The early June heat had been unbearable as she paced the parking lot trying to remember where she had parked the sleek Porsche. She had had too

much on her mind to remember the exact location, and anger
and frustration with Clay had erased any memory she might
have had.

She opened one eye and glanced down at her purchases.
At least fifteen boxes and bags were piled high on the carpet. They held three designer gowns, five expensive but casual outfits, a few day dresses, several teddies and night-
gowns in various shades of jewel tones and high heels that
cost more than a hundred dollars apiece.

She had done exactly what he had requested and spent
money on his credit cards. Thousands of dollars. The only
thing that kept guilt from baying at her mind's door was
that he had her jewels, which she now knew were worth
triple what she could ever owe him. But from now on, she
vowed, she'd never let her temper get the best of her. She
couldn't afford all this debt.

Still in the throes of anger, she'd gone the rest of the nine
yards and got a manicure, pedicure, facial and new hairstyle.
Carlo, the hairdresser, had bright brown eyes that had lit up
with the challenge before him. He had practically rubbed
his hands together in glee.

"You must tame your hair to do what you want, but you
must never take away its spirit!" he exclaimed with a slight
lisp as he trimmed and cut and shaped. And he had been
right. The hairdo was a masterpiece and well worth the ex-
orbitant amount he had charged. Wild, casually curled, it
was beautiful, but Katherine wasn't sure she could duplicate
what Carlo had created.

At least it would last for tonight.

Both eyes opened with that thought. She had to get ready!

She gathered the packages in her arms and rushed to her
bedroom, only to drop them on the floor as she reached for
the oversize brown manila envelope perched on her pillow.
Laura had scrawled Katherine's name across the front of it,
and she frowned as she opened the flap, wondering what on
earth Laura had done now.

Her frown turned to a grin and the grin to laughter. The note inside gave the explanation.

Katherine—Clay has always had others sign one of these, so turnabout's fair play. Use in case of emergency. Maybe it will be the very thing to wake him up. Good luck!

CLAY STEPPED OUT of the cab and stared at Laura's front door. A quick glance at his Porsche sitting in the driveway told him she had managed the powerful car without denting it. The Lincoln he had rented that afternoon was waiting at home for her. The key was under her pillow.

A shadowy form passed by the window, and Clay recognized it as Katherine's. Something about her drove him to the edge of frustration and back. She kept him in a constant state of turmoil, forcing him out of control in any situation where she was involved. Now, after several hours of soul-searching he knew himself better. He finally admitted—at least to himself—that he loved her.

He couldn't believe what he had done today, goading her and then throwing the cards and keys at her. She had declared her love for him so openly, so honestly, without all the machinations that other women he'd know had gone through. But then, she had always been that way. On any topic. There wasn't a lying bone in her body. She wanted him—and he was trying to punish her because he wanted her, too. But because their needs would put conditions on both of them, he couldn't let this relationship get out of hand. Conditions. Restrictions. The two words he hated most.

He walked up the sidewalk, his eyes seeking her through the filmy curtains. By the time he knocked, he was impatient to see her, be with her, talk to her and, perhaps, just once, get her under control so he could feel secure again.

But when she opened the door, he knew it wasn't to be.

She was wearing a filmy, midnight-blue blouse that hugged her slim shoulders and small breasts. Matching slacks outlined the rest of her beguiling figure. Her makeup was flawless, her lips full and pouting and damp, as if she had just darted her small tongue across them. Her hair billowed softly about her shoulders, and he itched to run his fingers through it. But it was her smile that stopped him in his tracks. "I thought you'd never get here," she said breathlessly.

"I'm early." His voice was barely above a whisper.

"I know, but it doesn't feel like it."

She opened the door wider and he stepped inside, closing it behind him and wondering how he was going to gain control of the situation. Not one idea came to mind, but those thoughts that did spring into his head filled his body with a tension that was almost unbearable.

They walked into the living room, Clay clenching his hands to rid himself of the urge to grab and hold her close. He wanted to absorb her so he'd never be without her again.

He could feel his body tighten, readying.... He turned and faced her. "Are you still willing to go through with this new relationship?" His voice was rough, demanding.

She nodded and her hair caught the glint of the lamp glow.

"Even though I'm marrying someone else and may never change my plans?" he goaded.

Her eyes narrowed slightly, her chin lifted an inch or so, but she nodded again.

"And what do you get out of this?"

She walked toward him until they were toe-to-toe, her eyes softening to a luminous shade of sea-fern. "You," she said softly, placing her small hand on his pounding heart.

He swallowed, then swallowed again. His heartbeat accelerated with her touch, and he knew she could feel it in the center of her palm.

Her green eyes widened and he was almost lost in them. "Is that because of me?"

"Yes." His voice was gruff.

"Do you react to every woman this way?"

His hands stayed clenched at his sides. "No."

"Why me, then?" Her other hand touched his chest, lightly pressing against his nipple.

"You know why." His voice was short, slipped.

"Are you angry?"

"Yes."

"With me?"

A grimace crossed his face. "With both of us."

"Why?" She frowned in confusion. Her tongue darted out to skim her upper lip.

He couldn't resist any longer. His hands spanned her waist, his fingers caressing the skin beneath the flimsy material. She was so small, so soft. So sensuous.

Her eyelids drifted down, a small smile barely tilting the corners of her full, parted mouth. "Clay?" she whispered, and he accepted the question with an answer of his own.

"You tempt too much," he growled accusingly as his lips covered hers, a moan echoing from his throat at the triumph of claiming her mouth as his prize.

It was heaven and hell together as he pressed her closer, devouring her will with his mouth. Then she answered his unrestrained passion with her own, her arms circling his neck as if to pull him closer to her.

Their tongues dueled and they savored the overwhelming passion they had unleashed. Their kisses were speaking a language they each understood completely.

Reaching down, he cupped her buttocks in the palms of his hands, raising and pressing her against him, showing her his almost overwhelming need. When he lifted his mouth from hers, his breath was hot, searing her with unspent passion. "Every time I'm near you, I go a little insane," he muttered hoarsely. "I react to you as I've never reacted to woman before—and I hate it.'' His damp forehead was pressed against hers as he tried to catch his breath and straighten out his jumbled thoughts. ''It's just not fair, Katherine.''

Her husky chuckle filled his mind. ''I could say the same thing, Clay, but I won't. You already have a big head.''

His brows rose. ''I might be sure of myself in business, but never when I'm around you. You send me spinning off balance.''

Her fingers traced the strong line of his jaw then his soft lips, her eyes drinking in everything she touched. ''I love you.''

He stilled, finally willing to accept her declaration. ''How do you know?''

She clasped his hand to her breast, and he could feel her quickened heartbeat. ''I just do.''

His frown stopped her fingers from traveling further, and when he spoke his voice was laced with sadness. ''I've never believed in love, Katherine. It always seemed more like an emotional trap than something wonderful.''

''You don't chalk all this emotion up to chemistry, do you?'' She tried to sound as if she was kidding, but her voice broke on the last two words, telling him just how important his answer was to her.

He tried to form the right words, but nothing came. He'd never been able to say the words before, and they wouldn't come forth now. The silence stretched.

''Clay?''

He shook his head, more from confusion than to form a negative answer. ''I don't know, honey. I just don't know anymore.''

Her hand covered his own heart, her small palm seeming even smaller against the breadth of his chest. ''So you've never been in love?'' He knew she could feel his response to her touch.

''No.''

"What about Magda?"

He sighed, pulling away from her, only to feel the coldness of her absence in his arms. He'd deceived her long enough, but this wasn't the time to discuss it. Later. After he made love to her, he'd explain it all. Perhaps then he'd at least have more control over her temper. A small voice inside him laughed hysterically. There was no controlling her, let alone her temper. "Change the subject."

She touched his arm. "I'm sorry, Clay, but she isn't right."

"And you are?" he chided gently.

She nodded, her hair brushing gently against her collar bones. "I think so. But if I'm not, it still doesn't mean she's right for you. It's not a question of one or the other. This isn't multiple choice, where there's a right answer or a grade score."

He couldn't help the rueful smile that claimed his mouth. "You certainly get to the point."

"So do you, when it concerns business." *But not our love,* her eyes seemed to say. "Clay," she began as he brushed away a tendril of her hair, then allowed his finger to play with the silken strand.

He smiled sadly. "I've never seen anything but hurt in the name of love. I'll never say the words, Katherine. If you can't handle that, let's call it quits now, before you get hurt."

"Would you mind if I was hurt?" she asked softly.

"Yes." His voice was gruff.

"Why?"

"Because I have enough on my conscience already. I don't want to add you, too." He cupped her face with his hands. "I want you so badly I ache, but I can't guarantee I'll feel the same way after I've held you in my arms night after night. I might want to walk away."

She flinched, but knew he was right. At least he was

honest. "And you couldn't do that with a clear conscience if I was hurt?"

"No."

She gave a heavy sigh before staring up at him again, her love shining enough to warm him all over. "I won't make it easy for you, Clay. I love you and I want to be with you. I want to touch you, hold you against my breast while you sleep. I want you to need me just as much as I need you, but I won't hang on if—or when—you say it's over. I have my pride, too."

He pulled her back into his arms. "Oh, Katherine," he groaned. "What the hell am I going to do with you?"

"Take me home and love me until dawn?" she whispered, wrapping her arms around his waist and tilting her face toward him as if he were the sun and she a flower. Possessiveness flowed through him, filling him with the need to keep her safe. Keep her in his arms. Keep her…

He shook his head again, only this time it was to shake out the nebulous ideas that were forming in the back of his mind. "Pack a bag, Katherine. We're leaving."

A smile slowly lit up her face and it warmed him all the way to his toes.

"Yes, sir," she murmured, placing a quick kiss on the corner of his mouth, tempting him almost beyond reason. Then she slipped out of his arms before he could grab her again, disappearing down the hallway toward her room.

It took every ounce of restraint he had to stand rooted to the spot instead of following and wrestling her to the floor, taking instant gratification. He could wait. He would wait. He was a man, not an animal.

He hoped he knew the difference, but he wasn't sure anymore.

KATHERINE'S INSIDES WERE SHAKING, but she ignored it. She had asked for Clay's love. She had begged to be a part of his life, and there was no reason to back out now, not when she was so close to what her heart desired. She was taking a gamble—one that she might lose—but there was no other choice left to her. For Katherine, it was either Clay or no one at all.

She glanced at him. The dimness of the car hid the grim creases around his mouth that had been there ever since she had walked back into the room, Laura's overnight suitcase in her hand.

He'd barely spoken since. She continued to watch him even though she made note of the direction they were headed. They had just turned off Loop 610 and curved toward Dominion Country Club. Soon they'd be at his town house.

She shivered.

"Cold?" He reached for the heater switch, but her hand covered his instead. He turned his palm over and captured her.

"No, I'm fine." She held on tight, afraid to let go just yet. His thumb began gently rubbing against her fingers, sending shivers up and down her spine.

"How do you feel?" he asked, really wondering whether or not she wanted to back out of this insane near relationship.

"Like a hot-fudge sundae."

His brows rose in question, his brown eyes darting to hers.

"I'm both hot and cold at the same time, waiting for the first bite to be taken." Her smile was stiff, and he squeezed her hand.

"I promise I won't jump your bones the minute we walk through the door."

"I wish you would."

"Why?"

She chuckled nervously. "Because then this tension would be over and I'd relax and enjoy your company."

He frowned. "If you don't want to follow through with this, just say so." His voice was clipped.

"I do," she whispered, her hand tightening on his. "I'm just nervous."

"We've done this before, Katherine," he reminded her.

"I remember," she chuckled ruefully. "But we didn't know we'd wind up that way. This time it's...it's..."

"Calculated?"

"Planned," she corrected softly.

He pulled off the highway and onto the access road, his hand leaving hers to grip the steering wheel. She waited—and prayed—that he would take her hand again, but he didn't. Her heart beat hard against her ribs. She was doing this all wrong. She should be seducing him, heaping praises upon his golden head, throwing grapes into his mouth and fanning his body with palm fronds.

A grin teased the corners of her mouth at the thought of him playing Julius Caesar to her Cleopatra. He'd make an autocratic Julius and she certainly was no Cleopatra!

"The first planned time is the most awkward, you know," she said aloud, reassuring herself far more than him.

"Is that right?"

"Oh, yes," she went on breezily. "After that, everything's a snap." She clicked her fingers as if to prove the point.

He chuckled. "You're incorrigible."

"No, but you're helping me become that way," she teased.

"I'm not too sure it's not the other way around."

"You? Innocent? Me, the seducer?" She pretended to think a moment. "Why not?"

Traffic became congested as cars backed up for all the lights through subdivision after subdivision and he looked over at her, curiosity lighting his eyes. "How would you seduce me?"

"Well," she said slowly. "First I'd kiss you, finding all

the secret places in your mouth that others might not have found. I'd feel your tongue against mine, feel the way you grew against my stomach when we're pressed together as I aroused you.

"I'd kiss your eyelids closed, then trail kisses down your jaw and nibble on your neck, smelling the scent of that aftershave you wear. Your ears would be moist with my whispered words of passion." She hesitated for a moment, then continued in an even lower tone. "I'd feel so close and need you so much that I'd have to rub against you, wanting you to be as close to me as you could get, knowing that you were craving the same thing I was. My hands would run through your hair, around the muscles in your neck and arms. I'd be hoping you were as ready for me as I was for you, but I'd wait until you felt empty and aching before I'd make my next move."

He cleared his throat. "Which is?"

"I'd undo your shirt buttons one by one, kissing every inch of skin as I went. I'd take your shirt off your shoulders, but I'd leave the cuffs buttoned so your arms were forced to hang at your side. You'd be unable to touch, to feel, to lead...."

The car jumped forward and he muttered something under his breath as he began the snail's march to the next light. She heard his shallow breathing and knew she'd hit a nerve—the same one that was making her breathless.

"I'd find each rib and indentation because you'd be my prisoner, mine to do with what I want. My fingers would run through your hair, feeling the texture and weight of it. I'd bury my face in your chest and let the curly strands tickle my nose. And then I'd capture your nipple with my mouth. You'd struggle a little, but your cuffs would hold you secure in my grasp."

A horn honked and Clay cursed under his breath as he stopped for another red light.

She stared at him, blotting out everything but his body,

his tension, his tight expression. His teeth were clenched, the small muscle by his jaw ticked like a meter. "Go on," he gritted.

She smiled triumphantly, feeling a power she'd never known before. He didn't want to listen, but he was responding anyway, against his will.

"I'd reach for your belt and unbuckle it, then unsnap your pants, letting them drop to the floor and cuff your legs so you couldn't walk away. My hands would slip underneath the elastic of your briefs while my mouth found your navel."

"Enough!" he practically yelled as he turned onto the street that led to his house. His knuckles were white against the black of the steering wheel. There was a pinched look around his mouth, almost as if he was in some kind of pain.

"Don't you want to hear the rest?" Her voice was as breathless as his.

"Hold that thought," he said through clenched teeth.

Driving up to the house, he reached for the garage door opener on his sun visor and pushed the button with an angry jab. Katherine leaned against her headrest, closing her eyes. She forced herself to drop the images she had created for Clay, making herself calm once more. Sanity returned slowly, bringing her surroundings back into focus. She'd blown it. She'd gone too far. Where had she found the nerve to *say* those things?

They pulled into the garage and the door came down behind them, leaving them in darkness. Clay turned to her, his voice rasping in the sudden quiet. "Katherine," he began.

But she was quicker. She opened the door and stepped out, standing by the side of the car. Her legs felt like rubber, her hands still shaking, only now they were shaking because of the erotic pictures she had painted. Her whole body was hot and spineless, and she clung to the door, praying he wouldn't vent his anger yet. Not until she was seated in the well-lit house and able to compose her features into some expression besides one of deep emotional hunger.

Without another word he stepped from the car and reached for her bag in the back seat. Then he flipped on the light and led her into the kitchen, closing the garage door behind him with a thud and a snap as he locked it securely.

She wanted to run, but she wasn't sure in which direction: toward him or away from him. The way her emotions were jumbled right now she could flip a coin and willingly do either one.

Clay walked toward her determinedly, not stopping until he almost touched her. Her eyes were wide, her lips parted as she stared up at him. He was so big, so strong, so—

His lips covered hers, sending his moan into the back of her throat as he devoured her with an appetite that knew no bounds. His roughness, his open, obvious arousal was an aphrodisiac to her. Her fingers clung to the back of his shirt as she answered him with the same desperate fierceness. Her tongue dueled with his before gentling and letting him take command.

He softened, too, savoring her taste, the strokes of his tongue slowing to imitate the actions of lovemaking. He clasped one breast in his hand, cupping her nipple in his palm and circling her flesh gently, teasing her to a heated pitch she didn't know was possible.

He nibbled her bottom lip. "You're an enchantress."

"You're Merlin."

"You're mine!" he said before claiming her mouth again, this time branding her with possession. She didn't know when her shirt was unbuttoned and removed, but the coolness of the air conditioning was a stark contrast to the heat of his touch. She snuggled closer to his hand, bringing forth soft murmurs that echoed in her throat.

He picked her up and carried her into his room, not letting her go until they reached the bed. Placing her in the center, Clay stood back, his eyes narrowed as he took in her disheveled appearance. "You look like you've already been made passionate love to."

"You don't," she said, finally finding her voice. She leaned back on her elbows and stared at him, not bothered that she was nearly naked from the waist up. "You're too dressed."

Without taking his eyes from her, he unbuttoned his shirt, then slipped it off, wadded it up and threw it in the corner. His buckle clicked, his snap unsnapped, his zipper unzipped. In one motion his pants and briefs were on the floor and he stepped out of them. He slipped off his shoes and yanked at the socks until both were disposed of, then stood magnificently naked as her eyes played over his strong, bare flesh.

"Are you frightened?" His voice was soft, and if she didn't know better, she would have thought he was vulnerable…as vulnerable as she was.

"No," she whispered. "Just unsure. Everything's so different."

He smiled and the whole room lit up. "And so wonderful. This time it isn't an accident of hormones, Katherine. We both know what we're doing, with no excuses except that we want each other," he said. He stretched out next to her, his eyes telling her even more than his words. With infinite gentleness he began the delightfully slow process of uncovering her partially clad body.

Her pants landed on the floor by his pants, her bra hit the side of the wall and disappeared behind the bed. She reached for the lacy edge of her panties, but he stopped her. "Not yet, sweet."

She halted, opening her eyes dreamily. "Won't it make it, uh, difficult this way?"

He chuckled, bending to tease the softness of her breast. "Interesting, to say the least."

His hand trailed over the flat planes of her stomach, then dropped to the feminine mound, and she couldn't hold in the light sigh that escaped. "That's it, darling, let the feeling overpower you," he murmured before finally capturing a rose-colored bud in his mouth and sucking gently in unison with his hand movement. She tasted like soft night flowers. So good. So very good.

Her own hands reached for him, trailing down to his taut stomach. Hearing him catch his breath at her touch made her even more brave. She wrapped her small hand around him, feeling the size and slick texture of his manhood. His moan fed her desire to learn more, but he grasped her hand, bringing it intimately back to her own body. "Show me. Show me what pleases you most."

She bit her lower lip. "I can't," she whispered, hoping he would understand.

"Shh," he reassured her, his lips scant inches from her ear. "It's all right. You will. Later."

Finally he slipped his hand underneath the elastic and found the moist warmth of her. She moved against his palm, her lips parting, her eyes half closed, consumed by the desire he'd awakened in her.

He sought her breast again, tugging at the budding softness with his mouth until he could feel it harden against his tongue. Her whole body tightened in expectation, but he refused to relent.

"Please," she moaned and he knew what she wanted, but wasn't yet ready to end his own torture. Katherine first. His Katherine...

She arched her back and a tense smile played over his mouth. His own body was drawn as taut as a bow string stretched to the limit.

As she reached the pinnacle, he encased himself in her, resting his weight on his arms as he took the first sweet plunge into the tight sheath of her body.

If he had ever doubted the existence of heaven, he knew better now. Heaven was in Katherine's arms.

CHAPTER NINE

CLAY PROWLED the darkness of his house, his naked body blending with the shadows and silence. A glance at the clock told him it was three in the morning, but his brain was as alert as if it were dawn and he was waking from an eight-hour sleep.

Katherine lay asleep in his bed, the sheet barely covering her trim buttocks. He couldn't help but look in every once in a while and make sure that she was still there. Waiting for him.

What a mess. Other women had thrown themselves at him for one reason or another, and he'd always been in control. Never, never would he have proposed such a ludicrous relationship to them.

Mistress. The word left a bad taste in his mouth. Live-in meant that she would share living and loving space with him. But mistress. That implied she was paid to work. In his bed. Exclusively.

Emotions flooded him at that thought. Oh, that's where he wanted her to be, all right. In his bed and no one else's. He wanted her there in the evening and waking with him in the morning. He craved her arms around him at every moment, stroking him, petting him, soothing him. Loving him.

Earlier, when he'd finally pulled the car key out from under the pillow, he didn't know who was more embarrassed. She had mumbled her thanks and he had nodded his welcome.

They made quite a pair. Both were embarrassed with the

situation. Katherine because it went against what she thought was love, and Clay because he wasn't sure what love was or how long it lasted. Consequently they both wanted something that was elusive.

He needed her to be there because she *wanted* to be, not because he was wealthy enough to afford her. And yet *he* was the one putting a price tag on his need of her. If she were any other woman it wouldn't bother him. But Katherine was different.

He hadn't cared enough for Magda to be frightened of the future. But it was as if Katherine held a marriage license in one hand and a leash in the other. The leash was for him.

He needed his freedom. *To do what?* a little voice asked.

To breathe, he answered, feeling the tension build inside him again. *To do what I want to do whenever I want to do it.*

But you won't let her have the same options! the voice chided. The voice was right. He'd die if he thought someone else touched her, held her, laughed with her in the dark of night. Loved her.

Love. He hated that word with a passion. Love was a patsy's word. It meant giving up all rights to do what he wanted and putting his emotional fate and happiness in someone else's hands. And that someone else might be kind, but they could be cruel. The end result was the same: he would lose control of his own life.

A sigh swept through the darkness to reach his ears and he strode to the door of his bedroom to check on her. The sheet had worked down to tangle in her legs, giving him a view of her slim waist and a sweetly rounded rump. So beautiful…

To hell with trying to analyze his situation in the middle of the night. Tomorrow was plenty of time. Right now he needed to be next to her, to reassure himself that she was really here, in his home and his care.

He slipped his feet under the sheet and reached out, pulling her sleeping form toward his. She turned, curling around the trunk of his body like a kitten wrapped around a ball of yarn. Her hand rested on his chest and he covered it with his own, then sighed and closed his eyes, more peaceful than he'd ever been before.

When the alarm went off, he awoke to find her gone. Her absence left a huge hole in the fabric of his contentment. A note was on her pillow and he squinted to read it.

Call me whenever you need me.

He crumpled the note in his fist, but it didn't make the loneliness any easier to bear.

CONSUELA EYED both Katherine and Clay narrowly as she answered the ringing phones. Very little got by the astute woman, but for once Clay hoped she'd keep her mouth closed. Katherine had been shy and nervous ever since she'd shown up in the office, and he didn't think she needed to have anything else upset her.

After fighting with himself all day, he finally gave in to his own demands as the office was about to close. He called Katherine into his office.

Staring out the window because he didn't trust himself not to reach for her, he spoke. "From now on I want you to spend the full night with me. I don't want you leaving without my knowing."

She took a step toward him, then stopped. He could smell her perfume and it wrapped around his senses. "If that's what you want."

"It is."

After a moment's hesitation, she slid her arms around his waist, her head resting against his back. "I'll see you again in an hour," she said softly, giving a quick, light squeeze.

Then she was gone. Clay rocked on his heels, feeling inordinately proud of himself. That had been almost pain-less.

She went to his house shortly after work, her suitcase in her hand.

Clay cooked dinner, then helped clean up—talking all the time. It was odd, but he'd never felt so free to express opinions with someone before. Her laughter rang in his head, her smiles lit his own eyes.

That night he undressed her slowly, savoring every movement. When they were both naked, he opened the drawer and drew out the earrings he'd been keeping for her. With hands that were tender, he placed them where they belonged—competing for beauty with her eyes.

They made love tenderly, saying with their hands and bodies what was never even whispered. Then they fell asleep locked in each other's arms until morning and the outside world and work intruded upon their world.

CONSUELA HANDED him a small stack of messages, then pushed the plate of goodies toward him. Clay sniffed. "What are they?"

"They're called temptation tarts. My next door neighbor, Vicky, always makes them."

His eyes darted up, narrowing. Consuela's expression was innocence personified. Katherine turned away, slipping her purse in the drawer without looking at either of them.

"I'll pass." He retreated to his office, just barely resisting the urge to slam the door.

All of Katherine's senses were focused on Clay until his office door was quietly closed behind him. Too quietly. Her shoulders sagged with the weight of his indifference. She knew. She knew he was afraid of love, afraid of commitment. Afraid of her.

A small part of her wanted him to feel that way; it meant that he cared at least a little. Maybe even a lot. But the other part, the bigger part, realized that he might run as far away from her as he could go. And that thought frightened *her*.

She loved him. After last night she realized just how

much. Her feelings were just as committed as if words from a preacher had been spoken. A terrible sadness invaded her. She had to face the fact that her love was one-sided. He would never let the barriers down enough to allow her into his life. His heart. Never.

"Katherine?" Consuela's voice filtered through all her thoughts, and she raised her head from the file she had been staring at but not seeing.

"Yes?"

"Beau wants to go over the contracts from that big sale the other day. That way you'll be able to follow what happens after the initial sale."

She smiled woodenly. "Sure. Thanks."

The older woman lifted up the box of cookies and offered her one. "And have one of these. You never know."

Katherine shrugged, but she knew there was hopelessness in her eyes. "Why not? I've got nothing to lose."

"No, not much, eh?" Consuela muttered, watching the young girl turn and walk toward the sales room. Her head went from side to side as she said a quick prayer in Spanish. But the prayer wasn't for the young girl. It was for a boss who wore blinders and still stubbornly thought he could view the entire world with that handicap.

CLAY SENT OUT for lunch, keeping his door closed to the outside world unless it intruded through the telephone. The less he saw of Katherine right now the better off he was. He needed time to think, to absorb the massive changes he'd gone through since he'd met and gotten involved with her.

He felt as if he'd turned a corner in his life and suddenly he couldn't recognize the streets or the neighborhood. He was lost.

At least two hundred times that day he rose from his chair intending to stride into the outer office and sweep the Irish imp into the circle of his arms and find peace there. Another hundred times he thought of calling her on the intercom and demanding she join him in the privacy of his office. By the end of the day he was exhausted from the effort of denying himself that which he wanted the most: Katherine Maureen O'Malley.

And he wasn't even sure why he was putting himself through the torture.

When his watch read five o'clock, he knew his waiting was over. He strode out the door, flicking his gaze toward her like a whip. "Ready?" he barked, frustration making his voice harsh.

She nodded, placing the last file in the cabinet and shutting the door.

"Don't forget your classes, Katherine. They're very important to a career. You never know when you'll need all that schooling to fall back on," Consuela stated, her back ramrod straight as she shot a disapproving look toward her boss.

He ignored her. "Do you have night school?"

Katherine nodded, her red hair caressing her shoulders and neck, just the way his hands itched to.

"I'll drop you off."

Again she nodded, and he held the door open for her. Watching her walk out, he felt himself hardening right under his secretary's eyes and there wasn't a damn thing he could do about it. Katherine's walk was sheer seduction of the senses.

"Good night, boss," Consuela sang.

His answer was a look that said he knew she knew and he didn't care.

"Where is your class?" He started the car and let the hot air blow out the windows at the same time the cold air came blowing out of the vents. Another sweltering San Antonio day.

"San Antonio College." She spoke quietly. Her hands on her lap were primly held together. "Tonight is beginning algebra."

"Fine." He put the car in gear and revved the engine; it still didn't match the power of his own inner motor. "When you're through we'll grab a bite to eat."

"I can make something when we get back to the town house, Clay. After all, I was a short-order cook and waitress far longer than I was a kid."

He stared straight ahead. "All right."

When they reached the entrance, Clay pulled over, but didn't park. He halted her movement to leave. "I'll be back at this same spot in ninety minutes." It sounded more like a warning than a statement.

She smiled, but the sadness that had been in her eyes all day was still there tonight. "Give me five minutes or so to get out of class."

"Right here," he said again, ignoring her plea for extra minutes.

Her hand came up and cradled his jaw, her fingers playing along his skin. He turned his head and kissed her palm, his tongue stroking the center. Her breath escaped and excitement seared through him, fed by the knowledge of the potency they created between them. Sexual power to be sure, but at least she wasn't the only one with the ability to upset and confuse.

"See you then," she whispered, and her hand dropped to the door latch. Then she was gone, striding up the wide sidewalk toward the opened doors. She was fascinating to watch....

He was double-parked and a horn honking reminded him of it. With short, stabbing movements he turned the car into the lane of traffic and drove around the downtown campus to a chain restaurant that specialized in breakfast twenty-four hours a day.

Reading his copy of the *Wall Street Journal* and ordering a cup of coffee helped to relieve those first few minutes of emptiness that he felt every time Katherine left his side. All

he had to do was fill the next eighty-five minutes and the
he'd have her back where she belonged.

It was the longest eighty-five minutes of his life. Studen
filled and emptied the booths, laughing and joking with the
friends. One or two of the older women tried to catch h
eye, but one look at his blank expression and they reluc
tantly turned away.

When his watch finally told him it was time for Katherin
to leave class, he gave a hefty sigh of relief.

Quickly, he paid his bill, then rushed to the car as if h
were going to a fire. In less than five minutes he was agai
double-parked in the same spot he had dropped Katherin
off.

The large double doors opened and a flood of studen
poured out. It took him a moment to find Katherine in th
crowd, but when he did, his brows froze into a frown. .
man was walking with her, his head bent down as he trie
to make a point about something or other. They stopped fo
a moment and let the people circle around them as he wro
something on a sheet of paper, talked to her again, the
grinned broadly.

Clay could feel his temper rising to an almost combustibl
level. How many men did she have hanging on her string
One? Two? Fifty?

By the time she reached the car and had slipped insid
he had gotten a grip on himself. Barely.

"Who was that?" he rasped, pulling into traffic.

"My instructor." She didn't try to pretend she didn
know who he was talking about. It wasn't worth the effor

"What was he saying?" His hands were clenched on th
wheel as he turned toward the loop.

She just looked at him and his stomach lurched. "He wa
telling me that I could be eligible for a scholarship."

"Really? Toward what?"

"An Associate's degree. Two years of an accredited ju
nior college education." She tried to keep her voice eve

but he could hear the small thread of excitement woven in it.

"Would you like that?"

"Sure. But it's impossible to go full-time. I'll just have to do it the way I've set out: two courses at a time."

"Why?" He glanced at her, seeing the mixture of excitement and defeat and fear, all at the same time.

Her brows rose as if she thought he was just slightly touched. "Because I can't afford to go full-time."

"You could," he answered gruffly. "I'll pay for it."

He felt her body stiffen. "No, thank you. I'll manage just fine my way."

"Think about it."

"Don't try to buy me, Clay." Her hands clenched in her lap, and he had to force himself not to cover them with his own and soothe her until the tightness ebbed away.

Instead he attacked. "Isn't that what I did when I hired you as a mistress? At your own suggestion, of course."

"I wouldn't want to put you out any more than you already are," she said quietly, unwilling to voice the obvious and start another fight. It wasn't worth it.

He glanced at her, wondering if she was being sarcastic, but saw nothing in her expression to confirm it.

The silence stretched and he was afraid to break it, for the first time realizing that he wasn't the only one in pain. He'd been so deeply immersed in his own tangled emotions that he'd failed to realize just how insulting he'd become over the past few weeks. He'd heaped insult after insult on her head in an effort to keep her at a distance.

He pulled into the driveway, pushed the button that opened the garage door and drove in. They stepped out and walked into the cool, air-conditioned kitchen. It wasn't until Katherine dropped her books on the table and turned, holding on to the cane-backed chair, that he realized he'd caused what he least wanted. A confrontation.

His gut tightened at the look on her face, his hands stiffening against his sides. He would not beg. He would not let her know what that pain-filled look in her eyes was costing him.

"Ever since we met, you've accused me of being after your money. No matter what I've said or done, you've believed it."

"That's not true," he managed.

But she waved his words aside. "Yes, it is and we both know it. Every move I've made toward you, you've equated with money. Your money."

"And you've spent it."

She nodded. "Yes. When I was told to do so, I did. I was hoping you'd realize that it was you who put those boundaries on our relationship. Not me. But it didn't work."

"Are you denying that you asked to be in my bed? To live with me?" His face felt like stone, his heart like lead. He hurt both of them with his words, but it was time to air them, to let loose the doubts and thoughts that kept them emotionally apart.

"I asked for all of those things and more. I received the things—I never got what I hoped for," she said, her wide green eyes brighter with the sheen of tears that glazed them. "You see, I took a gamble. I gambled on winning the one thing I wanted the most: your love. If I'd won, I'd have won the world. If I'd lost—well, I'd have lost my own happiness. It's apparent now. All the bets are in and the race is over. I lost."

He wanted to shout at her. *No! You didn't lose! I did!* He opened his mouth, but the words refused to spill out. Instead, he sneered. "Are you telling me you'd be just as 'in love' if I was a short-order chef in a truck stop? I doubt it, Katherine."

She winced, and he pushed again, hoping she would rise to the bait and force him into accepting her on her own terms. "You like wealth just as much as the next girl, don't you? And I just happened to be at the right spot at the right time. Lucky me.''

Her shoulders slumped in defeat. ''Good night, Clay. We'll continue this in the morning. I think we've hurt each other enough for one day.'' Her body rigid, she walked out of the room toward the stairs.

Not toward his room. Not toward his bed that they'd been sharing. Not toward his arms.

As he heard the tap of her steps on the stairs, his clenched fist hit the table. ''Damn!'' he muttered, frustrated with his inability to cope with her home truths—and for being such an ass to begin with!

He didn't know how long he stood there, listening to her pace the bedroom above. When he finally walked toward his own room, he realized he'd been holding his breath all that time. He had prayed for her to come to him when he was at his worst, to fit herself to his body, holding him in an embrace that would allow him to cry his love and tell her of her own courage.

He took an icy cold shower more to punish himself than to eradicate his need for Katherine. His mind couldn't conceive of not having Katherine in his life, but his pride refused to allow him to go to her.

Turning the lights out, he slipped between the sheets naked and lay in the center of the bed, wishing she was there to crowd him to the side.

He hated being estranged from Katherine, but he wasn't sure what to do. Apologize? Definitely. But what else? Anything that came to mind was worth a try.

KATHERINE WAS LEERY. All morning Clay had had a smile on his face and a gleam of mischief in his eyes. Sometime during the night he'd come up with a secret that seemed to please him. She tried to recall if she'd heard the phone or the doorbell last night, but she'd heard nothing. So what had happened to make him change his attitude so quickly?

She couldn't begin to guess, and that made her even more leery.

Consuela watched them both with an eagle eye, and Katherine knew that she was wondering, too. Clay touched Katherine's shoulder every time he walked by her desk. He touched her back every time she was in the salesroom, a large room in the back with blowups of some of their most expensive properties. He smiled at her every time she turned around. It was getting on her nerves.

By five o'clock, she was ready to kill him for making her so on edge.

That morning they had driven to work together at his insistence, so she resolved to question him all the way home. When five o'clock came, she was ready. The mischief in his eyes was matched by the determination in hers.

"Ready?"

She nodded, taking her purse out of the desk drawer and standing. "Are you?"

"Oh, yes," he murmured softly, for her ears only. "Very ready."

As soon as they drove out of the lot, Katherine turned in her seat and began her line of questioning. "What's going on, Clay? All day long you've acted as if you know a secret. What is it?"

"Have I intrigued you?"

"You've angered me," she said sweetly. "Is that the same thing?"

His chuckle reverberated through the Porsche's interior. "Not quite," he said finally. "But give me an hour or so and I'll see if I can't change your mind."

Katherine sat back, her arms crossed over her seat belt. She'd be *damned* if she'd voice any curiosity!

They drove through the usual afternoon traffic, but instead of aiming for home, Clay took the freeway to the Austin cutoff.

He glanced in her direction. "Aren't you going to ask me where we're going?"

"No."

He shrugged and picked up the sleek car phone that sat between the bucket seats. A few moments of cryptic conversation and they were pulling up in front of a well-known Italian restaurant. Clay drove around the back and gave two short honks. The chef, with profuse movements and even more profuse chuckles, set a large Styrofoam basket in the deep trunk. Then they drove away.

This time her curiosity couldn't be quelled. "What is it?" she asked, determined to get an answer.

"Dinner."

"Thanks for the explanation." She leaned back, surveying the roadside. The tantalizing aroma of pasta in rich sauce, garlic and other spices wafted through the interior. She tried to ignore it, but her stomach wouldn't cooperate; it growled daintily.

Clay glanced at his watch. "Good. We'll be there in time for sunset."

"Oh, wonderful," she cooed. "Then we have time to hide from vampires."

His brows arched. "Vampires? Aren't you being a little dramatic?"

"Aren't you?" she countered and was pleased to note his slight blush.

Another phone call and fifteen minutes later, Clay parked the car on a wide gravel driveway in front of a rustic log cabin. At least she assumed it was supposed to be a cabin, though to her it looked like a huge ranch house.

Just beyond the house she could see a trail leading through trees and sloping down to a dock where a cabin cruiser bobbed gently in the water. Katherine had seen the signs heralding Canyon Lake, but she hadn't really believed they were headed there. She'd been wrong. Clay had surprised her again.

He turned off the engine and stepped out of the car, pocketing the keys. Katherine stayed seated. "Coming?"

"Anywhere in particular?"

"We're here."

He reached in the trunk and pulled out the cooler and she had no choice but to follow. Her stomach was growling and it was no longer a dainty sound. "Are we renting a rowboat?"

"Something like that," he said, walking past the house and down toward the dock, careful to match his longer strides to her shorter ones.

"Is this place yours?" she asked, stepping carefully so that her heels wouldn't get caught in the spaces between the boards. It was silly to ask, but she didn't know what else to say.

"Of course," he answered, apparently surprised at her question. "Why?"

"I just wondered." She shrugged as he stepped onto what looked like an ocean cruiser to her. He set down the foam container and held his hand out to help her aboard. "Several of my friends have cabin cruisers," she said, "but theirs float in tubs."

His chuckle was delicious, sending shivers down her spine. So did his touch. His hand was warm and comforting and...sexy. His thumb rubbed against her palm and her body reacted immediately. Her breath shortened. Her muscles tightened.

"It's beautiful," she said, deliberately ignoring him as she looked around the deck. Lights flowed up from the downstairs of the cabin, shedding a pale glow on the pilot house. The sun was just getting ready to set and the sky was shot with pink and blue.

Everything on the boat was either sparkling white or deep gray, and in tip-top condition.

"I like it, but I don't get much of a chance to use it."

"Why?"

"Business keeps getting in the way."

"It seems to me you could conduct your business just as well here as over a restaurant table. In fact, it'd be more relaxing for some of your clients."

"I'd need a hostess to help me with the details."

"Like Magda?" Her voice was sweet, but the venom of the thought was just underneath the surface.

"Don't start, Katherine," he warned, for the first time all day, his frown appeared. "This is our time, let's not ruin it."

She had the grace to flush. He was right. This wasn't the time for a confrontation. A lethargy assailed her. She wanted peace from all the hassling of the past weeks. She needed time to just sit and stare at the sunset and speak nonsense. So much had happened to her that her energies were still running at full speed, while her mind was as tired as a two-year-old looking for a place to nap. Perhaps he would broach the subject of his canceled engagement and what her role in his life was supposed to be. Perhaps...

"Champagne?" He held a fluted tulip glass in front of her, his eyes silently asking her to just *be* with him.

She couldn't refuse. "I'd love it," she murmured, accepting the glass and giving a slight salute before sipping the bubbly liquid.

"Come sit." He led her to two gray-and-white-striped, padded chaise longues under the full back canopy.

Slipping off her shoes, she gave a sigh and began to sink to the cushions, but his hand still holding hers gave a tug. "Not there. Here," he said and pulled her onto his lap.

She barely kept the glass from spilling. "Cozy."

"Exactly the way I planned it."

She tipped her head back and smiled, snuggling against him. She heard his quick intake of breath. "Then why put out two chairs?"

"I didn't." He kissed the tip of her nose, his expression purposely bland. Not yet. Not yet. Every woman needed romance in her life.... "I asked Drake to ready the boat for guests. This was his doing."

"Who's Drake?"

"He lives two houses over and helps keep an eye on the property for me."

She sighed again, loving the feel of his free hand as it roamed up and down her arm. The sun played across the water, making red and black shadows dance for them. The peace invaded her. Water slapping softly against the side of the boat and an occasional bird call were the only sounds. Ever so slowly, darkness descended.

"Comfortable?" he murmured in her ear.

"Perfect," she said, wiggling her bottom against the seat. And against his side.

"Then stop that or we'll be exercising before we've eaten."

Her giggle filled the air, but the tense excitement that had been blossoming ever since they stepped aboard was heightened. His arm tightened around her, and she leaned into the strength of his body, loving the feel of him surrounding her. He was everything she could ever want in a man. Everything except that he refused to declare his love.... Stop! her mind cautioned. Not today. Not this moment. Later. Later.

When he kissed her, she melted into him. His hand reached and found the glass of champagne and made it disappear. She didn't care. He was intoxicating enough for her. Her hands couldn't stay still. Instead they strayed across his chest as she turned into his arms. Her fingers played with the buttons of his shirt, undoing them one by one. She wanted to feel his skin, to smell the scent of him, to rest her cheek against the strength of his heartbeat.

She felt rather than heard her dress zipper slide down. The cool breeze touched her skin at the same time as the warmth of his hand traced her back. "Mmm, you feel wonderful. So sleek and soft in all the right places," he said hoarsely.

She kissed his chest. "So are you."

"I hope not," he chuckled, and she blushed.

"I didn't say soft in the wrong places," she corrected, laying her hand lightly on his hardened desire.

And then she was sitting alone. He stood next to her, his hand outstretched. "Come on," he said.

"Where to?" She was dizzy with the need for him, and confused that he would leave her.

"Below. I don't want anybody with binoculars watching us."

CHAPTER TEN

HE PULLED HER into his embrace, giving her a light squeeze before leading her by the hand to the steep stairs that took them below. Vaguely she registered the living area, a small galley and a booth with a built-in dining table, but it was the last room that stunned her. The bedroom. It was larger than she could have thought possible, and a king-size bed dominated the room. Built-in dressers, a closet and side tables with lamps and books stacked haphazardly made up the rest of the furnishings. She reached out and stroked her hand over the spread; it was a dark fur that felt as luxurious as it looked.

Katherine glanced over her shoulder. Clay stood just behind her, his shirt undone, his tie hanging on either side of his collar. His eyes were ablaze, and his thoughts were transmitted to her as easily as radio signals.

With slow, studied movements, she let her dress fall in a puddle to the floor. She slipped the straps of her teddy off her shoulders and allowed it to follow the dress.

Clay groaned, and without another sound he shed his own clothes, then took her in his arms, kissing her as if there were no other way to communicate.

When he pressed her back against the fur, she went willingly. Her heart was beating so quickly it sounded like a trip-hammer in her ears. "Clay, I—" she began, but his firm lips stopped her.

"Shh," he murmured against her partially opened mouth. "Later. Everything can wait until later."

They kissed without reservation, their arms and legs and souls entwined in that inner space that makes two people one. Their movements matched perfectly, bringing pleasure to both. And their senses were so highly tuned to each other that they flowed together like the lapping waves outside. He coaxed her with his body and hands and tongue and she reacted with emotions and feelings she had never felt before. Then she lost herself in him.

Her last thought before shattering into a thousand pieces was that he *had* to love her. No one could do this to her, make her feel this way without that special ingredient.

Later that night, dressed in nothing but a teddy and the diamond and emerald earrings, Katherine sat cross-legged on the bed and grinned at Clay. He'd donned his dark blue, tight-fitting underwear, but that was all. His broad chest, well-developed arms and a smile was all he needed.

"What are you grinning about?" he asked, holding out a piece of hot garlic bread for her to taste.

She took a bite, then chewed and swallowed before answering. "How adorable you are."

His brows rose. "I've been called a lot things, but never that."

"That's because you've never let yourself relax before."

"I haven't had the time until recently." He swirled his fork in the mound of spaghetti in front of him and opened his mouth.

"You had the time," she corrected softly. "You just weren't willing to take it."

His eyes pinned her, looking deep into her soul. "Maybe," he hedged.

Her heart sank just a little. When would he learn to be unguarded with her? To be natural all the time instead of just those few moments when his actions loudly spoke the words he wasn't willing to say. He was so guarded.

"Maybe I didn't know how to relax until recently." He dropped his gaze and moved the plate to the nightstand.

"Did you know that on occasion people have *combined* business and pleasure? And very successfully, too, I hear."

He laughed. "Are you suggesting I try it?"

"Why not?" she asked before taking another bite of garlic bread.

"Why not, indeed," he repeated, sweeping away the rest of the dishes and reaching for her. "It's certainly something to think about." He pulled her with him to stretch out on the bed, molding her to his form and sighing deeply. "Some other time."

Pitching the bread after the spaghetti plate, she tried to stifle the yawn that worked its way out, but couldn't.

"Sleep, sweetheart," he murmured into her hair. And she did.

Two HOURS LATER, when she awoke, Clay was still there. Next to her. She edged closer and he moved, seeking the curves of her waist and hip, his fingers trailing lightly across her skin.

"You feel so delicate, so exquisite." His voice in her ear, husky with sleep, did crazy things to her libido. But making love wasn't all they could do.

She pulled away and undid each earring, setting them side by side on the nightstand closest to her. Clay watched greedily as her hands moved gracefully. He was entranced. As he tried to grasp her, Katherine slipped off the bed and unsnapped her teddy as she danced away. "I think you need to cool off, Mr. Reynolds," she teased throatily just before disappearing through the door.

Clay jumped up and followed, a chuckle caught in his throat. Would he ever be able to second-guess her? By the time he reached the deck, Katherine was poised on the edge of the boat, heart-stoppingly naked and in a perfect diving position. Her head was tilted toward him, twinkling eyes teasing. Taunting.

He crossed his arms and leaned against the bulkhead, still

feasting his senses. "Don't you think it might be wise to check the depth before diving?"

"I already did."

"When?"

"When we came on board I saw the post in the water. The water mark says twelve feet."

He grinned. "How perceptive."

"Aren't I, though." And then she disappeared, cutting cleanly through the air and into the water. Clay walked to the side and waited, his eyes scanning the lightly rippled surface for her.

When she appeared just five or six feet from the boat she looked like a sleek mermaid. Her smile was diamonds on black velvet, her skin translucent. "Come in," she called.

"Come out," he countered, and as she trod water they gazed at each other, both knowing the hunger was building to impossible heights. It curled in his groin and snaked through his blood. He needed her.

Without another thought, he dived in. Before he surfaced, he encountered her flesh, and his arms went around her waist as he broke from the water.

"Are you real?" she asked breathlessly, stroking his hair from his eyes before resting her hands on his shoulders.

"Very real." He pulled her closer, their legs entwined. "Feel me."

Then his lips captured hers and the water swirled around them as they sank into the moon-drenched water. For a fleeting moment Clay thought that Katherine brought stars with her wherever she was; on the boat—or below the shimmering surface of the water.

IT WASN'T UNTIL early morning that Clay realized just how wonderful this respite had been. His original plan had been to soften her up so she wouldn't be so angry with him when he finally confessed his broken engagement. He'd forgotten all about his confession.

She had taught him a few things instead. Her openness and charm had seeped into his very soul, but it was that same openness that scared the hell out of him. He made coffee with automatic movements, his mind consumed with the woman curled so enticingly in his bed.

He wanted to go slow and make sure this wasn't a fleeting form of happiness that would wear off and leave them both with sour tastes in their mouths. He wanted to move with caution as they entered this new phase of their relationship.

But what he really wanted was a guarantee that this would build into a lasting relationship, one that they would both be happy to share for the rest of their lives. Only there was no such an animal.

But he could try. In several months—perhaps a year— he'd know if this liaison was real or a mistake. Then—and only then—he'd ask her to marry him.

"Mmm," Katherine said as she walked into the room running her fingers through her riot of curls. She'd slipped into one of his old T-shirts. He could almost see the small scraps of lace she called panties.... "Coffee always smells more delicious than it tastes. Best smell in the world to wake up to." Her arms wrapped around his waist and she gave a hug before pulling away and reaching for a cup.

"You've got another hour before we have to get ready to leave. Why don't you go back to bed?"

She shook her head. "I want to see the sunrise and that should be taking place in another fifteen minutes or so."

"Sunrise?" He looked blank.

"Of course. It's when the sun comes up and brightens the day?"

"I know what it is. Why?"

"Because it's beautiful." Her voice was soft, her green eyes luminous.

She poured each of them a cup of coffee and they sat in the small plush booth and stared out the window, watching the dark of night slowly lighten to a dim gray.

This was peace. Once more he experienced that deep feeling of contentment. He'd known the pride of succeeding, the ups and downs of happiness and depression. But contentment was different. It had everything to do with the woman who sat next to him, her eyes bright with wonder and light.

"I love you." His voice was low and slow and meltingly soft.

She turned her head slowly, a stunned expression on her face. "Say that again."

"No. Once was enough." He smiled, his finger tilting her chin up so her lips were accessible to his. "But it's true."

"What does it mean?" she whispered.

His lips grazed hers. "It means shut up and kiss me."

And she did, until a loud voice caused them to jump apart.

"Hello! Anyone aboard?"

"Damn!" Clay muttered.

"Who is it?"

"Drake. As usual his timing is off." Clay stood and walked to the steps. "Down here, Drake, and you'd better have a damn good excuse for being the early bird."

"I do," the deep voice boomed. "Or I wouldn't bother with the likes of you."

The man who came down the stairs and shook hands with Clay was enormous, taking up practically all the available breathing space. Brilliant blue eyes highlighted a face covered with a dark beard and mustache.

"And how are your corn and green beans growing?" Katherine couldn't help asking. He wasn't green, but he was certainly a jolly giant.

His chuckle reverberated through the boat. "Just fine, thank you. I'm having a problem with my rutabagas, but Little Sprout seems to have a green thumb." His eyes twinkled as he scanned her small form perched on the booth seat. "Are you a little friend of his?"

She grinned. "Believe it or not, I'm a full grown person."

"What's the problem, Drake?" Clay broke in, apparently not liking the tone of the conversation. He hadn't even introduced them and they were cracking jokes.

Drake grabbed a cup and poured himself some coffee, then sat across from Katherine. Clay slid in beside her, his arm proprietarily across the back of the seat.

"Well, your engine is coughing. I think you might need an overhaul." He raised his dark brows. "Remember I told you last year that the carburetor and the fuel pump were both acting up?"

"I remember. Who do you recommend?"

The large man shrugged. "I've got one or two names in mind. I thought you might want them to bid on the job. Want me to find out and let you know?"

Clay nodded. "How long will the boat be out of commission?"

"Two weeks. Maybe three."

"Good enough." Clay stood, pointedly staring down at his neighbor. "We've got to get dressed and head back. Thanks for your help and advice."

Drake looked at his still-full cup and sighed regretfully, getting Clay's message. "And thanks for the delicious cup of coffee."

He stood and Katherine stretched her hand across the table. "It was good to meet you, Drake."

His clasp was warm and gentle, his eyes admiring. "You're one little fish I wouldn't throw back," he said, sliding a glance sideways to Clay.

"Drake," Clay warned, and the giant withdrew his hand.

"She's a keeper. Mind your manners," he muttered to Clay, and Katherine had to hold in a grin. Clay obviously couldn't see the funny side of his behavior.

Clay sat back down, slumping against the cushions. "Damn that man."

"Why?"

"Because he always tries to force me into decisions I'm not ready to make yet."

"The engine?" Katherine said, misunderstanding. "But he said it was acting up long before this."

Clay relaxed. She obviously didn't realize that his neighbor had been making a move on her. Drake was a ladies' man who played everything slow and easy, but got what he wanted every time. "You're right," he murmured, taking her back into his arms. His lips grazed hers. "Now where were we?"

"We were getting ready to go to work. Remember?"

He closed his eyes and groaned. "Right. Work." He opened one eye and looked down at her. "You wouldn't consider playing hookey, would you? I don't think the boss would mind."

Her hand trailed his jaw, but there was regret in her green eyes. "No, but the boss's secretary would be livid. She has a doctor's appointment this morning and there'd be no one there to cover the phone."

Clay kissed the tip of her nose. "You're off the hook for now, Katherine, but I won't forget where we left off."

"Neither will I, Clay," she promised, giving him a quick hug before formally ending the most wonderful night of her life.

When it was time to leave, Clay took one more quick tour around the interior, making sure everything was turned off and locked up. He glanced around the bedroom, spying the earrings that lay on the far nightstand. Picking them up, he remembered in his mind's eye how she'd looked last night dressed in nothing but those two pieces of jewelry, her skin translucent, her eyes filled with green fire. He had never felt so connected to anyone before!

He pocketed the earrings and finished closing up the boat. Later tonight, he decided, he'd give her back her inheritance. The earrings belonged to her and always would. Katherine and the earrings were inseparable.

THE DAY DRAGGED. Clay had a full calendar, but his mind was on a boat on Canyon Lake with a red-haired witch who had placed him under her spell.

And while one part of him wanted to hold her to him, the other part was scared to death of the commitment she represented. Never had he had his emotions in such turmoil, and that turmoil seemed to produce nothing but more chaos.

He kept telling himself that he suffered from that old fight-or-flight syndrome. And he wasn't sure which he was supposed to do. Drawn to her, he was also afraid of her. She was so strong and capable and honest. He'd never met anyone like her before. But would marriage turn her into the tyrant he'd known other women to be? Would she be bitter when business interfered? Would she pout when he couldn't give her her way when she wanted it? How much change would she undergo after a wedding ring was placed on her finger?

Time. He needed time to absorb it all and then he'd know the right thing to do.

When the workday finally came to a close, he gave a sigh of relief. He'd changed most of his appointments so that he could leave with Katherine. He'd even canceled a dinner he was supposed to attend. He wanted—craved—time with her.

He loved her. He'd said so. Once. That had to count for something.

"CLAY?"

"Mmm?" he asked, maneuvering through the afternoon traffic toward home.

"Where are we going?"

"Home. Did you want to go somewhere else?"

"No, I mean—where are *we* going? Are we going to continue to drift in this relationship or will it change into something else? What?"

He pulled into the garage and shut off the engine. "I

don't know." It was too soon for this. Too soon. "What were you expecting, Katherine?"

"I don't know." She opened her door and stepped out, going directly into the kitchen, refusing to look at him. Surely he could see that she was perfect for him! How stubborn could the man get? "I just know that I want to be with you forever, but you seem content to let us drift along with no sense of beginning or end."

"Is this a proposal?" He hadn't meant for his voice to be so hard, but she was pushing. He could feel his adrenaline pumping. Fight or flight. He began defrosting chicken breasts in the microwave, his attaché case still on the kitchen table.

"No." Her voice was stilted, stiff. She picked up a head of lettuce and showered it with water.

"What exactly do you want me to say, Katherine?" He turned on the broiler and readied a shallow pan. His movements were quick, decisive. Not at all like his brain. Damn! She was stubborn!

"I want—need—some kind of commitment. Obviously you aren't ready for that." She broke the lettuce into bite-size pieces.

When the breasts were in the broiler, he began slicing fresh tomatoes and small yellow squash. "You're right. I'm not ready. And neither are you."

"Don't speak for me, Clay. I know what I am and what I'm not." She set the table.

"You don't know a damn thing, girl. You're still living in some dream world where the fairy princess meets and falls in love with the prince and they live happily ever after! That's not real life." She dumped the lettuce in a large bowl as he reached for the salad tongs. While he tossed the salad, she sprinkled in the dressing.

"I know the difference, Clay. Believe me, you wouldn't fit into a suit of armor!" She put the salad on the table with a bang.

"And you're no princess!" Clay took the breasts out of the broiler and set them on the plate.

Dinner was a silent affair.

As a matter of fact, the rest of the evening was a war of silence. Clay lay in his own bed, listening to Katherine's footsteps as she paced the upstairs room, where she'd chosen to sleep.

Damn her! All she had to do was give him some time to sort this out.

He heard her footsteps on the stairs and he stilled. The footsteps came closer.

"Clay?"

Her soft voice melted away the anger and the indecision. She was right and he'd been wrong. He loved her. He'd loved her ever since he'd met her—he just hadn't wanted to admit it. Well, now was the time to make a commitment, but he was leery. She'd understand. He smiled, grateful that she had been adult enough to come to him.

Flipping on the side light, he sat up and watched as she walked into the room. A brilliant red T-shirt proclaimed it was good to hug a teddy, which brought to mind the black one he would always remember. Instead of the color clashing with her riot of curls, it turned them golden. He could feel himself grow and harden with desire for her.

"I need you to sign this," she said softly, holding out the papers clutched in her hand. Laura had given her the outline of a contract for her services and she hoped—prayed—that this would be the impetus to make Clay realize that they belonged together. In marriage.

"What is it?"

She took a deep breath, willing herself to be calm. "It's a rough draft of a contract that states when either of us is ready to end our relationship, I'll get a small settlement and won't sue. It also stipulates that you'll pay my clothing bills and a few other incidentals."

"We're going to build a contract?" His eyes scanned the sheets, turning icier with every word. He looked up, pinning her feet to the floor, his almost overwhelming anger plain to see. "What are the terms?"

"First of all, that I have a set of keys to your home."

"Agreed."

"That I also have a set of keys to both cars."

"Agreed." His eyes were still flinty. Her heart sank. He wasn't warming up to this idea at all.

She barged ahead. "That you agree to help me in any way necessary while I go for my college degree."

"Agreed."

"Every Sunday we go out for dinner. My choice of restaurant, and no combining business with pleasure on that day."

A muscle twitched at his mouth, and she prayed it wasn't the beginning of a temper tantrum. This was hard enough. "What if I don't like your choice?"

"I won't choose food you can't eat, Clay," she admonished sternly. "But I want to be well treated. Mistresses have their price."

"So do misters."

"What?"

"Never mind. What else?"

"You have to supply me with two weeks' notice and severance pay if you decide you want to terminate our relationship."

"A two week notice?" His voice was a roar.

She nodded. Had she gone too far? Could Laura have been wrong in assuming that this would make Clay realize what he and Katherine had?

"Severance pay?" He roared again.

She nodded again, her heartbeat pounding in her ears.

"What the hell are you planning to do with this money? Open a business?"

So he was already thinking of the end of their relationship. Tears prickled in her eyes, but she refused to let them fall. Later, she told herself. Later, when she was alone. "No. I just have to look out for myself."

"Yourself?" His tone was derisive enough to tear at her soul like a knife.

Her chin lifted stubbornly. "I may need to look for another benefactor."

Those words were tinder to the fire. Fury blazed in his eyes and she took a step away. Then his fury turned to a cold wariness she hadn't seen before. Would she never understand what to expect from him next? When he finally spoke, his voice was low and under control again. Barely. "You say you love me, then ask me to sign this document. You don't love me enough to trust me to take care of you?"

"You've only said the words once, Clay, and I'm supposed to be happy and reassured by that? With your obvious reluctance to even mouth the words I need to hear, you expect me to believe you'll take care of me? Won't that cramp your style with your new wife?"

Clay ran a hand through his hair. "Look," he said, patting the mattress beside him. "Come sit down and let me explain this."

"What?" Her smile was brittle. "That you broke up with Magda weeks ago, but didn't have the courtesy to tell me? Even after the most tender, wonderful, intimate night on your boat? How will you explain that you'd have me carry the guilt of taking another woman's man rather than live with being defenseless against a five-foot ogre with a G.E.D. for a high school diploma?"

His eyes narrowed. "You knew?"

She nodded. "I knew. Otherwise I wouldn't be here."

"Then why the contract? Why can't we just continue the way we are? As friends?"

"Because this isn't friendship!" *This is love* her heart cried. "Please read it."

"You aren't serious!"

Frustration warred with anger. "Why not? Why is it all right for you to draw up contracts with everyone you do business with, and it's not all right for me to do so?"

"Our relationship isn't business!"

"Then what is it? A living arrangement? Even renters sign leases!"

"This is sex! You set the rules yourself!"

Her eyes widened with the pain of his words. She closed them, praying for the strength to carry this argument to a conclusion and get out of here as quickly as possible. She didn't know how much longer her shaking legs would hold her. "Is it, Clay?" she asked. "Is that what this is all about? Sex?"

He balled the papers in his hand and threw them on the floor. "Dammit! You're trying to force me into making a decision that I'm not ready to make! And I won't sign a contract for that! You can consider this a two-week notice!"

Her tears were replaced by anger. Full-blown anger. "Great!" she cried around the lump in her throat. "Now I understand. The fine print doesn't have to be magnified for me to get the meaning." She pivoted, heading through the bedroom door.

"Where in hell do you think you're going?"

"To bed. *My* bed. This is one of my two nights off per week. Read the contract."

"I didn't sign the damn thing so it's not legal, you little idiot!"

"I'm abiding by it, anyway," she threw over her shoulder just seconds before slamming his door with a resounding bang.

He unclenched his hands and covered his face. What the hell had he just done?

A small voice laughed at him. He'd just chased off the woman he loved. He'd played the ass so beautifully he deserved an Academy Award. Clay Reynolds, who had always been in control, just lost it.

He had wanted her to come to him in love, because she couldn't do without him. He wanted her willing and warm and begging for his affection so he wouldn't have to show just how much he cared. He wanted her to give so he wouldn't have to. He wanted to cut his throat with a dull razor for being the stupid fool that he was.

It was early morning before he finally fell asleep. His last thought was that he had played the witless fool long enough. Tomorrow he would shove his pride aside and ask for her forgiveness. Perhaps, if he were lucky, he'd be able to admit just how stupid he'd grown in his adult life. And then he'd marry her so she couldn't pull a stunt like this again.

KATHERINE SLIPPED soundlessly out the door and into the dark early-morning coolness. The Lincoln sat directly in front, and she slid into the driver's seat.

Once she had decided on a course of action, she had packed quickly and efficiently, taking just what she needed for the next week or so and leaving the rest in paper bags next to the door. They'd be out of Clay's way and ready to pick up once she decided on her next step.

Before leaving, though, she had deposited a letter directly on top of the answering machine in his study, knowing he would check it in the morning since he hadn't done so last night.

She had pushed Clay too hard by asking him to sign that stupid contract. Instead of him laughing at it, he'd taken it seriously, losing his temper and dismissing her from his life. She would have given anything to retract that move, but it was too late. Too late for both of them.

She'd lost Clay, either because she wasn't right for him or because he just didn't care for her enough. She had always thought it was the former, but now she realized it was the latter. Either way, the results were the same.

And she couldn't stand the thought of staying and conducting a postmortem on their dead relationship, which would certainly have happened this morning. Apparently he was right. After bedding her, he was sated and ready to move on. Clay would have continued keeping that distance-serving wall up, and she would have become more hurt by banging her head against it.

No, this was the only way to end their relationship. Anything else would be more harmful to her, and she didn't think she could handle that. Her emotions were already too tattered.

He'd tried to buy her without the benefit of marriage, never seeing that she bled every time he offered his bribes, was wounded every time he denied her gift of love.

She parked the car at the curb and walked up the steps to Laura's front door. All she wanted was her own room and a good cry. And not necessarily in that order....

CHAPTER ELEVEN

CLAY SAT straight up in bed, his body slick with sweat. His gaze darted to the pillow next to him, then bounced around the room. Taking short, panting breathes, he tried to control his breathing. He'd had a nightmare about Katherine.

He slipped his feet off the side of the bed and strode naked toward her room. She had to be there. She had to be!

Her room was as neat as when she had first walked in. The closets were open to show they were empty, the bed made without a crease. Three paper bags of clothing stood by the door, the only remains of her visit. Visit. That was the key word. He'd treated her like a visitor and everyone else like old friends. But he hadn't been afraid of everyone else—just Katherine.

She had petrified him.

He now knew the whole contract thing had been staged as a joke to shake him out of his complacency with their relationship. Juvenile, but a joke, nonetheless. If he'd only treated it as such instead of allowing his anger to get the best of him, Katherine would still be with him right now. Instead, he'd fought her because he'd felt as if he was being backed into a corner.

She'd wanted a commitment as grand as her love for him, and he'd been reluctant to verbalize one. It wasn't a bad request. In fact, asking for him to love her in return was only honest. Just as she was.

He dropped to the edge of her bed, his head in his hands, as despair washed over him. He had been blind and stupid and now he was about to pay for the pain he knew he had caused her. She wasn't like any other woman he had known. She wasn't like his mother, and he wasn't like his father.

He'd seen his father die a little every time he'd been tongue-lashed by his mother. He'd seen his mother turn into a bitter woman because his father couldn't—or wouldn't—live up to his grand talk. Both had been vulnerable to love and neither had won. So they'd spent the rest of their lives together and miserable.

Clay had grown up an only child and just as frustrated as his parents. He'd spent most of his time away from the house, visiting David's family because he couldn't stand his own parents' constant bickering.

Then, over the years he began noticing that David's parents did the same thing. David's father was a mechanic who never had enough money to support six kids. And David's mother was unhappy working her life away as a civilian secretary at one of the air bases.

Then there was Laura. Her parents were wealthy and, though they never got along, money had allowed them to keep the necessary distance so they could at least be civil to each other....

But for the first time in his life it dawned on him that if any of their parents had ever separated they'd probably still have been miserable. One fed off the other, and each in his own way got something out of their bizarre relationships. Otherwise, they wouldn't have remained in them.

And Clay had thought he'd been so smart, refraining from anything that smacked of vulnerability when it came to females. He'd tried and discarded women like cheap pairs of pants, not really believing any of them were more emotionally involved than he was.

How many people had he hurt the way Katherine was hurting him? He was afraid to guess, but the idea wasn't at all pleasant. Now he was going to find out about hurt himself. Firsthand.

He had to explain to her, see her. He had to make her understand that he had been scared to death of everything she'd made him feel. That he'd built walls to defend himself against the emotions she evoked in him. And he'd done such a damn fine job of it, he had walled himself in and shut love out.

Filled with purpose, he stood. She must have gone to Laura's. Where else could she go? He'd confront her with what he'd learned about himself. She'd understand, he knew it. Then they'd get married. It was as right for them now as it would be a year from now. So why wait?

It was so simple that he smiled. Everything would work out....

IT TOOK KATHERINE an hour to stop the tears that felt as if they were being dredged up from her very soul. But finally she sat up from her bed in Laura's house and determinedly began to formulate plans.

She couldn't stay here. Clay would immediately guess where she was, and she'd have to go through the post mortem of their parting. She wasn't strong enough for that—not yet....

Picking up the phone, she dialed the only person she could trust besides Laura.

"Consuela? I have a favor to ask," she began.

CLAY BANGED on Laura's front door, impatience edging his voice as he called out. "Katherine! Open up! I know you're in there!"

There was no answer.

Only after minutes of knocking did he remember that Laura always kept a key in the fern plant hanging over the front balcony. Reaching in, he patted the dirt until he founded what he was seeking. With a sigh of relief, he unlocked the door and strode in, searching each room as he made his way to Katherine's. But when he reached the room, his footsteps halted and his heart thudded with fear.

The dresser was empty of cosmetics, the closet void of shoes. Everything was gone.

She was gone.

Where? Where could she go? Laura was the only friend he knew about, but apparently there were others.

Her brother? No, she wouldn't return to a job she hated, no matter how close she was to her brother. David? He wouldn't dare. Where? He pulled a blank.

Cursing under his breath, he called himself the biggest fool of all. He'd gotten what he deserved and it tasted like bile on his tongue.

He'd find her. He swore he would. And when he did, he'd hold her so tight she'd never be able to run again. Ever.

Turning, he strode from the house and jumped into his car. Maybe, just maybe, he'd drive up to the office and she'd be there, working away as usual.

He prayed so, but somehow he knew he was living in a fantasy world. The same one he'd been living in for thirty-odd years.

HE CRIED when he found her note later that evening.

Dear Clay,
I won't be your personal whipping boy. I've done nothing except love you and that isn't a big enough crime to be punished for. I hope you find whatever it is you're seeking.

For the rest of the week, Clay scoured San Antonio. He figured it wouldn't be too hard to find her. There weren't that many redheads in the Spanish-textured city. There probably weren't that many in the whole darned state. Or the country, for that matter. At least not natural ones with long bouncing curls that dared a man to tangle his fingers in the sweet luxury of it.

No one had seen her.

He'd even gone to San Antonio College and checked with her math professor. With a rigid nod and as few words as possible, the man had coldly informed him that Katherine had dropped out of school. Obviously he blamed Clay.

So did Clay.

Unending frustration and a terrifying depth of loneliness were now his constant companions. Everything he did or said emphasized just how many mistakes he had made in his personal life. He didn't even have any friends to turn to anymore, and his family... Well, his family would remain at a distance. At his wish. There were still too many bad tasting memories of his youth for him to turn to them now.

Shortly after her leaving, Clay had sat in the living room and listened to Katherine's favorite country-and-western station while staring at the jewels that would forever link him to her. Turning on the lamp next to him, he squinted to see the engraving on the backs of the earrings.

He could make out the crest, but time had worn the edges away. Several lines, obviously representing mountains, were on the left side of the shield while three stars formed a triangle on the right. Impatience made him mutter as he stalked to his desk and rummaged through the drawers until he found what he was looking for: a magnifying glass.

With the glass he could see the name Montclair just below the crest. He carefully placed that earring on the table and picked up the other one. Just as Katherine had said, there were initials and an inscription: A., *avec amour*, C.

So they had been given with love.

He didn't know the past history of these gems, but he was smart enough to realize that Katherine's parents had had a love just as strong as the original owners. A love that made all else trivial compared to that emotion.

He placed the earring next to its mate and dropped the magnifying glass on the sofa.

Katherine. Katherine. Katherine. His pulse thrummed the name in his ears. He loved her with all his heart and soul and he had never trusted her with his love enough to give it to her as a gift. No strings attached, just love.

He had to find her, to explain. She was everything to him. There would never be anyone else in his life who would make him face himself this way or help him to find happiness.

Katherine. Katherine. Katherine.

Picking the earrings up once more and holding them tight in his hands, he bent his head.

Whoever had been given the earrings first had been loved. And Katherine had received them in love, too.

Then she had given them to him.

He remembered Katherine sitting in his car as she placed the jewels carefully in his palm. He should have known then. She had faced and accepted her love for him, and he hadn't had the ability to see it.

He hadn't had the ability to love, either. But Katherine had been patient with him, teaching him what love was and that he was truly capable of that emotion. She had taught him the most important lesson he would ever learn.

He prayed it wasn't too late to show her just how much he loved her.

AT WORK, Consuela's all-knowing eyes kept condemning him, and for once he accepted that burden. She'd known from the first that Katherine wouldn't return to work. She'd even had a sixth sense concerning Clay's relationship with Katherine. And how much of an ass he'd been. There was nothing she could accuse him of that he hadn't already blamed himself for a thousand times over. It was a tough road that led adolescence to emotional adulthood—especially at the age of thirty-five.

But the one person he leaned on the hardest was Laura. She knew something, he was sure. She had to. She and Katherine had become best of friends, and neither Laura's relationship with David nor Katherine's with him had interfered.

For the fourth time in a week he tracked her down at David's home one evening. It was immediately apparent that they had come to an agreement, and love was once more in bloom. Clay tamped down his flaring envy as he watched the glances between them that spoke of an honest and true love. He finally believed in that commodity. It was a shame he'd learned so late.

"Have you heard from her at all?" Clay asked, his eyes pleading more than his words.

Reluctantly, Laura nodded her head. "But I—"

"I know," he interrupted tiredly. "You won't tell me where she is."

"Right."

"Is she all right?"

"She's fine."

"She hasn't gone back to her brother, has she? I don't think I could take it if I scared her back into that jerk's house."

"No." Laura chuckled. "I'd hog-tie her myself before she did something that stupid." The smile slipped from her face. "But your brain cells haven't worked very well so far, Clay," she admonished.

"Laura…" David warned.

But Clay waved a dismissive hand in the air. "No, David. She's right. I've been acting like a male pig all these years. Then when I finally meet the woman I want to share my life with, I force her into battle at every turn. I wanted her to prove herself worthy of me when I wasn't good enough for her." He leaned back, closing his eyes for a moment. Anguish, never completely gone, flooded him again. "Ironic, isn't it?"

"Sad." Laura's hand covered his on the table. "You've never spent much time on relationships before, have you, Clay?"

He shook his head, absently wondering where his words were pouring from now. He'd never opened up to anyone before, except to Katherine. "Every spark of energy I had went to business. I'm good at that," he said derisively. "But I can't seem to show the woman I love that I need her more than breath. It's hard to do when I keep breathing anyway."

He earned a chuckle from both David and Laura, but in his heart he knew he was right. He knew nothing about personal relationships and their intricate workings.

But David knew. "Did you goad her like you used to push the rest of us, making us prove ourselves until we told you we liked you even when you were a bas—" he glanced at Laura "—a stinker?"

Clay nodded. There was no use denying it.

"Then you deserve what you got," David said, his voice hard. "Take the time to look at yourself, man. You had this coming. You haven't made a new friend—personal friend— since college. You've been a loner for as long as I can remember. And your ideas about women were already well fed before then. It wasn't without justification, Clay, but you're smart enough to know that all kettles aren't black."

Standing, Clay clenched his hands in his pockets. "I'm well aware of my own shortcomings, or I wouldn't be here begging for help." His voice was low and harsh. "But none of us was raised without hang-ups of some kind. This one happened to be mine."

He stood and glanced at Laura, making certain David understood that he was referring to David's own hang-up about Laura and the fact that even when she returned, David had refused to seek her out. Laura had practically had to attack him just to get noticed. "We're all learning."

"Touché," David said softly as he watched his best friend walk from the room.

"You deserved that," Laura whispered in his ear, giving him a light kiss while she was at it.

"I know. I just didn't think he'd retaliate. He's been down so long that I didn't think he'd rise above it."

"Never underestimate our Clay, honey. He's had a tough lesson to learn, but it wasn't all his fault. Our fair sex had more than a little to do with it. His mother in particular."

David hugged her closely. "I'm glad to hear you admit it. It's about time you 'fessed up about your fairer—and supposedly—weaker sex. Men don't know the rules anymore, and it isn't until they realize that the women don't know, either, that they can ever begin to win."

Laura leaned back. "What's this thing about winning or losing? Men equate everything they do to those words. Can't more than one person win, and aren't there several ways to do so?"

Chuckling, David gave up. "You're right, I'm sure. And I'm certainly not going to argue the point with a pro debater. But I bet I could beat you in a wrestling contest," he declared with a leer.

She giggled, leaning her head on his shoulder and cuddling closer, knowing just what kind of an ending that would lead to. "It's a prime example of what I've been talking about. I contend that if I lose your wrestling contest, I win."

"Women's logic escapes me, but whatever you say is usually right on target." He sighed, pretending defeat as he stood with her tightly clasped in his arms. "Ready to prove your point?"

She wrapped her arms around his neck and kissed the strong, tanned column of his throat. "Ready."

KATHERINE AND CONSUELA finished wiping the kitchen counters, erasing the last traces of dinner for six in the older woman's large, old-fashioned kitchen. It was their night to clean, each two members of the family trading off this duty and almost every other chore to be done in the household.

Consuela's family was wonderful. They were rowdy and loving and full of fun, but they worked hard to ensure that each of them got ahead in a world that was filled with enough stumbling blocks to overwhelm a lone individual.

Katherine had lived with Consuela for almost two weeks now, and as soon as she received her next paycheck she'd be renting an apartment of her own. Last week she had returned Clay's car, parking it in front of the office with a short thank-you note attached.

Leaning her hip against the counter, she glanced around the slightly shabby room. "I'm going to miss it here," she mused aloud.

Consuela rinsed her washrag. "Then don't go. Stay."

Katherine smiled, but it didn't erase the sadness in her eyes. "I can't. It's time to stand on my own two feet." She glanced around again, taking in the often-scrubbed wallpaper that was as outdated as the paper at her brother's home. "But I'll still miss it."

Consuela folded the cloth neatly, then draped it over the faucet. "How is the job working out? Is that framerman training you properly?"

"Not as well as you were," Katherine teased, showing some of her old spirit. "But he's trying. And I'm learning."

"Hmph," Consuela answered. "You've got lots of smarts and they shouldn't go for the wrong things, young lady. You need that schooling."

Katherine pulled away from the counter and rinsed her own cloth. "I know. And I'll do it this September at the business school. By then I'll have enough money and be in my job long enough to prove I'm a good risk for another loan." She refused to think of her earrings. She had given them to Clay in love, and despite everything, they were where they belonged.

"Have you contacted Clay yet?" Consuela knew the answer to this, but it was the one question she asked at least three times a week.

"Not yet."

"When?" The older woman's sharp eyes took in the shadows under Katherine's eyes, the drawn, unhappy look that had been there since she'd arrived almost two weeks ago.

"Soon," she promised wearily. "I put a letter in the mail to him today."

"He's not himself anymore," Consuela muttered as she placed a full pot of water on the stove and turned on the burner. "I've never seen him like this. I don't like it."

"Is he angry?"

"No. He's just not the same. Like someone took all the stuffing out of him and threw it around the room. He sees it, but he's not interested enough to stuff it back into his shirt."

"Like a scarecrow?"

Her dark eyes pinned the younger woman. "Like a man who just lost the woman he loves. Nothing else matters except her."

Katherine turned and opened the refrigerator. Taking out a dozen eggs, she handed them to Consuela. "You're wrong. He made it more than plain that he wasn't in love. In fact, the last thing he needs is me."

Consuela took the eggs and began placing them in the pan. Lunch for six tomorrow would be egg salad. "Don't go by how he acts. He's always been that way. The boy was raised under rotten circumstances and he's grown his own armor around him. You were the first one he let in."

She thought of her own life and how hard it had been and felt herself bristling. "He lied to me about his engagement to Magda! Purposely! Besides, half of us have rotten circumstances. Why were his any different?"

"Well," Consuela sighed, reaching in the cupboard for two wineglasses and pouring a generous amount of ruby-red Mogan-David wine in both of them. She handed one to Katherine, then sat at the Formica-topped table. "His mother and father had big problems. Still do. But when he was young and impressionable, they fought and bickered over everything, especially him. His mother used him as a weapon against his father. Then she used him as a weapon against her own feelings. She would give him gifts, then swear that she had to pay for it out of private funds because his father kept her penniless. She'd tell him he just wasn't worth her poor saved-together money. Then she'd tell his father that he was worthless as a man, and if it wasn't for her, he wouldn't even have his son's love.''

''Was it true?'' Katherine's voice was almost a whisper.

''No, but I think he believed it anyway. And most of the time, Clay was in the middle, loving both of them, especially his mother, until she finally turned on him and tore him to shreds with her belittling tongue. Nowadays they call it emotional child abuse, but in those days parents were gods.''

Katherine leaned back, imagining Clay as a boy. It went a long way toward explaining his tendency to be a loner, not trusting anyone, especially a woman. No one except Laura and Consuela. ''How do you know this is true?''

The older woman's face turned to stone. ''Because I was their maid for over ten years. I saw it all. Some of it couldn't even bear repeating, it was so awful. I watched him retreat until there was no one to retreat from anymore.''

Katherine was stunned. Her mind churned over the story, her imagination recreating scenes she was sure had taken place. ''But…one woman, even his mother, couldn't have changed his life that drastically,'' she finally objected.

''It helped. From that point on it seemed that the women he chose had the same outlook as his mother had. Right up to Magda. They were all people who were selfish with their emotions, going through the actions of caring, but only when it suited them or when they needed something.'' Her voice was filled with derision. ''And not having any experience of what a real family was like or what more than one or two friends were for, didn't help.''

"I see." She slowly twirled her untouched glass. But it still didn't explain a lot of things.

Consuela gazed at her for a long silent moment. "None of us knows another person completely, Katherine, but I'd venture a guess that Clay just really didn't know how to deal with you. You see, he cared too much to know how to act and that scared him even more. When it comes to relationships, he's always been a cautious man." She stood and put her empty wineglass in the sink. "And that's my ration of philosophy for the night. It's time for my favorite program." She walked toward the living room where her family had gathered after dinner, her soft slippers scuffing against the linoleum floor. High-heeled shoes and office dresses were discarded the moment she walked into the house.

"Consuela?"

She halted at the doorway, looking over her shoulder in silent inquiry.

"How did you go from being a maid to being a head secretary?"

"Clay sent me to secretarial school the year he graduated." She grinned. "He knew it was what I wanted to do—just like you. I borrowed the money from him and by the time he opened his business, I was trained, experienced and ready to take on the job."

Katherine should have known. "For a man who hates love, he sure has enough people loving him," she muttered dourly.

Consuela laughed as she left the room, tossing one more remark over her shoulder. "*Niña*, nobody ever has enough people loving them!"

CLAY'S MUSCLES TENSED as he reached toward a particular letter in the pile of mail he'd been sorting through. He knew that handwriting well. He darted a glance toward Consuela who was sitting at the phone taking down a message, then he slipped the envelope into his coat pocket and walked into his office, shutting the door.

Fear and anticipation warred inside him. Was she ready to see him again? Was she telling him that he was no good? He was certain the answers were inside the sealed envelope, but he wasn't quite brave enough to open it and find out.

He glanced at the calendar on his desk. It was two weeks and three days since he'd seen Katherine last. A lifetime. A long, lonely, boring, depressing lifetime.

Every night he turned toward her side of the bed, his arms reaching out for her, only to find emptiness. Every evening he waited for the sound of her delight at certain music or a passage in a book that would please her enough to share it with him, only to find the room void of warmth. Every ring of the phone was a jump-start for his heart, and depression followed quickly to envelop him when he didn't hear her voice on the line.

Her earrings had become his talisman.

He'd had plenty of time to think. He'd been wrong so many times in his relationships, but now he knew why. No one ever received something without giving something in return. Money for goods. Love for love.

He'd spent his lifetime slowly shriveling up emotionally. The picture of his behavior until now wasn't pretty, and if Katherine hadn't come along to show him what he'd been missing, he doubted that he ever would have found the door to happiness.

The funny thing now was that he finally had the key, only there was no one on the other side of the door. Katherine was gone and he hadn't been able to find her.

Two swift raps on the door made him jump guiltily. Consuela didn't wait for his invitation, but peered around the door, her eyes bright. "Coffee and cookies?" she asked.

He looked at her warily. "What kind?"

Her face looked like a blank piece of wrinkled paper. "Wedding cookies."

"Forget it, unless you can deliver the bride."

"All in good time, Mr. Reynolds."

His eyes narrowed. He stared at her a silent moment before he asked the question to which he already knew the answer. He'd been so steeped in his own misery he'd overlooked the obvious. "You know where she is, don't you?"

"Yes."

"But you won't tell me."

"No."

"Why in hell not? Why does everyone protect her from me as if I'd eat her for breakfast?" His frustration was apparent in every movement of his body.

"Because you already had one try and you almost did."

Harsh words from the woman who knew him best. He sighed, leaning back in his chair and running a hand through his hair. "Go away, Consuela. Leave me alone."

Her head disappeared and the door closed softly. After several minutes he finally reached into his coat pocket and withdrew the letter, setting it on his desk and staring at it.

Another five minutes passed before he found the nerve to read it. With a silver letter opener, he slit the top, careful to not rip the folded papers inside. The handwriting was soft, feminine, flowing. Just like her. He forced his eyes to focus on the words, while his mind wanted to wander down memory lane and revisit the loving scenes the scent of her paper aroused.

Dear Clay,
The enclosed bills were charged on your account when you told me to buy whatever mistresses were supposed to buy. Now that I no longer hold that position, I'm not sure what to do with the clothing. Please send instructions via Laura. May I suggest that next time you

put a limit on your accounts? You could pay for years on the damage one person could do in a day.

I'm putting my life back together now and things are looking up. Please don't try to find me anymore, I don't think it would do either of us any good to rehash the past only to reach the same conclusion again. We'd both walk away with a headache and probably say things that are better left unsaid.

I wish you all the luck in the world.

Always,

Her name was a curlicued scrawl that flipped his heart over.

"Consuela," he barked into the intercom. "Could you come in here, please? And bring me all the cookies you have left."

"Right away, boss." When she appeared at the door, he was openly grinning.

"I want you to locate a Montclair Castle or family or whatever you can find. It's in France." He grabbed a piece of paper and scribbled something on it, then held it out to her. "This is a picture of the crest. It might help."

"But...how?"

"Call a travel service that specializes in Europe. Call the library. Call France!"

Her grin could have split the world apart. "Right, boss."

Leaning back, he stared out the window. If anyone could get the information, Consuela could. He'd find Katherine's dream, and then he'd tell Katherine....

After he'd drafted a reply to Katherine's letter, he left the office and played out the rest of his hunch. If Consuela knew where Katherine was, his bet was that she had found Katherine a job. And the one job that came to mind was in the office of the very people she had helped Beau sell the building to.

Later that afternoon he parked across the street from the

building and waited. His nerves jumped each time the door opened. Then she appeared, her red hair brushed sedately back, a black grosgrain ribbon holding it in place. Her navy-blue dress clung to her curves without being obvious, and tall high heels that he had begun to think of as her trademark slimmed her already perfectly shaped legs. He couldn't take in enough of her.

She joked with one of the other girls who walked out, but there was still an aura of sadness about her. He wanted to see her happy again.

Just as he was about to step from the car and confront her, another car pulled up and she slipped in. Anger rushed through his veins as he recognized the man behind the wheel. His best friend. David.

David's car moved away soon and disappeared down the street. Clay was slow. It took him almost a minute to realize he had to follow in order to find out where she was living. And after he'd gotten that information he'd attack David.

It wasn't until they reached Consuela's street that the truth hit him. Everybody that mattered to him was in on this conspiracy to keep him from Katherine. Consuela, David, Laura. They all thought he would hurt the woman he loved. He'd never felt so alone in all his life.

That deep sense of loneliness drifted over him like a heavy blanket. Katherine wasn't being coy when she had said she didn't want to see him. She had truly cut him out of her life.

He pulled the car into a driveway and turned around, heading for home. There was no sense in confronting Katherine. Or David.

He'd lost.

CONSUELA GAVE KATHERINE the letter as two of her girls were preparing dinner. "This is for you, *niña*," she said, holding out the envelope.

Katherine glanced at her friend, coming out of her reverie. "Me? From who?"

"Whom. Clay."

She still didn't reach for it. Her heart beat faster at the sound of his name. "You told him?"

"Only that I knew where you were."

"What did he say?"

Consuela dropped the envelope into her lap. "He wrote this letter while he ate an entire plate of wedding cookies." Her tone was smug.

"What does it say?" She stared at the white envelope in her lap as if it were going to bite. "Is he still angry?"

"Read it," Consuela ordered softly as she walked out of the small living room. "I need to change."

Katherine's hands shook as she lifted the envelope flap and plucked out the folded white sheet with Clay's company name at the top. She scanned the contents first, then read it from the top—word for word.

Dearest Katherine,

Missing you is now a habit I can't shake. Your scent and presence are all around me, filling my thoughts with visions of you. And instead of hating it, I find myself loving the hurt it gives me just to remember the times we had together. It's far better than feeling empty.

I stare at your earrings every hour, remembering the first time I met you. They capture the light in your eyes and remind me of the sparkle of your smile.

I was wrong. You weren't mine. You were never mine. I was yours.

Name your terms and come back to me.

Tears spilled down Katherine's cheeks even as she chuckled. The first two paragraphs were so beautiful, so unlike the Clay she had come to know, but the last line was a reminder of how much he still had to learn about personal relationships.

Damn the man! He still wouldn't admit that he loved her! Once, and in the throes of passion wasn't enough. She needed more. And so did he. The phone rang and she answered it, Clay's letter still clutched in her hand.

"Katherine? Laura. Clay left a card in my mailbox."

Her breath stopped. "What did it say?"

"Thanks for being such a wonderful friend to Katherine. No one on earth deserves your care more."

"How right he is," she stated between gritted teeth. If sympathy was what he was after, it wasn't going to work on her. "Next time you see him, thank him for me."

"Katherine, don't you think you could just see him once? He's so…"

"Broken-hearted? Sad? Depressed?" she asked sarcastically.

"All of the above."

"Like hell he is!" Her anger finally got the better of her. "He's maneuvering all of us around like he's playing chess! Damn that man! It's working and I resent it!"

"But Clay *is* depressed and lonely!" Laura defended. "And he *does* love you!"

"Only until he has me in his hip pocket again. Then he thinks he can go blithely off to fight dragons, making sure that I'm tucked safe and secure in the castle tower."

Laura's laugh tinkled over the wires. "I think he already knows that won't work," she corrected. "Right now he's looking for options. From you."

"I'll give him options," she threatened. How dare he manipulate the people who love him like this! "I'll give him more choices than he knows what to do with!"

"Go to it, lady," Laura cheered. "But see him. Okay?"

"Okay," she promised. "But he might wish he never saw me!"

"Katherine, the man has learned more lessons in a month

than most learn in a lifetime. Keep that in mind when you see him, won't you?''

"I'll give him a test to see how much he's grown," she returned. "And if he passes, I'll give him a star, but I'm still reserving the right to walk out."

"I'm praying he passes."

When Katherine hung up the phone, her mind was buzzing with alternatives that she checked and discarded. Then she smiled. One course of action would really knock him off base, which was exactly as it should be.

With hands that were suddenly calm, she dialed Clay's home number and waited for the answering device to click on. It did.

"Clay?" she said slowly, softly. "This is Katherine and I'd like to talk to you. Consuela knows where I am." She hesitated a moment for effect. Then with a voice that sounded as if it would break, she said, "I'll be waiting," and hung up.

Her emerald eyes gleamed. If Clay had declared war she couldn't be more ready. Only this time, if she played her cards right, they were both going to win—but not before Mr. Reynolds learned a lesson about the dangers of becoming a puppeteer. No one was going to pull Katherine O'Malley's strings unless she *allowed* them to!

CHAPTER TWELVE

CLAY PULLED INTO his driveway. It was still hard to believe that the woman he'd thought of as his substitute mother had been so afraid of his actions that she'd hidden Katherine from him. And his best friends! David and Laura both knew how Clay felt about her. How could they work so hard to keep Clay from the woman he loved?

He flipped the switch to activate the garage door opener, but he remained in the driveway. His hands returned to grip the steering wheel as if he were hanging on for dear life. The lump in his throat wouldn't disappear, but slowly anger welled up inside him, filling him and erasing the hurt.

Finally letting go of the wheel, he curled his hands into fists and hit the Porsche's wheel. Damn! He was sick and tired of being confused! But finally now, he wasn't anymore. Not since the morning he'd woken up to find Katherine gone.

Taking a deep breath, he forced himself to relax. He straightened his fingers and rested his hands on his pant legs. Then he reached inside his pocket, pulling out the small bag that held Katherine's earrings. He stared at them, feeling their weight in his hands. They were so small, but so very precious. Oh, not just because they were jewels, but because they were one of the first things about Katherine that had caught his eye. And she had given them to him in love. He was as sure of that as he was that they were created in the same name. His hand tightened.

It was time to act.

He put the car in reverse. Leaving his garage door opened, he sped down the quiet residential street and back toward the highway.

He was tired of being the emotional victim. Ever since he could remember he'd kept his business life and personal life separate. Compartmentalized. While his business flourished, his personal relationships never got off the ground. He'd allowed them to drift along rather than ending them himself. When he'd had to tell Magda that their engagement was over, it had almost hit him as hard as it had her. Had that been when he started to resent Katherine's emotional hold on him? He thought so. But try as he might, he hadn't been able to withdraw from her completely. She was in his blood. She belonged with him. For always!

He maneuvered the car down Consuela's street and pulled up to the curb. It was about time he took command of his personal life the same way he had his business.

His knock was loud and firm. His expression was bland, hiding the determination that flowed through him. His hands were steady. His eyes were clear with purpose. He knew what he wanted and he was going after it.

KATHERINE SHOOED Consuela back to the couch and her family's favorite situation comedy, before opening the door. Her jaw dropped and her heartbeat quickened when she saw Clay.

He took up all the room in the doorway. His hands were clenched into fists at his sides. His eyes were glazed with either anger or pain, she wasn't sure which. He was staring at her. It was the only reassuring thing about him: he wanted her and it came through in silent language.

"Are you ready?"

She looked at him, still confused. "Ready for what?"

"For this," he said and he reached out to draw her against him. "I've been patient long enough," he muttered before his lips possessed hers in a kiss that made her head spin.

He pressed her to him, and she reveled in the luscious feelings only he was capable of arousing. His tongue ravished her mouth, then softened to a most intimate caress. With his hands he rubbed her back as if impressing her softer image upon his own hard body.

She wrapped her arms around his neck and held on, her mind swirling. But there was something niggling in the back of her mind....

She pushed against his shoulders and he allowed her to pull away. Just a little. "Just what do you think you're doing?" she asked breathlessly, trying to stir up the anger she knew she was supposed to feel. "I just asked you to call, not to take me over as if I was a piece of land for development."

He frowned. "What are you talking about."

"My call? Isn't that what this is all about?"

"When did you call?"

Her eyes widened. "You didn't know?"

He shook his head. "But I do now. And it just confirms my feelings. You're coming with me."

"Where? Why?"

Clay glared down at her. "I'm taking you with me so we can have a long talk."

He was acting unyielding, but two could play at that game. She crossed her arms, her stance pure defiance. "I'm not going anywhere with you, Clay Reynolds."

"Yes, you are." His mouth clamped shut and he once more reached for her, picking her up in his arms as if she were the bride he was carrying over a threshold. With determination etching his features, he stalked down the front walkway. His grip was firm, holding her tightly but still being careful not to hurt her, even as she struggled.

"Put me down!" she screamed, pounding on his shoulder and back.

"What's going on?" Consuela's voice filtered through their anger, succeeding in stopping Clay.

He turned, meeting the eyes of the woman he'd known since childhood. "I'm taking Katherine for a long conversation." Her face, without the makeup she usually wore, was older and more tired. Her eyes locked with his, definite questions lurking there. Katherine didn't move as she watched with fascination the silent byplay between them.

Consuela's brows met over the bridge of her nose. "You're sure?"

"Positive." He grinned. "She'll call you in the morning and let you know all the gory details."

Consuela nodded, apparently convinced of the rightness of the thing. "Okay. I'll call her boss and tell him she's got an appointment."

Clay's eyes narrowed. "A long one. She may not be back."

Without realizing she was doing it, Katherine had wound her arms around Clay's neck. Suddenly she tightened her hands. "That's my decision, Clay Reynolds! Not yours."

He looked back at Consuela. "It's negotiable."

Consuela chuckled. "Isn't everything?"

With that Clay turned toward his car once more and didn't stop until Katherine was belted into the passenger seat. She sat quietly, suddenly docile, and waited for him to explain his bizarre actions. He had come to get her, not knowing she had called. He wanted her with him badly enough to take the chance he wouldn't be received well.

He started up the engine and drove quickly but surely out of the neighborhood.

"Well?" she said when she couldn't contain herself any longer. "Is there an apology in this?"

"No."

"Then let me out."

"Not until you hear what I have to say."

"Anytime soon?"

"In an hour." His mouth was grim, and she decided to go along with whatever he had in store. He had never hurt her, and she was positive he wasn't going to start now. Even Consuela trusted him. Katherine had confidence he'd do no more than break her heart.

She recognized the road. They were on their way back to Canyon Lake. Was he going to take her out in the middle of the lake until this "talk" was over? A delicious feeling flowed through her. It should have been fear, but she was honest enough to admit that it was excitement. She wasn't excited enough, however, to lose sight of the fact that he was only angry with her for leaving. There was no reason to get her hopes up. Clay would always be Clay: a man who'd had too many bad experiences with women to allow her to be part of the very essence of his life. And she would settle for no more than that.

The lake house was dark. Clay stopped the car in front of the door and turned to face her. "Ready?"

"You keep asking that," she said, frowning. "Yet you won't tell me what I'm supposed to be ready for."

He sighed. "Come on in. We can't talk here."

"Why not?"

"Because it's too cramped." He stepped out and walked around, opening her door for her. When she accepted his hand Katherine knew she'd follow him anywhere. She'd forget being contrary just because she didn't like his high-handed attitude; she wanted to hear what he had to say.

The house was as beautiful inside as she had imagined it would be. It might have been molded after a log cabin, but that was the only similarity between this house and any other cabin Katherine had seen. There were cathedral ceilings in every room, the white plaster contrasting with dark-stained pine logs. The furniture was contemporary instead of country as she would have expected. A loose-cushioned, white "playpen" couch sat in front of the rock fireplace that took up an entire wall. The other wall was glass that curved up to the ceiling, like a greenhouse, and the view of the lake was spectacular. A full moon bounced off the water and created diamond drops moving across the cove to the outer lake.

"Drink?" Clay asked, moving to the open kitchen in the corner.

"Please." She was going to need a little fortification.

"Wine?"

"Yes." She walked to the window, stepping around the plants that grew so profusely inside. Her back was to the room. Suddenly she could feel herself trembling from deep inside, the tremors working their way out through shaky hands and knees. But she refused to let him see....

"Beautiful view, isn't it?" Clay said as he handed her the glass. "It always calms me."

"And are you calm now?" she asked before sipping on the cool liquid.

"No. When you're around, I'm anything but." His voice had lowered, turning intimate and sexy. It reminded her of when he made love and whispered endearments in her ear. Her nerves tensed even more.

"Then I suggest we get this talk over with, so we can both go about our business. Separately." Was that her talking? She sounded so cool, so collected. Thank goodness!

He took a step away from her, retreating, and her heart sank. "Katherine, I love you."

"You said that," she replied, unable to keep the bitterness out of her voice. "Once, I believe. You just forgot to put the finish on it."

Piercing brown eyes dared her to look at him. She refused. "What's the finish?"

"The finish was something along the lines of loving me enough to sleep with me, but not enough to marry. Or to tell the truth to, or to live with forever. Or to trust."

"I just wanted to pick the time we came together and make up my own mind. Not be forced into it."

She finally turned, confronting him. Her eyes were blazing with anger and hurt, but she didn't care. "So I made the decision for you, Clay. I left so you wouldn't be put in a position of refusing me.''

"Were you asking me to marry you?"

His matter-of-fact tone drove her temper to the brink. "What the hell do you think I was doing? Of course I was!"

"Then I accept," he stated calmly, and her mouth dropped open.

She snapped it shut. "This is no time for jokes. Say what you have to say and let's get this over with.''

"I just did."

Katherine walked into the living room and placed the glass on a table. When she turned, Clay was standing where she had left him, his brown eyes sending her messages she couldn't begin to fathom. His sandy colored hair glinted in the overhead light and her fingers itched to run through the thick mass. But he was too far away....

Her pulse was erratic, her heart threatening to jump out of her body. "Let me get this straight. You're accepting my proposal of marriage, which I never formally issued, because you've finally decided all on your own that this is the time and place to marry.''

"I love you and I want to marry you."

"Then why didn't you ask me before I left?"

"Because I was fighting my feelings for you. You came into my life and, like a whirlwind, you turned everything topsy-turvy. I wasn't thinking straight so I relied on my old method and tried not to make any decisions at all." His voice vibrated through her soul, then filled her mind.

"Then why are you all the way across the room?" she whispered.

"Because if I come any closer to you, I'm going to drag you in there—" he nodded toward a partially closed door "—and make love to you until neither of us can move. Then we'd never get our feelings straightened out.''

She nodded as if she understood, when all she wanted him to do was exactly that. "Fire away."

He looked startled. "At what?"

"Your feelings. I've always worn mine on my sleeve, Mr. Reynolds. You're the mystery here. For instance, why wouldn't you tell me about Magda? Didn't you know how guilty I felt every time I lusted after another woman's man?" That thought brought back her anger. Thankfully. Anything was better than melting into a puddle at his feet!

"Because I resented the fact that you had such a tight hold over my heart. I used Magda as a weapon against you, only it didn't work." He looked so handsome. So contrite. So damned miserable. Her heart began to heal and he hadn't said more than a few words!

His eyes roamed her face hungrily. "I love you." His voice soothed her like dark, warm molasses. "I love you so much I ache with it."

"I thought you didn't believe in love." Her voice was shaking as much as her knees were.

"I was wrong. I was wrong about a lot of things."

"But now you've learned everything."

He shook his head, his eyes not leaving her face. "The only thing I've learned is that I don't know much about life and love. You've taught me that, Katherine."

Her eyes narrowed. Could this be some kind of trick? Clay had never been humble. "I'm happy for you."

"I've missed you. I can't sleep without you next to me. Everywhere I turn, your ghost is there, reminding me what a fool I was."

He took a step closer and, perversely, she wished he would retreat. She couldn't breathe. "We'd never make it. I don't have the education you do. I'm not that good with your clients, your friends. I'd embarrass you."

He took another step closer, determination filling his movements. "You can get an education, if that's what you want. Although you're smart in a sense most people never are. You have knowledge of people and their thoughts and emotions. You seem to have a sixth sense about it, and that can't be learned. You're great with my clients, open and honest. Not a 'yes' woman who would bore the hell out of them. My friends all adore you. Dave drives you to work. Consuela thinks you're one of her baby chicks. Laura considers you her best friend. Even Drake thinks you're the best thing in my life."

He took another step. "Embarrass me?" He shrugged. "Probably. But it only means that I'm a stuffed shirt on occasion and you're good for me. You shake me up, bring sunshine into my life, make me think of things I would never have thought of without you. You fill me with love and laughter and feelings that grant me peace."

"I'm a paragon of virtue," she muttered, wishing the couch cushion wasn't pressing against her thighs. The only direction to go was down. She sat. "But I think you've got the terms mixed up. I fill you with lust and possessiveness. I can handle the first one, but I'm not a thing to be owned, Clay."

His brown eyes turned heavy with sadness. "I know that now. Don't you think I knew how badly I was treating you? But I couldn't stop. I couldn't trust. I was waiting for you to prove me wrong—to prove that you wanted all the things I could give you instead of me, the person. Good and bad."

"You never gave me a chance to prove what I wanted," she said softly, the sadness in her eyes matching his. "I have nothing to offer you, Clay. No money or family or connections or education. So I gave you the only thing I owned. Me. It was my gift to you."

"And a pair of earrings with a history of love. Something you treasured beyond yourself. They've become my talisman these past few weeks. The only hope I had of your love."

"You knew?"

He nodded. "You wouldn't have parted with them if love—deep love—wasn't involved. I was just too stubborn and hardheaded to know it at the time."

"Smart man." Her voice was low, a lump in her throat causing her to swallow hard.

There was no happiness in his smile. "No. I was stupid. With the evidence in my hand, I still refused to see it." He closed his eyes. When he opened them again, she saw the vulnerability that he'd never allowed her to see before. "There's nothing I can do to change the past, Katherine. But I can change the future if you let me. We can. Together. Do you trust me enough to take my word for it?"

Her slow smile could have lit the entire room. "I think we could give it a try."

He pulled his gaze away from her just long enough to find the piece of paper he was looking for in his breast pocket. "With every contract offer, there's a counteroffer." He watched her beautiful face become lined with puzzlement. "This is my counteroffer."

Reluctantly she accepted the piece of paper, her heart dropping into the pit of her stomach. She unfolded it slowly. "It's a marriage license," she finally managed, her throat almost closed with knowledge.

"For us."

Katherine stared at it, tears in her eyes. She nodded her head and Clay pulled her into his arms. "Is that a yes or a no?" he asked, his mouth nuzzling the side of her neck. "Say something, dammit, before I go out of my mind!"

"Yes," she whispered. "Yes," she repeated in a stronger voice. "Yes!" she shouted, throwing her arms around his neck as if she'd never let go. Her buoyant spirits were out of control.

His kiss held the promise of everything bright and new and open and true. When she pulled away, she rested her head on his chest and heard the answer to her own quickened heartbeat in his.

"Do we sign any other kind of contract?" she whispered.

"To *hell* with contracts! This is a marriage—not a merger!"

Her fingertips slid over his well-formed lips, a small spritely smile on hers. "You win, Clay," she said with a sigh.

"Thank God, you little leprechaun." His voice was rough with feeling. "A friend of mine, a judge, has got the morning of the twenty-eighth set aside for our wedding."

"Suddenly you're making decisions left and right," she murmured, her hand busy with the buttons on his shirt.

"You're damn right," he muttered against her soft nape. "If you'd answered any other way, I was going to hold you here as my prisoner until you agreed."

"Such a novel idea," she purred.

"I have a better one. After the wedding we're flying to France for our honeymoon. We can do what your parents always wanted to do and trace the original owners of your jewelry."

"How?"

"Consuela found the Montclair Castle. It's a luxury resort now, and I've made a reservation for a two weeks' stay, starting the day after tomorrow and ending the first week in July."

"You're really taking time off work?"

"With Consuela keeping tabs on business, no one will miss me."

"At least for a while," Katherine said, her fingers teasing his neck.

"And you're taking back those earrings. I want you wearing them every time I make love to you. I saw them on you the first day I met you and I want to see them on you when I die."

Then Clay Settles Reynolds kissed Katherine Maureen O'Malley, sealing with his lips what had already been engraved upon his heart.

New York Times Bestselling Author

Stephanie Laurens

Four in Hand

The Ton's most hardened
rogues could not resist
the remarkable Twinning
sisters. And the
Duke of Twyford was
no exception! For when
it came to his eldest
ward, the exquisite
Caroline Twinning,
London's most
notorious rake was
falling victim to love!

On sale July 2002

HARLEQUIN®
Makes any time special ®

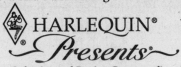

TRUEBLOOD, TEXAS

Coming in July 2002...

DYLAN'S DESTINY

by

Kimberly Raye

Lost:

One locket. A locket that certain
people want badly enough
to kill for, and Julie Cooper
is the only one who can lead
them to it. She's been running
for months with her baby.
But now she's tired.

Found:

Freedom. Dylan Garrett has
loved Julie from afar for years
and there's no way he's going
to lose her again. He'll do
anything to protect his love
and her precious son.

**It is up to Dylan to crack the case, so that he and Julie
can finally find their destiny...together!**

Finders Keepers: bringing families together

HARLEQUIN®

Makes any time special ®

Visit us at www.eHarlequin.com

TBTCNM11

The Trueblood, Texas
tradition continues in...

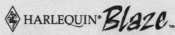

TRULY, MADLY, DEEPLY
by Vicki Lewis Thompson
August 2002

Ten years ago Dustin Ramsey and Erica Mann shared their first sexual experience. It was a disaster. Now Dustin's determined to find—and seduce—Erica again, determined to prove to her, and himself, that he can do better. Much, *much* better. Only, little does he guess that Erica's got the same agenda....

Don't miss Blaze's next two sizzling Trueblood tales, written by fan favorites Tori Carrington and Debbi Rawlins. Available at your nearest bookstore in September and October 2002.

TRUEBLOOD, TEXAS

HARLEQUIN®
Makes any time special®